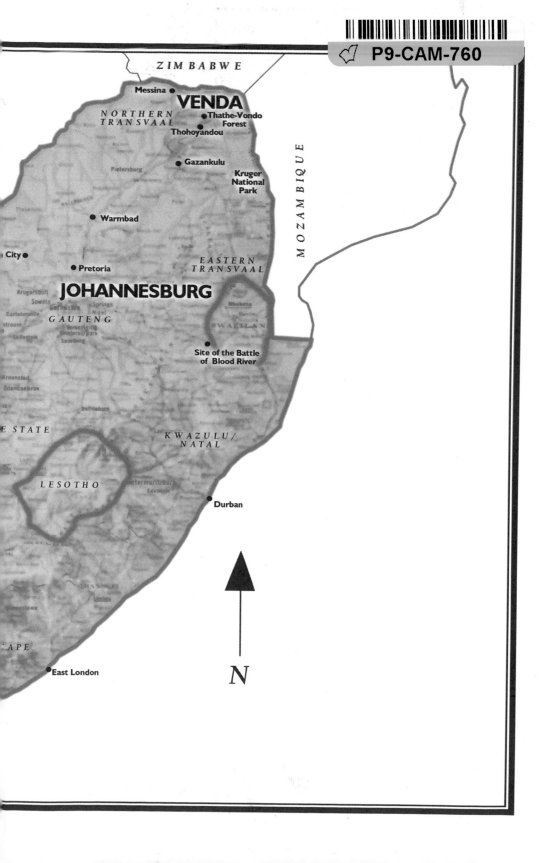

UBUNTU

A NOVEL BY

MARK MATHABANE

NEW MILLENNIUM BOOKS
North Carolina

First Edition

This is a work of fiction and is entirely the product of the author's imagination. Names, characters, events, places, philosophies, and incidents and dialogues, including those involving living individuals, are used fictitiously. They are in no way meant to be construed as real.

Printed in the United States of America

First New Millennium Books Printing: October 1999

10 9 8 7 6 5 4 3 2 1

Library of Congress Cataloging-in-publication Data

Mathabane, Mark.
    Ubuntu: a novel / Mark Mathabane – 1st ed.
        p.   cm.
    ISBN 0-9672333-0-5
    I   Title.
    CIP 99-09321
    813'.54—dc20

Book design by Keith Vest, author's photo by Gail Mathabane and both map designs by Paul Grantham.

For book orders contact:
New Millennium Books
341 Barrington Park Lane
Kernersville, North Carolina 27284
Tel: (336) 996-1703 Fax:(336) 996-3216
E-mail: books@Mathabane.com

Dedication

To my father, who fronted life without flinching – in the true spirit of Venda warriors. You were often hard to understand and difficult to get along with, but you taught me much about responsibility and honor.

And to all the freedom fighters who were murdered by apartheid security forces. Many of you still lie buried in unmarked graves dug by your cowardly killers who still walk free in the democratic South Africa you died for. But the story of your dauntless courage and sacrifice in the liberation struggle lives on. It is embodied forever in the unadulterated meaning of the impassioned cry:

"Amandla! Ngawethu!"
(Power belongs to the People)

1 MAKHADO warily made his way across Hillbrow, a seedy section of Johannesburg, the second largest city in Africa behind Cairo. It was around five o'clock. Rush-hour traffic clogged the narrow street, whose cracked sidewalks were swarming with prostitutes, pickpockets, drunkards, beggars, the homeless and glue-sniffing street kids. Stench from mounds of rotting garbage assailed Makhado's flaring nostrils, making him shudder.

Approaching a sleazy-looking bar, he quickened his pace. Dressed in a well-worn but neat plaid suit and clutching a frayed suitcase, he was anxious to get to the railroad station on Rissik Street to board the 8 p.m. train back to his village near Kruger National Park in the Northern Transvaal.

Outside the entrance to the bar, which was rocking with lively township jive music called *Mbaqanga*, several prostitutes in tight leather miniskirts, sharp-pointed high heels and garish make-up leered at him.

"I can make you feel young again, old man," one of them said with a coquettish wriggle of her large hips.

"I like being old," Makhado said tersely and kept walking.

Two long blocks later Makhado turned left into a side street lined with shops, restaurants and rundown residential and apartment hotels. He carefully zigzagged his way down the narrow sidewalk choked with hawkers selling all kinds of wares: shoes, sunglasses, suitcases, purses, pots, pans, dishes, fruit, vegetables, necklaces, bracelets, scarves, groceries, belts, ties, watches and mattresses. There was hardly any room for pedestrians. Makhado jumped off the sidewalk to avoid a rather aggressive turbaned hawker who was waving a pair of gigantic Nike sneakers while chanting in a thick West African accent, "Nice—Cheap—American."

Makhado shook his graying head as he came to a stop at a traffic light that was just turning from yellow to red. He was shocked by how overcrowded and rundown downtown Johannesburg had become since the abolition of apartheid, and by how much the area had been taken over by immigrants, legal and illegal.

Suddenly Makhado heard a loud scream. His pulse quickened and his sinewy muscles tensed. Barely seconds after hearing the scream he saw hawkers and pedestrians fleeing in every direction. Overturned tables scattered wares all over the sidewalk and into the street. Cars shot through the red light. Horns blared and tires screeched as brakes were slammed to avoid a pile-up in the middle of the intersection.

Makhado's big black eyes cast wildly about for the cause of the pandemonium. In an instant he saw it. About fifteen to twenty feet behind him, two armed men were attempting to carjack a red Mazda Millennia.

"The keys, bitch, or I'll kill you!" one of the carjackers hissed. His gloved right hand coldly aimed a nine-millimeter Makarov pistol at the head of the white woman in a light-blue dress cowering behind the Mazda's steering wheel. The second carjacker grabbed the back door handle, poised to jump in as soon as his partner had secured the keys.

But for some reason the white woman refused to budge. Her trembling hands remained glued to the steering wheel. Her screams for help grew louder and more desperate.

With an instinct born of his years as a warrior, Makhado sprang into action. Adrenaline surged through his veins. Heedless of danger, he dropped the suitcase and charged like a raging rhino down the now-deserted sidewalk. He barreled straight into the side of the unsuspecting carjacker, who was still holding the gun to the white woman's head.

Makhado and the carjacker fell hard onto the concrete pavement. The gun flew out of the carjacker's hand and clattered in the middle of the street. The second carjacker was so stunned by everything that instead of coming to his partner's rescue he turned and fled, disappearing around a corner.

Makhado wrestled with the fallen carjacker, who was much younger and had a jagged scar across the left cheek. Makhado's hands, unusually strong for a man nearing sixty-five, grasped the carjacker's throat in a vice-like grip. The carjacker gasped for air, his eyes bulged, and his limbs thrashed about wildly.

One of the carjacker's flailing elbows jabbed Makhado's left eye. Momentarily blinded, Makhado let go of the carjacker's throat. That was the break the carjacker needed. Dazed, he scrambled to his feet and ran down the street, minus his nine-millimeter, just as people who'd fled into nearby buildings for cover reappeared, seeing that the worst was over.

At that moment a black Opel Kadette came screeching around the corner, siren blaring. Two uniformed police officers from the Johannesburg anti-hijacking unit, one black and the other white, jumped out of the Opel, guns drawn. The white officer dashed toward the Mazda while the black officer quizzed onlookers about what had happened.

The white officer peered through the Mazda's half-open window.

"Are you okay, Miss?" he asked the shaken white woman, who was still clutching the steering wheel, breathing hard. She'd stopped trembling. Tall and slender, with shoulder-length honey-blonde hair and an aquiline nose sprinkled with a smattering of freckles, she looked no more than thirty.

"Ja," the woman replied softly in an Afrikaans accent, letting out a deep sigh of relief. Her marine-blue eyes, glazed with tears, kept blinking rapidly. "Thanks to that man over there." She half-raised her left hand and pointed at Makhado, who was standing in the middle of the sidewalk, surrounded by chattering and impressed onlookers.

"What's your name?" asked the white officer after holstering his gun and taking out a notepad. His tone sounded somewhat jaded. This was the tenth carjacking he and his partner had responded to since noon.

"Liefling," said the white woman. "Liefling Malan."

The officer jotted down the information. "Where do you live?"

"Cape Town."

"What are you doing in Jo'burg?"

"I was attending a human rights conference at Wits University. I'm on my way to the airport. This is a rental car."

The officer asked Liefling a few more questions, then he and his colleague, who'd also been asking Makhado questions, left abruptly following a dispatch. Another carjacking was reportedly in progress near city hall on Market Street and there were reports of an exchange of gunfire between the carjackers and the owner of a brand-new gray BMW 328i.

It was Friday evening and the limited resources of the undermanned and overworked Johannesburg police force were no match for carjackers in one of the most crime-ridden cities in the world.

Liefling got out of the Mazda. After making sure it was locked, she walked over to where Makhado was standing talking to a group of blacks who were congratulating him on his bravery and asking him all kinds of questions. Makhado was surprised to see Liefling coming toward him. He thought she'd have driven off by now, glad to be alive. The small crowd around Makhado dispersed as Liefling approached.

"Thank you very much for saving my life," she said gratefully, shaking Makhado's work-gnarled hand.

"You're welcome, madam," Makhado said tentatively.

"Please don't call me 'madam.' My name is Liefling. What' s yours?"

Having addressed white people as "madam" and "baas (master)" all his life in deference to their superior status under apartheid, Makhado instantly realized from Liefling's rejection of this form of address that she was different. He decided to let down his guard. She would not call him a "cheeky kaffir," as he'd been called many times by whites when he'd inadvertently violated the master-servant etiquette that was still very much alive in South Africa, despite black majority rule and the abolition of apartheid.

"Makhado," he said. "Makhado Samson Munyai."

"Where are you going, Makhado?"

"To the railroad station."

"Can I give you a lift?"

Makhado hesitated, then said, "No, thank you. I'll walk."

"But it's more than eight blocks away." She looked at his hand. "And you're carrying a heavy suitcase."

"Okay." Makhado followed Liefling to her Mazda. He instinctively reached for the back door.

"No, get in front," Liefling said from the driver's side.

Makhado cast a suspicious glance at Liefling. *What kind of white woman is this?* he wondered. *She's not afraid or ashamed to ride in the front seat with a black man.*

Guessing what Makhado was thinking, Liefling smiled warmly, revealing a set of perfectly straight, bright teeth.

"Apartheid is dead, Makhado," she said. "It's now okay for a black and a white to sit together in the front seat of a car."

"Old habits die hard, Liefling," Makhado said, smiling back as he tossed his suitcase on to the backseat. He climbed in beside her.

"Where are you from?" Liefling asked.

"Venda."

"Is it your first time in Jo'burg?"

Makhado nodded. "First time since I was endorsed out in 1979."

"Endorsed out? Why?"

"It's a long story."

"I'm eager to hear it, if you don't mind," Liefling said, fastening her seat belt. Makhado did the same.

Makhado coughed slightly to clear his throat. "Well," he began, "I first came to Johannesburg as a mineworker in 1960, two months after the

Sharpeville Massacre. For nearly three years I lived in a single men's hostel, separated from my wife and four children. Under the terms of my work permit, I could only see them once a year. During the Christmas holidays. It was very hard living like that."

"I can imagine," Liefling said with empathy as she started the car and rejoined traffic. "Influx Control was the cruelest apartheid law. The government used it to break up millions of black families."

"But I refused to let it break up *my* family."

"How did you do that? The law was so hard to get around."

"I left the mines."

Liefling signaled for a left turn as the Mazda approached a busy intersection. After her narrow escape from carjackers, her eyes were now on the lookout for suspicious movement from any of the pedestrians crossing the street, or the occupants of the cars next to hers.

"Didn't you lose your work permit?" she asked Makhado as the Mazda completed its left turn.

"I did. But at least I was reunited with my family."

"So you went back to Venda?"

"No. I couldn't go back. There was no work there."

"Where did you live?"

"I rented a shack in Alexandra."

"What did you do for work?"

"I worked at odd jobs here and there. Mainly illegally as a gardener. And my wife operated a *shebeen* (speakeasy). Life was okay. We even managed to send our youngest child to university, despite the fact that whenever I was between jobs, I was often arrested for the crime of being unemployed."

Liefling shook her head as she remembered the peculiar *crime of being unemployed,* which only blacks could commit, and the Catch-22 it entailed. During the apartheid era millions of jobless black men had been thrown in jail as "vagrants" and "undesirables." But to get jobs they first needed to obtain special permits proving that they had satisfied all the necessary laws for working in white areas, permits that the authorities refused to grant without the applicants already having jobs.

"In 1972," Makhado went on, "I was hired as a security guard for Barclays bank in Hillbrow. My employers petitioned the government to grant me a work-permit because I was one of their best employees. I got the permit. But one day in 1979, shortly after Venda was granted its so-called independence, the police raided my shack around 4 a.m. This time they arrested me for harboring my wife and children as illegal aliens."

As she turned left into Twist Street, Liefling fought back tears. Makhado's story had made her recall other wrenching stories of the pain and suffering wrought by the Influx Control law, a cornerstone of apartheid, under which the government had had the absolute power to decide which blacks could legally stay in "white" South Africa, and had made it a crime for migrant workers to live with their families. While a student at the liberal University of Cape Town (UCT) where she'd double-majored in Sociology and Literature, she'd done extensive research on the law's devastating impact on black families, black communities and the black psyche.

"I was taken to the notorious Number Four prison to await trial," Makhado said, anger slowly creeping into his usually calm voice at the recollection, despite the passage of many years. "When I appeared before the magistrate ten days later he ordered that my family and I be immediately deported back to Venda. I've been living there ever since. And in the rural areas time has sort of stood still. Many white people, who are mostly *Boers* (Afrikaner farmers), continue to cling to the old ways."

"You'd be surprised how many people in the cities still cling to the old ways," Liefling said, throwing a quick glance at the side-view mirror before switching lanes. "I recently broke up with a boyfriend because he called black people kaffirs."

Makhado turned his head and stared at Liefling in disbelief. He wasn't sure he'd heard her right. "You broke up with your boyfriend because he called blacks kaffirs?"

"I did."

"But many white people still call us kaffirs," Makhado said. "Not only that, but they still treat us worse than animals."

"I know," Liefling said, recalling two recent shocking racial incidents that had made headlines. Both involved farmers in rural areas. One had strangled and decapitated two of his black workers because one of them called him by his first name instead of 'baas"; another had shot and killed one of his black laborers because he mistook him for a dog.

"A lot of whites are still racist, Makhado," Liefling went on, "despite the end of apartheid. In fact, I've been called a kaffir-lover many times for speaking out against white racism."

Makhado was stunned by Liefling's frankness about her personal life and racial attitude. They were qualities he'd never encountered in a white person. He was eager to find out what made her so refreshingly different from other Afrikaners he'd known and come to hate for treating him and his fellow blacks as kaffirs.

2   **MAGNUS KRUGER's** face was livid as his right thumb jabbed the remote, turning off the color TV nestled in the center of the antique mahogany entertainment unit.

"Kaffir bastards," he swore aloud. "Now that apartheid is gone they think they can exterminate us. Not if I can help it."

Kruger, a retired general of the South African Defense Force (SADF), sat for some time on a brown leather sofa staring at the blank television screen. Tall and big-boned, with a shock of silver hair, sharp angular face and pale-blue eyes topped by bushy eyebrows, Kruger had just finished watching a news story about the arrest of three black men in connection with the murder of an Afrikaner farmer in Venda. It was the tenth white farmer killed in two months.

Kruger glanced at his gold Rolex watch. Nearly ten past six. He frowned. *Where the hell is he?* he wondered.

For the past hour and half Kruger had been waiting for an important visitor. He abruptly rose from the sofa and strode toward the L-shaped bar of his lavish King's Suite at the Palace Hotel in Sun City. While mixing half gin and half French Vermouth into a martini cocktail, he mulled over a maxim from his second favorite book, *The Art of War* by Sun Tzu. (His favorite was a leather-bound Afrikaans bible his mother, a British concentration camp survivor, had given him before she committed suicide). The maxim, which had jangled like a broken record in his mind since the African National Congress (ANC) ushered in black majority rule following the historic all-race elections of April 27, 1994, was:

SURVIVAL DEPENDS UPON UNCONDITIONAL VICTORY

Drink in hand, Kruger paced up and down the well-appointed living room. He recalled that that important maxim, which had served the Afrikaner people well since the pioneering days of the Great Trek in 1834, had been fatally disobeyed by National Party leaders who'd shrunk from using every weapon at their disposal—including biological and nuclear weapons—to preserve the system of Afrikaner power and domination known as *Baaskap.*

Kruger sipped his martini. *We should have held on to the bitter end,* he thought angrily. *Now Baaskap is gone. The once unthinkable has happened. The Vaderland – for which the Afrikaner people labored, sacrificed and died – is now ruled by kaffirs.*

To Kruger, whose life was governed by a mythological Afrikaner past in which race predominated, the word "kaffir" meant more than just "nigger." Its Arabic meaning of "infidel" was a powerful reminder of the indestructible covenant his Voortrekker ancestors, who saw themselves as the descendants of the Hebrew Patriarchs, had made with God after He'd led them to signal victories over *Die Swart Gevaar* (The Black Menace) on their way to the Promised Land. That covenant was to preserve *Baaskap* at all cost. Only white supremacy could insure the survival of the Afrikaner nation on the Dark Continent.

Kruger stopped pacing. He placed his drink on the bar's marble counter and took out a handkerchief from the top pocket of his neatly pressed light-brown safari suit with short sleeves. He blew his stuffy nose rather loudly.

Baaskap shall rise again, he vowed in his thoughts as he wiped his nose. *The Silent Brotherhood of Afrikaner Patriots shall liberate the Afrikaner people from corrupt and incompetent kaffir rule.*

Since the fall of apartheid, Kruger and his fellow white supremacists in *The Silent Brotherhood of Afrikaner Patriots*, a secretive neo-Nazi organization, had been laboring to effect such a liberation. They'd suffered a couple setbacks but, like their Voortrekker ancestors, they'd kept the faith. Now he hoped that the important visitor he was awaiting would help him and his brethren achieve their dream of an Afrikaner-only *Volkstaat*.

Kruger drained his drink, placed the empty glass on the counter, and then stepped through the French doors onto the balcony to take in the sights of South Africa's answer to Las Vegas. Despite his strict Calvinistic upbringing under apartheid, which had taught him to read the Bible twice a day and to shun gambling and bare flesh, Kruger was a regular visitor to Sun City's entertainment extravaganza called "The Lost City."

He didn't come, however, to ogle the barelegged showgirls, nor to play the slot machines and place bets on roulette wheels. He came mainly to conduct business, play golf and indulge in the resort's more innocuous Disneyesque attractions, which included ancient ruins; a lake complete with its own sandy beach, waves and palm trees; a national park replete with thousands of wild animals; and a volcano that erupted on schedule.

And he could afford such indulgences. He was the multimillionaire owner of Protect, Arm & Secure Inc., one of the largest private security firms in South Africa, which had offices in all nine provinces and the neighboring countries of Zimbabwe, Mozambique, Botswana, Namibia and Lesotho.

That morning he'd flown from the firm's headquarters in downtown Johannesburg in his private helicopter for a 10 a.m. meeting with a group of Japanese investors who wanted him to devise a security system for their new car manufacturing plant. After the meeting, during which the Japanese agreed to pay his steep price, he'd celebrated by playing golf at the superb 18-hole Gary Player Country club, shooting under par for the first time.

Energized by his success on the golf course, he'd spent the rest of the afternoon in a four-wheel drive Land-Rover called a *bakkie*, bouncing around the 500 square kilometers of Pilanesberg National Park surrounding Sun City snapping pictures of wild animals with his 35-mm Nikon.

He'd planned to leave Sun City at precisely five o'clock. At the last minute, however, he'd received a call from the important person he was now eagerly waiting for. Kruger grabbed the balcony railing with his large hands. He took a deep breath of the cool autumn air. He let it out slowly through a puckered mouth, while staring at the calming scene of the spectacular Valley of the Waves lake, whose surface reflected the golden hues of the African sun as it set beyond the nearby Pilanesberg range. The breath relaxed him some. He took a couple more.

The doorbell rang. Kruger raced to the thick mahogany door and flung it open. His eyes lit up when he saw standing in front of him a debonair-looking man with sleek raven-dark hair, a curved, arrogant-looking nose and the most intensely blue eyes.

"Reginald Hunter!" Kruger cried with uncharacteristic exuberance. He threw his arms wide open and wrapped his lanky visitor in a bear hug. "Is it truly you?" His stentorian voice had a guttural Afrikaner accent.

Hunter smiled broadly. "*Ja, mei bloedbroer,*" he said in a soft baritone with the distinct accent of someone from the American South, which made his saying "Yes, my blood brother," in Afrikaans sound a bit ridiculous.

A slim black leather attaché in his left hand, Hunter stepped into the brightly-lit suite. His eyes surveyed the lavish interior. "My, my, so this is what Sun City is famous for? How much does this palace cost a night?"

"Oh, about $2,500. Tax deductible, of course."

"Of course."

"Can I get you something to drink?"

"Gin and tonic, *asseblief*." Hunter leaned the attaché against the wall.

"With ice?"

"*Nee, danke.*"

Kruger let out an appreciative chuckle. "I see you still remember our *mooi moeder taal*." He poured the gin and tonic into a crystal glass.

"Thanks to the tapes you gave me," Hunter said, recalling how easy they'd made learning Afrikaans, the only Germanic language to have evolved outside Europe.

"I wish more people understood Afrikaans," Kruger said, handing Hunter his gin and tonic. "Then they would better understand the Afrikaner people and our determination to preserve our unique culture and heritage."

Hunter sipped his drink. "No doubt they would, my friend."

Kruger and Hunter sat down on opposite ends of the sofa. On the glass coffee table in front of the sofa was a bronze rhino statue, two long-stemmed candlesticks, a bowl of roasted unsalted nuts and an open box of aromatic Cuban cigars.

"So," Kruger said, placing his drink on a coaster in the middle of the coffee table. "How was your flight from South America?"

"Not bad at all," Hunter said. Feeling slightly warm, he took off his green sports jacket. "The jet I'm now using for long-distance travel is an airborne five-star hotel, my friend. I can't wait to show it to you."

"I'm eager to see it," Kruger said, looking Hunter over. "I still can't believe you're here, my friend. How long has it been since your last visit?"

"Oh, about fourteen years."

Kruger arched his bushy eyebrows. "That long?"

"Yep. When I was last here you'd just left the security branch at John Vorster Square to head a counterinsurgency unit of the SADF. And you took me to that special meeting, which inspired me to unite the various white supremacist groups in America into a single organization called The Brotherhood of American Patriots."

Kruger grinned. "Excellent memory," he said, fondly remembering the meeting he'd taken Hunter to in May 1984, which had marked a decisive turning point in his life. Over 7,000 members of right-wing and neo-Nazi Afrikaner groups had packed a hall in Pretoria to protest President P.W. Botha's constitutional reforms granting a limited franchise to Indians and to the mixed-race Coloreds in a tricameral parliament, while excluding the black majority. Amid fiery and defiant speeches, patriotic songs and waving banners and flags, the groups had launched the *Afrikaner Volkswag*, the Afrikaner People's Guard, following whose demise Kruger had formed *The Silent Brotherhood of Afrikaner Patriots*.

Kruger, who with Hunter had sat as honored guests in front of the stage, remembered three speakers in particular, whose message was at the core of *The Silent Brotherhood of Afrikaner Patriots'* mission. The first speaker was a university professor and a former chairman of the Broederbond, the secret Afrikaner society that for decades had championed and defended *Baaskap*. The professor, in a mild voice at odds with his racial fanaticism, had warned Afrikaners of the dangers of compromise, and had called on the Afrikaner nation to purify itself by returning to its cultural identity.

The second speaker was a notorious judge and a member of the AWB (Afrikaner Resistance Movement), a neo-Nazi group whose followers were fond of flaunting swastika-like flags. He'd described the Afrikaner history as one of war and not compromise, and had called on the *Volkswag* to rise and sweep away Botha's *verligte* (liberal) policies, warning that they threatened the very survival of Afrikaners as a distinct and superior race.

The third speaker Kruger vividly remembered because she was a woman who later became the wife of his pastor and close friend, Dominee Koos Muller. Her name was Wilhemina, and her fiery speech had brought the crowd to its feet. Wilhemina was a member of the Kappie Kommando, a militant union for Afrikaner women, whose badge was a Voortrekker bonnet. Compared by the press to the vengeful and ruthless Madame Defarge in Dickens's *A Tale of Two Cities*, Wilhemina had called for the purging of *Hensoppers* (sellouts) from the midst of the Afrikaner people, so that a new and stronger nation could be built with a sword in one hand and a Bible in the other.

"When the *Volkswag* failed to convince Botha to abandon his suicidal course," Kruger said, "I knew it was the beginning of the end. And I was right. Two years later the bastardized parliament repealed the Immorality and Prohibition of Mixed Marriages Acts which had protected the Afrikaner people against racial pollution. Then a year later Mandela was released. After that we lost the bloody country."

Hunter's eyes roved about the suite. "I see you've done well despite the end of *Baaskap*."

Kruger smiled. "Thanks to private security. It's the fastest growing industry in South Africa. When kaffirs took over, crime and robberies skyrocketed. Naturally, I was ready to capitalize on the situation, given my expertise in security matters. Now the firm, which is only five years old, has a forty-two percent market share and numbers among its growing clientele more than fifty major American, European and Asian corporations."

"Impressive," Hunter said. "So the recent article in the *Wall Street Journal* about the company being worth $90 million is true?"

"Depending on the exchange rate," Kruger said. "I believe it's now five rands to a dollar. So $90 million is about right."

Hunter's ever-roving eyes rested on a pair of huge elephant tusks standing like sentries on either side of a massive marble fireplace. "By the way, I very much enjoyed the time we spent at the bushveld camp in that homeland near Kruger National Park. What is it called by the way?"

"Venda. It's been reabsorbed into South Africa."

"And the bushveld camp—is it still around?"

"Ja," Kruger said, reaching for the box of cigars. "One of my close associates—Piet Viljoen, you remember him—the electrician?"

Hunter flashed a knowing smile. "Of course."

"He owns it now. He's upgraded it into an exclusive private game reserve. Really first class. It offers luxury chalets, cottages, lodges and Venda-style huts. And it caters—you'll love this—exclusively to our brethren from abroad who are seeking the wilderness experience. And since 1994 they and their families have been flocking in from all over Europe, Australia, South America and the former Soviet Union."

"The first Aryans-only private game reserve. I like that. It fits well with Pan-Aryanism."

"Would you like to spend some time there during your stay?"

"I'd love to," Hunter said. "But I have to be in Australia by tomorrow. I have an important meeting with a multimillionaire who's thinking of running for political office. From there I'll be flying to France, Germany and Austria to help our brethren prepare for upcoming elections."

"Are you still a political consultant?"

"Yep. Big time now. Scores of clients. All over the world. But I'll urge the Brotherhood to consider Viljoen's game reserve for our next annual meeting. It's a very important one and requires the utmost secrecy. We'll be planning strategy for the Second American Revolution."

"Secrecy shouldn't be a problem, my friend. The game reserve is very private. To this day what my counterinsurgency unit did there during the apartheid era isn't known. Not even by the kaffirs who work at the place."

Kruger offered Hunter a cigar. He politely declined with a wave of his small, almost feminine, hand. "Gave it up a long time ago. Doctor's orders."

"My doctor, too, told me to give it up. But I told him that life is too short for me not to enjoy one of its finer pleasures."

"That's Von Schleicher's philosophy," Hunter said.

"How's the old bugger?" Kruger asked, lighting his cigar.

"Not too well lately. He's almost eighty-two and recently had double bypass surgery. I'm now running the Brotherhood's day-to-day operations. He spends a great deal of time at his estate in the mountains of North Carolina. The mild climate is more agreeable to his delicate health. But he remains very devoted to the cause."

"I read in *Forbes* that he's now worth $25 billion," Kruger said with some envy.

"That was eight months ago," Hunter said brightly. "He's now worth $35 billion. The recent stock market surge has provided him with a whopping windfall. And he's devoting most of it to furthering the cause of white supremacy worldwide."

Hunter paused and scooped a handful of nuts from the bowl. He tossed a few into his mouth.

"One of the places he's most concerned about, of course, is South Africa," Hunter said, munching. "It remains dear to his heart. You do remember, don't you, how hard he lobbied the U.S. Congress and the Reagan Administration not to pass the sanctions bill back in 1987?"

Kruger nodded. "And the Afrikaner people are eternally grateful, my friend. Despite the disappointing outcome."

"And since your niggers came to power," Hunter said, "he's been paying a great deal of attention to how they are running things."

"Ruining them, you mean," Kruger said with particular vehemence, eyes flickering with anger. He abruptly got up and went to the bar, as if his anger needed another drink as a palliative. "Crime is out of control," he ranted, mixing another martini. "Afrikaners feel besieged. Law and order are disintegrating. Afrikaner farmers are being butchered like flies. Above all, miscegenation, the greatest threat against the survival of the Afrikaner people, is rampant."

Hunter got up and followed Kruger to the bar. He leaned his left elbow on the shiny marble counter and studied his irate friend.

"That's why I'm here, *bloedbroer*," he said soothingly. "I'm eager to help you liberate the Afrikaner people from nigger rule."

Highly pleased at the news, Kruger refilled Hunter's glass. He was about to ask exactly how Hunter planned to help but decided to postpone the question. Instead, he handed Hunter his drink and said, "Do you mind if we continued our most interesting talk on the balcony? It's such a lovely evening."

3 MAKHADO asked Liefling, "What kind of work do you do?"

"I'm a lawyer," she replied as the Mazda slowed due to bumper-to-bumper traffic along Pretoria Street.

"What kind of lawyer?"

"I represent victims of human rights abuses and their families before the Truth and Reconciliation Commission."

"Before the TRC?" Makhado was surprised that an Afrikaner would represent black victims of apartheid – the very system Afrikaners had for so long supported and defended.

"Ja," Liefling said.

His curiosity piqued, Makhado wondered if he should ask any more questions. He was still making up his mind when Liefling surprised him by asking, "What do you think of the TRC?"

The question caught Makhado somewhat off-guard. He fidgeted slightly in his seat, unsure how much of his true feelings he could safely reveal to a white person, no matter how liberal. He remembered too well the sting of past rebukes by white people offended by his "cheeky" questions.

But somehow, in a way he couldn't quite yet explain, Liefling forcibly struck him as accessible, human. He felt he could communicate honestly with her, rather than play his usual role of a humble and shuffling kaffir, who dared not look white people in the eye, and whose vocabulary was limited to "yes, madam" and "no, madam," and "ja, baas" and "no, baas."

"I've been following the TRC hearings very closely," Makhado said slowly, carefully watching Liefling's face for any sudden change in expression. "One thing baffles me. Maybe you could enlighten me about it."

"I'll try," Liefling said as the Mazda approached a fort-like structure perched on a hill in the middle of the city.

At the sight of "Number Four" Makhado shuddered. He recalled the many times during the apartheid era when he'd been brought to the dreaded prison, also known as The Fort, to await trial for violating Influx Control laws. At the Fort, which was used by the British to hold prisoners during the Boer war, he'd met men like Nelson Mandela, who were briefly jailed there for political crimes under the Sabotage Act, and other black men whose only crimes had been working without the proper papers, working with the proper papers but in the wrong place, riding in a white elevator, sitting on a white bench, drinking from a white water fountain, boarding a white bus or strolling in a white park. He especially remembered the Fort's racist policemen, who took pleasure in emasculating and torturing black men.

"Why is the TRC letting torturers and murderers off the hook?" Makhado asked, his eyes fixed on the high stone wall rimming the Fort.

"A lot of my clients have asked me the same question. The answer is quite complicated. Have you heard of the sunset clause?"

Makhado nodded. "The ANC should never have proposed it," he said firmly. "Not after what apartheid did to black people."

The "sunset clause" was a controversial proposal the ANC had made during the CODESA (Congress for a Democratic South Africa) talks on a peaceful transition to black rule. Reasoning that the white minority regime couldn't be dictated to because it was not a defeated enemy, the ANC had proposed amnesty for policemen and security officers, the honoring of the contracts of white civil servants, and the retention of many of them as policemen, military officers and judges. As a result former defenders of *Baaskap* now had the responsibility of safeguarding black majority rule.

"Without the sunset clause there would have been civil war," Liefling said. "And what South Africa needed was national unity and reconciliation."

"There can be no reconciliation without justice," Makhado said decisively.

"I agree."

"You do?" Makhado was surprised.

"Ja. That's why six months ago I quit a well-paying job at a private law firm to work with victims of human rights abuses and their families. I want to make sure that reconciliation goes hand-in-hand with justice. My father believed that strongly. That's why they killed him."

"Who killed him?"

"Death squads. He was an Afrikaner minister who fought against apartheid. He was murdered in 1989 while trying to help the families of victims of death squads find out what had happened to their loved ones. I intend to finish what he started."

"How will you do that? Few policemen and security force members are confessing the whole truth."

"I've been petitioning the TRC to deny amnesty to those who lie or give sanitized versions of what they did."

Liefling paused and glanced at the rear-view mirror. She quickly switched lanes before making a sharp left turn into King George Street. Makhado was impressed by her driving skills in the congested traffic of downtown Jo'burg on a Friday evening.

"And I sue those who refuse to testify," she said. "That's the best way to get justice under the new Constitution."

Makhado shook his gray head skeptically.

"I see you aren't a great believer in the TRC," Liefling said.

"I'm a warrior," Makhado said emphatically. "The only justice I believe in is an eye for an eye."

"Given what black people suffered under apartheid, I perfectly understand how you'd feel that way." Liefling saw the traffic light ahead turn red, but she was still so shaken by the trauma of the attempted carjacking that she did not come to a full stop. Because carjacking was so widespread in the second largest city in Africa behind Cairo, police turned a blind eye when motorists ran red lights or failed to stop at a stop sign.

"But my son supports the TRC," Makhado said. "It's hard to believe he does after what the police did to him."

"What did they do?"

"They detained him many times for his political activism," Makhado said. "One time he spent three months in solitary confinement at John Vorster Square, during which he was brutally tortured."

"What's your son's name?"

"Gideon. He's a schoolteacher. I just spent the week visiting him and his family in Alexandra. We watched the TRC hearings together on TV. We argued most of the time."

"Why?

"He's of the opinion that, despite its flaws, the TRC is good for the country. I strongly disagree. Especially after he told me that the government is so eager to have torturers and murderers testify that it's offered to pay their legal costs. Is that true?"

"I'm afraid it is."

"He also said that the families of victims, when they want to oppose the amnesty applications of those who tortured and murdered their loved ones, have to pay most of the legal costs out of their own pockets. Is that true also?"

"I'm afraid that's also true."

Makhado's chest heaved. His eyes smoldered with latent fury. "That's not justice!" He cried out in a bitter tone. "How can the poor, the unemployed and pensioners afford lawyers who charge between R250 and R400? My son said that these lawyers also want to be paid between R1, 500 and R2, 500 in court appearance fees per day. You know what? As a miner it took me more than two years to earn that kind of money. More than two years of hard labor."

"I share your anger and frustration," Liefling said with deep sympathy. "As a matter of fact, I gave a talk this morning at Wits University law school on the very issue. It was called, *'Justice and the TRC: The High Price of Being a Victim.'"*

Liefling drove cautiously through another red light. Makhado was silent for a while, simply staring out the window at the crowded sidewalks. Liefling could sense that he was angry. She thought it best not to say anything. She knew that a lot of blacks were unhappy with the whole issue of amnesty. They wanted to see former torturers and murderers punished. It was testimony to Mandela's leadership that he'd been able to persuade them to go along with the sunset clause and the TRC.

"Can you explain to me why many torturers and murderers refuse to apologize for the evil things they've done?" Makhado asked suddenly.

"Apologizing is not a condition for amnesty," Liefling said. "To be honest with you, many former security force members don't think that what they did was wrong."

"So what's to prevent them from undermining black majority rule?"

Liefling felt a chill run down her spine. As the Mazda turned left onto Rissik Street, she said to Makhado, "Why do you ask that?"

"I watch TV and read the papers," he said. "Former security force members have been stealing all kinds of sophisticated weapons from army barracks across the country. And many of them have also been implicated in drug dealing, money laundering, carjackings, taxi violence, crime syndicates and gunrunning. On top of that the military, the police force and the judiciary system are still filled with racists and white supremacists who have absolutely no loyalty to a black government. Then there are reports of plans by neo-Nazis to destabilize the country as part of a strategy to gain an Afrikaner homeland. Is all this pure coincidence?"

Liefling pursed her lips thoughtfully as the Mazda slowed on its approach to the busy railroad station. Makhado's probing question made her recall that back in 1993, after the signing of CODESA's historic power-sharing agreement between the ANC and the ruling National Party, there had been numerous plots by neo-Nazi elements within the police and the SADF to derail black majority rule. Guns had been poured into the townships to foment black-on-black violence. Death squads had roamed across South Africa firebombing houses and assassinating anti-apartheid activists. And there had even been efforts by neo-Nazis to assassinate top ANC leaders in order to ignite a race war.

She'd been an ANC activist then, freshly graduated from Wits law school and involved in efforts to register black voters. She remembered how serious these plots had been. As an Afrikaner she knew that there were many among her people who'd been prepared to see a bloodbath in South Africa rather than give up their power and privilege. One particularly harrowing plot had involved an AWB neo-Nazi who was arrested with a canister of cyanide in the trunk of his car, on his way to the reservoir which supplied water to Soweto, a township inhabited by over a million blacks.

Another plot, which brought South Africa to the brink of civil war, had involved the assassination of Chris Hani by an AWB neo-Nazi on April 10, 1993. Hani, who was the secretary-general of the South African Communist Party (SACP), had been chief of staff for the ANC's military wing, *Umkonto We Sizwe* (MK), during the liberation struggle. He was the second most popular black leader behind Nelson Mandela and was idolized by *Comrades*, radical black youths who rejected any compromise with the apartheid regime, and who clamored for guns to mount a violent revolution.

Liefling recalled how, when word of Hani's death spread, whites across the country had armed themselves as enraged *Comrades* went on rampage, setting fire to houses and attacking white motorists. Trapped inside the festering ghetto of Alexandra where she had gone to help register voters, she had to be smuggled out by black friends in the trunk of a Pontiac. She barely made it through burning barricades and an angry stone-throwing mob chanting "ONE SETTLER, ONE BULLET."

Mindful of all this, all Liefling could say in reply to Makhado's incisive question was, "Some neo-Nazis are coming forward and testifying before the TRC in the hope of being granted amnesty."

"What about those who aren't coming forward?" Makhado said. "Why aren't they taking advantage of such an unbelievably generous amnesty? What are they afraid of? What other plots are they still hatching?"

The Mazda came to a stop in front of the crowded entrance to the railroad station, about ten feet from a buxom Zulu woman who was selling woven baskets, beadwork and arts and crafts.

"You ask such tough questions, Makhado," Liefling said, smiling. "You should have been a lawyer."

"I might have been one but my father didn't believe in schools."

"Why?"

"He considered them a waste of time. Instead he sent me to the mountain school to become a warrior like himself, and his father before him. And when I killed my first lion at age fifteen, armed only with a spear, he took me aside and proudly said, 'No white man's school could have taught you such courage, my son. And life is for the courageous.'"

"How, then, did you learn to speak such good English?"

"From missionaries who worked among my people a long time ago. But unless I'm talking to white people I trust – a rarity – I always pretend I don't know how to read or write or speak good English. I speak only Fanagalo."

Fanagalo, which meant "Do it like this" in Zulu, was a lingua Franca with a simple syntax and a vocabulary of about a thousands words borrowed from Afrikaans, English and African languages. During the apartheid era, it was used by white mineworkers to give orders to black mineworkers from different tribes and nationalities, and outside the mines whites generally used it to speak to illiterate blacks.

Liefling smiled and shook her head. She was in awe of Makhado. For the first time she realized that she was in the presence of a very wise and very shrewd man. Makhado had perfected the black man's art of survival in a racist white world—where the wrong word or look could sometimes result in death—by playing the shuffling, humble and deferential kaffir who didn't know how to read and write, and who spoke only Fanagalo.

"Are you a Christian?" Liefling couldn't help asking.

Makhado shook his head. "No. I only believe in *Midzimu*, the gods of my

Venda ancestors. But I have no quarrel with Christians—so long as they respect my beliefs. My wife is a devout Lutheran and my son is a Bahai."

Liefling's face brightened. "That's interesting. My new boyfriend, who is black, is also a Bahai."

For the second time Liefling left Makhado totally stunned. "Your boyfriend is black?"

"Ja. His father is Zulu and his mother is Colored."

"What's his name?"

"Sipho. Sipho Radebe. He's a doctor."

"Where?"

"Half the time he's at Baragwanath Hospital, and half the time at a clinic in Crossroads, where his father grew up."

"So he commutes between Johannesburg and Cape Town?"

"Ja. But he's thinking of leaving Bara and concentrating on the clinic."

"Do you think you'll marry him?"

Liefling smiled. "If he asks me, I'd seriously consider it. I love him very much, despite the fact that we've only just met."

Makhado stared at Liefling for a long minute.

"You know," he said finally, smiling, "you're a very strange Afrikaner."

Liefling smiled back. "Why do you say that?"

"You're so different from other Afrikaners. You're so..." Makhado creased his prominent forehead, searching for the right word. "So.... African. That's it. So African."

"I regard myself as an African."

"You do?"

"Ja. That's one reason I rejected apartheid. I didn't believe all that nonsense about white superiority. The Afrikaner culture was not forged in Europe. It was forged right here in Africa. And it was heavily influenced by African cultures."

"That's very interesting. My son, who teaches history, says that one reason Afrikaners created apartheid was to hide their insecurity about their identity."

"He's right. We Afrikaners long to be accepted as Africans. But I'm afraid we won't be until we start behaving like Africans."

"What do you mean?"

"We must repudiate *Baaskap* and embrace the spirit of *Ubuntu*, which says that one is never fully human until and unless one acknowledges and affirms the humanity of others."

Makhado grinned. "You're very wise for one so young."

"Thank you."

Makhado glanced at the clock. It was almost seven-twenty. "I'd better get going. It's Easter and the trains will be packed."

Liefling reached for a handbag made of intricate Zulu beadwork, a gift from Sipho on her twenty-ninth birthday two weeks ago.

"It was really a joy meeting you, Makhado," she said.

"I feel the same way."

"And thanks again for saving my life."

"You're welcome."

"Here's my business card. If you should ever need help, please don't hesitate to give me a call."

"Thank you." Makhado took the card and put it in his wallet. He then opened the door, got out and retrieved his suitcase from the backseat. Passersby headed for the trains threw curious glances at him.

Liefling got out also. Without thinking twice about it, she hugged Makhado as onlookers gawked. The gesture of friendship and gratitude left Makhado speechless. It was the first hug he'd ever received from a white person – an Afrikaner woman at that.

"*Hamba gahle*," Liefling said, using the Zulu word for "go well."

"*Sala gahle*," replied Makhado, who knew all ten South African tribal languages from his stint as a miner. A genuinely warm feeling toward a white person flooded his heart for the first time. "And may your *Midzimu* protect you from further carjackings."

Liefling smiled and said, "*Giyabonga* (Thank you)."

Proud to have met the first white person who'd treated him as an equal, and to whom he could relate as a human being, Makhado walked with a jaunty step across the concrete pavement toward the entrance to the teeming railroad station.

She's indeed African, he thought. *No doubt about that.*

Makhado couldn't resist a backward glance at a woman who had made him reassess his view of Afrikaners, something he'd thought he'd never do. Liefling waved. Smiling, Makhado waved back vigorously before disappearing amid the hurrying throng headed underground to the packed trains.

4 KRUGER, very excited, asked Hunter, "How do you propose to help me, my friend?"

The two white supremacists were sitting on rattan lounge chairs next to each other on the wide balcony. It was a mellow evening, with very little humidity and a slight breeze. The sun was long gone. A fat silver-gray moon rested lazily on the brow of a distant hill.

Hunter crossed his long legs before replying. "Remember the letter you sent me, oh, about two years ago?"

"You mean the one in which I mentioned that *The Silent Brotherhood of Afrikaner Patriots* planned to launch a Fourth Boer Revolution?"

"Yeah, that's the one."

Kruger instantly became glum. "Those plans are currently on hold."

"Why?"

"Money. You may recall that they depended on my selling the firm. So far I haven't had a single decent offer. And I need money to make an Afrikaner-only homeland a reality, my friend. Big money."

"You'll soon have it, *bloedbroer*," Hunter said. "During my stop in South America, I met with a group of investors who were quite impressed by the profile of your firm in the *Wall Street Journal*. When they heard that I knew you, and that I planned to stop in South Africa to see you on the way to Australia, they asked if I could convince you to sell it to them. I immediately saw an opportunity to earn you a handsome profit. I told them that I was your overseas agent, that you'd received many attractive offers, and had rejected them all. But if the price is right, I said, I'll try to convince you to change your mind. You know how much I was able to get them to offer?"

"How much?"

"Guess."

"$100 million."

"Guess again."

"$150 million?"

Hunter leaned back in his chair. "How does one billion strike you?"

"One billion rands?"

"No, my friend, one billion dollars."

Kruger's eyes bulged like a squid's. "One billion dollars?" he muttered slowly. "Are you serious?"

Hunter flashed a self-satisfied half-smile. "I'm serious, my friend. I wouldn't be here if I weren't."

"But that's five billion rands! Ten times the firm's market value!"

"I told these investors that your firm is worth more, *bloedbroer*. I told them that it's the best for their kind of business."

"I-I-I don't know how to thank you," Kruger stammered gratefully.

"The best way to thank me is to ensure that the Fourth Boer Revolution succeeds."

"With that kind money it can't possibly fail, my friend," Kruger said, hardly able to contain his excitement. "Crime, violence and affirmative action are stampeding more and more Afrikaners back into the *laager*. Even the *verligte* ones. *The Silent Brotherhood of Afrikaner Patriots* plans to mobilize them into such a powerful political force that the ANC will finally let us set up our own *Volkstaat*."

"The ANC will never allow you to secede," Hunter said, grim-faced.

"Section 235 of the Constitution guarantees us the right, my friend."

"It does?" Hunter was genuinely surprised. Out of disdain, he hadn't bothered to read the historic document that, in the name of national unity and reconciliation, guaranteed even right-wing and neo-Nazi groups whose members had been implicated in torture and murder during the apartheid era the right to field candidates in local, provincial and federal elections.

"Ja," Kruger said brightly. "Wait a moment." He leaped to his feet and ran inside. He returned a few moments later with a well-worn copy of the new South African Constitution. He didn't bother to sit down. With the eagerness of a child, he read Hunter the following excerpt in the forceful and resonant voice that had won him prizes during debates at Stellenbosch University:

> The right of the South African people as a whole to self-determination, as
> manifested in the Constitution, does not preclude, within the framework
> of the recognition of this right, recognition of the notion of the right to

self-determination of any community sharing a common cultural and language heritage, within a territorial entity within the Republic or in any other way determined by national legislation.

Hunter waved his left arm dismissively. "That's constitutional claptrap. I repeat, the race-mixers in the ANC won't let Afrikaners secede."

"Why not?" a sullen Kruger said, sitting down.

"Because it would mean a return to the homeland system envisioned by the creators of Grand Apartheid. Don't forget, my friend, that we Southerners fought a bloody civil war over the issue of secession."

"Afrikaners are prepared to do the same, if need be," Kruger vowed.

"Who will do the fighting?"

"What do you mean?" Kruger asked, a confused look on his face.

"I mean where are the patriots brave enough to take on the black hordes, as your Voortrekker ancestors did at the memorable Battle of Blood River?"

Kruger bristled. "Are you impugning my patriotism?"

"No, my friend. You and I are of the same ilk. We are *Bittereinders*, as your forefathers who refused to surrender to the British during the Boer War called themselves. Because of our devotion to *Baaskap* and white racial purity, we'd rather die than surrender. That's why we're leaders. It's your men I'm concerned about."

Despite his evident relief at being exonerated from the charge of cowardice, Kruger felt it necessary to say, "What makes you doubt the loyalty of men who nobly defended apartheid? Don't forget it was the bloody politicians who sold out the Volk to kaffirs. *They* negotiated the ignominious surrender. My men were prepared to find to the bitter end."

Hunter ignored Kruger's wounded chauvinism. He understood his fellow white supremacist's bitterness and rage. As a Klansman, he'd felt the same emotions when the South capitulated to Yankees during the 1960s civil rights struggle, rather than fight a second civil war to protect the Southern way of life that had included an American version of apartheid.

"I hear what you're saying, my friend," Hunter said soothingly. "But like the rest of the world I've been closely following the TRC's witchhunts. I've never in all my sixty-one years seen such a stampede by Aryans to snitch on each other. Absolutely revolting. Especially the groveling before haughty niggers and begging for forgiveness. Forgiveness for what? For defending your birthright by whatever means necessary? How shamefully detestable!"

Eyes flashing, Kruger shot back. "Your facts are wrong. None of my men have testified or applied for amnesty. Not a single one." He demonstrated the number by wagging a finger.

"But many in the SADF have."

"Am I responsible for the entire fucking SADF?" Kruger hissed.

"Of course you aren't. But what's to prevent members of your unit from applying for amnesty as the deadline approaches, thus exposing you and derailing plans for the Fourth Boer Revolution?"

Kruger hadn't thought of that. So confident was he of his men's loyalty that the farthest thing from his mind was their betraying him. He abruptly stood up and walked toward the edge of the balcony, his hands clasped behind his back, his large jaw firmly set. For a long while he said nothing.

Hunter got up and joined Kruger. His intense blue eyes seemed aglow with mystical fanaticism. He gently laid a hand on Kruger's right shoulder. "*Bloedbroer*," he said, almost in a whisper, "don't you see that this TRC shit is nothing but a deadly trap to exterminate the Afrikaner people under sweet-sounding names?"

He's right, Kruger thought, recalling the spate of murdered white farmers.

"Haven't you figured out your niggers yet?" Hunter went on with growing intensity. "First they humiliate you before the whole goddamn world while being applauded for their so-called humanity. Then they turn around and butcher your farmers, rape your women, make prostitutes of your daughters, hijack your cars, invade your homes, and defile your schools, your culture and your heritage with all kinds of liberal experiments. All because Afrikaners are not men enough to take up arms and defend their birthright and honor. Instead, they stampede each other in order to rat before that gnome Tutu and his fellow inquisitors."

"I know what you mean," Kruger said quietly. He turned and faced Hunter, a confident look on his face. "But I assure you members of the Thathe Vondo death squad won't rat."

"And why not?"

"They are *regte*, true, Afrikaners. They swore a sacred oath to *bly op die bus,* to maintain their code of silence. And breaking that oath is punishable by death. They know I won't hesitate to kill anyone who squeals."

Hunter was apparently reassured. He changed the subject as he walked toward a potted bougainvillea with lush green capes. He leaned over, opened one of the large purple bracts and peered at the small delicate flower inside.

"Can you come to the U.S. at the end of the month?" he said, without looking at Kruger, as if addressing the flower. "I want to introduce you to our rising stars who've infiltrated the Republican and Democratic parties and are poised to help bring about the Second American Revolution."

"I wish I could. But I'm getting married."

Hunter jerked up and stared at Kruger, stunned. "You're what?"

"I'm getting married."

"Why in the world are you making a damn fool of yourself at your age?"

"Sixty-two is not too old to have a wife, my friend," Kruger said, smiling complacently. "I'm still virile, even without taking Viagra."

Hunter managed a small laugh at this witticism. "Who is she?"

"She's someone I almost married forty years ago. But she ended up marrying someone else. Now she's a widow. She's the only woman I've ever considered marrying. My mother adored her."

"Well, happy matrimony," said Hunter, a confirmed bachelor.

"The only problem, my friend, but it's a minor one, is that she's *verligte*."

"She's a liberal!" Hunter said in utter disbelief.

Kruger gave a sheepish nod.

"In heaven's name why are you marrying a goddamn liberal? Aren't there enough *verkrampte* Afrikaner women?"

"She was *verkrampte* before she married her first husband, who turned her into a *verligte*. But I'm confident I can turn her back into a *verkrampte*."

Hunter was skeptical. "How?"

"She's a disillusioned liberal. South Africa is full of them. Carjackers, rapists and robbers don't care if you're a liberal. And the racism directed against whites has shocked her into realizing how wrong she was in assuming that blacks don't hate. She's told me as much."

"Typical of liberals," Hunter sneered. "We have them in America too. Their naiveté and idealism have blinded them to the realities of the world in which we live. Blacks and whites are eternal enemies, my friend. When one is the master, the other must be the slave. That's why total separation is the answer. How old is this woman you're planning to marry?"

"Fifty-eight. But she looks half her age. A former beauty queen. From one of the most respected Afrikaner families in the country."

Kruger took another puff of his smoldering cigar and continued. "Her mother, who died about three years ago, was in the same British concentration camp with my mother during our war of Independence. And her father was a Boer war commando leader who later became a senior member of the Broederbond – our version of the Klan, which unfortunately has now been disbanded. Her pedigree is impeccable, my friend. She's of pure Afrikaner blood. And in these race-mixing days that's important."

"Very important," Hunter said emphatically. "A husband who's worthy of the title can always change his wife's politics to suit his own taste and comfort. But contaminated blood can never be changed."

In a celebratory mood, Kruger and Hunter returned inside. They had a couple more drinks before a chauffeured bulletproof limo took them to the Pilanesberg Airport, about 7 km northwest of Sun City, where Kruger's JetRanger helicopter and Hunter's retrofitted L-1011 Tri-Star jet were parked.

"It's more than an airborne five-star hotel," Kruger said in evident admiration as Hunter showed him around the luxury jumbo jet with its richly-paneled interior, lavish bedrooms, showers with gold fixtures, private office, conference room with TV monitors and laptop computers, and state-of-the-art communications center uplinked to an orbiting satellite.

"Von Schleicher bought the jet a year ago after I told him we'll need our own Air Force One to use as a secure command center during the Second American Revolution," Hunter said proudly. "It's capable of cruising at 560 mph for distances of up to 4,000 miles without refueling. I've named it Aryan Force One."

"I look forward to welcoming Aryan Force One to an Afrikaner-only homeland to join us in celebrating the magnificent achievement," Kruger said with a confident smile as he prepared to leave.

"Before I forget, where do you plan to establish the Volkstaat?"

"In the Orange Free State, where our forefathers settled after God answered their prayers for their own Vaderland."

"We'll be honored to come," Hunter said. "And I'll let you know soon when the representative of those investors can come to finalize the deal."

The two supremely confident new-Age white supremacists embraced for some time on the steps of Aryan Force One before Kruger disembarked. Shortly thereafter the jumbo jet taxied down the runaway and took off on its journey to Sidney, Australia.

Without delay, Kruger boarded his helicopter, which was piloted by Wolfgang Erasmus, a bearded, sallow-faced former member of Kruger's death squad. Its rotor blades spinning rapidly, the helicopter lifted off into a cloudless night sky bejeweled by stars, headed for downtown Johannesburg. Kruger planned a brief stop at his office before proceeding to the important late-night meeting of the *Uitvoerende Raad*, the Executive Council of The Silent Brotherhood of Afrikaner Patriots.

He couldn't wait to brief his fellow neo-Nazis on the unexpected three billion rand offer from the South Americans, which, if everything went well, would bring them a step closer to realizing their dream of creating an exclusive homeland for South Africa's six million Afrikaners.

5   **MAKHADO** struggled to squeeze his bulging suitcase into the narrow metal rack above the seat. It wouldn't fit. Frustrated, he looked about the crowded and stuffy third-class compartment of the train from Johannesburg to Messina, searching for a space large enough for his suitcase, which was packed with food and clothing for his extended family back in Venda.

There was none. The train was packed with passengers, mostly Venda and Shangaan migrant workers headed home for the Easter holidays. Most were carrying huge boxes and suitcases filled with purchases they'd made in the city of goods hard to find in the impoverished former homelands: warm blankets, Primus stoves, children's clothing, shoes, candles, sacks of mealie meal, sugar, cooking oil, cheap radios and TV sets.

Suddenly Makhado heard a familiar voice behind him call his name. He turned and looked about. He broke into a surprised smile at the sight of his fellow villager, Lucas Nzhelele, sitting about three rows back.

"There's room over here," the clean-shaven and compactly built Nzhelele said in a loud voice, waving. Makhado hurriedly jostled his way down the crowded aisle to where Nzhelele was sitting next to the befogged window. There was just enough room in the rack above the seat for Makhado to stash his suitcase. Sighing with relief, he sat down next to Nzhelele.

"This is a miracle, my friend," Makhado said. "I was in Hillbrow just this afternoon looking for you. There was no one at the address your wife gave me."

"I left Hillbrow about three weeks ago."

"You did? Why?"

"I could no longer afford the rent. I was laid off from my job as a security guard at Arm, Protect & Secure Inc. They said I was too cheeky when I asked for a pay raise."

"Did you find another job?"

"No."

"Where have you been living?"

"With friends in Soweto. But now I'm going home."

"For good?"

"Ja. I'm sick and tired of the city. It's grown too violent. And there are no jobs."

"I know what you mean," Makhado said, placing snuff under his tongue. He extended his snuffbox to Nzhelele, who took a pinch and did the same.

"I plan to open a mountain school once I get home. What about you? I thought you said you'd never again set foot in Jo'burg again after they endorsed you out. What made you change your mind?"

"Gideon just bought a new house in Alexandra. He asked me to come down and conduct the ceremony asking our *Midzimu* to protect it from harm."

The uniformed black conductor on the crowded platform blew his whistle. Last-minute passengers scrambled aboard.

"By the way, thanks very much for saving my aunt's life," Nzhelele said gratefully.

"I'm glad I was home when the mob came after her."

Nzhelele's 66-year-old aunt, a *nganga* (traditional healer), had sought refuge at Makhado's kraal after she was set upon by an enraged mob of villagers accusing her of being a witch. The mob, which wanted to burn her alive, blamed her for the brutal murder of a 14-year-old girl whose mutilated body was found in the nearby forest. The girl's lips and genitalia had been torn off, and her heart and tongue had been ripped out. The gruesome manner of the killing suggested that the body parts were to be used to concoct potions called *muti*.

"Exactly how did you pacify the bloodthirsty mob, my friend?" Nzhelele asked. "I never got the full story."

"It helped that I'm the village elder," Makhado said. "The mob, which was made up mostly of women and children, listened when I pointed out that your aunt dealt in a different kind of *muti* as a *nganga*. Her potions, I said, are made from roots and herbs. They regularly heal the sick in our village, who go to her because the clinic is so far away, or because they have no money, or because they don't trust western medicine. And as you know, it's impossible for the same *nganga* to perform good and evil deeds. The *Midzimu* won't allow it."

"That's true."

"Interestingly," Makhado said, "a week after your aunt was almost burned alive, an unemployed man from the next village confessed to killing the poor girl in order to sell her body parts to witchdoctors. He's now in jail awaiting trial for murder in Thohoyandou."

As the train slowly chugged out of the station, the two long-time neighbors talked at length about their hopes that the ANC government would finally bring much-needed improvements to Venda, one of the poorest regions of the country, where many people still had no running water or electricity, lived in mud huts, walked on dusty roads and had little access to jobs, clinics or schools. Both agreed that poverty and illiteracy made it easy for desperate people to blame their woes – lack of a job, an illness, death of a loved one and so on – on witchcraft.

An hour later, the train pulled into the station in Warmbath, a sleepy town 90 km north of Pretoria, which was famous for its salubrious mineral springs. Makhado and Nzhelele purchased two cans of Castle Laager beer from a train vendor. Amid hearty laughter, as the train left Warmbath, Makhado and Nzhelele began reminiscing about their many experiences at the mountain school, both as pupils and as teachers.

"Do you have enough pupils to open a mountain school?" Makhado asked. "So many of our people today are westernized. They no longer consider it necessary that their sons be made into men the old-fashioned way."

Nzhelele sipped his beer. "That's changing. I expect more than sixty initiates from the townships alone to enroll this winter."

"More than sixty? How did you manage to sign up that many?"

"Well, while I was living in Jo'burg I spent a lot of time talking to Venda families in the townships about the importance of tradition. I told them that if they didn't send their sons to the mountain school to learn about honor, respect and courage, then they shouldn't be surprised if they emulate carjackers and *tsotsis* (gangsters). Remember how back in the old days young men proved their manhood by killing lions? Now today's young men prove theirs by killing people and hijacking cars."

Thinking of Liefling, Makhado nodded. "That's so true."

"But wait until they get to the mountain school. I'll whip them into shape, or my name isn't Nzhelele."

Makhado smiled. "I know you will, my friend," he said, patting Nzhelele on the shoulder.

"And you should come and tell the initiates stories about famous Venda warriors," Nzhelele said. "I'm sure they know next to nothing about the bravery and sacrifices of the like Makhado, your namesake."

"If such stories will spur them to emulate his courage and sacrifice," Makhado said, "I'll gladly come and talk to them."

KRUGER's large and ornately furnished office was about a block away from Johannesburg Central police station, formerly known as John Vorster Square. From his window on the top floor he had a clear view of the blue monolithic building that was a dreaded detention and interrogation center during the apartheid era, and was named after his hero, arch-segregationist John Vorster.

A former Prime Minister and member of the pro-Nazi *Ossewabrandwag* (Ox-wagon Guard) during the Second World War, Vorster had been responsible for the development of South Africa's formidable Gestapo-like security apparatus that for decades safeguarded *Baaskap* by keeping the black majority cowed and controlled using a battery of draconian laws and an elaborate network of black collaborators, *impimpis* (informers) and *askaris* (double agents).

But Kruger wasn't thinking of his days as head of the security branch at John Vorster Square as he sat behind a massive oak desk, a phone in his right hand and a thick stack of files piled high in front of him.

"I won't be coming down tonight, honey," he said. "I have to work late." He was speaking to his fiancée of nearly four months.

"I understand, darling," his fiancée said in a somewhat disappointed voice. The two were talking in Afrikaans. "It's just that I haven't seen you in over a week. I miss you very much."

"I miss you too, darling. But I've been very busy."

"Will I see you tomorrow night?"

"Definitely. And we'll celebrate."

"Celebrate?"

"Ja. I finally clinched that deal with the Japanese."

"Wonderful."

"There's more. A group of investors from South America are interested in buying the firm. Guess how much they're offering?"

"Five hundred million rands?" Kruger's fiancée said, recalling that he'd once mentioned the figure as the firm's market value.

Kruger smiled as he said, "One billion."

There was a brief pause. "Did you say one billion rands?"

"No. One billion dollars. Five billion rands at today's exchange rate."

"You're kidding me?"

"I'm not."

"Why, that's absolutely marvelous, darling!"

"So I thought we should celebrate by going to that Mozart concert you told me about two weeks ago. Afterwards we can have dinner at your favorite restaurant."

"Delightful. I can't wait to hold you in my arms."

"Me too."

"I love you very much, Magnus."

"I love you too, dear. So sleep tight and I'll see you tomorrow."

Smiling broadly, Kruger replaced the receiver and returned to the problem he'd been grappling with when his fiancée had called. His conversation with Hunter still fresh in his mind, he wanted to make sure that the men of the Thathe Vondo death squad didn't panic and scuttle his plans, given the rash of last-minute applications from members of other counterinsurgency units as the deadline for amnesty approached. It was three and half weeks away.

Once again Kruger put on his silver-rimmed reading glasses, resting them on his broad, slightly-peeling nose. Under the bright light of a green banker's lamp, he resumed reviewing the top-secret files of the fifty men who'd belonged to the death squad he'd headed from February 1986 to December 1993. He'd recruited the men, all bonafide Afrikaner nationalists with at least one Voortrekker ancestor, from commandos in the Northern Transvaal. Commandos were self-defense units in the rural areas made up mostly of military-trained civilians who coordinated their activities with and received logistical support from the police and army. Commandos became an integral part of the SADF's counter-revolutionary strategy during the 1980s. The men in Kruger's death squad were mostly farmers and policemen from the Venda and Shangaan homelands, which abutted each other.

Following the disbanding of the SADF's counterinsurgency units shortly before power was transferred to the black majority, Kruger had helped the men resume normal lives. He'd helped them find ways to earn a living in a society that no longer guaranteed them one because of the color of their skin. He'd arranged for discreet Afrikaner therapists to help them deal with the psychological trauma of what they'd done and endured in the defense of *Baaskap*. He'd give farmers on the verge of bankruptcy loans at generous terms. He'd provided policemen who couldn't stand working for blacks jobs in his security firm. Most important, he'd helped every one of the men to keep together their families, the nucleus of the Volk.

They are once more productive and respectable members of the Afrikaner community, Kruger thought with satisfaction as he studied the dossiers of the fifty men. *And they owe it all to me. They should remain loyal.*

Kruger, an avid student of Nazi history throughout his long military career, thought of another reason why the men of the Thathe Vondo death squad should remain loyal. They'd undergone no program similar to de-Nazification. Such a program would most likely have purged them of their deeply-held belief in *Baaskap*, which they'd acquired growing up in verkrampte households and attending Afrikaner-only schools, where they'd been taught to bear any burden and make any sacrifice for the Afrikaner nation, God's Chosen People.

More than that. Before he recruited them, the fifty men, terrified by the prospect of black majority rule, had joined the AWB, which had championed *Baaskap* and demanded an Afrikaner-only homeland.

Kruger rose and walked over to the wet bar. Feeling reassured that the men of the Thathe Vondo death squad would remain loyal, he made himself a martini. Sipping, he wondered if it might not be time to inform the men of his plan to launch the Fourth Boer Revolution, especially now that he was about to obtain the wherewithal to finance it.

So far, only three former members of the Thathe Vondo death squad knew of his closely guarded plan. The three – his associates at the firm – were Ludwig Botha, his chief of communications, Piet Viljoen, his director of personnel, and Jan Barnard, his strategic planner. All three were members of the *Uitvoerende Raad,* the Executive Council that controlled The Silent Brotherhood of Afrikaner Patriots.

If I tell them, they'll bly op die bus, Kruger thought as he walked back to his desk, drink in hand. *They'll scorn the TRC's amnesty offer, knowing that in an Afrikaner homeland they won't be publicly humiliated and prosecuted for what they did defending Baaskap. On the contrary, they'll be feted as heroes.*

Kruger resolved then and there to tell the rest of his men as soon as he'd sold the firm to the South Americans. Then he'd invite them to join his secret Boer army, particularly because they were already familiar with the ruthless methods he'd used during the apartheid era to wage war against *Die Swart Gevaar* in defense of the Afrikaner nation.

Kruger had one more drink before locking away the files in a wall safe behind a painting depicting the Battle of Blood River, a seminal event in Afrikaner mythology, on which Kruger had a particular fixation. He then left for the home of his close friend and pastor, Dominee Koos Muller, in Houghton Estate, an exclusive suburb of Johannesburg, where the Executive Council of The Silent Brotherhood of Afrikaner Patriots regularly held its clandestine meetings.

6

THANDO KHOSA towered above the makeshift podium as she prepared to introduce her two guests speakers. Five eleven, with almond-shaped hazel eyes and shoulder-length--cornrowed hair, she resembled a Shangaan princess in her stylish traditional dress called a *mucheka*, large hoop earrings make from cowry shells, and wrists covered with copper and silver bangles that jingled at the slightest movement of her long ebony arms.

Thando beamed with satisfaction as she surveyed the crowd packed inside the Phutadichaba (Gathering of Nations) Community Center – a non-profit organization devoted to caring for the aged, abused women and children – for an urgent meeting she'd called two weeks ago. She was surprised at the huge turnout.

As a community activist and Phutadichaba's programs director, she was aware of the apathy and busy-ness of many residents, and hadn't expected this many people to show up. In the past she'd barely managed to fill half the hall for a meeting, no matter how important the issue. Now it was standing room only, and there were at least a dozen newspaper, radio and TV reporters covering the event.

I'm glad they take the issue seriously, Thando thought, adjusting the microphone in front of her. *And they should.*

She threw a quick glance backward at the two persons seated in straight-backed metal chairs behind her on the dais. They were Detective Malusi Radebe of the Johannesburg Police Department, and Dr. Ndicheni Mudau, a sociologist at Venda University who'd served on the Commission on Witchcraft and Ritual Violence in the Northern Province. She and Thando were currently serving on the Commission on Gender Equality.

Thando's attention returned to the restive crowd in front of her. She leaned into the microphone.

"I'm very glad you all could come, ladies and gentlemen," she began, speaking with a noticeable Shangaan accent. Because of a mediocre sound system, her alto reverberated inside the hot and stuffy hall. But people were still able to hear her clearly. "I didn't expect so many of you to show up because the issue we'll be discussing tonight is still very taboo."

Bothered by a slightly sore throat, Thando paused and sipped water from a plastic tumbler. An old woman in the front row coughed loudly.

"But as a community we can no longer afford to bury our heads in the sand," Thando went on. "The issue of muti-killings must be confronted head-on. Too many of our children are becoming victims. And what future does our community and South Africa have if we do not protect our children. Tonight we are going to hear from two people who will help us address the issue. Without further ado, I'll introduce our first speaker, Detective Malusi Radebe, who was recently chosen by President Mandela himself to head a task force investigating muti-killings. Detective Malusi tells me that in a couple weeks he'll be addressing a Parliamentary Committee in Cape Town on this very important issue. Here he is, ladies and gentlemen. Let's give him a warm Alexandra welcome."

The crowd applauded as Malusi stood up and headed toward the podium. Dressed in a double-breasted brown suit, white button-down shirt and blue tie, he hugged Thando, who then sat down.

"Thank you very much," he said in fluent Zulu as he pulled several pages of notes from the inside pocket of his jacket. "I would like to thank Thando for arranging this very important meeting. There is no more serious problem facing our young nation that the scourge of muti-killings. In the past three years alone, over 2,000 children have been reported missing. Many of them were victims of muti-killings."

Malusi placed the notes on the podium.

"Contrary to popular belief, muti-killings are not limited to the rural areas," he went on. "There have also been reports of muti-killings in the townships and suburbs. The problem is nationwide. I'm here to inform you that the government has made muti-killings a top national priority."

Malusi flipped a page and then continued, "President Mandela has asked all police stations across the country to immediately devote extra manpower to investigating muti-killings. He's also asked the Defense Force to provide my task force with access to planes and helicopters. That means that we can fly anywhere in the country on short notice to investigate any muti-killing case."

Malusi paused and wiped his sweaty brow with a cotton handkerchief.

"But the government and the police alone can't fight this national scourge," he continued. "You as citizens and parents have to become involved. Take extra care of your children. Make sure you know where they are at all times. The task force is working with communities and schools across the country to come up with programs to teach children about safety."

Malusi took a sip of water from a tall glass.

"I'm glad to say that here in Alexandra we've received excellent cooperation, thanks to the efforts of Thando and Professor Gideon Munyai. In the coming weeks, I'll be traveling across the country to assess the magnitude of the problem so I can make a request for the necessary funds during my appearance before Parliament. One final thing, anyone with information about any missing child should immediately contact my office. There are pamphlets and brochures about the task force just outside the hall. Thank you."

The audience applauded. Thando rose and thanked Malusi, who then sat down. She proceeded to introduce the second speaker.

"Dr. Ndicheni Mudau has had a very busy day," Thando said. "This morning she gave a speech at a conference on human rights at Wits University, and then another one in the afternoon at a women's conference in Soweto. And she has a flight to catch to Durban tonight, where she's scheduled to give yet another speech tomorrow morning. But she's generously agreed to join us. I'm privileged to call Ndicheni a dear friend and comrade. Both of us were fellow students at Alexandra Secondary School and freedom fighters during the liberation struggle. And now we are comrades in an equally important battle: the emancipation of women. Please give Ndicheni a very warm welcome."

Ndicheni rose as the audience clapped and gave her a standing ovation as a former MK warrior. She hardly seemed the ruthless guerilla fighter who'd been considered public enemy number one by the apartheid government after she blew up a police station in Venda, killing two policemen. Short and petite, with a serious, dark-skinned face, she was dressed in a checkered two-piece business suit and a matching scarf.

"Thank you for that very warm welcome, my brothers and sisters," she began, as the applause died down. She glanced at the notes as she'd scribbled on a yellow legal pad. "In the interest of time I'll be brief. I know that the streets aren't safe at night, especially for women, who I notice are the majority of the audience. I'll address three basic areas concerning muti-killings. My extensive research shows that muti-killings are on the rise because a lot of people are desperate. They are desperate for money, for love and for miracle cures. Instead of people earning money through hard work, they want potions to become millionaires overnight. And instead of women relying on their intelligence and charm to get a man, they want love potions. And instead of men being monogamous and wearing condoms to guard against AIDS, when they catch the incurable disease, they want a magic cure. And who do such desperate people turn to?"

Ndicheni paused for dramatic effect. The hall was silent, except for an occasional raspy cough. It was clear that the audience was transfixed. They'd never heard such blunt, honest talk before about so taboo a topic.

"They turn to charlatans and quacks who infest the traditional healing profession," Ndicheni said with intensity, gesturing with her small hands. "These bogus *ngangas* promise miracles to people if they use muti made from human body parts. They tell the desperate business-owner that if he buries a human hand at the entrance of his *spazza* (lean-to store) it will attract legions of customers and turn the spazza into an OK bazaar."

The crowd roared with laughter.

After it died down, Ndicheni continued. "They tell the desperate woman that if she drinks their special muti, she'll find everlasting love. They tell the desperate criminal that if he drinks their muti, he'll have the courage of warriors like Makhado and Shaka."

The last statement provoked peals of laughter. Even Ndicheni's usually taciturn face crinkled into a faint smile.

"And, finally, they tell the desperate AIDS victim that if he drinks their special muti and sleeps with a virgin, he'll be cured of the disease."

A murmur of outrage rose from the audience. Ndicheni paused and cleared her throat.

"How can the community protect itself against such charlatans and quacks?" she asked rhetorically. "Education is the key. We must separate fact from superstition. We must learn to distinguish between legitimate traditional healers, who have a place in African society, and charlatans and quacks, who should be avoided like the plague. Finally, these charlatans and quacks must be prosecuted to the fullest extent of the law. Not only that, but the government must do a better job of combating poverty, which often makes people desperate and therefore easy prey to quacks and charlatans. Thank you very much."

Ndicheni, true to her manner of being brief, sat down to loud and sustained applause. A question and answer session followed, lasting about twenty minutes, after which the crowd dispersed. Ndicheni promptly took a taxi to the Johannesburg International airport for her flight to Durban. Malusi gave Thando, whose Toyota Hilux was in the shop for a brake job, a lift to her flat on Fourth Avenue, about thirteen blocks away. It was growing dark but the streets were teeming with life as most people didn't own cars.

"Thanks for inviting me to speak at such an important meeting," Malusi said as his Chevrolet Marquis left the Phutadichaba Community Center on Seventeenth Avenue.

"Thank you for taking time from your busy schedule to come."

As the Marquis turned left into Vasco Da Gama Street, Thando said, "There's a question I've been meaning to ask you."

"Fire away."

"It's very personal."

"I don't mind."

"How did you end up working for the security branch during the apartheid era?"

"That *is* very personal," Malusi said with a smile, revealing a gap between his front upper teeth. "To tell you the truth, I applied for the job. Being a cop gave me more power than a black man could ever have under apartheid."

"But that power was used against your own people?"

"At the time I didn't consider blacks my own people."

"Despite the fact that your father was Zulu?"

"Despite that. I was filled with self-hatred and angry at the world. I believed all that propaganda which said that Coloreds and Afrikaners were *bloedbroers* because they share the same culture and language."

"What made you change?"

"It was a gradual thing. I think the change began after my mother died from breast cancer. I was very close to her. Before she died, she begged me to remember my roots. My brother, who was studying in America at the time, also kept telling me to let go of my anger. And then in the 1980s more Coloreds joined blacks in the struggle against apartheid. When the police began detaining, torturing and killing them also, I realized that Coloreds were still oppressed, despite their privileges and light skin. When I realized that, I secretly joined the ANC. I became a spy. I passed on highly classified information about the security branch's counterinsurgency activities in the Western Cape and Jo'burg. I'm told the information saved many lives."

"Wasn't it dangerous being a double-agent?"

"It was. Several times I was almost caught. But it was the least I could do to help the struggle."

The Marquis stopped to let a group of churchgoers cross the street.

"And you, what made you join MK?" Malusi asked after the churchgoers were safely across and the Marquis moved again.

"My parents' assassination. They were killed in 1989 when their house was firebombed by death squads."

"I'm sorry."

"It's okay."

"Has the TRC revealed who actually carried out the bombing?"

"No. But I'm determined to find out. That's one reason why I'm working with Liefling at the Ubuntu Resource Center."

"How is it going?"

"Frustrating. Many of our cases are going nowhere because we can't find witnesses. But hopefully that will soon change. David Schneider just joined us. You know David, don't you?"

"The TRC investigator?"

"Former."

"You're very lucky. He was one of the best investigators the Commission had. He helped them crack a number of important cases."

"Liefling is ecstatic. We desperately need to find witnesses before the amnesty deadline passes. Especially for our current case. It's a very big one."

"What is it about?"

"We are trying to help more than a hundred families in Alexandra find out what happened to their loved ones who were victims of death squads."

"That will be tough, given the code of silence among security force members."

"I know."

After a thoughtful pause, Thando said, "I'm concerned about your brother Sipho."

"Why?"

"He works too hard . He hardly has time for anything else."

The Marquis turned left onto Fourth Avenue. The Avenue was congested with pedestrians and honking cars and taxis, reducing traffic to a crawl.

"I too am concerned about his work load," Malusi said. "I told him that he should choose between Bara and the clinic in Crossroads. He can't continue working at both places. He'll burn out. And he's only thirty."

"Bara alone is bad enough," Thando said.

"Maybe now that he's dating Liefling he'll choose the clinic so they can spend more time together. Especially since both love Cape Town."

"I hope so. Liefling is madly in love with him. But she hates long-distance relationships. For instance, she was in town today but Sipho was so busy he couldn't even have lunch with her. Then as she heading for the airport she was almost carjacked in Hillbrow."

Malusi looked worried. "No. Is she all right?"

"She's fine. She called me before boarding the flight back to Cape Town. Gideon Munyai's father, Makhado, foiled the carjacking."

"Really?"

"Ja. Despite the fact that the carjackers were armed and he wasn't. He took them on and they fled."

"Quite a brave man."

'He's a warrior."

"The Jo'burg police department needs warriors like him to effectively fight crime. Unfortunately it's riddled with corrupt officers. Some of them are even involved in committing crimes."

"I read about that in the paper. Is it true that some of them are into drugs?"

"Big time. One of my tasks is to ferret them out."

"Here we are," Thando said as the Marquis pulled in front of her apartment. "Thanks a lot for the ride."

"Don't mention it."

She grabbed her briefcase from the backseat and got out.

"Please don't hesitate to call on me should you, Liefling and David need any help," Malusi said.

"Thanks, I'll remember that."

7	**LIEFLING** arrived at the Cape Town International airport shortly before 11 p.m. She took the Intercape Shuttle to the railroad station in downtown Cape Town, where she caught the last train to Stellenbosch, about 45 km away. She looked forward to seeing her mother, whom she hadn't

visited in nearly three months because of work.

As the Metro train chugged under a starry sky between the dramatic mountains and undulating valleys of the wine route, Liefling dialed her answering machine using her cell phone. There were four messages. The first was from a *New York Times* reporter confirming their interview for noon the following day. The second was from a Xhosa woman thanking her for helping her file a claim with the TRC's Reparations Committee for the murder of her husband and son by the police. The third was from Thando, telling her that the community meeting on muti-killings went very well.

The fourth was from Sipho. He again effusively apologized for missing lunch, and hoped that she'd had a safe trip, despite the carjacking attempt. He looked forward to seeing her in Cape Town tomorrow night and accompanying her to the AIDS black-tie fundraiser at the Waterfront Hotel.

As she turned off the cell phone, Liefling fondly remembered meeting Sipho at another fundraiser – this one for a battered women's shelter in Crossroads – a little over two month ago. They'd hit it off immediately. Both, it turned out, lived only a couple blocks apart in Sea Point, one of the most densely populated suburbs in Africa, loved jazz, eating out, surfing, backpacking and taking relaxing walks in the spectacular Kirstenbosch Botanic Gardens, where Sipho's mother ashes were scattered after she died from breast cancer in 1978.

Liefling wasn't surprised that she was now madly in love with him. Yet it wasn't typical of her to fall in love at first sight. And despite her liberal views, she'd never expected to fall in love with a black man.

But Sipho was special. An idealist and workaholic like herself, he was unlike any of her previous boyfriends, all of whom had been white. He was romantic, funny, sensual, vulnerable and – what she most liked about him – he was unafraid to openly express his innermost feelings. And, rare for a black man, he was a feminist and refreshingly colorblind.

She recalled their first date, and the openness of their conversation about race, an issue that was constantly on the minds of South Africans now that the TRC hearings had provoked a heated debate of the country's racial past. The debate had put a lot of whites – including liberals – on the defensive, with the result that few of them dared reveal their true feelings on the issue when talking to blacks, afraid of saying "the wrong thing" which might paint them as racist, or offend the sensibilities of blacks.

But Sipho hadn't been the least offended about her candor as the two of them sat at a corner table near the stage of the Green Dolphin. The trendy restaurant, one of the most popular in Cape Town, was beneath the Alfred & Victoria Waterfront Hotel. It served a range of entrees with jazz names complemented by its nightly feature of live jazz entertainment Sipho had ordered an Ellington antipasto and Liefling a Goodman salad with baked Salmon. The wine was Paarl Chardonnay, properly chilled.

They had been listening to the mellow jazz band and feeling each other out for some time when, halfway through their meal, Liefling said to Sipho, "Do you consider yourself Colored or black?"

Sipho stopped eating and looked at Liefling, her face radiant in the subdued candlelight. "I consider myself human," he said.

Surprised by the directness and simplicity of Sipho's answer, Liefling smiled. *He's right,* she thought, sipping her wine. *We are all human. A good person is a good person, regardless of color, race, religion, nationality, creed or sexual orientation.*

"Well, let me phrase it another way," Liefling said, putting down her wineglass. "How did you come to have such light skin?"

"I bleached it," Sipho said, grinning impishly. "During the apartheid era there was such a premium placed on white skin that many blacks were constantly bleaching their faces so they could pass for Colored. I simply went overboard with the bleaching, I guess."

"Seriously, now."

"Well, my grandpa was white."

"Really?"

"Actually he was Afrikaner."

"Afrikaner?"

"Ja."

"And your grandmother?"

"She was part Cape Malay, part British, part Dutch, and part Xhosa. Officially she was classified as Colored. But she was so light-skinned a lot of people thought she was white."

"Where did they meet?"

"Here in Cape Town. My grandma, who was from Mannenberg, was studying marketing at the University of the Western Cape (for Coloreds). To support herself she worked as a nightclub singer. And my grandpa, who was from Johannesburg, was an aide to a cabinet minister."

"Did you grandfather know she was Colored?"

"He did. But he didn't care. He was *verligte* and loved my grandma. Of course he kept the news a secret from his *verkrampte* family. They got married and moved to Pretoria, where my grandpa had a high position in the Department of Interior. My mother got a job at an Afrikaner bank. They had three daughters – all of them very light-skinned – whom they sent to Afrikaner schools. They were very happy. That happiness, however, was shattered when their neighbors, who apparently were suspicious about my grandma's racial classification, called the police."

"You're kidding."

"I'm not. Officials from the South African Bureau of Racial Affairs (SABRA) came and investigated the matter. And when they found out that my grandma was indeed Colored, my grandparents were charged with violating the Prohibition of Mixed Marriages Act and the Immorality Act."

Sipho noticed that the color had drained from Liefling's face.

"Should I continue?"

"Yes, please," Liefling said softly.

"Their marriage was instantly annulled. Both were dismissed from their respective jobs. They were also kicked out of the white neighborhood and their daughters were thrown out of the white school. It was too much for my grandpa – especially after his family disowned him. He shot himself."

"Oh, my God…"

"After his death my grandma moved back to Cape Town. She, my mother and my two aunts were reclassified as Coloreds."

For a long time Liefling said nothing. Tears stood in her eyes. She made no attempt to dry them. Finally she spoke, in a voice full of anguish. "I feel so ashamed."

"Why?"

"Well, my grandpa was one of the biggest champions of the Prohibition of Mixed Marriages Act and the Immorality Act."

Sipho raised his eyebrows. "He was?"

"Ja." Liefling said, her voice cracking. "Excuse me."

She got up and went to the Ladies Room, where she broke down and cried. Minutes later she came back, having regained her composure. But her face was flushed and her eyes were pink at the edges.

"I'm sorry, honey," Sipho said, tenderly holding her hand.

"I'll be fine."

"Who was your grandpa?" Sipho couldn't help asking.

"His name was Francois. He was chaplain to a guerilla unit during the Boer War. After the war he became an influential member of the Broederbond. He also was a fervent admirer of Hitler."

"Really?" Sipho said, leaning back in his chair.

"Ja. He called him a great man who gave the German people a calling. He strongly identified with their plight following the Treaty of Versailles. He compared it to the Treaty of Vereeniging, which Afrikaners were forced to sign in order to end the Boer War. A die-hard nationalist, he was vehemently opposed to the treaty."

"So he was a *Bittereinder*?"

"Ja. And he never forgot that Germany had backed the Afrikaner cause. So during the Second World War he joined the pro-Nazi *Ossewabrandwag*. In fact he and John Vorster were interned together at Koffiefontein as Nazi sympathizers. After the National Party came to power in 1948, my grandpa urged it to adopt its own version of the Nuremberg laws. Which it did with the Immorality and Prohibition of Mixed Marriages Acts."

Liefling paused and sipped her wine. "The irony is that the first person charged under the Immorality Act was a dominee from the Northern Cape."

"Is that so?" Sipho said with surprise, leaning forward.

"Ja. He was caught red-handed with a domestic worker in a garage his parishioners had built for him next to his house. My father heard a lot such stories from my grandpa. Some of them involved very powerful Afrikaners. Including members of the Broederbond itself."

"Why weren't they more widely known?"

"They would have undermined apartheid. How could the government justify saying that blacks and whites had to live in separate neighborhoods, attend separate schools and churches, ride separate buses, have separate toilets and belong to separate homelands when Broederbond members themselves were regularly sneaking across the border to apartheid-free Swaziland and Botswana in order to satisfy their lust for black women?"

"It would be funny if apartheid's obsession with race hadn't created so much suffering and pain," Sipho said reflectively, twirling his empty wineglass. "As you were talking, I was reminded of a girl I dated when I was at the University of the Western Cape. Her name was Marie. Though both her parents were Colored, she was darker skinned than myself. She came from a wealthy family. Her father owned a chain of bottle-stores around the Cape Flats area."

Sipho paused and took a sip of water. "Her entire family belonged to the Colored Labor Party," he continued. "One time during dinner with her parents I indirectly criticized her father for supporting Botha's constitutional reforms. I said they were only designed to co-opt Coloreds and Indians, and to divide them from blacks. Marie was furious with me. She wanted to know why I was so worried about blacks instead of focusing on the needs of 'our people.' By 'our people' she meant Coloreds."

"What did you say?"

"I reminded her that my father was Zulu and that my mother had been ostracized by her Colored relatives for marrying him."

"Really?"

"Ja. They accused her of degrading herself."

"They said that despite what happened to your grandparents?"

Sipho nodded. "Marrying a black was an unspoken taboo. It didn't matter that my father had won a bursary to study medicine at UCT. My grandma and aunts even refused to come to her wedding. It devastated my mother, for she was very close to the three of them."

Liefling was surprised to notice a tear in the corner of Sipho's eye. She reached across the table and touched his hand, all the while thinking of the pain, suffering and humiliation the issue of race had caused countless South Africans. In particular she thought of the Population Registration Act of 1950, which her grandfather had also championed, and under which officials at SABRA often used such arbitrary measures as the "pencil" and "eyeball" tests to determine if a person was black, white, Colored, Indian and so on. During the pencil test a pencil was run through one's hair. If the pencil got entangled, that was positive proof of being black, because blacks are supposed to have kinky hair.

The eyeball test required the examining officer to carefully scrutinize the applicant's features to determine which racial characteristics predominated. According to the law, a white person was anyone who "in appearance obviously is, or is generally accepted as a white person, but does not include a person who, although in appearance a white person, is generally accepted as a Colored person." Anyone who contested their racial classification could appeal to a special board headed by a judge or a magistrate. And each year a cabinet minister reported to Parliament on the number of those reclassified. On February 1980, P.W. Botha's Minister of Interior had given the following answer to a question about the year's reclassification results:

> A total of one hundred and one Colored people became white; one Chinese became white; two whites received Colored classification; six whites became Chinese; two whites became Indians; ten Colored people became Indians; ten Malays became Indians; eleven Indians became Colored; four Indians became Malays; three Colored people became Chinese while two Chinese were reclassified as Colored people.

"Racial classification taught a lot of South Africans to hate themselves," Sipho said. "My brother and I, for instance, when we were young, actually hated the fact that we were part black."

"Why?"

"Well, shortly after my father died, my mother was diagnosed with breast cancer. We left Soweto, where we'd lived while my father was doing his residency at Bara, and moved back to Cape Town. My mother was pretty ill at the time. Feeling guilty, her relatives took us in and cared for her. My brother and I enrolled at the local Colored primary school. But it was tough adjusting to the Colored way of life after living among blacks in Soweto. Our fellow students constantly teased us for speaking Zulu. And they constantly cracked jokes about how primitive Zulus were. They were fond of saying that the only reason the Boers slaughtered so many of them at the Battle of Blood River was that Zulus were too stupid to realize that one can't fight bullets and cannons with assegais and shields. And then they'd make jokes about our African names."

Sipho paused and stared into the flickering flame of the candle. "How we hated those Zulu names," he said slowly, with a faraway look in his soulful brown eyes. "It didn't matter when my mother told us that they were beautiful names, that Sipho meant 'Gift' and Malusi meant 'Shepherd.' All we wanted was for her to change our names to Andries, Paul, John, Robert. Anything but Sipho and Malusi. She refused. She told us that those names were a way of keeping my father's memory alive."

"How did he die?"

"Well, in his second year of residency at Bara, he became quite an activist. Especially against segregated medical care. He'd seen the horrors at Bara and wanted to do something to change the status quo. He was quite ahead of his time. He began speaking out and organizing protests to integrate medical care. On November 23, 1974, when I was only six, he was arrested during what the government called an 'illegal demonstration' and taken to John Vorster Square. Three days later he was dead. The police said he'd suffered a heart attack."

Liefling blinked back tears and looked away. She could feel a lump in her throat. She said softly, "Was an inquest ever held?"

"It was. But the judge cleared the police of any wrongdoing. And it was tough to prove anything because my father did have a weak heart. After he died my mother, despite the ravages of cancer, redoubled her efforts to make us proud of our Zulu heritage. She reminded us that Africa belonged to Africans. But it took us a long while to believe that. Especially my brother. He was so desperate to distance himself from blacks that he joined the police force after graduating from high school."

"Really?"

"Ja. But he later changed and joined the ANC. He took great risks as a spy in the fight against apartheid. I respect him a lot for redeeming himself."

The conductor's announcement that the train was now arriving at Stellenbosch station jolted Liefling from her reverie about his first date with Sipho and their intense conversation about race. She wiped the tears that had formed in her eyes at the recollection, then peered out the window. She saw her mother standing on the platform next to a bright lamppost, smiling and waving. She smiled and waved back. Liefling looked forward to spending time with her. At the same time she wondered how her mother would react to news that her only child was deeply in love with a black man.

8   **DAVID SCHNEIDER** shook his head in disbelief as he surveyed the scene inside the casualty ward at Chris Hani Baragwanath hospital, the largest hospital in the world. The ward or "intake room" resembled a battlefield. The wounded and the dying were everywhere. Groans and shrieks of pain filled the hot and stuffy air.

One drunken man with a broken arm threatened to shoot someone if he wasn't attended to. A young pregnant woman who'd been waiting for hours to be seen hollered with each painful contraction. A bruised and scantily dressed toddler shivered beside his mother on the bench where they had been waiting hours for treatment following a car accident.

The doctor, a red-haired intern in her mid-twenties, from the UCT medical school, scurried from patient to patient, determining whether an injury was life threatening or not. She stuck a red "urgent" sticker on a young black woman with a knife embedded in her chest.

"OR 3!" the doctor shouted. The tired and overworked nurses immediately wheeled the woman to Operating Room 3.

David marveled at the dedication and courage of the hospital's staff. He recalled reading an article in *The Star* about the harrowing conditions at the hospital popularly known as Bara. Staff members had been mugged, their cars had been hijacked, nurses had been raped and doctors had been shot. As a result, the hospital, which the previous year had seen more than 500,000 patients, treated nearly 3,000 gunshot victims and delivered more than 11,000 babies, was severely understaffed.

On this particular Friday night four surgeons, four interns and eight nurses -- all on a 24-hour shift – were working the casualty ward. Before the weekend was over, they would have handled nearly 1,000 patients.

From the crowded wooden bench where he was sitting, David kept glancing at the swinging doors. For the past two hours he'd been anxiously awaiting news on the condition of a black man he'd brought in with multiple gunshot wounds. David prayed he would live.

Suddenly the door swung open and a light-skinned surgeon with dark curly hair walked in. Exhaustion was written all over him. There were smudges of fatigue under his soulful brown eyes, and his broad shoulders slouched a bit. He'd been awake thirty straight hours and had just performed complicated surgery. He was still wearing a green cotton surgical scrub suit and a pager was attached to his slim waist. David immediately stood up and accosted him.

"Will he make it, doctor?"

"Yes," the surgeon said with a tired smile. "We removed all the bullets. He's in the intensive care unit and should make a full recovery."

"Thank God," David muttered.

"Are you his employer?"

"No. I happened to be driving along N1 headed home when I saw him lying in a pool of blood on the side of the highway. Looks like a robbery victim. A suitcase next to him had been ransacked."

"Good thing you brought him to the hospital immediately," the surgeon said. "Otherwise he would have bled to death."

"Will you make sure the hospital staff contacts his next of kin when he comes to?"

"Certainly. By the way, I never got to ask you your name."

"David Schneider. I'm a human rights lawyer."

"I'm Dr. Sipho Radebe," the surgeon said, shaking David's hand. "You don't happen to know someone named Liefling Malan, do you?"

David's eyes lit up. "As a matter of fact I do."

"She's a good friend of mine."

"Really?"

"Ja."

David picked up his briefcase. "I was with her this morning at a human rights conference at Wits."

"Then you must be the David who will be working with her at the Ubuntu Resource Center."

David nodded. "I can't wait to get started."

"She's delighted you've come on board," Sipho said as he and David walked toward the swinging doors. "She and Thando can use a top investigator like you. The SADF's code on death squads must be broken."

"I'm no miracle worker. But I'll try my best."

"By the way, did you know Liefling was almost carjacked in Hillbrow?"

An expression of grave concern clouded David's boyish-looking face, with its mop of unruly dark hair. "No. Is she all right?"

"She's fine. A Good Samaritan like you, a Venda man named Makhado, thwarted the carjacking. But she was a bit shook up."

"I can imagine."

"I can't wait to be with her. I'm flying to Cape Town tomorrow morning. But then I have to be back here Monday morning for two more days of surgery before flying back to Cape Town to my other job."

"You have another job?" David asked, incredulous, as he and Sipho walked through the swinging doors.

"Ja. I also perform surgery at a clinic Crossroads. A lot of doctors are emigrating, as you may be aware, so those of us who are left have to pick up the slack. It often means commuting across the country and working long long hours."

Suddenly Sipho's pager squealed and was followed by an announcement over the hospital speaker system:

Dr. Radebe, Code Blue, ICU, Dr. Radebe, Code Blue, ICU.

Sipho shrugged. "Back to work," he said matter-of-factly. "Nice meeting you." He shook David's hand.

"Nice meeting you too." David watched as Sipho raced down the crowded hallway toward the ICU, his white coat flying behind him. He marveled at his dedication and thought, *I can see why Liefling is in love with him.*

DOMINEE MULLER's mansion was an impregnable fortress. A fifteen-foot brick wall topped with electrified barbed wire rimmed the twenty-room mansion, which occupied ten thickly wooded acres. Two stern-faced guards with close-cropped blond hair, armed with Uzis, sat inside a bulletproof glass booth behind an electronically controlled gate. Hidden cameras were strategically located around the perimeter of the wall. Kruger's firm had provided the elaborate security, which had given Muller's home the distinction of being one of the few in Johannesburg never to have been burglarized.

After Kruger had identified himself, the guards opened the spiked gate and let his black limo through. The limo cruised slowly along the winding tree-lined driveway until it came to the three-story mansion whose stone facade was illumined by powerful spotlights. Kruger, a cowhide attaché in his right hand, stepped out of the limo and bounded up the stone steps to the ponderous door.

Mrs. Wilhemina Muller, a large woman with brown hair pulled severely away from her square face and pinned in a French twist, stood silhouetted against the door waiting for him. The former president of the Kappie Kommando had been alerted of Kruger's arrival via short-circuit TV.

"*Welkom*, General Kruger," she said, smiling pleasantly. "Nice to see you again, Mevrou Muller," Kruger said, kissing her cheek.

Mrs. Muller ushered Kruger inside the brightly-lit foyer. "They're waiting for you in the library."

"Thank you."

"Where's your fiancée?" asked Mrs. Muller as she led Kruger along a broad carpeted passage toward the back of the mansion.

"She's back home preparing for our wedding at the end of the month."

"Is that so? Please tell her to give me a call if she needs any help. It's been many years, but I still remember how nerve-wracking it was preparing for my own wedding to Koos."

"I'll tell her," Kruger said as they reached the thick oak door to the library.

Mrs. Muller headed back to the living room, where she was playing hostess to two dozen women sitting around a blazing fireplace sipping tea and making small talk while their spouses conducted important business.

As soon as Kruger entered the enormous paneled library, the two dozen dark-suited and grim-faced men seated around the conference table rose as one. They saluted him with shouts of *"Vryheid vir Afrikaners* (Freedom for Afrikaners)!" Smiling, Kruger greeted each member of his inner circle, who'd flown in from all parts of South Africa, and whom he'd personally chosen to shape the destiny of the Afrikaner people in the new Volkstaat.

They included members of the most ruthless covert units of the apartheid era security forces: Koevoet, Vlakplaas, Military Intelligence (MI), the State Security Council (SSC), reconnaissance regiments, the police security branch, the Civil Co-operation Bureau (CCB) and the National Intelligence Service (NIS). Every one was a die-hard Afrikaner nationalist, wore triple-7 swastika armbands and was prepared to die for the Vaderland.

"Sorry I'm late, gentlemen," Kruger said, taking his seat at the head of the oblong conference table made from imported mahogany.

"We haven't been waiting long," said Muller, a vole-faced Dutch Reformed Church minister who'd become a sort of celebrity among neo-Nazis for his refusal to join his fellow dominees in issuing an apology for the church's past racism and complicity in apartheid.

Kruger wasted little time in getting to his main point.

"The hour of deliverance has come, *bloedbroers*," he said. "God has answered our fervent prayers. Our American bloodbrother, Reginald Hunter, whom I met with this evening, brought us great news."

Kruger proceeded to relate his conversation with Hunter and the incredible offer made by the South American investors for his firm. As soon as he ended, his listeners applauded vociferously, smiling with deep satisfaction.

"When will the deal be finalized?" asked Muller, leaning forward in his soft leather chair.

"As soon as the South Americans send their representative," Kruger said. "In the meantime, gentlemen, we must, with all deliberate speed, begin laying the groundwork for the Fourth Boer Revolution."

Heads bobbed around the room in agreement. At the end of the brief meeting Muller uttered a short but impassioned prayer. Afterwards the twenty-four men sang *Die Stem Van Suid Afrika* (The Call of South Africa), the patriotic Afrikaner national anthem, as one by one they proceeded to the head of the table, which was draped with a huge triple-7 swastika flag.

Their right hands placed on Kruger's Bible, they pledged their lives, fortunes and sacred honor to protect the interests of the Volk and to fight for an independent Afrikaner nation, in much the same way as their predecessors had done over fifty years ago as *Stormjaers* (Stormtroopers), the military wing of the Ossewabrandwag.

During the Second World War Stormjaers, who numbered among their ranks the future creators of apartheid, blew up pylons, railway tracks, post offices, shops and banks. They also beat up Jews and soldiers. These acts of sabotage and intimidation were meant to demonstrate the Afrikaner Nationalists' vehement opposition to South Africa's decision to enter the war on the side of the Allies and their ardent support of Hitler's cause. They believed that if Hitler defeated England then the Commonwealth, of which

South Africa was then a part, would crumble and they would be able to proudly proclaim an Afrikaner Republic.

Kruger, then a youngster, had actually cried when he heard that his idol, whom he'd expected to conquer the world, had committed suicide in a Berlin bunker. The Fuehrer's death had come as a double blow to Kruger. A couple months earlier his favorite uncle, a stage actor and a Hitler fanatic, had been killed while furthering the Nazi cause. The uncle, who'd often captivated the impressionable Kruger with his animated readings of *Mein Kampf*, had been one of the Stormjaers' chief saboteurs. He was shot while attempting to blow up a train loaded with troops headed for North Africa. Ironically, most of the troops aboard were Afrikaners, disparagingly called *Rooi Luises* (Red Lice) by Nationalists for their loyalty to the Smuts government and for their having taken the Africa Oath to fight abroad alongside English-speakers, Coloreds and Africans.

After the twenty-four men had made solemn pledges to defend Baaskap to the bitter end, Kruger proceeded to administer the chilling oath that bound them together as members of the Uitvoerende Raad. It was the same oath sworn by Stormjaers over fifty years ago. With his right hand on the Bible, and Kruger pointing a pistol at his chest and Muller pointing another at his back, each of the men, grim-faced, slowly recited the following words in Afrikaans:

> *"If I advance, follow me.*
> *"If I retreat, shoot me.*
> *"If I die, avenge me.*
> *"So help me God."*

9 LIEFLING, her forehead beaded with sweat, jogged at a steady pace along a stretch of oak-lined streets on the southern end of Stellenbosch, the second oldest town in South Africa behind Cape Town and the citadel of Afrikaner politics and culture during the apartheid era. The town held many memories for her, both happy and bitter. It was the place where her parents had met, and where she was born on February 22, 1970. She'd lived contentedly in the bucolic town until her family was ignominiously driven out in 1976, following her father's repudiation of apartheid.

Though she'd vowed never to return to Stellenbosch because of the way her family had been treated, she'd been back several times because of her mother, Freda, who'd relocated there after an absence of nearly twenty-five years. Freda lived in a white-gabled Cape-Dutch bungalow dating back to 1688, the year Liefling's maternal great-great-grandfather, Rene de Villiers, arrived in South Africa from France with two hundred fellow French Protestant Huguenots fleeing religious persecution under Louis XIV.

A bit winded and achy after jogging almost seven miles in the nippy morning air, Liefling stopped and sat on a park bench overlooking the university. A nearby clock struck eight. Her eyes followed groups of white students, and a few black ones, hurrying from the nearby residential halls called hostels to classes in the largest predominantly Afrikaner university in the country, with over 17,000 students.

Despite having seen the sight many times since apartheid was abolished, Liefling still found it amazing. When she was a child blacks were barred from the university under the ironically named Extension of University Act of 1959 which mandated segregated universities. Liefling watched a black couple make its way across the courtyard to the Theological Seminary where many a segregationist and champion of Baaskap, including her own father before his life-changing transformation, had lectured on the Biblical and moral justification to apartheid.

If Dad were alive he'd be stunned by the changes, Liefling thought.

Feeling thirsty, she got up and walked across Merriman Avenue to a water fountain inside the modern-looking J.C. Smuts building for Botanical Sciences. The building was named after a famous Stellenbosch University alumnus and one of Liefling's heroes, General Jan Christiaan Smuts. A former Boer War guerilla leader, Smuts nevertheless had been hated and mistrusted by many Afrikaner nationalists. They'd accused the Cambridge-educated soldier and statesman of being an Anglophile and of selling out the interests of the Volk by denouncing the Broederbond and its aspirations for an Afrikaner Republic.

Liefling recalled that Smuts's decision to enter the Second World War on the side of Britain and its allies had led nationalists to found the pro-Nazi Ossewabrandwag and its military wing, the Stormjaers, of which Liefling's grandfather, Francois, became a *Hoof-Generaal* (High-General).

In one of history's ironies, Smuts had jailed scores of Stormjaers during the war, including Francois, only to see his former prisoners oust him and his United Party from power in the 1948 general election and usher in apartheid. And twelve years later, on October 5, 1960, the Nationalist Party, campaigning on the slogan *"Ons Republik nou, om Suid Afrika blanke te hou* (Our Republic now, to keep South Africa white)," had garnered the backing of 59% of voters on a platform of leaving the Commonwealth and declaring South Africa a Republic. It was the ultimate repudiation of Smuts, who'd worked hard to keep South Africa within the Commonwealth.

But Liefling chose to remember Smuts, whose biography was one of her favorite books, not as a traitor. Rather, she saw him as a complex man, a flawed visionary who, despite his insistence on maintaining segregation within South Africa, had believed in reconciliation between Afrikaners and the English, had helped rid the world of the Nazi scourge, and had brought about world peace as a signatory to the charter establishing the United Nations on June 26, 1945.

Liefling took a sip of the cool water. As she left the J.C. Smuts building, she wondered how she'd have turned out had her father not repudiated apartheid. Her parents were Stellenbosch alumni, and she'd been expected to become a *Matie* after graduating from an Afrikaner-only high school, as did most children from elite Afrikaner families. But she was barred from the university after her father's rejection of apartheid.

I certainly wouldn't be a lawyer representing blacks, she mused as she crossed a small square of manicured grass. After a brief stop at a kiosk to buy several morning papers, she walked a block or so to her mother's bungalow on Dorp, the town's main street which was lined with historic buildings and magnificent ancient oak trees, which had given the town its Afrikaner name of *Eikestad*.

Upon reaching the bungalow, Liefling immediately soaked her aching body in the claw-footed enamel tub filled with steaming hot water while reading the *Argus*, the liberal English newspaper published in Cape Town. As usual, the TRC hearings dominated the headlines. Former Prime Minister P.W. Botha was again defying a subpoena to testify about what he knew regarding death squads and human rights abuses committed under his leadership.

But the article that caught Liefling's attention was about a former askari named Joe Mamasela. An MK guerilla who later worked for the South African security police, Mamasela had just given sensational in-camera testimony before the TRC exposing a notorious SADF death squad called Vlakplaas, whose members had apparently tortured and murdered scores of ANC activists and MK guerillas.

Liefling wondered if the exposure of Vlakplaas would finally crack the code of silence surrounding SADF death squads. If it did, it would benefit her current case, which was going nowhere because of a lack of witnesses.

After reading the Mamasela story, Liefling folded the slightly wet paper and got out of the tub. She grabbed a soft green towel and slowly dried her tanned skin. She then put on a pair of bleached denim jeans, a white T-shirt with an Ubuntu Resource Center logo, sandals and an exquisite necklace and dangling earrings made from cowry shell – the last two gifts from Sipho. She went into the small but cozy kitchen, where her mother had just finished preparing an elaborate breakfast. She took a seat at the small round oak table next to the refrigerator whose door was festooned with recipes, snapshots and messages.

"Did you have a good run?" Freda asked in Afrikaans. A former music teacher, her voice was well modulated and pleasant.

"Ja," Liefling said, pouring herself a glass of fresh-squeezed orange juice. "But it was tough. I had to push myself. I haven't run in over two months."

"That's because you've been spending a lot of time in Jo'burg. I don't know why. You'd have been killed yesterday if that brave old man hadn't come along. What's his name again?"

"Makhado."

"I'm still surprised he came to your rescue," Freda said, turning off the gas-stove burner. "Few blacks nowadays would risk their lives for a white person."

"He's different. He's the most remarkable black man I've ever met."

"More remarkable than Nelson Mandela?"

"He's up there with him."

"You were extremely fortunate, dear," Freda said, bringing the food over to the table. "If I were you I'd start carrying a gun."

"You know I hate guns."

"I hate them too, but I want to live. I know a lot of people who are alive today because they carry guns."

Not wanting to argue with her mother or to make her unduly worried, Liefling said resignedly, "Okay, I'll get one."

"You won't regret it," said Freda, who owned a palm-sized Beretta she always kept handy in her purse. She was relieved that her daughter, who'd long resisted her entreaties to start carrying a gun, had finally relented. The majority of white women in South Africa, as a matter of survival, regularly packed guns and thronged firing ranges to learn how to use them.

Freda placed in front of Liefling a large pastel plate filled with steamed vegetables and an omelet with melted Gouda cheese.

"Looks good," Liefling said.

"Thank you."

Freda took out of the oven a tray of piping hot scones and placed them on a hotpad in the middle of the table.

"By the way," she said, "while you were out running I heard an announcement on the radio. When I heard your name, I stopped to listen. Is it true that you've started a legal service center in Alexandra for the families of victims of death squads?"

"Ja. It's called the Ubuntu Resource Center."

"Why have it in Alexandra and not Cape Town? It's a lot safer here."

"You know why I chose Alexandra, Mom."

Freda didn't immediately reply. There was a look of concern on her face.

She unfastened her checkered apron and placed it on the back of a nearby chair. She sat down across from Liefling, who at five eight was three inches taller. Freda looked remarkably youthful for fifty-nine, despite using little make-up. Only the faint lines under her bright hazel eyes betrayed her age. She had short, raven-black hair that accentuated her high cheekbones and small mouth.

"Just because your father was murdered in Alexandra is no reason for you to risk your life, you know," Freda said softly, unfolding an embroidered cloth napkin and spreading it on her lap. There was a note of frustration in her voice.

"You forget that Alexandra was Dad's adopted home after he was kicked out of the Dutch Reformed Church," Liefling said, sipping her juice. "And I'm determined to finish the work he was doing when he was murdered."

"Isn't it too much work for just one person?" Freda said, buttering a scone. "I seldom get to see you because you're always busy. I haven't seen you in over two months."

"I now have two colleagues."

Freda sipped her cranberry juice. "Who are they?"

"Thando Khosa and David Schneider. Thando is program's director at the Phutadichaba Community Center in Alexandra. And David is a lawyer and a former member of the TRC investigative committee."

"How will the center be funded in these tough economic times?"

"Mainly through donations and fund-raising. The Coalition for International Justice has promised to fund the center for a year. And I'll be hosting fund-raising parties from time to time. And to save on operating costs, I'll be sharing offices with Thando."

Freda studied her daughter thoughtfully. "Is it true you broke up with Derek Prinsloo?"

"Ja," Liefling said tersely.

"May I ask why?"

"Do you really want to know?"

"If you don't mind. I thought you two were headed for the altar."

"He's a spoiled brat and a racist."

Freda was surprised. "What makes you say that?" She recalled the athletic and blonde-haired Derek as a courteous, charming and highly successful criminal lawyer from a well-respected and powerful Afrikaner family. He'd played scrumhalf for the Stellenbosch University rugby team, owned his own helicopter and had taught Liefling how to fly. She thought they made a perfect match.

"Well, when I told him I was quitting my job to represent the families of victims of death squads before the TRC, he became very angry."

"Why?"

"He said that the woman he planned to marry shouldn't degrade herself. I asked him what he meant. He replied that his parents expected me to behave like a proper Afrikaner once I became his wife. 'And a true Afrikaner never persecutes fellow Afrikaners for the sake of kaffirs,' he said. I told him that I didn't like his using the word kaffir. He became furious. 'Kaffirs are still kaffirs despite the end of apartheid,' he yelled. 'And it's either me or them.' I told him to fuck off."

"Mind your language, my dear."

"Sorry."

"I'm not surprised he reacted that way," Freda said, daintily cutting a piece of steamed asparagus seasoned with Hollandaise sauce. "A lot of Afrikaners are calling you names and accusing you of persecuting your own people."

Liefling became defensive. "I'm not persecuting anyone," she said, her eyes flashing in anger. "I simply want to make sure that torturers and murderers tell the whole truth before being granted amnesty. And victims of human rights abuses and their families have a constitutional right to sue any policeman, politician or security force member who refuses to testify before the TRC."

"But surely you know that a lot of Afrikaners are opposed to the TRC. They believe it's out to punish and humiliate them for the sin of apartheid."

"They're wrong," Liefling said passionately, leaning forward as she spoke. "They should be thankful that they have the TRC instead of the Nuremberg Tribunal. Apartheid was not just a sin, Mom. It was a crime against humanity."

"I don't disagree. I'm simply telling you what people are saying."

Liefling and her mother ate in tension-filled silence for some time. A clock on the wall ticked. Liefling suddenly felt guilty. She looked at her mother and said, apologetically, "I hope I'm not an embarrassment to you, Mom."

"Why do you say that?"

"Oh, you know, you're now living in a very verkrampte town. I know how vicious Afrikaners can be against those who dare step out of the laager.

I haven't forgotten what they put you through after Dad repudiated apartheid."

Freda sighed and looked at her daughter. "I admit I endured hell after we were ostracized from the Afrikaner community because of what your father did. I wasn't at all prepared for it. That's why I became so depressed. I couldn't handle being shunned by my own family, losing all my friends, being called names by total strangers, and being harassed by the security police."

Freda paused to wipe a tear. The memories of her ostracism and persecution for her husband's rejection of apartheid were apparently too much. Liefling reached across the table and clasped her mother's hand.

"But I've since developed a thick skin, my dear," Freda said. "Just like you have. And even though I'm now eager to rejoin the Afrikaner community, because that's where my roots are, I won't stand to hear my daughter insulted by anyone, whoever they are. No one has called you names to my face. They know I'd give them a piece of my mind. And as for being an embarrassment, you'd be one if you didn't do the right thing because of what people say."

Blinking back tears, Liefling affectionately squeezed her mother's hand. "I knew you'd understand, Mom."

"So, what's your latest case?" Freda asked.

Liefling freed her hand from her mother's and said excitedly, "It's my most important one so far. And the toughest. Winning five cases in a row has made me famous and brought me more clients. I'm currently representing about two hundred families from Alexandra whose loved ones were murdered by SADF death squads. I'm trying to find out which security force members applying for amnesty were involved."

"Any luck?"

Liefling drained her juice. "None so far," she said, pouring herself a second glass. "The code of silence among SADF death squads is impregnable. And despite our running ads on radio and in newspapers, no witnesses have come forward to identify which security force members applying for amnesty belonged to death squads."

"So where do you go from here?"

"Our hopes hinge on David. He's a top investigator. He's currently working on ways to break the SADF's code of silence on death squads."

Suddenly the phone rang.

"Oh, bother," Freda said, wiping her mouth with the napkin. "I'll be right back." She got up and went into the living room. Minutes later, she returned.

"That was Tina," she said brightly.

"Who's Tina?"

Freda sat down. "Don't you remember her?"

"No." Liefling glanced at the clock. She realized she'd have to leave shortly if she was to catch the 10 a.m. train back to Cape Town so she could be in time for her noon interview with the reporter from the *New York Times*.

"Tina, your tennis coach at the Sandton multiracial school."

"Oh, Tina Uys! I remember her."

Liefling fondly recalled the former world-class player who'd played at Wimbledon and the U.S. Open. Tina had broken the Afrikaner taboo of marrying an Englishman, and then compounded the "crime" by joining the Black Sash, a group of mainly middle-class and middle-aged English-speaking housewives from the northern suburbs of Johannesburg.

Moved by a common humanity with blacks, Black Sash members had courageously helped illiterate blacks apply for jobs and permits and arranged legal representation for those facing deportations for violating Influx Control laws and for activists detained without trial under the Suppression of Terrorism Act.

"Is she living in Stellenbosch too?" Liefling asked.

"Ja. Her husband James—you remember him, don't you—the *Rand Daily Mail* sports reporter?"

Liefling nodded. "Sure."

"He was killed by carjackers in Jo'burg two years ago."

"Oh, how terrible. Was Tina with him?"

"Ja. She barely escaped alive. I told her Jo'burg was too dangerous and suggested she move to Stellenbosch. At first she didn't want to. She said Stellenbosch was too verkrampte. But after her apartment was burglarized eight times in two months she changed her mind. She's been living here almost six months."

"Does she like it?"

"Very much. She even has a new boyfriend, a very liberal-minded economics professor. And they're engaged."

"Wonderful," Liefling said. "I'd love to see Tina again, but I'm afraid I have to get going. My train leaves in forty-five minutes."

"Why don't you stay another day so you can have dinner with us at De

Volkombuis. Afterwards we're going to a Mozart concert. Then we'll go to church together in the morning. I'll drive you back to Cape Town in the afternoon."

"I'd love to stay," Liefling said, rising from her chair. "But I have a noon interview with a journalist from the *New York Times*. And tonight I'm attending an AIDS fund-raiser at the Waterfront."

"Then I guess you'll have to wait until your next visit to meet my fiancé."

"Your what?" Liefling cried, abruptly sitting down.

Freda gave an impish smile. "I'm getting married."

10 **LIEFLING** stared at her mother for almost a minute.
"You're joking," she said.
"I'm not."
"Who's the lucky man?"
"Someone I almost married before I met your father," Freda said, then paused, as if studying her daughter's reaction.

"Is his name a secret?" Liefling asked, a curious smile on her full lips, aware of her mother's penchant for harboring secrets, especially love-related ones.

"No. His name is Magnus Kruger, the owner of a security company called Arm, Protect and Secure."

Liefling took a long hard look at her mother. "You're joking, right?"
"No, I'm not."
"But he's one of the richest Afrikaners in the country."
"Do I deserve less after the privations I endured with your father?"
"How long have you and Kruger been seeing each other?"
"Almost three months. He just bought a lovely estate about five miles from here. We met at the annual banquet for *The Society for the Preservation of the Afrikaans Language*."

Liefling saw the radiance in her mother's eyes and thought, *It's been a long time since Mom has been this happy.*

She recalled Freda's battle with clinical depression following Christiaan's death in 1989, and her abuse of prescriptive drugs and alcohol. After her recovery in 1993 she'd left Johannesburg, the source of so much pain and hardship in her life. She'd moved back to Stellenbosch, the town where she was born, to be once more among the joyful scenes of her childhood and near her ailing and widowed mother, from whom she'd been estranged since Christiaan repudiated apartheid.

"I'm very happy for you, Mom," Liefling said.

"Are you really?"

"Of course I am. Why shouldn't I be?"

"I thought you'd object to Magnus becoming your stepfather."

"Object?" Liefling stared at her mother in total surprise. "Why in the world would I object?"

"Oh, I thought you might be bothered by the fact that he used to be a general in the SADF. Part of the apartheid system. I know how much you hated it for what it did to black people and to *verligtes* like your father."

"I don't believe in guilt by association. There are many good Afrikaners who were part of the SADF. They had a job to do, even if it was a distasteful one. And a lot of them are now part of the reconstituted South African National Defense Force (SADNF)."

Freda sighed with relief. "I'm glad to hear you say that, dear. You know, after your father was killed I thought I'd never fall in love again. But Magnus is very special."

"But isn't he a bit too conservative for you?"

"Funny, Tina said the very same thing. But I'm not marrying him for his politics, my dear. I'm marrying him for love. He's kind and pampers me like a queen. And if you want to know the truth, lately I've become something of a *verkrampte* too."

Liefling rolled her eyes. "That's news," she said coolly. "Why?"

"Just look at what's happening to South Africa. Crime and violence are endemic. You yourself were almost killed in a city that used to be one of the safest in the world."

"Are you suggesting that apartheid shouldn't have been abolished?"

"Of course not. Apartheid was immoral. It was evil. It had to go. But for democracy to survive in South Africa, people must feel safe. That's why I'm for the restoration of the death penalty."

Liefling decided to change the subject rather than engage her mother in a debate over the death penalty, which Liefling opposed on the grounds that most of the crime committed by blacks had its roots in the apartheid legacy of poverty and unemployment.

"When is the wedding?"

"Next Sunday here in Stellenbosch. At the *Moederkerk* where your father used to preach. You'll come, won't you, dear?"

"Of course. Can I bring my boyfriend along?"

Freda's eyes lit up. "You have a new boyfriend?"

"Ja."

"Great. Bring him along."

Realizing she'd spoken too spontaneously, Liefling coughed slightly before saying, "There's a minor problem."

"What's that?"

"He's not Afrikaner."

"Well, I don't mind if he's English."

"I didn't say he was English."

"Oh." The awkward pause that followed made Liefling's heart pound and her mind race. She wondered how best to finally break the news to her mother that she was dating a black man. Another part of Liefling was angry for having to worry about what her mother thought. It was her life, after all. She could not spend her life trying to be "a good Afrikaner girl" in her mother's eyes. She had to make her own decisions. Failure to do so was partly what had led her to please her mother by dating Derek, a "perfect Afrikaner catch," despite her instincts telling her that they were incompatible.

"What race is he?" Freda asked at last.

"Why should it matter?" Liefling said defensively.

"I'm curious."

"He's human."

"What's that supposed to mean?" Freda snapped in exasperation.

"He's a human being whose father happens to be Zulu, and whose mother happens to be Colored."

The color drained from Freda's cheeks. She blinked, then stammered, "You mean he's black?"

"Ja." Liefling felt suddenly strong now that she'd finally told the truth. She stared boldly at her mother, waiting for her reaction.

"That's quite a surprise," Freda said slowly, groping for words, trying to sort out her true feelings from the reaction Afrikaner society expected of her. "You've never dated a black man before."

"And he's never dated a white woman before."

"No doubt. What other white woman would risk so much to…." Freda stopped herself short. Seeing the hurt expression on her daughter's face, she immediately regretted her words, which her upbringing had forced out of her. "I'm sorry, honey. I didn't mean it that way."

"Never mind," Liefling said flatly.

There was an awkward silence. Freda pulled her chair closer to Liefling, making its metallic legs scrape the linoleum floor. She tried to restart the conversation. "What's his name?"

"Sipho. Sipho Radebe."

"Why have you kept him a secret?"

"I just met him recently. And both of us have been very busy."

"Is he a human rights lawyer too?"

"No. He's a doctor."

"What kind of doctor?"

"A surgeon. One of the best in South Africa. He studied in America. He divides his times between Baragwanath Hospital and a clinic in Crossroads, where his father grew up."

"Where did you meet?"

"At a fund-raiser for a battered women's shelter."

"Nice place to meet. Is he from a large family?"

"No. He's the youngest of two. His brother is a detective with the Johannesburg police. He was recently in the news when President Mandela nominated him to head a task force on muti-killings."

"I think I read about him in the *Argus*," Freda said. "Won't he be testifying before Parliament on the issue?"

"Next month."

Freda was silent for a while.

"I want an honest answer, Mom," Liefling said, looking her mother squarely in the face. "Does the thought of my being with a black man disgust you, as it does so many white people?"

"Liefling!" Freda said, almost reproachfully. "Do you think I'm a racist?"

"Frankly, I'm not sure. Especially since you just told me you were becoming more verkrampte."

"So what? Not all conservatives are racists, you know. And not all liberals are in love with blacks. Some of the worst racists I know were liberals in the anti-apartheid movement. They loved blacks only as long as they didn't marry their daughters or acquire real power. I personally don't care who you date as long as he's a good person and respects you."

"Oh, Mom," Liefling said joyfully, relieved. She leaned across the table and planted a kiss on Freda's left cheek. "I'm sorry for thinking you'd changed."

"Just because I'm marrying a verkrampte doesn't mean I'm going to give up my own identity, honey," Freda said. "I didn't after I married your father. But I don't know how Magnus views interracial relationships. I've only known him a couple months. Also, a lot of his friends are verkrampte. It might be kind of awkward if Sipho attended the wedding. You know what I mean."

"I understand. I'll come alone. The last thing I want to do is spoil the wedding of my best friend and favorite mother."

Freda smiled. "Thanks for understanding, dear. But I look forward to meeting Sipho."

"Why don't we all three have lunch sometime after the wedding?"

"I'd like that."

On the rattling train back to Cape Town a jubilant Liefling leaned back in her seat, a book of Afrikaner poems on her lap and a happy smile on her face. She gazed wistfully out the window at the lovely valleys pied by a patchwork of white-gabled Cape-Dutch manor houses and vineyards whose vines were a riot of autumn colors. She thought, *I'm so glad to see Mom happy again. She deserves to be after all she's been through. And I can't wait to meet Magnus. He sounds like a nice man, despite being verkrampte.*

KRUGER's limo pulled up in front of Freda's bungalow at ten to five in the afternoon. The sky was a leaden color and rain had been forecast but hadn't yet begun falling. The chill in the air penetrated the bones. Kruger was impeccably dressed in a cashmere overcoat with a blue double-breasted Christian Dior blazer, a white Ralph Lauren button-down cotton shirt, a red silk bow tie and matching scarf, white flannel slacks and a pair of black wingtips. Thin black leather gloves were stashed inside the pockets of his overcoat.

After saying something to his chauffeur, Kruger got out and headed toward the four-foot high white picket fence. He frowned at the smallness of the house it rimmed.

Once we're married she'll be mistress of a house ten times this size, he thought as his black wingtips clattered along the stone walkway. Reaching the door, he remembered that he'd asked Freda to move in with him but she'd insisted that they first get married. He liked that about her. She was still traditional, despite her verligte politics.

Whistling, he rang the doorbell. Freda answered almost immediately.

"Wonderful to see you, my dear," Kruger said. "You look lovely, as always."

Freda smiled. There was a time in her life when she dreamed she'd never hear such compliments again. "Please come in."

Kruger entered the small but neat living room, which was modestly furnished in the country-style with a rust-colored sofa and loveseat in the middle. Several potted plants lined the windowsill next to an upright piano.

Kruger planted a kiss on Freda's rouged lips. "I missed you," he said.

"Me too. When did you get in?"

"My jet landed in Cape Town about an hour ago. Luckily it took my chauffeur less than an hour to get here, despite rush hour traffic."

"You haven't been home yet?"

"No. I came straight here. I changed on the plane. That outfit looks stunning on you, my dear," Kruger said, admiring Freda's green silk chiffon tank with hand-sewn beads and sequins, which nicely complemented her black velvet pants and crystal link necklace.

"You think so? Liefling helped me choose the combination."

Kruger glanced about. "Is she here?"

"No. She was here last night. She left this morning."

"Why didn't you ask her to stay and go to the concert with us?" Kruger asked, taking off his overcoat and hanging it in the hallway closet. "I'm anxious to finally meet my future step-daughter."

"I asked her to stay."

"And she wouldn't? Is she avoiding me?"

"Of course not. She's attending a big fundraiser tonight. Can I get you something to drink?"

"A martini please."

Freda went to the kitchen. Kruger sat down on the loveseat and flipped through a copy of *Fair Lady* magazine on the coffee table. Minutes later, Freda came back with two martinis. She handed one to Kruger and sat down beside him.

"Thank you," he said. "Did you finally tell her about us?"

"Ja."

"Does she have any objections to our getting married?"

"Your fears were unfounded, darling. She doesn't hate the SADF. As a matter of fact, she's as eager to meet you as you are to meet her."

The doorbell rang. Freda immediately got up from the sofa.

"Are you expecting anyone?" Kruger asked in surprise.

"I invited Tina and her boyfriend to come with us to the concert," Freda said, looking at Kruger. "You don't mind, do you?"

"Not at all, dear."

Kruger was lying. He couldn't stand Freda's verligte friend and her even more verligte boyfriend, who'd caused quite a stir in Afrikaner circles with his articles criticizing as racist right-wing clamors for an Afrikaner homeland.

Freda opened the door and ushered in Tina Uys and her boyfriend, Paul Strydom. Tina hardly resembled a former world-class tennis player. She was short and had gained a little weight. Her comely face had just enough make-up on, and her dark hair, streaked with gray, was neatly done up in a bun. Her limpid light-brown eyes had that calm introspection of someone who'd endured persecution but was never broken. She was wearing a white mink coat and a simple black dress with no jewelry except for a pair of dolphin-shaped gold earrings. Her slightly chubby and sandy-haired boyfriend was dressed as professors generally dress. His tweed jacket was a bit rumpled, and somewhat mismatched with a light-blue shirt and a red tie. Kruger greeted both newcomers with extreme politeness.

"What can I get you to drink?" Freda asked as Paul helped Tina take off her mink coat.

"A bloody Mary for me, please," Tina said.

"Vodka for me," Paul said.

"Please have a seat," Kruger said.

Tina and Paul sat down on the sofa across from Kruger.

"That was an interesting article you wrote for the *Star*," Kruger said to Paul.

"Thank you."

"But I must say I strongly disagree with your arguments."

"Really?"

"Ja. Afrikaners do have a right to their own homeland under the Constitution. They have a right to preserve their own identity, culture, language and heritage."

Paul's mischievous brown eyes brightened. This was his favorite subject.

"Everyone has that right, General," Paul said. "Zulus, Vendas, Shangaans, the English, Coloreds, Indians and so forth. And if everyone began demanding their own homelands, we'd be back to the old days of Grand Apartheid. Is that what you want?"

That was precisely what Kruger wanted, but he wasn't about to admit that openly. Instead, he said, "Don't you think Afrikaners have a right to ensure their own survival as a people?"

"They have every right to do that. But they can do that within a unified and democratic South Africa. Not by seceding."

"Even if they're being discriminated against?" Kruger asked.

"What do you mean by that?" Tina jumped in.

"I'm talking about affirmative action," Kruger said, looking at Tina. "Qualified Afrikaners are being passed over for jobs in every sector of the economy. And this discrimination will never end until and unless they have their own homeland where at least merit will determine who gets a job."

Tina surprised Kruger by laughing aloud. "I'm against discrimination of any kind, General, including discrimination by blacks. But I think it's a bit hypocritical of Afrikaners to now criticize affirmative action when they themselves were the beneficiaries of apartheid -- the most extensive affirmative action program ever undertaken in the history of South Africa."

If Kruger had not been such a master at hiding his true feelings, he would have exploded. Instead, he said with a calmness he was far from feeling, "I don't know what you're talking about. Merit is what accounts for the Afrikaners' accomplishments and rise to power economically."

This time it was Paul who answered Kruger. "I'm afraid you're wrong, General. I wrote my doctoral thesis on the massive affirmative action program the National Party implemented after 1948 to help Afrikaners. It originated within the highest ranks of the Broederbond itself. Surely you haven't forgotten discriminatory laws like the Jobs Reservation Act, which prohibited blacks from holding so-called 'white jobs.' And you couldn't have forgotten that after the National Party came to power, English-speaking South Africans were purged from the civil service and replaced by members of the Broederbond who'd sworn to protect the interests of the Volk. Talent counted for nothing in getting a job or a promotion. One simply had to be a loyal Afrikaner. That's why, within a generation, the National Party was able to create a solid Afrikaner middle-class and to virtually wipe out poverty among Afrikaners."

Kruger had no adequate rebuttal. He knew Paul was right. That had been the signal achievement of *Baaskap*, an achievement the ANC government now threatened to undo with its own affirmative action program. Black economic empowerment had swelled the ranks of poor Afrikaners. Many were now crowding homeless shelters, lining up at soup kitchens, begging in the streets. Worse, some Afrikaner women were now so poor they felt no shame committing the unpardonable sin of selling their bodies to kaffirs!

Because of this, Kruger hated verligte Afrikaners like Paul and Tina. They were traitors who'd sold out the Volk. Kruger was so furious with them that he might have lost his composure if Freda at that moment had not opportunely reappeared with the drinks.

She'd overheard the heated discussion from the kitchen and had been growing concerned. She'd sensed a looming and potentially ugly confrontation, which she was sure would ruin their evening. So, like a good hostess, she deftly changed the conversation.

"What do you think of the orchestra that's playing tonight?" she asked Paul, a music buff.

"I heard that they play Mozart exquisitely," he said.

For the next half-hour, until they left for dinner at De Volkombuis, they discussed music and the arts. Freda heaved a sigh of relief. Knowing how adamant Kruger was on the subject of Afrikaners having their own homeland, and how equally stubborn Paul and Tina were that the idea was racist, she knew she'd avoided a disaster. And the last thing she wanted a week before her wedding was a bitter argument between the man she loved and was eager to marry and the woman who was her most-trusted friend and matron-of-honor. Little did Freda know that a greater disaster loomed involving her husband-to-be and her beloved daughter.

11

PIET VILJOEN tightly gripped the steering wheel of a bakkie, splattered with red mud, as it bounced up a rutted dirt road headed for Makhado's kraal. Beside him sat his close friend and business associate, Jan Barnard. The two men wore short-sleeve khakis, khaki shorts, thick ankle-high socks and snub-nosed black boots. Barnard was short, with thick sideburns and a puffy face the color of veal. Viljoen had the built of a wrestler and green reptilian eye that never seemed to blink.

Because rural travel nowadays was extremely dangerous, Viljoen and Barnard were heavily armed. R5 semi-automatic rifles were slung over their shoulders, and each carried a loaded Glock 19 pistol concealed in a Galco Scorpion rig holster made of premium saddle leather. Each also had a cold steel XL Voyager knife with a razor sharp blade capable of cutting through bone.

"The bloody ANC could at least pave the fucking roads," Viljoen said. "My bloody arse is sore."

"Nobody cares about improving rural roads, man," retorted Barnard. "The corrupt kaffirs are busy lining their own pockets with public funds."

"You're bloody right," Viljoen said. "Homeland kaffirs had it bloody good under apartheid. My brother-in-law used to be high up in the department of Plural Relations. He was in charge of implementing the policy of Parallel Democracies. He told me that each year the government gave millions of rands in foreign aid to independent homelands such as Venda."

"That's true."

It didn't occur to Viljoen that the governments of the so-called "independent" homelands had been so riddled with corruption and nepotism that very little of the millions the apartheid regime annually spent propping them up actually ended up being used to improve the lives of rural blacks. Also, it didn't occur to Viljoen that a sizeable portion of the ANC government's budget, which could have been used to improve the roads he was complaining about, went toward paying the hefty pensions of former apartheid civil servants like himself and Barnard, as part of the "sunset clause."

"Ah, here we are," Viljoen said with relief as the bakkie came to a stop at the main entrance to Makhado's kraal, which consisted of a cluster of thatched mud huts arranged in a semi-circle and enclosed by a fence made of thorny branches. Beyond the huts were fields sprouting dried stalks of maize, and beyond the fields was a thick forest edged by hills. Several scrawny goats, sheep and cattle grazed languidly in the shimmering afternoon heat.

Viljoen and Barnard jumped out of the bakkie and approached a group of about fifteen barefoot black children playing in the dusty courtyard.

"I hope the old kaffir is around," Viljoen said to Barnard, who was trailing behind, amused by the crude toys the children were playing with, which included "cars" made of chicken wire and soccer balls and dolls made from rags. Barnard was used to seeing white children playing with expensive toys, including the latest video games.

Yet they seem to be having a good time, Barnard thought. *It doesn't take much to satisfy kaffirs.*

At the sight of the two heavily armed white men, the children fled toward the huts. Only a tall, thin boy of about fourteen, who had brown teeth from drinking well water, didn't run away. He simply stared impassively at the approaching white men.

"Hey, pickaninny!" Viljoen yelled. "*Kom hierso!*"

After a moment's hesitation, the boy warily approached the two Afrikaners.

"Is Makhado home?"

"Yes."

Viljoen was surprised that the boy didn't say "yes, baas," as Makhado always did.

"Go tell him baas Viljoen wants to talk to him," he said to the boy, whose name was Vutshilo, which meant "Life" in Venda.

Vutshilo ran toward the largest of the five huts, which stood in the middle, near a huge baobab tree. Minutes later Makhado came shuffling across the dusty courtyard, wearing bib overalls and sandals made from discarded car tires. His demeanor was completely changed from that of the proud Makhado who'd rescued Liefling from carjackers in Johannesburg several weeks ago. Eyes cast down and his voice low and servile, he said to Viljoen, "What's the matter, baas?"

"I wish you had a bloody phone, that's what's the matter," Viljoen said brusquely. "Then I wouldn't have had to drive twenty miles on bad roads to let you know that I plan to open the game reserve early this season."

"Sorry, mei baas."

"I want you to do repairs around the game reserve. Several of the lodges need fixing."

"Ja, baas."

"And the viewing hut near the watering hole has a damaged roof. Fix that too."

"Ja, baas."

"This time I want you to hire only ten girls to clean the lodges, chalets and huts and wash the linens."

"Only ten, mei baas?" Makhado said in a plaintive voice. Last year Viljoen had hired two dozen.

"Ja, only ten," Viljoen said emphatically. "I can't afford to hire more. And this time I can only pay them R20 a day instead of R30. The economy is bad, you know."

"And it's all because of the bloody ANC," Barnard said with a chuckle.

"Okay, mei baas. I'll tell them."

"You can start work next week. I'm off to attend an important wedding this weekend. After that I'll be in Johannesburg for about two more weeks. And while I'm away, I want people to work, not sit around on their bloody arses watching TV and wasting electricity, understand?" He wagged a finger at Makhado.

"Ja, baas."

"Here are the keys," Viljoen said.

"Thank you, baas," Makhado said, accepting the cluster of silver keys with both hands, like a child receiving candy from a parent.

Viljoen and Barnard climbed back into the bakkie and left.

Makhado spat after them.

*****

LIEFLING and Freda stood at the bottom of a spiraling mahogany staircase, watching couples dance across the marbled floor of the enormous ballroom, from whose high ceiling dangled a gigantic crystal chandelier of 18th century French design. It was evening and the wedding reception was in full swing.

Liefling couldn't believe that just a few hours ago, in an elaborate ceremony held under a huge white tent on the manicured lawn of Kruger's magnificent estate, witnessed by one hundred invitation-only guests from the elite of Afrikaner society and presided over by Dominee Muller, she'd proudly given her mother away.

"You look lovely, Mom," Liefling said as she admired her mother's elaborately embroidered Shantung wedding dress with an illusion neckline and sleeves covered in delicate Alencon lace.

"Oh, thank you, sweetie," Freda said, adjusting her glittering two-carat diamond wedding ring. "You look lovely too." Liefling was stunningly dressed in a black evening gown by Chanel that sharply contrasted with her tanned skin and blonde hair. "And I'm so glad that you and Magnus have hit it off so well."

"To be honest with you, I didn't think we would," Liefling said, entwining the long fingers of her hands, which were covered with white gloves. "But he completely surprised me. He's not as verkrampte as I thought he'd be. And he's funny and very charming."

"I thought you'd like him once you met him."

"Who are those men talking to him?" Liefling pointed with her eyes at three men dressed in tails who were standing about thirty feet away, deep in conversation with Kruger.

"Oh, those are his business associates," Freda said. "The one on the left is Piet Viljoen. The one to his right is Jan Barnard. And the handsome blond in the middle is Ludwig Botha. Why do you ask?"

"Ludwig is quite rude," Liefling said.

"What makes you say that?"

"He's been hounding me all evening for a date. He won't take no for an answer."

"You're a very lovely woman."

"I also happen to have a boyfriend."

A moment later, a beaming and clean-shaven Kruger, dressed in a crisp black custom-made tuxedo and silk shirt with gold cufflinks, joined Liefling and Freda. He kissed both of them on the cheek.

"Shall we dance, my dear?" he said with an ingratiating smile. He bowed slightly and extended his right hand to Liefling.

"With pleasure," she said, curtseying.

Freda smiled as she watched her husband and daughter whirl around the dance floor to Strauss' Blue Danube waltz, played by an orchestra on a raised stage at the far end of the huge ballroom.

What more can a woman ask, Freda thought with a joyful smile, *than to have a loving daughter and a doting husband.*

VILJOEN blocked the path of the sandy-haired man in a rumpled tuxedo as he left the bar, a glass of champagne in his right hand.

"Are you Paul Strydom?" he asked.

"Ja, how did you know my name?" asked a tipsy Paul in Afrikaans.

"I'm Piet Viljoen."

"Nice to meet you." Paul proffered his hand.

Viljoen didn't shake it. Instead he said coldly, "Why do you hate your own people?"

Paul frowned. "I don't hate my people. What makes you think I hate my people?"

"Of course you do," Viljoen retorted. "I read that bloody article you wrote in *The Star* in which you call Afrikaners who want their own homeland racist. You are racist, too, man."

"I most certainly am not," Paul said angrily, weaving slightly.

"Don't kid yourself," Viljoen said. "Everyone is a racist. Whites, blacks, Indians, Coloreds. When push comes to shove, we all prefer our own kind. And we all do what we can do to protect the interests of our own kind."

"I'm a South African," Paul said. "The only interests I'm prepared to protect are South Africa's. And Afrikaners like you will be better served by remaining in South Africa instead of dreaming of some mythical Vaderland."

Viljoen's face turned crimson. His green reptilian eyes flashed with rage. He would have punched Paul in the face if he had not suddenly remembered where they were.

Viljoen sneered. "Okay, kaffir-lover, you and your kind can remain with your kaffir brothers and sisters in the bloody new South Africa. We don't need traitors like you in the Volkstaat."

Despite being drunk, Paul was taken aback by what he considered a gratuitous insult from someone he didn't even know. He was momentarily struck dumb. By the time he recovered his senses, Viljoen had disappeared into the thick crowd of revelers. All Paul could do was to tell Tina about the strange encounter with Viljoen.

KRUGER said to Liefling, "Isn't your mother lovely?"

"She sure is."

"I'm the luckiest man alive."

Liefling smiled as she and Kruger dipped, glided and stepped across the dance floor to the fast rhythm of the Viennese waltz. For a moment she wished she were dancing with Sipho instead of Kruger. She remembered how well they'd danced together at the AIDS fund-raiser. At the same time she knew that his appearance at a wedding full of verkramptes would have caused a scandal and ruined her mother's happiest day.

"I hear you'll be honeymooning on a yacht," she said to Kruger.

"Yes, my dear. We'll be cruising around the Indian Ocean in *The Henrietta,* a 197-foot yacht I bought last year. It's named after my mother."

"How long will you be away?"

"About two weeks. We plan stops in Madagascar and the Seychelles Islands. I'm looking forward to having some time alone with her. I've been so busy with the firm I've neglected her, poor thing. I want to make it up to her. She tells me she hardly took any vacations with your father because of the banning orders."

"That's true," Liefling said. "For almost ten years the apartheid regime forbade Dad to leave our home or travel abroad, even for a vacation."

"Well, I told your mother that we'll take as many vacations as she wants."

Liefling smiled gratefully. Kruger effortlessly whirled her around.

"You're a wonderful dancer, my dear," Kruger said.

"I took lessons in high school. I haven't had many opportunities to practice since then. This is wonderful."

"It is indeed." Kruger smiled down at Liefling's upturned radiant face.

The two continued dancing until the waltz ended. There was thunderous applause for their sterling performance from onlookers.

Liefling and Kruger left the dance floor and headed back to Freda, who was talking to Tina and Paul.

Freda kissed Kruger on the cheek. "You were marvelous, honey."

"I simply rose to the occasion, my dear," Kruger said. "Liefling is a superb dancer."

"She puts the rest of us to shame," Tina said.

"I'm not a bad dancer either," Paul said. He gulped another glass of champagne, set the empty glass on the snowy tablecloth and extended his arm to Tina. "Let's dance, my dear."

"Not while you're drunk."

"I'm not drunk," Paul slurred.

"You are," Tina said. "Besides, I feel a bit light-headed from the champagne."

The band struck up a polka. Paul grabbed Tina's arm. "Then let's dance the drunken polka, baby."

Liefling laughed as she watched Tina and Paul – both of them giggling – head for the dance floor, which was quickly getting crowded with vivacious and drunken couples.

"I feel rather warm," Liefling said suddenly, wiping her brow with a silk handkerchief. "I think I'll step outside for a little while and get some fresh air."

"Mind if I join you?" Kruger asked.

"Not at all."

Liefling and Kruger stepped onto the portico of the 50-room Norman-style chateau overlooking a valley through which meandered the Eerste River. Beyond the river loomed the dramatic Hottentot Mountains, silhouetted against a bright full moon. The night air was crisp but not cold. Liefling felt invigorated by the fresh air.

"What a beautiful and peaceful spot for a house," she observed dreamily.

"I thought so too when I was growing up in this valley over fifty years ago," Kruger said with a touch of nostalgia, standing inches from Liefling. "It has always been my dream to come back and settle here. As a matter of fact, if your mother and I had gotten married back then, our plans were to start our own winery near here, on land my grandfather owned. But as fate would have it, my family moved away and your mother ended up marrying your father."

"Well, if she hadn't, I wouldn't be here."

"Of course, my dear." Kruger said with a small laugh.

For a while Liefling and Kruger stood in silence, staring at the moon, breathing the fresh air, and listening to the mysterious sounds of the night. Inside the ballroom the orchestra merrily played on.

"Your Mom told me you broke up with Derek Prinsloo," Kruger said suddenly.

Liefling immediately felt uncomfortable. "Ja," she said softly.

"That's unfortunate. He's such a nice young man."

"You know him?"

"His father is my lawyer."

"I didn't know that."

"I hope you won't consider this question impertinent. But why did you and Derek break up?"

She wanted to tell Kruger the truth, that they'd broken up because of Derek's insistence on calling blacks "kaffirs," but she decided against it, unsure how Kruger would react.

"We are very different," Liefling said evasively.

"I hope you don't mean politically. A lot of couples, including your mother and I, are on opposite sides on many political issues. But we're deeply in love."

"It was more than political differences," Liefling said.

"Are you seeing anyone?"

Liefling didn't know what to say. Did her mother tell Kruger that she was dating Sipho?

She was still pondering how to respond to Kruger's question when a voice behind her cried, "There you are." It was Mrs. Muller, who was garishly dressed in a frilly purple gown bedecked with eye-like jewels.

"My dear Magnus," she said, "Koos is looking all over for you. He wants to propose a toast."

"Excuse me, my dear," Kruger said to Liefling, then headed inside with Mrs. Muller.

Liefling breathed a sigh of relief. She didn't know what she would have said had Kruger asked about Sipho. She wondered how he would react if he knew she'd rejected the advances of his handsome business associate, Ludwig Botha, in part because she was dating a black man.

12 LIEFLING was awakened from a deep sleep by the loud ringing of a telephone. It was shortly before noon on Monday. She was sleeping late, recovering from the wedding festivities and a slight hangover from too much champagne. She was back in her two-bedroom flat overlooking the foam-flecked Atlantic Ocean in Sea Point, an old Cape Town suburb densely populated with high-rise flats, apartments, hotels, restaurants and trendy bars.

Liefling groped for the phone on the cherry nightstand. The alabaster aluminum blinds were drawn and the room was in semi-darkness, despite the brilliant sunshine outside.

"Who is it?" she asked groggily, squinting from a splitting headache.

"It's me, Ludwig."

"Ludwig who?"

"Ludwig Botha. From the wedding last night, remember me?"

Liefling hoisted herself up against the curved headboard. "What do you want?" She had half a mind to hang up on him.

"Is it true you're dating a kaffir?"

Liefling was too angry and too astonished to respond.

There was a long pause. Then Botha said, "It's pathetic that such a beautiful Afrikaner girl like you would let herself be fucked by a kaffir."

"Go fuck yourself, you bastard." Liefling slammed down the phone. Furious, she decided to call her mother. Freda was in her bedroom, busy packing her clothes neatly into a fat brown leather suitcase for her honeymoon cruise. She and Kruger, who was in his office down the hall making last-minute calls, were leaving that afternoon.

"Mom, did you tell anyone at the reception last night about me and Sipho?"

"No," Freda said. "Why do you ask?"

"I just got a call from that asshole Ludwig Botha. He knows."

"I didn't tell him."

"Did you tell Magnus?"

"I didn't tell him either."

Liefling was surprised. "You didn't? Then why did he ask me about Derek last night?"

"I didn't tell him about your break-up with Derek."

Liefling got out of bed and went to the window with the cordless phone still pressed to her ear. She opened the blinds and blinked as bright sunshine flooded the room, which was, as usual, messy.

"I wonder how he knows," Liefling said, looking down at the street below. There was a lunch-hour crowd at her favorite Indian restaurant across from her flat.

"I wonder too, dear."

"Wait a minute," Liefling said, remembering. "I think I know how he could have found out. He told me yesterday that Derek's father was his lawyer."

"He is," Freda said.

"Then he must have found out through Derek," Liefling said. "He stopped by my flat a couple weeks ago to pick up his stuff. Sipho was here. I thought he'd make a scene, but luckily he didn't. I guess he told his father, and his father told Magnus."

"Well, like I said, it's nobody's business whom you date, honey," Freda said. "And I'll tell Magnus to tell Ludwig to stop pestering you."

"Thanks, but don't worry. I can take care of him."

"Well, I guess I'll see you when Magnus and I get back in two weeks," Freda said. "And don't forget, I'm still hoping to take you and Sipho out to lunch."

"I'll check with him to see which day would be best. He's coming down today."

After hanging up, Liefling put on a pair of jeans and a T-shirt, had a Tuna sandwich with salad, then settled down at the kitchen table to read the piles of transcripts from recent TRC hearings held across the country, searching for clues about death squads.

Around three in the afternoon Liefling heard a loud knock on her door. She left the kitchen table and rushed to the door, thinking it was Sipho, who was supposed to be arriving from Johannesburg that afternoon.

She opened it and let out a cry of amazement: "Thando! David!" Liefling stared at her two colleagues. "What are you doing here?" she asked as she embraced Thando and then David.

"We thought it best to come down and talk to you in person," David said.

"Anything wrong?" Liefling asked as she ushered David and Thando into her messy flat. Books, newspapers, files, music CDs and clothes were scattered on the sofa, coffee table and carpet.

"Can we sit down?" Thando said. "We have something very important to tell you."

"Sure." Liefling hurriedly removed stacks of transcripts from the table and tossed them onto the sofa.

"Girlfriend, you're messier than I am," Thando said, smiling.

"I haven't had time to clean," Liefling said as the three of them sat down at the kitchen table. "I've been working non-stop for the past two weeks. Don't forget we still haven't broken the SADF's code of silence on death squads. And the amnesty deadline is less than a week away."

"That's why we're here," David said, reaching for his brown leather briefcase. "I think we may finally have a breakthrough."

MAKHADO stood facing about two hundred people desperate for jobs. The crowd was packed inside a ramshackle church on the outskirts of the village. Except for Nzhelele and two or three other men, there were no able-bodied men in the audience. Most of them had gone to faraway cities in search of work. And with the unemployment rate among South African blacks hovering close to 50 percent, many of the men had not found jobs and therefore hadn't been able to send the all-important remittances on which their wives, children and extended families depended.

Makhado knew this, and it made his task doubly heart wrenching and difficult. Viljoen needed only ten workers, down from the two dozen he'd hired the year before. Makhado had agonized over how he'd go about choosing the ten workers. He'd discussed the matter with Nzhelele, who'd given him some important advice.

"I'm glad you could all come," Makhado said to the crowd of women. Most had infants tied to their backs with blankets. Small children fought and ran about their mothers' legs, screaming or crying. Some children squatted and stared vacantly, too malnourished and weak to move or speak. The hot and stuffy church felt like an overheated catacomb. Sweat dripped down Makhado's face.

"I'll be brief," he said in a loud voice. "Viljoen needs workers."

An excited murmur arose from the crowd.

"But he needs fewer workers than last year."

The excited murmurs turned to disappointed groans. The women desperately wanted work, any work, to feed their starving families.

"I had a hard time deciding what criteria to use in picking the ten workers he wants. I finally decided that I'd pick those women with the most children. But only on one condition: that we all pool part of our earnings into a small fund to enable those families without sources of income to borrow from it. Do you all agree to this scheme of helping each other?"

The women assented, amid a hullabaloo of bawling infants.

"Work at Viljoen's game reserve starts in two days," Makhado said. "I'll continue to canvas for work at other private game reserves and bushveld camps. In the meantime, let's all do our best to keep our community together during these trying times."

LIEFLING muttered, "I don't believe it. It's not true."

Her face was blanched with shock.

"I'm afraid it's true," David said with lawyerly somberness.

Suddenly feeling dizzy, Liefling slowly rose from the kitchen table where she'd been sitting with David and Thando barely ten minutes ago. With unsteady steps, she staggered toward the French doors leading to the small wrought-iron balcony. David and Thando immediately sprang up from their chairs and rushed to her side, thinking she was about to faint.

"No," Liefling said softly, waving them away. "I'll be fine. I just need some fresh air."

She stepped onto the balcony. Immediately a cool breeze buffeted her face. She took several deep breaths and felt a bit better. Her face regained its color and she was no longer trembling, despite her sweaty palms. She leaned onto the railing of the balcony and stared out into space for several long moments. Her back was toward David and Thando, the bearers of the news that has shaken her so. They remained standing by the kitchen table, watching her with sympathetic eyes through the open French doors.

After several minutes, Liefling returned to the kitchen table. "I just can't believe it." She shook her head as she sat down. "My stepfather a member of the Civil Cooperation Bureau?"

"Not just any member, mind you," David said, relieved that Liefling was okay. "He was very high up. One of its leaders."

"And there was nothing civil or cooperative about what the CCB did," Thando said, her oval face set and traces of anger creeping into her normally calm voice. "It sponsored death squads."

The word "death squads" made Liefling shudder. She looked anxiously at David as he reached into his briefcase and removed a small black notebook. He quickly flipped through it.

"And according to my sources," David said, glancing at his copious notes, "Kruger joined the CCB around 1986, shortly after the organization was formed. He remained a member till 1993, when the organization was finally disbanded."

"And during those seven years," Thando added, "scores of anti-apartheid activists and MK guerrillas were killed by CCB agents, hundreds more disappeared, and dozens of houses were firebombed, including my parents'."

"Are the sources credible?" Liefling asked weakly, still stunned by the revelation. She couldn't believe that the urbane man whose wedding she'd just attended, the charming man she'd danced with during the reception and who'd made her mother the happiest she'd ever been in years, could have been responsible for the most ruthless death squads in the history of South Africa.

There must be some mistake, Liefling thought. *There must be.*

"Who are your sources?" Liefling asked.

"One of them is a *Mail & Guardian* journalist who is working on an expose about the CCB," David said.

Thando leaned forward in her chair and said, "I know the journalist, Liefling. She is one of the best. She was among those who broke the story about the Vlaakplaas death squad."

"Not only that," David said. "I cross-checked her information with copies of documents from the National Archives and from my sources inside the TRC investigative committee. In the documents Kruger's name appears in the minutes of several top-secret meetings of the State Security Council."

David retrieved copies of the documents from his briefcase and handed them to Liefling. While she perused them, he continued, "You'll notice there's a list drawn up by the SSC of 'politically sensitive people' who must be neutralized and eliminated as part of the SADF's total strategy against the liberation movement. Tell me what neutralize and eliminate mean? Especially in the context of what happened in places like Alexandra during the struggle, when dozens of activists and MK guerrillas were killed by faceless assassins?"

Liefling didn't answer. Instead she placed the documents on the table, next to a lovely blue vase filled with a dozen red roses from Sipho. Lips tightly pursed, she was thinking of the disastrous consequences if the revelations about Kruger being a high-ranking member of the CCB turned out to be true. Part of her continued to cling to the faint hope that there was some big awful mistake that would soon become apparent.

"Is there any evidence linking my stepfather to a specific CCB death squad?"

"That's what I'm currently investigating," David said. "And I need your help."

Startled, Liefling looked at David and said, "What kind of help?"

"My sources within the TRC investigative committee gave me the names of several policemen they believe may have belonged to a CCB death squad Kruger knew about. But so far the policemen are clinging to a code of silence. I mean to expose them."

"How?"

David didn't immediately reply. Instead he flipped through his notebook till he came to a page marked "Biko's Case" at the top.

"When I was still with the TRC I often tried exposing several policemen linked to death squads using a tactic I learned from the Steve Biko case," he began, glancing at his notes. "The policemen who killed him were also clinging to a code of silence, remember?"

Liefling nodded.

"And they would've maintained that silence had not a TRC investigator begun calling them anonymously and warning them that the TRC already possessed information about what really happened to Biko during his detention."

Liefling shut her eyes as if to erase the indelible and harrowing details of the final hours of the Black Consciousness leader Stephen Bantu Biko. The details had shocked the nation when they were finally revealed in their entirety during an amnesty hearing for Biko's killers. On August 18 1977, Biko, who'd been banned from engaging in any political activity and from meeting with more than one person at a time, was stopped at a police roadblock set up especially for him on the outskirts of Grahamstown in the Eastern Cape. The police – who apparently had been tipped of Biko's movements by an informant – charged that he was on his way to distribute "inflammatory pamphlets" inciting blacks to riot.

He was immediately detained under the catchall Section 6 of the Suppression of Terrorism Act, which permitted the indefinite detention, for purposes of interrogation, of anyone "thought to be a terrorist, or who had information regarding the activities of terrorists."

Twenty-six days after he was detained, Biko was dead from massive head injuries. The police had attempted to cover up the truth of how Biko had died by saying that he'd turned "wild" after being confronted with "evidence" that he was a "terrorist," and had repeatedly bumped his head against a wall while being restrained.

The truth was sickening. In reality Biko had been stripped naked, "in order to prevent him from hanging himself by his clothes," his legs were clamped in leg irons, and he was hauled to security police headquarters where five white policemen began interrogating him. When he refused to confess, they repeatedly bludgeoned him until he lost consciousness. Then they threw him into the back of a Land Rover and drove him more than 1000 kilometers to a prison hospital in Pretoria, where he died "a miserable and lonely death on a mat on a stone floor of a prison cell," as the lawyer for the Biko family put it.

"The truth about how Biko died would never have been known if the policemen hadn't been bluffed," David said. "The thought that one of them had squealed panicked them. Within days they all started scrambling to save their own skin by coming forward, applying for amnesty and confessing the whole truth."

"You still haven't explained how I can help," Liefling said.

"Where's Kruger?"

"He and my mom just left on their honeymoon. They'll be gone two weeks."

"Good, that gives us enough time to try and expose the policemen who may implicate your stepfather."

"You still haven't told me how I can help?"

"I want you to confront your stepfather when he gets back from his honeymoon," David said.

"Confront him about belonging to the CCB?"

David gave a solemn nod.

"Why on earth should I do that?"

"Because we must give him every opportunity to come forward and confess, "David said. "I personally don't like the idea, but in whatever we do we have to stick to the spirit and letter of the TRC's mandate at all times. Those suspected of committing human rights abuses must be given a chance to apply for amnesty."

"David is absolutely right," Thando said. "If we don't give Kruger the opportunity it'll seem like we are on some kind on vendetta against the SADF and are ignoring the national interest. Don't forget that the ANC government fully supports the TRC process. I wouldn't be here working with you guys if I hadn't been given the opportunity to confess the human rights abuses I committed as a cell leader for MK and been granted amnesty. Kruger deserves a similar chance to come clean. Whether he takes it is another matter."

David looked at Liefling and said, "I bet you he'll take it if you tell him about the *Mail & Guardian* story."

"What if he doesn't take it?" Liefling asked.

"Then play a little psychological game with him. Tell him that the TRC has received secret amnesty applications from members of a CCB death squad who intend to implicate him during in-camera testimony. Remind him of what Mamasela did to members of the Vlakplaas unit."

"What if he doesn't swallow the bait?" Liefling asked.

David gave Liefling a serious look. "Then we have no choice but to file a criminal lawsuit against him."

Liefling gasped. "A criminal lawsuit? Are you serious?"

"I'm serious. It's our only way of forcing him to testify."

Liefling shuddered. She was convinced that such a lawsuit would ruin her mother's marriage and rapture their relationship, a relationship she highly prized. She prayed that David's plan to bluff Kruger into testifying would work. But what if it didn't? What if Kruger called their bluff? Did she have the courage to file a lawsuit against her powerful stepfather?

13	**THANDO** bustled about her small but nicely furnished two-and-half bedroom flat. She was getting ready for work and preparing breakfast for herself and her daughter. It was 6:10 a.m. Thando felt exhausted from working long hours and getting little sleep since the trip to Cape Town to see

Liefling three days earlier.

Many times she'd wondered if it was worth it working practically seven days a week for the Phutadichaba Community Center and the Ubuntu Resource Center. The two non-profit organizations paid her very little and left her little time to spend with her thirteen-year-old daughter Mkondeleli. If it weren't for Sidney, her former husband, who paid generous child support, Thando didn't know how she'd manage.

Having completed only Standard Nine, several times she'd considered returning to school to get her Matric certificate. Only by finishing high school and going to college, she thought, could she improve her chances of getting a well-paying job in the new South Africa. But each time she hadn't followed through. She felt that her community work was too important to give up. She could always go back to school. But the elderly and abused women and children urgently needed help, as did the victims of human rights abuses and their families. So she tried her best to cope, comforting herself with the thought that the sacrifices she was making were her contribution toward rebuilding her shattered community and creating a better and safer environment for her daughter.

Mkondeleli was the pride of her life. She was a top student at Bovet Community School, and loved learning at a time when many kids were dropping out and getting pregnant or involved with drugs, gangs and crime.

Thando smiled as she served Mkondeleli a breakfast of scrambled eggs, whole-wheat toast and a glass of skimmed milk. Tall and ebony-skinned like her mother, Mkondeleli was too engrossed in her homework at the square kitchen table to notice the food or her mother who watched her with evident pride.

Thando marveled at the courses her daughter was now taking: Calculus, Biology, History, Literature and Physics. She remembered that when she was attending high school in the 1970s, black students were precluded from taking many of these courses under the inferior Bantu Education. Its creator, Dr. Hendrick Verwoerd, a future Prime Minister, had said in Parliament in 1954, speaking in support of the government taking over the running of black schools, which had previously been operated as mission schools:

> *When I have control of native education, I will reform it so that the natives will be taught from childhood that equality with Europeans is not for them. There is no place for natives in European society above certain forms of labor.*

Thando recalled the small part she'd played in destroying this education for servitude. Now her daughter and millions of other black children had the incentive to work hard at school, knowing that meaningful jobs awaited them in an apartheid-free South Africa, where there were no longer Job Reservation laws to deny them employment opportunities because of the color of their skin.

Thando sat on a chair across the table from her Mkondeleli. As she ate her oatmeal sprinkled with brown sugar, she recalled her own girlhood dream of wanting to be a nurse, like her mother, not the guerilla fighter that she subsequently became. Like most black students back in the early 1970s, she had been apolitical, even though her grandfather had been an ANC activist and had helped organize the Alexandra bus boycotts of the 1940s.

But when, on June 16, 1976, police opened fire on 10,000 unarmed black students in Soweto who were demonstrating against Bantu Education and its latest decree that henceforth black children be taught in Afrikaans, Thando had had something akin to an epiphany. She'd become aware of the connection between knowledge, power and oppression. She'd realized that the enforcers of apartheid weren't content with denying blacks their political rights. They also wanted to enslave their minds. Enraged, the next day, June 17, she's urged her fellow students to boycott classes and take to the streets in solidarity with their Soweto brethren.

The decision had changed her destiny. Hunted down by the police as a "terrorist," she'd fled the country through Botswana, ending up in an ANC refugee camp in Zambia. In 1983 she was on the verge of joining a group of bright exiled students the ANC was sending to schools across Europe, America and the Soviet Union when she heard that her parents had been killed when death squads firebombed their house.

Thirsting for revenge, she'd begged to be allowed to join MK, eager to infiltrate back into South Africa to help destroy the apartheid system. After distinguishing herself during boot camp, she had been among those sent to the Soviet Union for more sophisticated training in urban guerilla warfare. It was while there that she met and fell in love with Sidney. A year and half later she was pregnant with Mkondeleli, and two years later she found out she had ovarian cancer. She had radical surgery at a hospital in Harare that eradicated the cancer but left her unable to have any more children.

Mkondeleli put away her books in a brown schoolbag with her name on it, which meant "Endurance" in Venda. As she began eating her breakfast she said, "Why don't you and Dad get back together, Mom? It would make life so much easier for you."

"Some things can't be undone, Mkondeleli," Thando said, slowly stirring condensed milk into her steaming black tea.

"But each time I visit him he says he still loves you. Don't you love him?"

Tears welled in Thando's eyes. She stopped stirring her tea and bit her lower lip. "I still love him. I've never stopped loving him."

"Then why don't you get back together?"

"There are things that happened between us that make it impossible."

Curious, Mkondeleli stopped eating and asked, "What happened?"

Thando glanced at the kitchen clock. It was almost 7:30. "If you don't hurry and finish your breakfast you'll be late for morning class. And Professor Gideon won't be too pleased if his favorite student arrives late."

"Okay." Mkondeleli resumed eating. "But I hope you'll tell me someday. Whenever I ask Dad, he says I should ask you."

"I'll tell you someday, dear child. I promise I will."

Suddenly there was a sharp knock at the door, and then the voice of a woman sobbing. Thando knew that once more her daughter would be late for school because another woman had been abused and was seeking help.

LIEFLING watched her mother as she sat next to Kruger, aglow with happiness after her two-week honeymoon.

I don't know if I have the strength to go through with it, she thought.

The three were having a sumptuous breakfast in the chateau's elegant breakfast room overlooking acres of woods, gardens and vineyards. It was almost nine. The sky, covered with wooly nimbus clouds, augured yet another rainy day, maybe a thunderstorm. A light drizzle was already falling.

The breakfast room, heated by logs sizzling in the marble fireplace, was pleasantly warm. Its large breakfast table, covered with an embroidered lace tablecloth, was decked with platters of fresh fruit, poached eggs, ham, scones, fresh fish, vegetables, freshly baked bread, kettles of steaming rooibos tea and coffee, trays of butter and tins of jams and marmalade.

Liefling had little appetite. Throughout the meal, she kept thinking about how to confront Kruger regarding allegations that he used to be a high-ranking CCB member. Several times – at dinner the night before and when she and Kruger finished playing tennis at the chateau's indoor clay court – she'd attempted to bring the matter up, but each time her courage had failed her when she thought of her mother.

How can I spoil her complete happiness? Liefling thought, watching her mother laugh and gently stroke her new husband's arm. *Especially when we have no proof that Magnus has done anything wrong except belong to the CCB?*

Freda, wearing a blue silk robe and her freshly washed hair still damp, leaned over and kissed a slightly sunburned Kruger on the left cheek, all the time smiling at him.

I haven't seen Mom this happy since I was five, Liefling thought to herself. It was December 1975 and she, her father and Freda were backpacking in Australia. Upon returning to the inn where they were staying, her father had received a call from a high-ranking member of the Broederbond. The caller had informed him that, because of his blue blood Afrikaner pedigree and vigorous defense of apartheid over the years, he'd just been promoted to head the *Moederkerk* in Stellenbosch, which administered to the spiritual needs of the elite of Afrikanerdom. Being named pastor of the mother church was considered a stepping stone to higher things.

Liefling remembered how overjoyed her mother had been. The promotion meant that her husband was now poised to play a prominent role in guiding the destiny of the Afrikaner people. With his oratorical skills, brilliant mind and pedigree, she thought, he might someday be Prime Minister. After all, several former professors and dominees had gone on to become Prime Minister.

But that was not to be. Six months after her father's promotion, Soweto exploded. Black students rebelled against being taught in Afrikaans. The government responded with a brutal and bloody crackdown. The Sunday after June 16, 1976 Christiaan had stunned the world by denouncing the crackdown and repudiating apartheid in front of his shocked parishioners, who included several senior members of the Broederbond. Christiaan was instantly fired from his new post and stripped of his membership in the Broederbond. He, Freda and Liefling were ostracized from the Afrikaner community and shunned even by their own families. They moved to Johannesburg to try to rebuild their shattered lives.

Liefling recalled the hell her mother had endured following their ostracism from the only community she'd ever known. She became chronically depressed, abused prescription drugs and alcohol and once even contemplated suicide. Only thoughts of her daughter left alone to fend for herself in a hostile world had prevented Freda from taking her own life.

She sacrificed so much for me, Liefling thought as she poured herself a cup of herbal tea. *Without her I wouldn't be what I am today. I owe her a great deal. She deserves to be happy. And Magnus has made her happy.*

Liefling wondered if confronting Kruger with the allegations of being a CCB member would ruin that happiness, and possibly so infuriate him that he'd dump her mother and she'd kill herself.

Liefling couldn't bear the thought. But immediately she thought of all those grieving families who'd lost loved ones to CCB death squads. She thought of the promise she'd made to them, after hearing their wrenching stories, that she'd leave no stone unturned in finding out the truth about what had happened to their loved ones, and in finding their remains so they could be buried properly. She thought of her father's courage in risking everything to do what was right.

I can do no less, Liefling thought as she sipped her tea. *I must confront him.*

She was about to when Kruger looked at her and said, "So, how's work at the Ubuntu Resource Center, my dear?"

"What?" Liefling said distractedly, caught off-guard.

"I asked how's work at the Ubuntu Resource Center?" Kruger repeated, reaching for a cup. "Your mom tells me you've been spending a lot of time in Jo'burg lately."

"Fine. Just fine."

"Is it rewarding?" Kruger said, eyeing Liefling carefully.

"What?"

"What's on your mind, dear?" Freda asked, concerned. "Ever since you arrived yesterday you've been quite absentminded."

"I noticed the same thing too, dear," Kruger said, pouring tea into his cup.

"I just have a lot on my mind related to work," Liefling said evasively.

"My question is about your work," Kruger said. "Do you find it rewarding?"

"Oh, yes, it's very rewarding," Liefling said.

"I'm glad," Kruger said, sipping his tea and studying her face over the rim of his cup. "I'd hate to see you waste your talents, my dear. Not many women who graduated at the top of their class from one of the best law schools in the country end up working for next to nothing."

"I told her so," Freda said, reaching for a piece of pink grapefruit. "Especially after what I went through to keep her in school following Christiaan's death. Working at three jobs, taking out loans, denying myself everything."

"I appreciate what you've done for me, Mom," Liefling said. "But we all have to sacrifice to help heal our new nation."

"I totally agree," Kruger said. "That's why I'm selling my firm. I'm planning to use the proceeds to help the Afrikaner people. So many of them have lost their jobs, farms and homes since apartheid ended. They're angry and bitter. If they aren't taken care of, the ANC might have a revolution on its hands."

"How much is your firm worth?" Liefling asked, already thinking about how much to sue him for, should it become necessary.

"Oh, about three hundred million rands."

That would more than take care of the education of the children of victims of CCB death squads and build their families decent homes, Liefling thought.

"Magnus is being modest, as always," Freda said. "A group of South American investors want to buy the firm for three billion rands."

Liefling choked on her tea, then hastily wiped her mouth, struggling to hide her shock.

"The deal is not yet finalized, my dear," Kruger cautioned, as he began eating an omelet stuffed with spinach ad melted Gouda cheese.

"There's something you can do for the good of all South Africans, not just Afrikaners," Liefling said.

Kruger abruptly looked up from his plate. "What, my dear?"

Liefling threw a quick glance at mother, who was also looking at her, puzzled. *Should I say it?* she thought feverishly.

Anxious to get it over with, she decided to be blunt. "You can tell the TRC all you know about the CCB. The information will go a long way toward helping restore a sense of dignity to the grieving families who lost loved ones to CCB-sponsored death squads. Many of them are my clients. They want to find out where the bodies of their loved ones are buried so they can exhume them for proper burial according to tribal customs. But so far the code of silence among CCB members has prevented the truth from coming out on this important issue. As a former high-ranking member of the organization, will you please help?"

Liefling thought she detected a stunned look on Kruger's face, but it was so fleeting she wasn't sure. But the shock on her mother's ashen face was unmistakable.

"Are you accusing Magnus of being involved with death squads?" Freda demanded indignantly, putting her silver fork down on the plate of fine bone china.

"I'm not accusing him, Mom. I'm merely pleading with him to testify before the TRC about what he knows regarding the CCB. According to media reports, the organization sponsored death squads."

Freda stared at Kruger. "Is that true, dear? Do you know anything about the CCB? Were you ever a member?"

Kruger didn't immediately reply. He deliberately wiped his mouth with his napkin, while his steely gray eyes focused like a pair of lasers on Liefling. A sardonic smile playing on his thin lips, he said, with a calmness in his voice that surprised even Liefling, "Who told you I was a CCB member, my dear?"

"The *Mail & Guardian* plans to run a story detailing your involvement with the paramilitary organization," Liefling said.

Freda was aghast. "When?"

"In tomorrow's paper."

"Oh, my God," Freda said. "Is it true, Magnus? Were you ever a member of the CCB?"

Kruger again ignored his panic-stricken wife. Realizing the predicament he was in, and not wanting to sound panicked too, he was eager to find out how much Liefling knew. He recalled the following maxim from Sun Tzu: *Lure your enemy with baits into revealing his stratagem.*

"I *was* a member, " Kruger said.

14

FREDA stammered in astonishment. "You were a member of the CCB?"

"Ja," Kruger said. "But it was totally innocent."

"The CCB was far from innocent," Liefling interjected angrily. "It sponsored death squads that killed hundreds of anti-apartheid activists and MK guerrillas, both inside the country and abroad. And many of the bodies of the dead still haven't been found."

"You misunderstand me, Liefling," Kruger said calmly but firmly. "I meant my involvement with the CCB was totally innocent. As a lawyer you should know the difference between those two simple statements."

"There's no difference to me," Liefling said icily.

Kruger smiled faintly. "Do you know anything about the CCB besides the lies and distortions put out by the biased, leftist and anti-SADF media?"

Liefling had no immediate reply.

"Then I'll tell you," Kruger said. First he slowly poured himself another cup of the medicinal rooibos herb tea, of which he drank several cups each morning as a palliative for his sinus problem.

"It's important for you to listen to what I'm going to say with an open mind," Kruger began. "Remember that during the 1980s we were in a state of war. The country was teetering on the brink of anarchy and disintegration. The ANC, through its armed wing, *Umkhonto We Sizwe* (Spear of the Nation), and the Pan African Congress, through its armed wing, *Poqo* (Standing Alone), were determined to end apartheid through violent revolution. The National Party wanted apartheid abolished, but gradually and peacefully. To be able to do so, it relied on the SADF and the police force to maintain law and order while it carried out fundamental reforms. The last thing the government wanted was a civil war. It would have had horrendous consequences for both blacks and whites."

"But what about the – "

"Let me finish," Kruger cut her short, clearly annoyed at being interrupted.

Freda nervously studied her fingernails. She hated the tension that was building between her daughter and her new husband.

"In pursuit of its revolutionary Marxist-Leninist goals, the ANC did things it now regrets," Kruger said. "In seeking to stop the ANC, the government also did things it now regrets. It is in that context that you should judge the activities of the CCB."

"But the ANC never sponsored death squads, Magnus," Freda said, surprising Liefling, who'd expected her to take Kruger's side or to at least remain silent.

She is still verligte, Liefling thought with inward relief.

"That's not entirely true, my dear. The term 'death squad' is being used selectively by leftist papers such as the *Mail & Guardian*. It's never used when referring to ANC operatives who tortured, murdered and executed innocent people. The papers call them freedom fighters. I grant you that some rogue elements within the CCB committed human rights abuses. There's already been evidence of that from testimony by members of the Vlakplaas unit. But there's overwhelming evidence showing that ANC and PAC operatives committed more human rights abuses than all the CCB's rogue units combined. That's why of the 7060 applications received by the TRC for amnesty, over two thirds are from ANC and PAC operatives."

Liefling had heard enough. Outraged, she flung back her chair and abruptly stood up. Almost yelling, she said, "How dare you suggest that the ANC and the PAC --"

"Please sit down, my dear, and permit me to finish," Kruger said with a calmness he was far from truly feeling. "You'll have your say. I know you're an ardent ANC supporter. I also know that your father, whom you dearly loved, was a hero and a martyr to the movement. I personally have nothing against the ANC. If I did, do you think I'd have married your mother, who was once a member?"

"Please sit down, Liefling," Freda said softly, "and let Magnus finish."

Still furious, Liefling hesitated, then complied.

"I was present at the State Security Council meeting in May, 1986, when the decision was taken to create the CCB," Kruger said. "I saw the evidence of ANC atrocities and plans to commit more. Those plans were part of a 'People's War' waged by the ANC following a visit by its high-ranking leaders to Vietnam in 1978. There they consulted with the Vietnamese on how they'd fought the Americans and driven them out of Indochina. This 'People's War' consisted of what the ANC officially called 'The Four Pillars of the Revolution.'"

Kruger paused and sipped his rooibos, which was now cool. He glanced at Freda, who was riveted. He smiled inwardly, aware that he was winning her sympathy, which he knew he needed on his side in the looming battle against Liefling.

Cultivate allies when fighting against a formidable enemy, said Sun Tzu.

Kruger continued. "These pillars were: one, the all-round activity of the underground structures of the ANC; two, the united mass action of the people; three, the armed offensive; and four, the international drive to isolate South Africa. The CCB, and other groups such as Military Intelligence and the National Intelligence Agency, were formed specifically to counter the first three pillars, particularly in light of how devastating their effects were."

"Devastating in what way?" Liefling demanded.

"I'll give you an example, my dear," Kruger said. "At the time the CCB came into being, there had been a marked increase in ANC attacks on so-called soft targets, that is, civilians. Bombs were being exploded in shopping malls, parks, churches, playgrounds, buses and train stations. Farmers in rural areas were being butchered. Limpet mines were maiming and killing dozens in the countryside. There was also a marked increase in the number of MK cells in the townships, whose goal was to render them ungovernable. To achieve this, a new and more gruesome method of dealing with so-called collaborators and impimpis was introduced by the ANC."

"Are you referring to necklacing?" Freda asked with a shudder.

"Yes, my dear," Kruger said. "The same method used in murdering your first husband. And why did militant blacks wrap a gasoline-soaked tire around Christiaan's neck and then ignite it? Because he was white. And the ANC and the PAC, in an effort to ignite a race war, had promulgated the inflammatory slogan, 'One Settler, one Bullet.'"

"I don't believe black militants murdered my father," Liefling said.

"You don't?" Freda said, surprised. "But those two ANC militants confessed to the murder before they were hanged."

"Who do you think killed Christiaan, my dear?" Kruger asked, looking at

Liefling.

"Death squads."

"That's preposterous," Freda said. "ANC militants did."

Kruger looked at Freda. "I understand why Liefling is in denial, my dear. She hates the SADF. That's why she'd on this witch-hunt for death squads that never existed. And let's not forget that most of her clients are the families of ANC and PAC militants. But the evidence is incontrovertible, my dear. Members of the ANC and the PAC did commit gross human rights abuses. And they didn't care which whites they targeted. That's why they even murdered *verligtes* like your husband Christiaan and that American Fullbright Scholar who was stabbed to death in Guguletu. What was her name, by the way?"

"Amy," Freda said. "Amy Biehl."

Liefling said nothing. Kruger's cunning twisting of the facts to bolster his arguments left her speechless. And her mother, Liefling sensed with dismay, was starting to believe Kruger.

"I know how you feel about the ANC, Liefling," Freda said, looking at her with sympathetic eyes. "But the group, which I once supported, is guilty of horrible crimes. No two ways about it. The ANC and the PAC have admitted before the TRC to bombing churches, to torturing innocent people and to murdering and executing those suspected of being police spies."

"And evidence shows that necklacing was the preferred method of committing murder by ANC and PAC operatives in the townships," Kruger said. "Between 1984 and 1989, 399 black people died as a result of necklacing. An additional 372 were burned to death in their homes or after petrol was poured over them and they were torched."

"The ANC categorically condemned necklacings," Liefling said.

"Belatedly, my dear. After it realized that it was losing the public relations war. Yet even after the ANC condemned necklacing, its structures within the townships continued to use the gruesome method. Why? Because it was highly effective in the ANC's campaign of terror and intimidation. That's why high-ranking ANC leaders published those outrageous statements about necklacing in *Sechaba* (The Nation). They defended necklacing – or at least tried to. They wanted the deaths of so-called collaborators to be so grotesque and horrifying that no one would even think of helping the police maintain law and order."

Freda's small frame again shuddered. The necklacing of Christiaan had precipitated her disillusionment with the anti-apartheid movement. That disillusionment had deepened after the ANC came to power and crime and violence escalated and scandals and charges of corruption, incompetence and nepotism dogged its fledgling government.

Liefling noticed the shudder and frowned slightly. She wanted to say something in defense of the ANC but didn't want to interrupt Kruger. She feared alienating her mother by appearing rude. She felt it was important to have her mother on her side, especially if it became necessary for her to file a criminal lawsuit against Kruger in order to compel him to testify before the TRC.

"Now I'll come to the CCB and my role in it," Kruger said, leaning back in his chair, confident that he was winning the argument. "The CCB was made up of civilian and demilitarized personnel who were appointed under contract. I was asked to come on board strictly as an advisor because of my extensive knowledge of security matters. Yes, I attended several SSC meetings. But my presence at those meetings was to act as a liaison between the military and civilian commandos, who, as you know, had formed self-defense units in the rural areas. Those units protected innocent white farmers and their families from increasing attacked by ANC and PAC guerrillas infiltrating into South Africa, mainly through Zimbabwe and Mozambique. That's why I traveled to Venda from time to time."

"Are you saying you won't testify about CCB death squads?" Liefling asked impatiently.

"You keep on harping on the issue of CCB death squads, my dear," Kruger said with a faint smile. "I know nothing about any death squads. Is it fair to expect me to testify about something I know nothing about?"

Kruger felt confident saying this because he knew full well that most CCB files, especially those about death squads, had either been destroyed during the final days of apartheid or were in his possession.

"Liefling," Freda interjected impatiently. "Magnus has told you he knows nothing about CCB death squads. Why won't you believe him?"

"What if the *Mail & Guardian* article proves he's lying?"

"What if it's the *Mail & Guardian* that is lying?" Kruger said. "The paper has lied before on other so-called sensational exposes about the SADF. And it has had to retract its libelous stories and apologize."

Liefling decided to play her trump card. "I'm not relying only on the *Mail & Guardian* story," she said.

Freda stared at her. "What other evidence is there?"

"I've heard that several former policemen belonging to a CCB death squad that was based in Venda are planning to give in-camera testimony implicating their leaders. If Magnus is implicated, he'll be forced to testify."

If Liefling had been watching Kruger when she said this, she'd have noticed his eyes flicker with concern when she mentioned a CCB death squad based in Venda. As it was, she was watching her mother.

"Who will force him to testify?" asked Freda.

"I will," Liefling said. "If he refuses to testify, he leaves me no choice but to file a criminal lawsuit against him."

"You wouldn't dare!" Freda screamed.

"If Magnus forces me to, I will," Liefling said with quiet determination. "I made a promise to the families of victims of CCB death squads that I'd do whatever I could to find out who killed their loved ones. If that person or persons refuse to testify before the TRC, I promised I'd sue them. That's why I'm begging Magnus to testify. If he does, he'll be granted amnesty if he's committed any human rights abuses. And my clients are prepared to forgive him."

"Are you accusing Magnus of being a torturer and murderer?" Freda said, aghast. "Are you?"

"No," Liefling said calmly. "I'm not accusing him of anything – not yet. I'm simply asking him to help grieving families by revealing what he knows about an organization whose death squads were responsible for the torture and murder of their loved ones. He was a high-ranking member of that organization. My clients want the truth. Only the truth can lead them to the bodies of their loved ones. Is that too much to ask?"

"Go ahead and sue me, my dear," Kruger said. "I won't give in to your blackmail. Not in a million years. But if I were you, I'd remember one thing before filing any lawsuit. Lawsuits are heard in criminal court, not before the TRC, which everyone knows is biased against Afrikaners and former SADF members like myself. In criminal court you have to produce witnesses. And I can't wait for my lawyers to cross-examine your witnesses, my dear. That is, if you have any."

Kruger paused and sipped the last of his tea. "But I'm convinced you don't have any witnesses," he went on. "Because there was nothing to witness. You're bluffing. You think you can scare me into testifying. But I'm one Afrikaner who doesn't scare easily, my dear."

The tension inside the room was so thick it made Liefling feel suddenly hot. She could feel the scorn in Kruger's voice as he said, "And one thing more, my dear. I pity you. I pity you because you've forgotten your roots. You are no longer an Afrikaner. I don't know what you are. I don't even think you yourself know what you are. But I assure you, one of these days you'll find out that there's nothing more suicidal than belonging nowhere."

With that cryptic warning, Kruger abruptly got up from his chair and left the table. Dumbfounded, Freda watched him go up the spiral staircase to their bedroom on the second floor.

Freda glared at Liefling. "Do you see what you've done? Do you see what you've done? You've made him mad. If I'd known you were going to be so rude I wouldn't have invited you to come over and spend the night."

"I'm sorry, Mom. But I just had to confront him."

"Confront him about what – about lies?"

"They're not lies, Mom. Magnus admitted that he was a high-ranking member of the CCB. You heard him."

"So what? A lot of people were high-ranking members of the CCB. That doesn't make them guilty of torture and murder."

Feeling totally frustrated by her inability to get through to her mother, Liefling finally blurted out, "Why are you so naïve and blind about this man? Just because he's charming and pampers you like a queen doesn't excuse what he may have done."

"I think you should leave now," Freda said tersely. She got up and followed Kruger to the bedroom. She found him just getting off the phone. He was still wearing his burgundy camel jacket and soft leather slippers.

"Is Liefling still in my house?" he asked as soon as Freda walked in. "If she is I want her to leave immediately."

"I've already told her to leave."

"I just spoke to my lawyer," Kruger said, walking toward the closet. "He's as shocked as I am about your daughter's outrageous accusations. He's meeting me at my office at noon."

Kruger didn't say anything more. He simply stepped into the huge walk-in closet to pick out the navy-blue business suit he intended to wear that day. Freda, noticing that he was still upset, felt it best not to say anything. She went into the bathroom to remove her curlers, crying as she did so.

LIEFLING rose and went to the guestroom she was occupying on the third floor, shortly after her mother left the breakfast room. There were tears in

Liefling's eyes as she packed her overnight bag. Within minutes she was dressed in her usual jeans, T-shirt and sneakers. She didn't even say goodbye to her mother. She got into her old white Honda Accord and drove off.

Kruger watched her leave through the mullioned bedroom window. He waited about ten minutes, and then got into his limo and left for Cape Town. As soon as he was gone Freda, distraught and wanting to talk to someone she trusted about what had happened, called Tina. Tina wasn't home. Then Freda recalled that Tina had told her she might be accompanying Paul to Durban, where the renegade Afrikaner professor was giving a talk at the university on another of his favorite subjects: the controversial issue of paying reparations to victims of apartheid.

Freda, tears in her eyes, slowly dressed. But she didn't feel like attending her book-club luncheon. All she could think about was what the disaster at the breakfast table portended. Just when she had finally found happiness. Just when she felt her daughter and Kruger were getting along. This had to happen. She wondered if Liefling would indeed carry out her threat to file a criminal lawsuit against Kruger.

If she does, Freda thought with bitterness, *my marriage is ruined. I must find a way to stop her.*

15

GIDEON MUNYAI stood next to the blackboard, a piece of white chalk in his left hand. About fifty pupils in neat navy and white school uniforms sat attentively in front of him. They were crammed three to a desk because there were not enough desks at Bovet Community School, a school attended mostly by children of Venda and Shangaan families.

Despite a lack of desks, computers and textbooks, Bovet had some of the most dedicated students in the township. That was the main reason why Gideon, one of the best teachers in the country, had rejected lucrative offers to teach at better-funded private schools in order to remain at Bovet. To prove his faith in the school, he'd enrolled his own two children there, even though he and his wife, a staff nurse at the Alexandra Clinic, could afford to send them to one of the many multiracial private schools in Johannesburg's rich northern suburbs.

Gideon was by far the toughest teacher at Bovet and, surprisingly, the most popular. He taught History, a popular course with a generation of students raised on TV and Nintendo, and with little knowledge of what blacks had experienced during 300 years of oppressive white rule. The history course taught by Gideon was far from the sanitized Bantu Education history black teachers had been required to teach when Gideon was still attending school. It was rather a history he knew his students needed to understand if they were to overcome the legacy of Baaskap and develop pride in themselves as Africans. Decades of apartheid had told them that blacks were inferior, and that Africa had been a Dark Continent overrun by savages and heathens before the white man arrived from Europe with the torch of Civilization and Christianity.

This morning Gideon was focusing on the history of the liberation struggle, tracing it all the way back to the 19th century, when the different African tribes had resisted inroads by whites into their sovereign territories. He'd assigned his students, who were in Sixth grade, a section in the history textbook to read overnight, and he was now asking questions to test their comprehension of the material. He'd just asked a tough question when there was a soft knock at the door.

"Come in," he said in a booming voice, a bit annoyed by the interruption.

The door slowly opened and in walked Mkondeleli. She was clutching her brown schoolbag full of books and looked quite embarrassed at being late.

Gideon glanced at his wristwatch. "Why are you late, Mkondeleli?" he said sternly. "You've never been late for morning class before."

"Just before we were about to leave, a woman who'd been badly beaten by her husband came to our house seeking my mother's help. So my mother couldn't drive me to school as usual. I had to walk all the way here."

Gideon knew Thando very well, and he greatly admired the work she was doing for abused women and children, while at the same time being a single parent. He also knew that given the high incidents of rape in the ghetto, it was dangerous for young girls to walk alone to school.

"You can sit down," he said.

"Thank you, sir." Mkondeleli squeezed into one of the front desks, which she shared with two other girls. She took out her history textbook just as Gideon turned to the rest of the class and asked, "Now where were we?"

A tall boy in a green blazer with orange stripes who was sitting in the back row raised his right hand.

"Yes, Robert?"

"You'd asked why the Venda people were the last tribe to be conquered, and if there are any similarities between black resistance against colonialism in the 19th century and black resistance against apartheid in the 20th century."

"Yes. Can anyone give me the answer?"

Mkondeleli's right hand shot up.

Gideon smiled. Mkondeleli was always eager to answer tough questions. That's why she was his favorite student. Unlike a lot of female students, she didn't hide the fact that she was smart. And she wasn't shy about asking questions when she didn't understand something. As a result she excelled in just about every subject, including Math.

Gideon had recommended her for a government bursary after she'd expressed interest in becoming an engineer. Gideon remembered that when he was a student there were hardly any black engineers in South Africa. The profession was restricted to whites under the Job Reservation Act which reserved all skilled jobs for whites.

"Tell us the answer, Mkondeleli," Gideon said.

Mkondeleli, who like Gideon was near-sighted and wore glasses, stood up and faced the class. She was a confident public speaker like her mother.

"There are three reasons why the Venda people were the last to be conquered. First, the Soutpansberg region where they lived was mountainous and thick-forested. It provided excellent fortifications for their villages. Second, the malaria-carrying tsetse flies made the lowveld area unattractive to white settlers and their livestock."

"Good. And what is the third reason?"

"The valor of Venda warriors such as Makhado, the Lion of the North, struck terror into neighboring tribes, colonialists and Boers alike. Under his leadership, the Venda people won many memorable battles, and it was not until 1898 that a Boer army of 4,000 finally defeated them. But even in defeat, Makhado was respected by the Boers."

"Why?"

"Because he was a worthy foe, a true warrior like Shaka."

Gideon beamed with satisfaction. Yes, Mkondeleli would go far. He could see a lot of her mother in her – the directness, the self-confidence, the encyclopedic knowledge of African history.

"Sir, can I also answer the second part of the question?" Mkondeleli asked.

"Certainly."

"There *are* similarities between black resistance against colonialism and black resistance against apartheid. Freedom fighters against apartheid had to have the spirit of warriors like Makhado and Shaka."

"Please explain what you mean," Gideon asked, folding his arms across his broad chest to listen.

"My mother often tells me that the reason apartheid lasted so long is that the security force that defended the system relied on a sophisticated network of collaborators, *askaris* and *impimpis* in their ruthless war against the liberation movement. Anyone who joined or supported banned groups like the ANC or the PAC was instantly imprisoned or killed. As a result, a lot of people remained apolitical, especially after the Sharpeville Massacre, during which the police killed 67 Africans, many of them shot in the back as they fled for safety. Then came the Soweto Uprising of 1976 and everything changed. Spurred by the bravery of their children, black men and women joined the liberation struggle by the droves because they feared dishonor more than they feared jail or death."

Gideon raised his eyebrows. "What do you mean by 'dishonor'?"

"Dishonor means not doing the right thing because you're afraid to go to jail or to die. My mother tells me that she never set out to be a freedom fighter. She wanted to be a nurse. But when she heard that the police were shooting innocent students who simply wanted a better education system, she joined the struggle. She became convinced that apartheid would never end until black people stopped being cowards ruled by the fear of death."

"Well done," Gideon said. "You may sit down now."

Gideon proceeded with the lesson. But Mkondeleli's words kept echoing in his mind. They reminded him of a pivotal moment in his life, when the fear of death had made him commit a cowardly deed which had haunted him ever since and made his soul die a thousand deaths. He wondered if he'd ever have the courage to confess the cowardly deed. More important, he wondered if he'd ever have the opportunity to atone for it, and thus redeem his soul.

LIEFLING'S cell phone rang shortly after she left Kruger's mansion. She hoped, for a fleeting moment, that it would be her mother calling to inform her that Kruger had changed his mind and would testify before the TRC. Then she dismissed the thought as impossible.

"Hullo darling," said a familiar mellifluous voice.

Her face instantly brightened. "Sipho! Are you in town?"

"No. I'm still at Bara. It's been quite hectic. I've been operating since last night. I'm afraid the earliest I can come down is tomorrow morning. Do you mind picking me up from the airport? I need to be at the Clinic for a couple operations. My car is in the shop."

"Okay."

"Thanks. By the way, how did your visit with your mother go?"

"It was a disaster."

"What happened?"

"It's a long story. I'll tell you all about it tomorrow."

Liefling hung up. After the confrontation with Kruger, she looked forward to spending time with someone who loved and understood her, someone who never failed to reassure her that what she was doing was worthwhile, despite the long hours, the death threats, the self-doubt, and the sacrifices. She knew that she needed Sipho more now following the fallout with her mother.

Please God, she murmured as she turned on the radio to a classical music station, *don't make me have to choose between my mother and doing the right thing.*

KRUGER was deeply troubled throughout the forty-minute drive to Cape Town. The confrontation with Liefling had left him shaken, despite the self-control he'd shown at the breakfast table. The possibility that Liefling might actually expose him made him feel desperate.

Desperate times call for desperate measures, he thought, recalling a saying from Sun Tzu.

For the first time it occurred to Kruger that he might have to kill his stepdaughter. The thought didn't surprise him. He'd killed before, many times, in order to insure survival of the *Volk.* But Kruger knew that killing the daughter of the woman he adored would require careful planning and faultless execution – precisely the skills he'd honed from following Sun Tzu's advice during his years with the Security Branch and as leader of the Thathe Vondo death squad. He hoped he wouldn't have to do it. But he knew he'd do it if he had to. It all depended on whether or not Liefling actually took steps to file a criminal lawsuit against him.

I'll soon find out, Kruger thought as the limo approached downtown Cape Town. He couldn't wait to talk to his lawyer, Willem Prinsloo, a notorious judge during the apartheid era, who had sentenced many an ANC and PAC guerilla to death by hanging. Prinsloo was one of two members of the *Uitvoerende Raad* whose advice Kruger implicitly trusted, mainly because, Prinsloo had helped shape his destiny. In 1968 Kruger had been a demanding boot camp instructor in counterinsurgency tactics at *Voortrekkerhoogte* (Voortrekker Heights) military base near Pretoria, where young white men were trained before they were sent to fight 'On the Border.' His methods – derived from his diligent study of Sun Tzu's *The Art of War* – of teaching squeamish soldiers how to kill without remorse had caught the attention of his superior, who was a member of the Broederbond.

The superior had recommended him for admission to the secret society, surmising that it needed ruthless, fearless and decisive men like Kruger to uphold *Baaskap* by keeping *Die Swart Gevaar* at bay.

To be admitted into the exalted ranks of the Broederbond, Kruger had to meet its exacting standards. Those standards required that each member strive for the eternal existence of a separate Afrikaner nation with its own language and culture; give preference to Afrikaners in economic, public and professional life; uphold the Afrikaans language in his home, in his job and in the community at large; be a Protestant; and, lastly, have nothing in his person, character or behavior that would preclude him from brotherhood.

Kruger had failed to meet the last standard. His application would have been summarily rejected if Prinsloo had not intervened. He'd argued successfully that there were mitigating circumstances in Kruger's failure to meet the standard, and had urged his colleagues on the bond's Executive Council to admit Kruger.

"I assure you, my fellow Broeders," Prinsloo had said passionately and, as it turned out, prophetically. "This man is a *regte*, true, Afrikaner. The sins of his father should not be held against him. He's a *Bittereinder* if I ever knew one. He'll fight until his last breath to protect the interests of the Volk."

Kruger reached downtown Cape Town just as lunch hour began. The streets, restaurants and cafés thronged with tourists, politicians and workers. Kruger's limo turned left into Adderly Street, which led to the entrance to the parliament building. As the limo drove past the *Groote Kerk*, Kruger turned his eyes away from the building. He had the strange habit of never looking at the first Dutch Reformed Church in South Africa, where his father had been dominee. It reminded him of a past he wanted to forget, and the shame and humiliation he had felt when he had learned of his father's scandalous deed.

But he could never forget. Nor could he forget the man whose inflexibility had led him to cast the deciding vote when the Broederbond had sat in judgment of his father following the scandalous deed. The Broederbond's decision was final and without appeal. It had stripped his father of his position and had forced him and his family to flee Cape Town, just when Kruger was looking forward to marrying Freda, the love of his life.

But Kruger didn't blame the man. He'd done what he had to do as a *regte* Afrikaner. His inflexibility had been an indispensable part of ensuring the survival of the *Volk*. Kruger recalled that he too had adopted a similar inflexibility. And, over the years, it had led him to punish swiftly, ruthlessly and without remorse all those who'd threatened the survival of the *Volk*.

After passing the church, Kruger's limo turned right onto Wale Street. He frowned at the sight of the diminutive and gray-haired Bishop Desmond Tutu, dressed in his trademark purple robes and gold pendant, shaking hands with visitors on the steps of St. George's Cathedral. Tutu, who was chairman of the TRC, had recently made an impassioned last-minute plea to former members of the security forces in the Civil Cooperation Bureau, the State Security Council and Military Intelligence, to come forward and apply for amnesty before the May 10th deadline, only four days away.

I'd rather die than bow down before you, Kruger thought with a sneer. The limo turned right into Queen Victoria Street and cruised past the planetarium and the Natural History Museum. As it took the curve into Grey's pass, Kruger's car phone rang.

"Kruger speaking."

"Hi, darling," Freda said. "It's me."

Trying his best to sound gentle, Kruger said, "I thought you were at the book-club luncheon, honey."

"I didn't go."

"Why not?"

"I'm still very upset about Liefling's threat to file a criminal lawsuit against you."

"Don't worry. Prinsloo will take care of everything."

Freda didn't like the fact that Prinsloo was getting involved. She wanted time to talk to Liefling, convinced that she could get her to change her mind and desist from filing the lawsuit. But she was afraid of upsetting her new husband by raising the issue. All she said to him was, "Do you still want me to go ahead with preparations for the *braai* on Sunday, despite what happened this morning?"

"Of course, my dear."

16

GIDEON often went home for lunch to save money. His wife Nomhle usually left him an extra plate of whatever they had had for dinner the day before. Gideon would then heat the food in the microwave, then have it with his favorite soft drink, Fanta.

Today, however, he had no appetite. He sat at the table staring at the plate of curried chicken, porridge and vegetables in front of him. His agitated mind was on the front-page story of the *Mail & Guardian*, about Kruger's membership in the CCB and possible involvement with death squads.

Gideon couldn't believe that the opportunity he'd long prayed for to redeem his soul had finally come. And yet, for some reason, he was afraid to seize it. As if to screw up courage, he recalled what Mkondeleli had said in History class about honor. He again read the front-page story in the *Mail & Guardian*. The story was accurate, all right, but it lacked incriminating details linking Kruger directly to death squads.

He thought for a long while. Suddenly he sprang to his feet, dashed across the carpeted hallway to the living room, picked up the phone and dialed a number. He waited, heart pounding.

MAKHADO was busy fixing a broken fan inside the main office of the private game reserve when the phone rang. He glanced at the clock on the wall. It was almost noon. Viljoen normally didn't call until around five in the afternoon, when Makhado was about to leave. And the delivery trucks weren't due until tomorrow. Wondering who it could be, Makhado picked up the phone.

"The Thathe Vondo private game reserve," he said in a suitably deferential voice, assuming it was a white person.

Gideon let out a great sigh of relief when he heard his father's voice. "Hullo, Baba," he said in Venda, "It's me. Gideon."

Makhado's face brightened when he realized the caller was his son. His voice relaxed. "Hullo, son. Are you calling from school?"

"No, from home. It's lunch hour."

Makhado sensed a certain urgency in his son's voice. "Is anything wrong?"

It took a while for Gideon to answer. And when he did, his voice was full of anguish. "I need to talk to you, Baba."

"Go ahead. Viljoen is not here."

"No, not now. I'm planning to drive to Venda this coming Sunday. I called because I wanted to make sure you'd be home. I should arrive around four in the afternoon."

"I was planning to accompany your mother to Elim Hospital to visit her sick uncle. But I can stay behind if it's that important."

"It's very, very important, Baba. It's a matter of life and death."

KRUGER'S limo reached the Victorian mansion housing the Cape Town offices of Arm, Protect & Secure Inc. just as the noonday cannon atop Signal Hill was being fired. The tradition dated back to the days of the British occupation of the Cape. The heavily guarded two-story mansion was at the end of a quiet tree-lined cul-de-sac near the top of Signal Hill, which separates the old inner city suburbs known as the "City Bowl" from the older suburb of Sea Point. The mansion commanded a breathtaking and strategic view of the entire city. The location made surveillance and the transmitting of coded messages from the huge satellite dishes on the grounds relatively easy.

The two stern-faced guards at the entrance recognized Kruger and let him through, and within minutes he was in his spacious office on the second floor.

He was there barely half an hour when his secretary buzzed him. "*Meneer Prinsloo is hier, Generaal.*"

Kruger was surprised but pleased at how quickly Prinsloo had made it to

Cape Town from Pretoria, where he'd been attending an engagement party for his son.

"Send him in, please."

Moments later the door opened and in walked a large florid-faced, silver-haired man. Kruger put aside the newspaper he'd been reading, rose from behind his massive oak desk and eagerly shook hands with Prinsloo.

"Can I get you something to drink?" Kruger asked.

"Brandy, please."

While Kruger was preparing the drinks, Prinsloo lowered his large frame onto the Italian leather sofa in the middle of the room and admired the intricate patterns on the expensive oriental area rug. His double chin and beady blue eyes gave the seventy-year-old Prinsloo a piggish appearance.

Kruger poured the brandy. "How was Derek's engagement party?"

"Splendid. I like his fiancée very much. I had my doubts about her after what happened with Liefling. But I was quickly reassured. She's very Afrikaner. Hardly a trace of liberalism."

"I'm glad." Kruger handed Prinsloo his drink and then sat down in an upholstered armchair across from him.

"Did you have time to talk to your contacts within the TRC about the matter we discussed this morning?"

"Ja. I called them as soon as I got off the phone with you."

Prinsloo paused and sipped his brandy. Kruger stared at him expectantly.

"They confirmed my suspicions. None of the applications for amnesty are from members of the Thathe Vondo death squad."

Kruger heaved a deep sigh of relief.

"Not only that," Prinsloo went on, "but none of the cases scheduled for in-camera hearings involve any policeman or farmer from the Venda area. In other words, members of the Thathe Vondo death squad haven't broken their sacred oath."

"So the fucking kaffir-lover is lying."

"Definitely."

Kruger leaned back in his chair, a questioning look on his face. "Why would she lie?"

"I suspect there are a couple of reasons. The obvious one is that she's attempting to make you panic. She knows she's got no evidence against you except the article in the *Mail & Guardian*. But it's too flimsy to be the basis of a successful criminal lawsuit. I read it on the plane."

Kruger got up and walked toward his desk near the window. There were several newspapers scattered across it. He picked up a copy of the *Mail & Guardian*, which he'd been reading while waiting for Prinsloo.

He waved it in front of Prinsloo. "If this is all the evidence she's got, then she's more of a *domkop* (fool) than I thought."

Prinsloo smiled wryly. "She's desperate."

Kruger started pacing, the paper still in his hand. His brow was knit, deep in thought. It was clear that something was still gnawing at him. Again Sun Tzu was telling him to be careful, not to be too hasty in dismissing as cunning a foe as his stepdaughter.

"I wish there was a way to be absolutely sure that this is all she knows," he said, returning to his chair. He placed the paper on the coffee table.

Prinsloo said nothing. Instead his flipper of a hand disappeared inside the pocket of the jacket of his well-tailored gray suit. He brought out a monogrammed gold cigar case, flipped it open and offered Kruger a cigar.

Kruger took one. "Thanks."

Prinsloo lit both cigars using a slim gold cigarette lighter, also monogrammed. "I'm absolutely convinced that's all the kaffir-lover knows," he said after a puff.

Kruger looked at him, a bit surprised. "You are?"

"Ja. I haven't been a judge and a lawyer for more than fifty years for nothing," Prinsloo said smugly. "After we talked I had my office do a little background check on the Ubuntu Resource Center and its staff. Did you know that your stepdaughter has two partners?"

"No."

"I believe you know both of them. One is a kaffir bitch named Thando Khosa. She used to be with the MK cell in Alexandra. Big time terrorist."

"I remember her," Kruger said. He puffed lazily on his cigar.

"The other is a former TRC investigator named David Schneider."

Kruger flinched as if he'd received an electric jolt. His eyes flashed angrily. "That liberal Jew bastard is working for her?"

"Ja. He joined the center about a month ago. And I have reason to believe that he's behind the lawsuit threat. It's a tactic he used a lot when he was still with the TRC. As a matter of fact, he tried it against several of my clients. But I advised them not to panic. In the end he either backed off, or the courts threw out the lawsuits as frivolous."

A sardonic smile twisted Kruger's thin lips. For a long while he was silent, thinking. Finally, he said to Prinsloo, grinning, "My friend, I knew I could rely on you. You know what you just did?"

"What?"

"You just saved the Fourth Boer Revolution. What you just told me about David has given me a brilliant idea about how to throw a wrench into Liefling's little blackmailing scheme."

Prinsloo smiled.

"And on Friday, my friend, I'm meeting the representative from South America to finalize the sale of the firm. The Fourth Boer Revolution is right on schedule. Nothing will stop it. Least of all a desperate kaffir-lover."

"So there'll be a lot to celebrate at the braai on Sunday."

"Indeed."

FREDA was worried as she undressed to go to sleep. It was around eight-thirty. Kruger had told her that he wanted to go to bed early since he had to fly to Jo'burg the next morning, where he would be for several days on business. All evening she'd been wondering why Kruger was so uncommunicative about the one subject that was uppermost in her mind: What had Prinsloo advised him to do about Liefling's threat to file a criminal lawsuit against him?

She wondered why throughout dinner Kruger had made no reference to the subject whatsoever. They had talked mainly about preparations for the *braai* on Sunday. Several times she'd fought the urge to ask him bluntly. Afraid of possibly upsetting him, she'd refrained.

She put on a silk slip, brushed and flossed her teeth, and got into bed. Kruger did the same after putting on his flannel pajamas. He reached for the leather Bible on the nightstand and Freda reached for a mystery novel.

Several minutes passed. No longer able to bear the suspense, she closed the book without reading a word, placed it back on the nightstand, turned to Kruger and finally asked, "Darling, what did Prinsloo say about the lawsuit?"

Kruger was silent for a long while, deep in thought. Finally, he put down the Bible, turned and faced Freda.

"My dear," he said, "Do you know much about Liefling's partner, David Schneider?"

"Not that much. All I know is that he's Jewish and that he used to be a TRC investigator."

"Well, there's more to him than that."

Kruger proceeded to tell Freda about David. When he finished, Freda, stunned, said, "I can't wait to tell Liefling what you just told me about David, dear. As a matter of fact, I'll call her first thing tomorrow morning. I'm sure once she finds out the truth about him, she won't file any lawsuit against you."

"I hope you're right, my dear," Kruger said.

He reached over and began caressing Freda's breasts while kissing her passionately. She moaned in response, then gave herself willingly to the man she adored, the man who at that very moment was planning how to kill her daughter, and how to use her as an alibi to cover up the deed.

LIEFLING, after a long and tiring day, was asleep in a darkened room. She moaned as she rolled on the waterbed, dreaming that she and Sipho were making love. They were alone on a beach somewhere on the East Coast of South Africa. It was sunset and, as they lay on the golden sand, the warm ocean spray of the Indian Ocean kept lapping their entwined naked bodies.

Suddenly the loud ringing of the telephone interrupted Liefling's dream. She opened her eyes and blinked at the digital clock. It was almost midnight. Thinking it was Sipho, who'd promised to call as soon as his shift was over, she groped for the phone on her nightstand and answered groggily.

"Hullo?"

She heard nothing at first, then rapid breathing, followed by a calm, suave voice that made her skin tingle. "We are watching you, kaffir-lover."

"Who is this?"

"And this is what we do with kaffir-lovers."

There were several gunshots, then the mysterious caller hung up.

Liefling slammed down the receiver and unplugged the phone. She sat on the bed naked, hugging her knees to her breasts, trembling with a mixture of fear and rage. That was the twenty-fifth death threat she'd received since she announced that she'd be representing victims of death squads before the TRC. She'd unlisted her phone, informed the police, changed her number, but the calls hadn't stopped. She wondered if they'd ever stop.

<table>
<tr><td>**17**</td><td>**LIEFLING** and Sipho were cruising along the highway in her Honda, headed for the Crossroads squatter camp, the location of the clinic where Sipho was a part-time surgeon. Crossroads was one of the most notorious of the Cape Flats Townships. With its endless sprawl of shacks, it was also</td></tr>
</table>

one of the impoverished, which is one reason why Sipho worked there. Another reason was because Crossroads was where his father grew up after his family moved there from Natal to look for work.

During the apartheid era the squatter camp was overcrowded with refugees from poverty who'd been lured to Cape Town by the promise of menial jobs. But most ended up spending their working lives fleeing the police so they and their families wouldn't be arrested and endorsed back to the homelands, where there was little work and where they couldn't eke out a living farming the exhausted land.

Now, with the abolition of Influx Control laws, the overcrowding had worsened. More and more waves of refugees from poverty were daily pouring in. This time they came not only from the former Xhosa homelands of the Transkei and Ciskei, but from Mozambique and other parts of Africa, making the squatter camp one of the most overcrowded on the planet.

Violent crime, much of it drug-related, was rampant in the ghetto, and Sipho's Clinic was one of the busiest, which is why, though exhausted from his stint at Bara, he felt compelled to begin his day early.

"I received another death threat last night," Liefling said as the Honda neared Crossroads.

"Who this time?" Sipho asked, a concerned look on his tired face.

"It could be anyone. Relatives or friends of the cops I got convicted for torture and murder. Afrikaners who hate my guts. My stepfather's goons."

The Honda left the highway and turned left onto a potholed street.

"What did your stepfather say when you confronted him with the allegations?"

"He denied them. And he did so very cunningly."

"What do you mean?"

"He put me on the defensive about ANC human rights abuses."

"Why do you think Kruger refuses to testify?"

"Because he has something to hide, that's why. But the irony is that my clients are prepared to forgive him if he's guilty of any crime. All they want is to find out where the bodies of their loved ones are buried."

"I'm playing devil's advocate here. But couldn't he be afraid that the truth might lead your mother to divorce him?"

Liefling laughed. "Divorce him? You must be kidding. She's so in love with him that nothing short of his having tortured and murdered people would make her divorce him."

Liefling turned left into a narrow side street. The clinic was about half a mile away. On either side were rows of tightly packed shacks made from wattle branches, plastic sheets, pieces of wood and cardboard, which were a fire hazard and offered little shelter against the freezing rain and wind of the wet Cape winters. Entire families lived in these tiny hovels without electricity, running water, sewer or heat.

"What if he did personally torture and murder people?" Sipho asked.

Liefling knitted her brow. "That's a tough question. Knowing how my mother abhors violence of any kind, I think she'd draw the line there."

"What about you?"

"Well, if he expresses remorse and asks for forgiveness, I'd forgive him. I know that people on both sides of the apartheid struggle did horrible things they now regret and are sorry for. Take Thando, for instance. While she was an MK leader she ordered the execution of collaborators and impimpis. She planted bombs that maimed and killed innocent people. But she confessed everything and asked for forgiveness. She was granted amnesty, and now she's doing wonderful things for the Alexandra community. People can change."

"I agree," Sipho said. "My brother did change."

The Honda pulled up in front of the clinic complex, which consisted of four trailer-like buildings behind a high barbed wire fence. The clinic's dusty courtyard was already teeming with patients, despite the early hour. Most were knife and gunshot victims.

Sipho leaned over and kissed Liefling. "I'll give you a call as soon as I'm done."

"Do you know when that will be?"

"Around five."

"Okay. I should be done with reading the TRC transcripts and with working out. Maybe we can have dinner together and then catch a movie."

"That will be great. I need to relax." Sipho grabbed his duffel bag and got out. Liefling watched in admiration as Sipho was recognized and greeted warmly by many of the clinic's patients.

He's so selfless, she thought as she left the clinic, remembering that Sipho had rejected offers from private clinics and hospitals to work in Crossroads. *Dad would have been very proud of him.*

LIEFLING stopped at a Pick 'n Pay Supermarket to get groceries for the fund-raising party on Sunday. When she returned to the flat she found two messages on the answering machine. One was from David and the other from her mother. Freda was coming to the Waterfront to do some shopping in the afternoon and wondered if they could meet and talk.

Liefling picked up the phone and dialed her number.

"Hi Mo."

"Hi."

"What do you want to talk me to about?"

"Your stepfather."

"What about him?"

"It's too important to discuss on the phone. Can we meet around two at the Waterfront? I'll be done with shopping."

"How about three-thirty? My aerobics class ends at three."

"Three then."

Putting down the receiver, Liefling wondered if Kruger had changed his mind and now wanted to testify. She prayed he had. But deep in her heart she doubted he would.

He's too proud, Liefling thought. *Just like most Afrikaners.*

Liefling was about to leave the kitchen to clean up her messy bedroom when she remembered the second message. She dialed David's number. David was with Thando, who'd stopped by with more affidavits from families in Alexandra. Both of them got on the speakerphone.

"I'm meeting my mom this afternoon," Liefling said. "She wants to talk to me about my stepfather."

"Is he willing to testify?"

"I don't know. Probably not"

"Then let's sue the bastard," David said.

"Sue him?" Liefling cried. "Are you crazy? We have no proof that he's guilty of any crime."

"Liefling is right, David," Thando said. "We'll simply be wasting precious time and money we could be devoting to other cases we have a better chance of winning. Besides, Kruger might counter-sue us for defamation of character."

"I tell you the bastard is guilty," David insisted.

"But where's the proof, David?" Liefling said. "Even the *Mail & Guardian* story didn't provide any. All it said was that Kruger was a CCB member and that he attended several SSC meetings where words like 'neutralize' and 'eliminate' were used in reference to opponents of apartheid. But no court can convict him on such flimsy evidence."

"Liefling's right David," Thando said. "If we dragged him to court now we'd only be making fools of ourselves."

"And you've tried exposing those former policemen your TRC sources said might have belonged a CCB death squad Kruger knew about," Liefling said. "It hasn't worked."

David was adamant. "I'm sure Kruger was involved in death squad activities. And I'm sure there are witnesses out there who can prove it."

"Okay," Liefling said. "I'll make a deal with you. The minute you find me a witness – just one – who can implicate Kruger, I'll file the lawsuit. But not a minute before. Is that fair enough?"

"It's a deal," David said.

GIDEON stared at the phone next to the color TV in the darkened living room. He was glad that Nomhle had taken the children shopping at the Rosebank Mall. He needed to be alone in order to make the most important phone call of his life. He'd wanted to make it yesterday, shortly after he'd read that article in the *Mail & Guardian* about Kruger. But for some reason he'd been afraid of consequences.

Now that he'd spoken to his father and had had time to think over the matter, he knew he had no choice but to make the phone call. It was his only opportunity to atone for the cowardly deeds he'd done and to redeem his soul.

His trembling right hand, its palm sweaty, slowly reached for the sleek black phone. He glanced at the number on the business card next to the phone, though it was unnecessary. He'd memorized the number.

He dialed it slowly. He listened to the phone ring five, six, seven times. He wondered why nobody was picking up. Maybe it was an omen that he shouldn't go through with the call. He was about to hang up when a voice said, "David Schneider speaking."

Suddenly Gideon was tongue-tied. His heart pounded.

"Hullo?" he heard David say.

Gideon made no response.

"Hullo?"

Gideon took a deep breath, then said in Afrikaans, "Are you still looking for evidence implicating General Kruger in death squad activities?"

Gideon heard David catch his breath.

David, who was fluent in Afrikaans, said, "*Ja, ons soek dit.*"

"I have such evidence."

"*What is jou naam?*"

There was a long pause, then Gideon said, "I'm not ready to give my name."

"How do I know you're not a prankster?"

"I'm not a prankster. I'm one of two remaining askaris who served on a death squad headed by Kruger."

"Did you say headed by Kruger?"

"Ja. Originally there were ten of us. But eight are dead."

"*Dood?*"

"Ja. Kruger had them killed for doing what I'm doing. That's why I'm scared." Gideon thought he heard a click. "Are you taping this?" he said anxiously.

"*Nee.*"

There was another long pause.

"What kind of evidence do you have?" David asked gently.

"It's too explosive to mention over the phone. All I can tell you now is that Kruger operated one of the most ruthless CCB death squads. More ruthless than Vlakplaas. It killed dozens of activists and MK guerillas."

"Can we meet and talk?" David asked.

Gideon hesitated. "Not yet," he said. "I need time to think about this. I'm real scared. Kruger will kill me like the others if he finds out I plan to rat."

"The more reason for us to meet. I can arrange to have you placed in a witness protection program."

There was a long pause.

"No. I'll call again."

"When?"

"I don't know."

KRUGER sat at his office in downtown Johannesburg, talking to Botha,

Barnard and Viljoen, who were smoking and drinking. The afternoon sun streamed in through the large window and dappled the long mahogany table around which the four men sat. They were all in a jovial mood.

"The meeting with the representative of the South American investors is set for Friday in Sun City," Kruger said, lighting a cigar.

"I still can't believe we'll be getting three billion rands for the firm, General," Viljoen said. "How did Hunter manage that?"

"He's a very persuasive man."

"What's the latest on your kaffir-loving stepdaughter?" Botha asked. "I had one of my buddies give her a call last night just to make her think hard about filing any lawsuit."

Kruger smiled. "She won't. Prinsloo assured me that without any witnesses she has no case against me. Not even a circumstantial one. But just to make sure, I've taken certain precautions."

"What precautions?"

"I've told her mother some very interesting things about that kaffir-loving Jew, David Schneider. You should have seen her reaction." Kruger laughed aloud at the memory, then puffed on his cigar, admiring the swirling blue smoke. "She promised to talk to Liefling."

"About what?" Viljoen asked.

"About dropping the lawsuit. As a matter of fact, she told me they'll be meeting this afternoon at the Waterfront."

"Do you think the kaffir-lover will drop it?" asked Barnard.

"After she hears what I told her mother about David, I have no doubt she will."

18

LIEFLING and Freda strolled along the paved walkway of the Waterfront's pier. Freda had just finished shopping at the Waterfront's expensive boutiques, and Liefling had just finished doing aerobics at the Fitness and Living Well Center where she'd been a member since moving to Sea Point three and half years ago. She was dressed in a blue Adidas warm-up suit and a pair of white Nikes.

It was a balmy day, and the afternoon sun sparkled on the placid water. Robben Island, where Nelson Mandela had been a prisoner for over two decades, breaking rocks and lugging seaweed, was visible in the distance. A ferry packed with tourists churned its way back from the island about eleven kilometers away. It passed Freda and Liefling just as a flock of screaming seagulls careened overhead.

"Your threat to sue Magnus has put a strain on my marriage," Freda said from behind a pair of sunglasses. She was dressed in a peach Anne Klein sweater and black slacks, and carried a burgundy purse.

"I thought you were going to tell me Magnus had agreed to testify," Liefling said.

"Testify! Where's the proof that he knows anything about death squads? I read the *Mail & Guardian* article. There's nothing in it implicating Magnus in any wrongdoing."

Exasperated, Liefling looked at her mother. "Do you really think he could have belonged to a secretive group that was set up specifically to repress black people without knowing the methods it used? I find that hard to believe."

"Have you forgotten that your own father once belonged to the Broederbond, the most secretive of all groups? It also repressed black people. Yet he didn't know everything it authorized in the defense of apartheid. Only a handful of people knew. And after the Soweto Uprising, when he realized that the Broederbond was prepared to sanction even the cold-blooded murder of innocent schoolchildren in order to uphold *Baaskap*, he repudiated apartheid. Don't you think that Magnus could be in a similar situation regarding the CCB?"

Liefling didn't answer. Instead she brushed away a strand of blond hair that the breeze had thrown across her face.

"If you can't prove your wild allegations," Freda said, "please stop bothering my husband. You know, I'm starting to think you have some kind of vendetta against him."

Liefling stopped and glared at her mother. "What vendetta?"

"Who knows."

"I have no vendetta against him, Mom. And you know that. Why would I?"

"What about David?"

"What about him?"

"Doesn't he have a vendetta against my husband?"

"Of course he doesn't."

"I wouldn't be so sure if I were you."

Liefling stared at her mother. "What do you mean?"

Freda lowered her voice. "I've recently learned some shocking things about David that make me very suspicious of his motives in abruptly quitting the TRC to join you."

"What shocking things?"

"Did you know he blames Magnus for the death of a girl he once dated?"

This was news to Liefling. "What girl?"

"I don't know her name. But she was black. She died while in police custody at John Vorster Square. From a heroin overdose."

"A heroin overdose?"

"Ja. According to Magnus she was a hardcore drug-addict. While in police custody, she suffered an epileptic seizure induced by contaminated heroin. Do you know who smuggled her the heroin?"

"Who?"

"David."

Liefling laughed. "I've never heard anything so outrageous in my life," she said. "Why would David have murdered her?"

"To silence her. The police had found stashes of heroin in his Hillbrow flat. Apparently he was a big time drug dealer. To build a case against him, the police needed a witness. So they picked up the black girl he'd been shacking up with. Two days later David visited her in jail on the pretext of wanting to arrange for her defense. The next day she was dead. Magnus believes that David gave her the contaminated heroin in order to silence her."

Liefling slowly shook her head. "David would never do such a thing. He's innocent."

"If he's innocent, my dear, why didn't he tell you any of this?"

Liefling had no answer.

"I know why," Freda said. "It's because he wanted to use you, honey. The same way he used that poor black girl. There's a lot of shocking things he didn't tell you about for that very reason. Let's sit down and I'll tell you more."

They were abreast a park bench overlooking a dozen moored boats and yachts. Liefling mechanically sat down next to Freda on the wooden bench, still wondering how much of the story, if any, might be true.

"Listen, honey," Freda said, touching her shoulder sympathetically. "I know you mean well. You don't hate Magnus. You simply want to help those grieving families. And there's nothing wrong with that. But there are other ways you can help than by letting yourself be used by a consummate con-artist."

"David is no con-artist."

"How much do you know about him?"

"He's Jewish and lives in Soweto. He used to work for the TRC as an investigator. His parents were members of the South African Communist Party. Death squads using a letter bomb assassinated his mother in 1984. The following year his father, who was in exile in Zimbabwe, died in a suspicious car accident believed to have been engineered by South African death squads."

"There's your motive. Revenge."

"But David is not a vengeful person, Mom. He's very tolerant, open-minded and generous. For instance, his parents left him R2 million. You know what he did with most of the money?"

"What did he do?"

"He gave it to black charities. I tell you he's a good human being. Tell me, how many white people with money would give it away and go live in Soweto, of all places?"

"There could be another reason he's living in Soweto," Freda said.

"What reason?"

"So it can be easier to deal drugs."

"That's rubbish," Liefling said angrily. "David is not a drug dealer. And he was never arrested on heroin charges. He'd have told me about these things when I interviewed him for the job."

"Well," Freda said, "confront him about what I told him. Then give me a call. If Magnus is lying, then I owe David an apology."

DAVID laughed loudly. "So Kruger is up to his old dirty tricks again," he said, speaking to Liefling on the phone. "Yes, it's true that I was arrested on heroin charges. But that was fifteen years ago."

Liefling was sitting on the floor of her bedroom, nervously running her fingers over a patch of beige carpet.

"Why didn't you tell me?" she asked, upset.

"I didn't think it was necessary."

"Not necessary?"

"The heroin was planted. During the apartheid era the police were always planting drugs in the homes of activists. Then they could arrest us and discredit us in the media."

"What had you done?"

"I was making a great deal of noise regarding the suspicious death in police detention of Dikeledi Motsei. She was a classmate of mine at Wits. She and I were actually quite close."

"You mean you were dating?"

"Ja. And the Immorality Act goon squad from the SABRA raided my flat in Hillbrow a couple of times. One time they took sheets, my briefs and Dikeledi's panties as criminal evidence. At the police station a guy named Swanepoel interrogated us in order to find out if we'd made love. I told him it was none of his fucking business. They released us. Next thing I knew the police booked me for heroin possession."

"What happened to Dikeledi?"

"Two weeks later the security branch arrested her and pressured he to testify against me. She refused. When I visited her at John Vorster Square, she told me that they'd brutally beaten her but she wouldn't sign a fake confession saying I was a drug dealer. Then they threatened to revive a 1976 case against her."

"What case?"

"It involved the necklacing of a white sergeant in Soweto on June 17, the day after the police opened fire on those unarmed students. Dikeledi had been a leader of the mob that attacked the sergeant who was head of the notorious security branch in Soweto. But my father successfully defended Dikeledi on murder charges."

"How did she die?"

"The official police report -- and you know how reliable those were during the apartheid era – said that she'd died from overdosing on contaminated heroin."

"Where did she get it?"

"The bastards injected her with the stuff, of course."

"Against her will?"

"Sure. Some of these guys were like Nazis, I tell you. You've heard policemen confess during TRC hearings how they secretly poisoned detainees and then covered it up. They even wanted to poison Nelson Mandela, for God's sake."

"I know," Liefling said, recalling the many dirty tricks the security police had played on her and her family after her father repudiated apartheid. They'd poisoned her favorite dog, a golden retriever, and sent her an ANC T-shirt laced with poison oak, to which she was severely allergic. Her skin had itched for a whole month and had huge welts that punctured and oozed pus.

"Believe me, Liefling. I didn't kill Dikeledi. I loved her very much. And both of us never, ever used hard drugs. Sure we smoked some *dagga* once in a while. But marijuana is nothing like heroin."

He waited for a response. Liefling didn't answer. She simply stood up and stared out her bedroom window, trying to understand. She was silent for a long while. She studied the patterns of light that the sun's rays, filtered by towering trees, cast on the street below.

You believe me, don't you?" David said anxiously.

"I believe you," Liefling said.

David sighed with relief.

But you haven't connected Dikeledi's death to my stepfather."

"The bastard killed her," David said with clenched teeth.

Liefling gasped and gripped the phone tighter. "What?"

"Kruger murdered Dikeledi."

"What makes you say that?"

"He was head of the security branch at John Vorster Square at the time of her detention. And he participated in every interrogation."

"But my mom says an independent inquiry cleared the police of any wrongdoing in Dikeledi's death."

David laughed. "An independent inquiry also cleared Biko's killers of any wrongdoing. And the truth only came out before the TRC."

"But why didn't you tell me all this about Kruger before?"

"I didn't want you to think I'd agreed to work with you because I was waging a personal vendetta against the bastards for what he did to Dikeledi.

Especially when I found out that he had become your stepfather. And without witnesses, I didn't think you'd believe me even if I told you."

"Why do you think that we can nail Kruger this time? We have no without witnesses linking him to death squads."

"I think we're about to get one," David said.

"What do you mean?"

"When you called I'd just finished talking to an *askari* who says he has evidence implicating Kruger in death squad activities. And he's eager to testify."

"What evidence?"

"It's too explosive to discuss over the phone," David said. "Why don't you come to Jo'burg tomorrow. I'll tell you and Thando in person."

"I'll catch the first plane out," Liefling said with a pounding heart.

"And come ready to file the lawsuit," David said. "After you hear what the askari told me about your stepfather, you won't have any more doubts about his guilt."

19

LIEFLING gazed impatiently out the window of the South African Airways 737 jet as it began its initial descent into Johannesburg International airport. Minutes later, it touched down with a puff of smoke on runway 2. Liefling glanced at her watch. It was precisely 7:30 a.m.

The 737 taxied to gate number 6. Clutching a gray Samsonite garment bag and a fat briefcase stuffed with newspapers, files and documents, Liefling was among the first passengers to disembark from the full flight. She found David and Thando waiting for her outside the crowded gate.

"How was your flight?" Thando asked.

"I slept most of the way," Liefling said.

"Lucky you. I didn't get much sleep. I worked till two and had to get up at six to help my daughter with her homework."

"Any luggage?" David asked.

"No. This is all I have."

South Africa's largest and busiest airport was bustling with travelers. Most of them were black business executives, politicians and tourists -- a stark contrast to the apartheid era, when the only blacks to be seen around at the airport were those cleaning it.

"I wish my grandmother had lived to see the new South Africa," Thando said as they headed for the parking lot. David had detoured to the lavatory.

"Why do you say that?" Liefling asked.

"She used to work at the airport as a charwoman. She couldn't read. And there were 'WHITES ONLY' and 'NON-WHITES ONLY' signs all over the place. I remember her telling me how terrified she was all the time of getting fired for disobeying the signs."

Liefling recalled the ubiquitous "SLEGS BLANKES" and "NIE BLANKES" petty-apartheid signs that had segregated blacks and whites in public spaces, in accordance with the Reservation of Separate Amenities Act of 1953.

"When I was growing those signs were very normal," Liefling said. "I was taught by my parents and at school that blacks and whites didn't belong together. That blacks were inferior to us. And that if we mixed with them we'd catch all kinds of diseases and sink to the level of savages."

"Interesting," Thando said. "I, too, thought whites were savages."

"Really?"

"Ja. The only white people I came in contact with as a child were the police during brutal raids to enforce Influx Control laws. And they terrified me so much I'd pee on my little dress at the sight of them. Especially the big Boers with hairy arms and red faces."

The two women reached Thando's white 1994 Toyota Hilux. It was parked in a crowded lot close to the terminal. The Toyota, a donation to the Phutadichaba Community Center from an American philanthropic group, had the following commandment painted on both sides in huge black letters:

THOU SHALT NOT HIJACK

Liefling smiled and pointed at the sign. "Does it work?"

"It's worked so far," Thando said. "One time carjackers stopped me at an intersection in Soweto. They were heavily armed with AK-47s. I thought the Toyota was gone. Instead, their leader said to me, 'The reason we aren't taking this Toyota is because my men almost died laughing when they saw that sign.'"

"I didn't know carjackers had a sense of humor," Liefling said as Thando unlocked the Toyota. "The ones who almost hijacked my car a month ago would have shot me if Makhado hadn't come to my rescue."

The two women got in and circled back to David.

"Talking about Makhado," Thando said, "we have an open invitation for dinner with his son Gideon. He and his wife Nomhle told me they're eager to meet you. Especially after they heard that your boyfriend is a Bahai."

"I'd like to meet him too," Liefling said. "And I have no dinner plans for tonight. Sipho is working the evening shift."

"Okay. I'll phone Nomhle as soon as we reach Alexandra."

They pulled up to the curb outside the terminal. David climbed in and they left the airport.

As the Toyota raced down Eleckron Highway, Liefling said to David, "So what evidence does our mystery witness have against my stepfather?" she asked.

David looked a bit disheveled from having stayed up late working on the case, but there was excitement in his brown eyes.

"Plenty," he said, leaning forward. "He called me again since I last spoke to you. He says that Kruger actually headed the most ruthless dead squad in the entire CCB. He says it assassinated dozens of anti-apartheid activists and MK guerillas and firebombed scores of houses and buildings."

"What!" Liefling cried. "I don't believe it."

"I know it sounds incredible."

"Did he give his name?"

"No. But he spoke fluent Afrikaans."

"Is he Afrikaner?"

"It sounded like it."

"And he said he used to be an askari?"

"Ja."

"Then it's unlikely that he's an Afrikaner."

"He could be Colored."

"He also could be black," Thando said. "Don't forget there are blacks who are fluent in Afrikaans."

"How do you know he's not just another prankster?" Liefling asked. "We've had quite a few such calls in the last couple weeks."

"I'm convinced he's legit. He provided specifics only an insider would know."

"Such as?"

"The code-name of Kruger's death squad. It was named Thathe Vondo. And he says it was made up of fifty policemen and farmers, all bonafide AWB neo-Nazis. He also knew that the death squad operated from a remote bushveld camp in Venda from 1986 to 1993, when it was disbanded."

"That would explain why Kruger was always visiting Venda," Liefling observed thoughtfully.

"Not only that," David continued. "Our mystery witness also gave me the names of about three dozen MK guerrillas who were captured, tortured and then executed by the Thathe Vondo death squad."

"Among them were ten members of my MK cell," Thando said. "They disappeared while infiltrating back into the country through Venda."

The Toyota entered Lombardy East, a previously working-class white suburb adjacent to Alexandra. Liefling's family had lived there after her father, following his ouster from the white Dutch Reformed Church, accepted a position with a black church in Alexandra. Lombardy East now had a significant population of middle-class and professional blacks.

"You said this askari is willing to come forward and testify," Liefling said as the Toyota climbed a winding hill.

"Ja. But only under certain conditions."

"What are they?"

"First, he wants you to file the lawsuit by tomorrow morning."

"By tomorrow morning – why so soon?"

"He wants to have time to apply for amnesty. Don't forget the deadline is next week."

Liefling had a dubious look on her face. But she decided to say nothing until David had finished.

"That's not all. After you file the lawsuit he wants you to call a press conference for that very afternoon and tell the world why you filed the lawsuit. During the press conference he expects that you'll be asked if you have witnesses and who they are."

"He's damn right," Liefling said.

The Toyota soon reached the outskirts of Alexandra. The ghetto was shrouded with a blanket of smog from a thousand *mbawulas* (braziers) and coal stoves. The roadside teemed with black men and women hurrying to their jobs at the outlying factories, and clusters of jobless young men huddled around smoldering trash fires.

David went on. "When asked to name your witnesses, the askari wants you to say that you've tracked down several members of the Thathe Vondo death squad who are willing to testify against Kruger in return for amnesty."

"He's very clever," Thando said. "He's trying to throw Kruger off his scent by attempting to implicate one of his men. That would explain why he speaks in Afrikaans. I bet you he's black."

"That won't work," Liefling said. "Kruger will soon find out who he is. He's better off coming in from the cold. We can arrange to place him in a witness protection program."

"I suggested that," David said. "But he said he had reasons for wanting things done his way. At least for now. So will you file the lawsuit?"

Liefling was silent for a while, then said, "It's risky. I've never filed a lawsuit without being sure of my case. We have no witnesses, no tangible evidence. Only the word of an askari we've never met."

"I know," David said.

"But I'll file it."

"You will?" David almost shrieked with joy. "Great." A broad grin spread across his face. "Thank you, Liefling. I promise you won't regret it."

"I hope not," Liefling said. "I'm doing this in part because I care very much about my mother's marriage and happiness. I want to give my stepfather, if he's committed any human rights abuses, enough time to apply for amnesty."

"That's fair enough," David said.

Liefling turned to Thando. "Do you think you can arrange a press conference for three tomorrow afternoon?"

"Sure," Thando said. "I'll start contacting journalists right now."

She removed a cell phone from her purse and began dialing.

Liefling looked at David. "We have a lot of work ahead of us between now and tomorrow. I sure hope our mystery witness keeps his word and comes forward once we file the lawsuit. If he doesn't, we're in deep shit."

"He will," David said confidently.

20

MAKHADO and the ten women finished work at the Thathe Vondo private game reserve around five. After tramping ten miles through bush country in humid weather, half the distance to their village, they reached a small bridge spanning a turbulent, crocodile infested river.

Makhado saw the women safely across, then as they stood on the other side of the river, he said, "I must leave you now. This is the final week at the mountain school. I promised Nzhelele that I'd stop by and address his initiates."

"Thank you for bringing us this far," said Nzhelele's wife, a tall and dark-skinned woman named Beauty. "We should have no problem finding our way home. There's still a bit of light left."

"Tell my wife where I've gone so she won't worry," Makhado said.

"We will," Beauty said.

Makhado watched the women as they wended their way along the narrow footpath leading to the village on the other side of the mountain. They sang as they walked. Their plaintive songs were about the hardships of being women: bearing many children, putting up with philandering husbands, and working for thankless white people. After they disappeared behind a cluster of trees, Makhado turned and jogged eastward along the river, headed for the mountain school about eight miles away. He made such good time that he reached it just before dusk.

The mountain school stood in the middle of a clearing deep in the forest, behind a high enclosure of thorny branches. The branches were a boundary indicating that everything taking place within the school was to be kept secret.

Makhado saw about one hundred half-naked young men squatting around a huge fire in the middle of the enclosure, not far from the huts where they slept without blankets on the earthen floor. The aroma of roasting Bushbuck and Impala meat filled the air. After a day of exercises and trials to build their strength and teach them endurance, courage, obedience, hunting and fighting, the young men were about to eat dinner. Feeling hungry, Makhado smiled. He looked forward to stuffing himself before relaxation time, when the young men would be learning songs and performing rituals meant to create solidarity among them.

Makhado approached the fire using a path lined with twenty-four poles arranged in pairs, which was reserved for the initiates and their teachers, who were called *Shepherds* or *Fathers*. Uninitiated visitors to the school were required to go around the poles and cross the path five times in order to reach the visitors' entrance on the right side of the path. They were forbidden from using the initiates' entrance on the left side.

When they saw Makhado, the young men rose and stood in silence as a mark of respect. Nzhelele had told them of Makhado's coming. They gazed at him in awe as he spoke to Nzhelele. None of the young men had ever killed a lion, and here in front of them stood a living legend, the only man to have killed two lions by the time he'd graduated from the mountain school.

Makhado joined Nzhelele and several *Shepherds* and *Fathers* on wooden stools near the crackling fire. His serious eyes surveyed the young men. Their hard, bulging muscles impressed him. But he was even more impressed by something else he saw flickering in their eyes: the manly courage young boys developed after weeks of hardship and discipline at the mountain school. He knew they were now men, ready to confront life without flinching.

After the hearty meal, Makhado, as he drank homebrewed beer made from fermented sorghum, regaled the initiates with stories of warriors whose heroic deeds were legendary among the African people.

DAVID finished packing his briefcase. He grabbed his suede jacket from the hanger behind the door. Liefling and Thando, both exhausted, looked up from a table strewn with newspaper articles, affidavits, TRC transcripts, documents, fruit, bags of peanuts, chips and bottles of water and juice. Since arriving at the Phutadichaba Community Center from the airport, the three had been working non-stop preparing the criminal lawsuit to be filed against Kruger. It was now almost seven.

"See you guys tomorrow morning," David said.

"Say hi to Hannah," Liefling said.

"I will," David said. "I can't wait to see her perform. You know, we've been going out two months now and I haven't been to one of her performances."

"David!" Thando said playfully. "That's naughty of you."

"You guys have kept me quite busy. I have no social life left."

"What play is she in?" Thando asked.

"Hamlet. She's playing Ophelia."

"I should take my daughter to go see it. She loves Shakespeare."

"Say when, and I'll get you free tickets," David said.

"When," Thando said.

All three of them laughed.

"Enjoy your dinner, guys," David said. "Tell Gideon and his wife that I regret not being able to make it. But I look forward to seeing them another time."

"I will," Thando said.

David was almost out the door when Liefling remembered something.

"David, don't forget we have to be at the Magistrate's court at exactly nine o'clock so we can file the lawsuit. So don't stay out too late."

"I'll be there," David said. "I won't miss it for the world."

David strode to his beat-up Volkswagen parked outside the office. He was so comfortable around blacks that he was not afraid to drive alone in the ghetto, even at night – something few whites ever dared to do.

NOMHLE smiled with satisfaction as she watched Liefling enjoying the African meal she'd cooked. She and Gideon had never had a white person over for dinner, so she'd gone out of her way to impress their guest after Thando had told her that Liefling loved African food. Nomhle had cooked pap, curried chicken viscera and *murogo* (greens) in peanut sauce.

Liefling had been dubious about eating the chicken giblets, heart, liver and intestines – until she tasted them for the first time. Then she'd asked for seconds.

While the adults sat around the dinner table, Mkondeleli and Nomhle's two children, Pinkie and Joshua, sat in the living room eating as they watched *The Cosby Show*, one of the many American re-runs popular with South African audiences.

"My father-in-law told me that your boyfriend is Bahai," Nomhle said.

"Ja," Liefling said.

"So are Gideon and I."

"Why did you two join?" Thando asked, looking at Nomhle, who was busy serving carrot cake, vanilla ice cream and rooibos tea for dessert.

Nomhle looked at her husband.

"Well, Nomhle and I have friends who are Bahais," Gideon said. "They kept urging us to join but I kept resisting. You know how skeptical I am of religions in general. Then one day Nomhle and I attended one of their meetings in Sandton. I was amazed at how progressive and humanistic the Bahai religion is."

"What exactly do Bahais believe?" Thando asked, stirring honey into her tea.

Nomhle answered. "They believe in universal education, a universal language, one government, the equality of the sexes, and the abolition of racial, religious and ethnic prejudice."

"Quite progressive," Thando said, impressed.

"You should join," Nomhle said.

"No, thank you," Thando said. "I'm happy being an agnostic."

"What about you, Liefling?"

Liefling stopped eating her carrot cake. "I haven't been to church in years," she said. "But Sipho wants me to become a Bahai."

"You should," Gideon said. "You belong there."

"Why do you say that?"

"Well, you are a genuine progressive, for one," Gideon said. "You really made an impression on my father. He hasn't stopped raving about your Ubuntu."

"And that's quite a compliment," Nomhle said. "My father-in-law is generally unimpressed by white people. All his life he's had bad experiences with them. But when I spoke to him the day after he rescued you, he kept going on and on about how much Ubuntu you have. He said you were the first Afrikaner who's treated him as an equal. When you told him you didn't want to be called 'Madam' he let down his guard. You shattered many of the stereotypes he used to have about Afrikaners."

"To be honest with you, until then he had me completely fooled. I thought he was illiterate. You can imagine my surprise when he spoke to me in perfect English, and asked me very probing questions about the TRC."

"My grandpa was like that," Thando said. "He'd never let white people know he was intelligent until he was sure he could trust them."

"Why is that?" Liefling asked.

"Because a lot of white people resent and fear intelligent black people," Gideon said.

"Why?"

"They consider us economic threats. That's why during the apartheid era Bantu Education and the Jobs Reservation Act insured black servitude."

"You're right," Liefling said. "When I was growing up a lot of white children were taught that blacks were inferior and uncivilized. We were even taught that blacks had smaller brains and were therefore incapable of learning complex subjects like math and science."

There was a brief pause as people ate. After the meal, Liefling and Thando prepared to leave.

"Before I forget," Nomhle said to Thando, "I finally managed to convince my mother to provide you with an affidavit about my brother's death."

"Great," Thando said.

Seeing the puzzled look on Liefling's face, Thando said, "I've been eager to get the affidavit to add to our case. Nomhle's brother, Vusi, was a member of my MK cell. Incredibly brave. He was captured, tortured and brutally murdered while he was on assignment to blow up the local police station. The bloody bastards sent his mother his severed right hand pickled in a jar with a note that read: 'This is what happens to terrorists.'"

"That's sick," Liefling said.

Nomhle said, "My mother changed her mind because I told her you were her last best chance of ever finding the rest of Vusi's body so we can bury it properly."

The topic was making Gideon quite uncomfortable. He excused himself and went to the bathroom. When he got there he threw up. There were tears in his eyes. As he was wiping his face with a *waslap* (facecloth) to remove any tell-tales signs of his distress, he said to his image in the mirror, "You coward. You must testify against Kruger. Even if you end up getting killed."

21

KRUGER studied the odd appearance and mannerism of his South American guest. He was a heavyset man with beefy jowls and sleek dark hair. Thick tar-black sideburns framed his florid Santa-like face. He was wearing a well-tailored navy-blue suit, white silk shirt and gaudy tie. He spoke good English, albeit with a heavy Spanish accent that sometimes made it difficult for Kruger to understand what he was saying.

It was around one thirty on Friday of the first week in May. The two men were seated at a secluded corner table in the Crystal Courtyard Restaurant in the Palace Hotel in Sun City. A pony-tailed waiter in a tuxedo brought Kruger and his guest a bottle of chilled vintage Cape Chardonnay in a cooler. He poured a little of the wine into one of two crystal glasses and gave it to Kruger to taste. Kruger slowly swirled it like a connoisseur, sniffed it and then took a sip.

"Excellent," he said to the waiter, who smiled and poured more wine into Kruger's glass, then into that of his guest.

The waiter jotted down their orders for lunch on a notepad and disappeared into the kitchen.

"So, how do you like South Africa?" Kruger asked his guest in a casual tone.

"It's depressing," said the South American with evident disgust. "I remember when it used to be clean and orderly."

"When were you here?"

"In 1983. On a safari. I must say I can hardly recognize it. It's interesting to see what happens to a country when whites are no longer in charge."

"It turns into a banana republic," Kruger said.

"How can you stand living in a place ruled by niggers?"

"I can't stand it."

"Do you intend to emigrate like the others?"

"Never," Kruger snapped.

"Then good luck."

Kruger was about to say something when the pony-tailed waiter arrived with their entrees. Kruger had ordered his favorite – *boerewors* sausage, wild rice and vegetables with a delicious tangy sauce. The South American, apparently not concerned about weighing nearly 250 pounds, had ordered baked pork chops with apple and sage stuffing.

The waiter served them and left.

"So, what questions do you have about the firm?" Kruger asked as they began eating.

The South American didn't immediately answer as his mouth was full of pork. After chewing a bit, he wiped his greasy mouth with a lace napkin then said, "Let me first ask you if you have any questions about the people who sent me."

"I'm curious about one thing," Kruger said. "The letter Hunter gave me didn't state what business they were in."

"That was omitted intentionally," said the South American. "In case the letter fell into the wrong hands. That's how we normally conduct business."

"I see."

"I thought you'd have guessed the nature of our business by now."

"Is it not private security?" Kruger asked, feigning innocence.

The South American emitted a short laugh. "Stop joking, will you. Do you think they'd be willing to pay three billion rands for your firm if they were into private security? It would take forever to recoup their investment."

"What business are they in?" Kruger asked, even though he knew.

The South American's beady eyes glanced about the half-empty restaurant. Satisfied that no one was within earshot, he said in a low voice. "I represent a conglomerate that considers South Africa of strategic importance to its multi-billion dollar business worldwide."

"What's the name of the conglomerate?"

The South American leaned forward and whispered, "The Cali Cartel."

Kruger wasn't in the least surprised to hear this. He'd known all along that South American drug lords considered South Africa not only a lucrative market for cocaine and its cheaper and more potent and highly addictive derivative, crack, but also the perfect place to set up manufacturing plants for the production of the two drugs before shipping them to the rest of Africa, Australia, and the Far East.

And involvement in drug-trafficking wasn't anything new for Kruger. During the apartheid era he'd let members of the Thathe Vondo death squad dabble in drug trafficking as a means of augmenting their low pay. His rationale was that as long as the drugs were destined mostly for kaffirs, they were simply another means of neutralizing *Die Swart Gevaar*.

"What use will my firm be in such a business?" Kruger asked after taking a bite of his boerewors.

"South Africa is a very dangerous place, my friend," the South American said. "As a matter of fact, I'm told that Johannesburg now ranks behind only Moscow and Mexico City as the most crime-ridden city in the world. So you see, the Cartel needs to be able to protect its valuable merchandise and safely transport it to its various destinations. Your firm is perfect for doing that. It has excellent infrastructure across Southern Africa, and a sophisticated communications network."

The South American paused and stuffed his mouth with several more pieces of pork. Kruger watched him indulgently. He couldn't believe his windfall. Three billion rands for a firm whose market value was a fifth that much!

"You also have extensive connections with policemen, politicians and judges," the South American said, draining his wine and reaching for the chilled bottle in the wine cooler. "Isn't that right?"

"That's right."

"Am I correct in assuming that these connections are part of the deal, and that you'll make all the necessary arrangements to discreetly inform these policemen, politicians and judges about the firm's new owners?"

Kruger nodded perfunctorily.

"I'm glad we agree on that important point, General," the South American said, pouring himself more wine. "Connections with policemen, politicians and judges are very important. Word has reached us that the ANC government plans to crack down on drug-trafficking and drug-related violence."

"They always promise to crack down," Kruger said dismissively. "But they never do. They can't. They're incompetent kaffirs. Afrikaners knew how to enforce law and order."

"That may be true, but in our business it's better to be safe than sorry," the South American said. "The Cartel has been very successful in South America, Latin America, Europe, North America and the former Soviet Union precisely because it's always prepared. So if these terms are agreeable to you, I'll fly back tomorrow and present my report to the Cartel. Then a deal will be finalized with Hunter and three billion rands will be wired to your account. I assume you have an account in Switzerland."

Kruger nodded.

"Good."

Kruger saw nothing to object to. The sooner he had the money in his hands, the sooner he'd be able to start implementing plans for the Fourth Boer Revolution. Now, more than ever, he was convinced it would succeed. Not only would he have ample funds to bankroll the revolution, but also once the Cartel began flooding drugs into South Africa they would wreak more instability and violence than all the neo-Nazi groups he could put together. What a godsend. He silently thanked Hunter.

I must give him a call after the meeting and express my gratitude, Kruger thought. He was about to say something to the South American when the maitre d' approached the table.

"There's a call for you, General," he said.

"Thank you." Turning to his guest, Kruger said, "I turned off my cell phone and they still find ways to interrupt me. Please excuse me for just a moment."

"Certainly," the South American said.

Kruger rose, pulled his cell phone from the inside pocket of his blazer and pressed the auto-dial button as he stepped out of the dining area into a less noisy atrium.

"I thought I told you I didn't want to be disturbed," Kruger said in exasperation to the man who answered.

"I didn't want to bother you, General," Botha's raspy voice said on the other side of the line, "but a very important matter has just come up."

"What is it?" Kruger asked impatiently.

"There was a strange news bulletin on TV about fifteen minutes ago. Apparently your stepdaughter is holding a press conference this afternoon in Alexandra."

"So what?" Kruger snapped. "She's been holding goddamn press conferences ever since she began persecuting her own people."

Botha coughed slightly. "This one is different."

"What do you mean?"

"She plans to announce on national TV that she's filed a three billion rand lawsuit against you on behalf of the families of victims of death squads."

The statement struck Kruger like a sledgehammer. He was so stunned and angry he couldn't speak for several minutes. Finally, he said in a low, hissing voice, "Are you sure?"

"The news bulletin was repeated shortly before I called you."

There was another long pause.

"When is the press conference?" Kruger demanded.

"Three o'clock."

Kruger glanced at his watch. It was 1:45.

"I'll be there."

Kruger pressed "end," dropped the cell phone into his inside pocket and quickly returned to the table, his face flushed.

"What's the matter?" asked the South American, who'd now finished his meal.

"I have to leave immediately. Something important has come up."

"Do we have a deal?"

"Yes. I mean no. I...I need a little time to think about it."

"The Cartel doesn't like waiting. It means lost revenue. Don't forget there are plenty of other security firms who'll snap at a tenth of what the Cartel is offering you. To be honest with you, if it hadn't been for the fact that the Cartel owes Hunter and Von Schleicher a favor, they wouldn't be willing to pay you that kind of money."

"Can you call me next Friday?" Kruger said. "I promise I'll have a final decision by then."

"Okay. A week. No more."

LIEFLING sat on a straight-backed chair behind a podium sprouting microphones like insect antennas. She anxiously panned the throng of chattering reporters crowded inside the small conference room of the Phutadichaba Community Center. Her heart pounded as she realized that in a just a few moments she'd be answering their questions about the most sensational criminal lawsuit in the history of the new South Africa.

Liefling wished she'd mustered the courage to tell her mother of her decision to file a lawsuit against her husband. Now it was too late. Liefling consoled herself with the thought that her mother wouldn't have understood, even if she'd told her.

Not when she's madly in love with Kruger, Liefling thought. *She'd have done everything to stop me. And I doubt if I'd have had the strength to resist her entreaties.*

Liefling's thoughts turned to another matter worrying her. *What if our mystery witness is nothing but a sophisticated prankster?*

Liefling willed herself not to think of the possibility that their only witness might be a fake. Her thoughts returned to her mother. *She's so happy. And she's been through so much. Now I'm about to ruin everything for her.*

As she watched the TV crew set up its camera and lights near the podium for a live broadcast, Liefling murmured silently to herself, *Please forgive me, Mom. I must do the right thing. You yourself said that. Oh, God, I sure hope I'm doing the right thing.*

Liefling glanced at David, who sat calmly in the chair next to hers, dressed in his favorite olive-green suit, white button-down shirt and red bow tie. David seemed completely unaware of the turmoil raging within Liefling's heart. He was busy scribbling a note on a small pad with his Mount Blanc fountain pen. He tore off a sheet and handed the note to Thando, who was standing behind the podium waiting for the hubbub from the reporters to die down before speaking.

Liefling cupped her mouth with her left hand and leaned toward David. She wanted to say, "David, I don't know if I can go through with this." Instead, the words that spilled from her quivering lips were, "I'm so bloody nervous."

David touched her hand reassuringly. "Don't worry, you'll do just fine."

Liefling didn't think so. She knew that after the press conference her life would never be the same. She'd be vilified by many. She'd receive more death threats. And God only knows how her mother would react.

Torn by conflicting emotions, Liefling wondered if she possessed the strength to face what lay ahead. What if David's strategy of using the lawsuit to force Kruger to testify didn't work? What if our mystery witness didn't deliver? It was clear that without him they didn't have a case against Kruger who, with his millions – no, billions – could afford to hire the best legal defense in the country, if he hadn't already done so. Not only that, but what would happen to them if the courts dismiss the lawsuit as frivolous? And what if Kruger turned around and sued them for defamation of character?

Liefling was saved from torturing herself any further by the thought of Thando. She raised her eyes toward her.

She's such an inspiration, Liefling thought, admiring the self-assured black woman she'd come to trust and love like a sister. She still couldn't believe that Thando had spent most of her thirty-five years as a guerrilla fighter for MK, nor the courage it took her to confess the human rights abuses she'd committed.

I owe it to her and to the victims of apartheid to go through with this, Liefling thought. *Above all, I owe it to Dad.*

| 22 | **GIDEON** sat on a sofa in a darkened living room watching TV. This was the moment he'd been waiting for, and dreading, since arriving home from work half an hour earlier. He was glad it was Nomhle's day off and that she'd taken Pinkie and Joshua to see the latest Disney movie at a |

theater in Sandton. As he watched the unfolding press conference, Gideon concentrated on one face: Liefling's. He wondered what she was thinking and feeling. Was she as torn as he was? Was she as riddled with doubt and guilt? He wished he could speak to her, reassure her that all would be well, that he would deliver on the promise to provide the evidence necessary to implicate Kruger in death squad activities.

Gideon loosened his tie and kicked off his size twelve black Bostonian shoes. He adjusted his thick horn-rimmed glasses, then reached for the bottle of Fanta on the glass coffee table. As he sipped, Gideon wondered why he hadn't revealed the truth to everyone around the dinner table last night. It had been the perfect moment. It would have ended years of agony and a double life. Was it because subconsciously he was afraid that at the last minute he might not go through with what he'd vowed to do?

His fear was real, but he felt compelled to keep his promise to David. Makhado had risked being killed by carjackers to do the honorable deed of saving Liefling. Gideon felt he could do no less to bring peace to the families of victims of death squads, who would continue to suffer as long the spirit of their loved ones remained shut out from the realm of their ancestors because they'd never been properly buried. He must testify. The time for hiding, for lying, for excuses, was over. He was no longer an askari. He was now a free man, a Bahai who valued his soul and his humanity.

I should have told Liefling what actually happened to her father, Gideon thought as the camera zoomed in on Liefling behind the podium, conferring with David. *After all, I was the last person to see him alive the day he was murdered.*

For some reason Gideon wished Nomhle were sitting close beside him on the sofa watching the press conference, holding his hand, telling him she loved him, despite everything. He needed her reassurance, her understanding.

But would she have understood if I had revealed the truth about what really happened to her brother Vusi? And would Thando have understood if I had revealed the truth about who'd betrayed all those MK cadres who were captured and executed by the Thathe Vondo death squad?

Suddenly Gideon began crying. He cried uncontrollably – deep heart-rending sobs that shook his large frame.

Please, God, he wailed in Venda, *give me the strength to do the right thing. Give me the strength to tell my father everything on Sunday. And above all, give me the strength to testify against Kruger, despite the risks.*

Gideon wiped his tears with a white handkerchief and his gaze returned to the TV, just as Thando began introducing Liefling.

KRUGER's helicopter landed on the rooftop heliport of Arm, Protect & Secure just as Liefling prepared to speak. Even before its single engine had come to a complete stop, Kruger was already out the door.

He hurried across the concrete rooftop, down a flight of winding stairs and within minutes reached his office at the end of a long, narrow corridor. Inside he found Botha, Viljoen and Barnard seated around the shiny mahogany conference table. Their impassive faces, along with their dark suits, gave them the look of attendants at a funeral wake.

"Has it begun yet?" Kruger asked, hurriedly hanging his coat on a brass hook behind the thick mahogany door.

"You're just in time," Viljoen replied, raising a pair of reptilian eyes up to the 27-inch TV perched above a glass cabinet filled with the latest surveillance and security equipment offered by the firm. His voice sounded edgy, scared. "Your stepdaughter is about to speak."

"Well, let's hear what the kaffir-lover has to say," Kruger said. He leaned back in his burgundy leather chair, propped his black wingtips on the edge of the table, and fixed his eyes on Thando as she introduced Liefling.

FREDA stretched languidly on a lounge chair, resting. She'd just finished her daily lap swim in the chateau's heated indoor pool. A copy of *Long*

Walk to Freedom, Nelson Mandela's remarkable autobiography, lay open on the glass-topped end table beside her. She'd spent the morning making final preparations for the braai on Sunday. Following a quick lunch at *De Volkombuis* with a friend from her university days, she'd returned home and swum laps for forty-five minutes.

Now she was waiting for Kruger. He'd called her earlier in the day from Sun City and said that he'd be arriving late that afternoon. He'd promised her they would enjoy a quiet candlelight dinner to celebrate his selling the firm to the South American investors. A she dozed on the lounge chair, listening to the lulling sounds of water lapping softly against the side of the pool, her thoughts turned to her life as mistress of Kruger's magnificent estate.

Everything seemed like a fairy tale. Though they'd been married for almost two months, she was still unaccustomed to such a luxurious and pampered lifestyle.

She couldn't help contrasting her present marriage with her last. After Christiaan had repudiated apartheid, they'd tumbled from the ranks of the upper middle-class to the near destitute. They'd been evicted from their comfortable ten-room church-owned home, which had come with a pool, a large garden and two fulltime maids and a gardener. Their parents had disinherited them both. No white churches, not even the few liberal ones sympathetic to his plight, dared hire Christiaan, largely out of fear of being harassed by BOSS, the Bureau of State Security, for giving succor to someone deemed a traitor by the all-powerful Broederbond.

Without any significant savings or source of income, Christiaan and his family would have been rendered homeless if they had not received help from an unlikely source. The congregation of a black church in Alexandra, moved by Christiaan's courage, had invited him to become its interim pastor. The church's activist pastor had recently been detained indefinitely without trial under the Suppression of Terrorism Act for leading a march to protest the massacre of schoolchildren following the June 16 Soweto Uprising. The church had offered Christiaan a modest salary and the use of its two-bedroom manse.

Freda recalled how Christiaan, despite her vehement opposition, had accepted the offer. But when Christiaan had applied to the authorities for permission to move to Alexandra, he'd received a bizarre response. He was told that even though the government occasionally made exceptions to the Group Areas Act in order to accommodate the needs of religious institutions, the only way he and his family could be permitted to live in a non-white area would be if they applied to be reclassified as Coloreds.

Freda shuddered when she recalled that Christiaan had been prepared to accept such a degrading condition, which was clearly instigated by the Broederbond and meant to humiliate and punish him. She'd threatened to divorce him rather than be reclassified as Colored. Their marriage was saved by the timely generosity of an anonymous donor, who offered to purchase for Christiaan and his family a three-bedroom house -- with no pool and definitely no servants -- in the working class neighborhood of Lombardy East.

Freda recalled how, in her new home, she had been forced to learn to cook, clean and wash laundry because they couldn't even afford a maid. They had used Christiaan's meager earnings as interim pastor to enroll Liefling at a multiracial private school in Sandton because free Afrikaner public schools in the area had refused to let her enroll, on orders from the Broederbond. Between raising Liefling, housekeeping, adjusting to a radically different lifestyle and coping with severe depression, Freda had had little time for anything else.

Now here she was, mistress of a mansion with twenty bedrooms, six full-time maids a butler and four gardeners. She had all the time in the world to play tennis, go shopping, read, write letters to friends, attend book-club luncheons, get massages, facials, manicures, or simply relax, as she was now doing.

It's all a dream, she thought, fluttering her eyelids open and staring at the giant tropical plants surrounding the heated pool, from whose surface a thin mist of steam was rising. *I'll wake up someday and find it all gone. Just like Cinderella.*

Freda's reverie was suddenly disturbed by a familiar voice. She turned and noticed that Emma, one of her Colored maids, was standing beside the lounge chair. Freda wondered how long she'd been standing there, afraid of disturbing "Madam's" afternoon nap.

It will take the maids some time to realize that I'm not like other madams, Freda thought. *It's not always necessary for them to be this deferential. I won't snap at them if they act too familiar.*

"What's the matter, Emma?" Freda asked in a kindly voice.

"Mrs. Uys is on the phone, Madam," Emma said in Afrikaans, the mother tongue of South Africa's Coloreds. "I told her you were taking a nap but she insisted I wake you. I'm so sorry to disturb – "

"No need to apologize. Let me talk to her."

Emma handed Freda the black cordless phone, then left.

Freda pressed the receiver to her ear. "Hi Tina. This is Freda."

"Are you near a TV?" Tina asked excitedly.

"No. Is *Felicia* on?"

Felicia was the most-popular talk show in the country, hosted by Felicia Mabuza, a black woman who'd been called South Africa's *Oprah*.

"Not yet. But get to a TV quickly. Your daughter is in Alexandra about to give a press conference."

"What?""

"I was surfing the channels waiting for *Felicia* to start when all of a sudden I saw Liefling. I'm looking at her right now. She's sitting behind the podium, next to a man named David Schneider."

"Did you say David Schneider?" Freda tossed aside her damp towel and rose from the lounge chair.

"Ja. Do you know him?"

"Ja. Who else is there?"

"The room is packed with reporters with cameras and microphones. There are also several TV crews. There's a black woman named Thando Khosa at the podium now, and she's introducing Liefling."

"Oh, my God!" Freda cried, a chill running down her spine. "She's done it! She's done it!"

"Done what?" Tina asked.

"I'll tell you all about it later," Freda said, breathless. "Can you please come over?"

"What's wrong, Freda?"

"Just come over, please. And hurry." Freda grabbed her robe and slipped it on as she ran to TV in the living room.

23 THANDO said, "Thank you all for coming on such short notice." Her friendly brown eyes beamed with evident satisfaction at the huge media turnout. She couldn't remember ever seeing this many journalists attending a press conference in Alexandra, except when President Nelson Mandela had visited the township shortly after his release from twenty-seven years in prison in 1990.

"Since the TRC began holding hearings into human rights abuses committed during the apartheid era, it has sharply divided South Africans," Thando said in a confident, warm voice, facing the sea of attentive journalists. "Some people accuse the Commission of persecuting former SADF members. On the other hand, there are those who charge the Commission with letting torturers and murderers off the hook. But a few brave people have risen above these divisions to embrace a higher standard. That standard calls for reconciliation and forgiveness, yes, but it also calls for justice. Liefling Malan is one of the brave ones."

Liefling felt overwhelmed with gratitude toward her friend and her kind words. David reached out and patted Liefling's hand.

Thando continued. "Liefling is a very special human being. When I first met her four months ago I immediately sensed that she is filled with what Africans call Ubuntu – that special quality that is at the core of our humanity, whether we are black or white, Jew or Gentile, Gay or Straight. She is very much like her late father, Christiaan Malan, who was one of the heroes of the liberation struggle and was murdered her in Alexandra while helping the families of victims of death squads."

Thando paused, looked back at Liefling and smiled.

"Liefling has picked up where her father left off," she went on, her voice growing more passionate. "She gave up a lucrative job to start the Ubuntu

Resource Center at a time when few lawyers – black or white – are interested in representing the poor. She's been vilified as a traitor by many whites for seeking justice for the victims of apartheid. She's received countless death threats. Her courage and selflessness, ladies and gentlemen, prove that the struggle for justice has little to do with the color of one's skin. It has everything to do with the color of one's heart -- one's Ubuntu."

Cameras clicked and paper rustled as reporters captured Thando's intense face and jotted down every one of her heartfelt words.

She continued. "It's now my deepest pleasure to introduce to you Liefling Malan, a dear friend and a comrade for justice, who will tell you about our first major lawsuit."

Liefling blinked back tears, deeply moved by Thando's eloquent introduction. She reached under her chair and retrieved a thin, black folder. Her legs suddenly felt weak as she rose, unsure if she was doing the right thing. She didn't want to hurt her mother. Then she thought of Thando's touching words.

I can't let her down, Liefling vowed. *I can't let my clients down. Mom, please forgive me.*

She took a deep breath and confidently walked toward the cluster of microphones, determined to do the right thing, whatever the cost.

FREDA slumped at the edge of a beige leather sofa in front of the 52-inch Toshiba projection TV in the living room. Though touched by Thando's eloquent introduction of her daughter, Freda kept wringing her hands and pursing her lips. Her heart raced as she watched Liefling rise and walk toward the cluster of microphones.

"Please don't do it, sweetie," she murmured frantically. "Please don't do it."

GIDEON watched breathlessly as Liefling headed for the microphones. He fidgeted nervously with his can of Fanta.

LIEFLING gave Thando a hug and whispered, "Thanks for those very kinds words."

"Be strong, girlfriend," Thando whispered back, then sat down next to David.

Be strong, be strong, Liefling chanted inwardly as she stood before the cluster of microphones and looked out at the sea of expectant faces.

With slightly trembling fingers she unfolded the black folder and placed it in the middle of the podium. She pushed her neatly trimmed blonde bangs away from her eyes and adjusted the skewed lapel of her black Armani pinstriped suit, which was nicely complemented by a silk blouse and a scarf with the gold, green, black and white colors of the new South African flag.

"I'd like to join Thando in thanking you all for coming on such short notice," she said slowly, almost hesitantly, in a soft English accent with traces of Afrikaans. "I called the press conference to announce that at nine o'clock this morning, after a great deal of soul-searching, I filed a lawsuit for three billion rands at the Johannesburg Magistrate Court against my stepfather, General Magnus Kruger. The lawsuit charges him with operating a death squad between 1986 and 1993, which tortured and murdered dozens of anti-apartheid activists and MK guerillas and firebombed scores of houses, schools and churches."

There were audible gasps across the room. Reporters scribbled and cameras clicked furiously.

FREDA cried out, "Oh, my God!" then buried her face in her hands and wept.

KRUGER bellowed, "The fucking kaffir-loving bitch!" He slammed his fist on the conference table and glared with hate-filled eyes at Liefling's image filling the TV screen.

LIEFLING said, "The decision to file the lawsuit was the toughest I've ever made in my life. But I gave my stepfather plenty of opportunity to come clean before the TRC after the *Mail & Guardian* exposed him as a high-ranking member of the CCB. He's repeatedly refused."

She paused and took a deep breath. Her stomach was churning, but she tried her best to remain calm and focused. She was aware that every word she uttered, and every gesture she made, were being noted and conveyed to millions of listeners and viewers across the country and around the world. Even reporters from CNN and the BBC were covering the sensational press conference.

"Many will question my motives for suing my stepfather," she continued, her voice gaining in confidence with each sentence. "Let me make it clear that I have nothing against his politics. There are a lot of *verkramptes* who are devoted to the new South Africa. Neither is the lawsuit an indictment of the South African Defense Force. There were many men and women who performed their duty with honor and restraint, even while defending an indefensible system."

Liefling flipped a page.

"I filed the lawsuit solely because of my obligation to the grieving families of the victims of CCB death squads. I want to help them find out what happened to their loved ones. I want to help them find their bodies so they can be properly buried. And if the truth about death squads is exposed, then the integrity of the spirit of Ubuntu, which is crucial for healing our divided land, will be upheld. As my late father said, those who tortured and murdered in the name of apartheid must be held accountable. If they are not, justice will have miscarried. And without justice, there can be no reconciliation or respect for the rule of law in the new South Africa."

Again Liefling paused. This time for dramatic effect.

"But let me stress this very important point. The lawsuit is wholly consistent with the TRC's mission. My stepfather can stop it from going to trial," she said, staring straight into the TV camera, as if she knew Kruger was watching. "All he has to do is to agree to tell the TRC everything about his role in the CCB. If he does, not only will I drop the lawsuit, but if he's committed any crimes, he'll be eligible for amnesty for confessing the truth. But if he doesn't change his mind and testify before the TRC, then I'm determined to prosecute the lawsuit, come what may. I'm now ready to answer your questions."

Thando and David looked at each other and smiled. Liefling's remarks, despite her nervousness and conflicted emotions, were concise, clear, to the point and superbly delivered. Both marveled at her enormous courage.

GIDEON couldn't believe what he'd just heard from Liefling's mouth. Eyes glued to the TV as Liefling took questions from reporters, he thought, *I never thought she had the courage to file a lawsuit in behalf of black people. Especially against her own stepfather -- one of the most powerful men in South Africa.*

Gideon recalled Thando's eloquent introduction of Liefling, his father's impressions of her, and his own impression of her during the dinner.

She is indeed a special human being, Gideon thought. *She's one of the few white people I can honestly say has Ubuntu.*

Gideon then thought about the call he'd made to David two nights ago. *I'm glad I suggested the press conference. Now that Kruger has been exposed, it's up to me to help convict him.*

	LIEFLING pointed a finger at the reporter from *The Star*, Johannesburg's leading English-speaking daily, to start off the Q & A.
24	

"How many families are involved in the lawsuit?" asked the reporter.

"Two hundred," Liefling said.

"Is it true that all of them are from Alexandra?" asked a reporter from the *Alexandra Times*.

"Ja."

"Why only Alexandra when there are victims of death squads all over South Africa?" asked a reporter from the *Sowetan*, the country's largest black newspaper.

"The center has limited resources. We can't represent everyone."

"What's the name of the CCB death squad you're accusing General Kruger of operating?" asked a reporter from *Die Burger*, an Afrikaans daily that was the National Party's mouthpiece during the apartheid era.

"It was code-named Thathe Vondo."

"Do you know who, besides your stepfather, belonged to it?" the reporter from *Die Burger* followed up.

"It was made up of about fifty policemen and farmers," Liefling said. "And it operated out of a remote bushveld camp in Venda."

"You're leveling very serious charges against General Kruger," said a reporter from the *Cape Argus*. "Do you have any witnesses?"

"Ja," Liefling said. "Several members of the Thathe Vondo death squad have contacted me and offered to testify against General Kruger if I'll help them apply for amnesty before next week's deadline."

"Will you help them?"

"Ja. And I'll do my best to represent them."

"What are their names?" asked a reporter from CNN.

"I cannot divulge them at the moment," Liefling said. "It might endanger their lives."

"Are they black or white?" asked a reporter from the BBC.

"They're Afrikaner."

"How many are they?"

"More than one."

"Is that all the evidence you have?"

"No. David and Thando are working around the clock gathering affidavits from the families of anti-apartheid activists and MK guerillas who were tortured and killed by the Thathe Vondo death squad. We intend to use the affidavits to corroborate the testimony of our witnesses."

"How will the lawsuit affect your relationship with your mother?" asked a reporter from SABC TV. "Especially because she recently got married to General Kruger."

The question Liefling had dreaded caught her somewhat off-guard, even though she'd expected it. For several moments she said nothing. When she finally spoke, her hands clutching the podium to steady herself, her voice trembled a bit.

"I love my mother very much," she said, staring straight at the camera, for she had a feeling that her mother was watching. "She suffered a lot after my father started speaking out against apartheid. And after he was killed, she sacrificed a great deal to make sure I became educated. Without her I'd never have become a lawyer. That's why it wasn't easy for me to file the lawsuit against someone she deeply loves. The lawsuit was a last resort. If my stepfather agrees tomorrow to appear before the TRC and confess the truth about his role in the CCB, I'll drop it. I've also contacted Bishop Tutu, in the hope that he can convince Kruger to testify. But if Kruger won't, then I'm determined to see to it that justice is done. I can only hope that my mother understands that I didn't file the lawsuit to hurt her in any way. I love her very much. I filed it because it's the right thing to do."

Liefling's eyes suddenly grew misty. Noticing that her friend was on the verge of tears, Thando deftly stepped to the mike. She wrapped her arm around her friend's shoulder and said, "Liefling has had a long and emotional day, ladies and gentlemen. David will be more than glad to answer the rest of your questions."

Thando hustled Liefling out of the conference room into an adjacent office. David went to the podium and fielded further questions.

*****

GIDEON watched Liefling being led away from the podium by Thando as photographers captured the scene. *She'll definitely need me,* he thought. *But can I risk death in order to help her convict Kruger?*

Gideon turned from the TV and studied a gallery of framed black-and-white photographs on the far wall. The first photo showed him beaming as he shook hands with his hero, Nelson Mandela, the day the President presented him with a plaque for being named Alexandra's Teacher-of-the-Year. He'd won the honor two previous times, and was a strong contender again this year - his twelfth teaching at Bovet.

Next to the Mandela photo was a framed certificate from the Sandton City Rotary Club for a program Gideon had begun three years ago to educate students about the dangers of drugs. The centerpiece of the gallery was a grainy black-and-white photo of his father as a young man. Makhado was resplendently dressed in his warrior garb, and his right foot rested on the neck of a dead male lion. Lutheran missionaries had taken the photo shortly after he'd killed the lion, a man-eater that had been terrorizing villagers for some time and was responsible for mauling three women on their way to church.

I wish I were as brave as you, Baba, Gideon thought, recalling how his father had rescued Liefling from armed carjackers. *You never flinch in the face of danger.*

Gideon remembered his plan to go to Venda on Sunday to see his father. His prayer was to somehow stay alive between now and then. He knew that, as soon as the press conference was over, maybe even before, Kruger and his henchmen would be working overtime trying to find out who was planning to expose them. He was living on borrowed time.

He reached for his large brown briefcase and snapped it open. He took out two thick bound notebooks with black vinyl covers and placed them on the coffee table.

As he re-read portions of the diaries he'd secretly kept as an askari, it occurred to him that he'd forgotten something very important. Why not contact the remaining askari and persuaded him to also testify against Kruger? The testimony of two would surely be better than one. Also, should anything happen to Gideon, the other askari would be around to testify. Gideon liked the idea so much he immediately picked up the phone. He was about to dial the other askari's number when a thought made him freeze.

KRUGER snapped, "I've seen enough!"

Viljoen promptly turned off the TV.

Kruger rose abruptly and violently shoved back his chair. Eyes ablaze with fury, he began pacing the length of the office.

Viljoen, Barnard and Botha followed his movements with nervous eyes as he strode across the room. The three men had been the nucleus of his CCB death squad, and now held high-ranking positions in his security firm and within The Silent Brotherhood of Afrikaner Patriots.

Seated on the left side of the conference table was the fifty-six-year old Viljoen, the firm's strategic planner and head of its Northern Transvaal offices, which were located in the Venda town of Louis Trichardt. Before joining Kruger's death squad, Viljoen had been a police brigadier in Venda, where he'd overseen the brutal crackdown on student-led protests by the dreaded Venda police during the late 1970s and early 1980s.

Kruger had recruited Viljoen for his extensive connections with corrupt homeland officials, whose cooperation he'd needed to pacify rural communities sympathetic to ANC and PAC guerillas infiltrating into South Africa from Zimbabwe and Mozambique. Viljoen had been nicknamed "The Electrician" by fellow death squad members because he loved using electric shock to extract confessions from reluctant prisoners during interrogations. He was divorced from his wife of twenty-five years, whom he began battering shortly after joining Kruger's death squad. She had custody of their four children, and he was saddled with steep alimony payments, which he loathed to pay, despite the fact that he was now a millionaire.

Next to Viljoen sat the fifty-four-year old Barnard, the firm's chief of personnel. The twice married but childless Barnard was a failed farmer. He used to own a tea plantation in the former Shangaan homeland of Gazankulu. After it went under in 1972 he became, successively, a mercenary in Rhodesia, a big-game hunter and a gunrunner to Renamo rebels fighting the Marxist Mozambican government during that country's bloody and protracted civil war. In 1982 he'd joined the National Intelligence Service, one of the apartheid regime's most violent units. Kruger had recruited him mainly for his tracking abilities and his intimate knowledge of the cultures of the Venda and Shangaan tribes, whose languages he spoke fluently, and whose homelands abutted each other.

Opposite Barnard sat Botha, the firm's director of communications. At forty-six he was the youngest of the four men and had been Kruger's right-hand man since his days as head of the security branch at John Vorster Square. A former member of the fearsome *Koevoet* counterinsurgency unit of the SADF, Botha was an extravagant playboy with the looks of a matinee idol: chiseled body, blond hair and Paul Newman-like blue eyes. But the good looks masked a ruthless and sadistic streak fueled by a long-simmering hatred against those connected with the gruesome killing of his father in Soweto back in 1976.

Kruger stopped and turned to look at the three men. He could tell they were deeply concerned about the possibility of being exposed.

They're waiting for me to outline a plan to prevent such a possibility, he thought. *I can't let them down.*

Kruger resumed pacing. He came to a stop before the large window. Hands clasped behind his back, he gazed down at Commissioner Street, one of the main thoroughfares snaking between the skyscrapers of downtown Johannesburg. Its narrow sidewalks were bustling with hawkers, mostly foreign blacks from as far away as Nigeria, Uganda and Ethiopia, who'd been lured to South Africa by the opportunity to prosper in the new democracy, legally and illegally.

Swarms of harried black commuters jostled their way past the vendors. They were hurrying to squeeze into overcrowded trains headed for the South Western Townships, which lay beyond the mine dumps yellowed by the cyanide used in gold extraction. The townships made up the bleak urban sprawl better-known worldwide by its acronym SOWETO.

Rush-hour traffic on Commissioner was a pandemonium of honking cars and taxis. From time to time flying squad cars from the Johannesburg anti-hijacking unit raced past with screaming sirens, on their way to the latest carjacking, robbery or shooting.

Deep in thought, Kruger was oblivious to all the hubbub. Questions besieged his mind. How did Liefling find out about the existence of the Thathe Vondo death squad? How much did she know? Were his men really planning to squeal or was she bluffing?

There was no doubt that if the lawsuit went to trial, there could be no deal with the Cali Cartel. And until and unless he had the money, he couldn't lay the necessary groundwork for launching the Fourth Boer Revolution. And time was running out.

Suddenly a maxim from *The Art of War* flashed across his harried mind: *When standing on desperate ground, fight.*

It was clear to Kruger that his situation was desperate. There was only one way he knew how to fight: he had to completely destroy whatever threatened him and the survival of the *Volk*.

He pondered ways to kill Liefling.

He thought back to the days when he was head of the security branch at John Vorster Square. With a touch of nostalgia, he recalled how easy it had been back then to eliminate his enemies. All he had to do was to arrest them under the catchall Suppression of Terrorism and Communism Act and bring them to the soundproof, off-limits room on the 10th floor of the dreaded police headquarters. There he'd torture them into signing "confessions" that they were ANC and PAC terrorists seeking the violent overthrow of the apartheid state on orders from Moscow, Peking and Havana. He'd then present these "confessions" as "evidence" against them in court to secure a death sentence from a sympathetic judge like Prinsloo. If anyone died during torture, as frequently happened, Kruger had no problem coming up with a suitable cover-up.

Coroners, witnesses and judges -- part of the vast and secretive network of *Baaskap* defenders -- would be rounded up. They would back up bogus police reports stating that victims had slipped and broken their necks while taking showers; had hung themselves by their shoe laces and belts; had rammed their heads against brick walls while being restrained; had suffered epileptic seizures induced by an overdose of drugs smuggled to them by their liberal lawyers; or had jumped out of the 10th floor window to their deaths on the pavement below in a desperate act of martyrdom.

Those were the days, Kruger thought. *Back then, I would have swiftly dealt with the fucking kaffir-lover. And no one would have traced her death to me.*

But apartheid was gone. With it had gone the vast Gestapo-like security apparatus built by John Vorster, Kruger's idol and mentor, with the intent of investing guardians of *Baaskap* with the absolute power they needed to eliminate their enemies and cover it up completely.

I must find a way to stop the kaffir-lover before its too late, Kruger thought, staring at John Vorster Square. *I'll never let her derail the Fourth Boer Revolution. Never. Not when I've come this far.*

25

MAKHADO, perspiring, drove the final nail into the roof. He wiped beads of sweat from his brow with the back of his hand and took a deep breath. At last he was done repairing the *Molwareng Sky Bed*, a hut on stilts with a kitchen, built well above the ground and overlooking a water hole. It would enable visitors to the private game reserve to have an excellent view of the "big five" animals: lions, elephants, leopards, buffaloes and rhinos.

It had taken him more than three hours to repair the hut, which had suffered serious water damage from a leaky roof during the off season. He wished Viljoen hadn't been such a miser, and had agreed to his suggestion that they install a new roof before the rainy season.

But rich people are often stingy, Makhado thought as he took a sip of water from a plastic bottle.

After gathering his tools, he climbed down from the roof and walked back to the private game reserve's main visitor center. It was about three miles away from the hut, and the tropical afternoon sun was torrid. Yet Makhado was so fit that, though he was two months shy of his sixty-fifth birthday, he not only didn't feel the effects of the humid heat, but his pace was so rapid that he reached the center in less time than it would have taken a man half his age. It was about four-thirty, almost time to leave.

Makhado headed straight for the main lodge where the ten Venda women usually gathered after completing their chores. Upon entering, he found the women crowded around a large color TV. They were wearing colorful *mucheka* dresses and their heads were covered with skillfully tied *doeks*. Their arms and legs were adorned with copper and silver bracelets. Most of the women wore no shoes – they couldn't afford them. The women had just finished cleaning the lodges, chalets and Venda-style huts, along with washing and ironing the linen and scrubbing the pots and pans in the huge kitchen.

Watching TV was a luxury these poor women -- who ranged in age from sixteen to sixty -- never enjoyed at their homes. Unlike Makhado, who had a small color TV that Gideon had bought him two years ago and was powered by a generator, most of the women couldn't even afford a radio.

So whenever Viljoen was away, Makhado let the women watch a little TV. It was one of the few joys they had in a life of perpetual toil and child bearing and rearing, a life about which they seldom complained.

"*Va kho vona mini* (What are you watching)?" Makhado asked in Venda as soon as he entered the lodge. He marveled at how spotlessly clean it was. Everything in it had been dusted and polished, including the blades of the two ceiling fans hanging from the vaulted ceiling.

"We wanted to watch *Felicia*," said Beauty. "But the show hasn't begun yet. So we were watching a press conference that's taking place in Alexandra."

"Alexandra?" Makhado said, curious. He put his toolbox down on the shiny hardwood floor.

"Ja," Beauty said. "Isn't that where your son Gideon lives?"

"It is."

Makhado glanced at the TV and felt a jolt of recognition. There on the screen was Liefling, the woman he'd rescued from hijackers nearly four months ago, being led away from the podium, almost in tears.

"What happened to her?" he asked in a concerned voice, sitting down on a barstool.

"Poor thing," Beauty said in a sorrowful voice. "She's just filed a lawsuit against a death squad leader who happens to be married to her mother. She must love her mother very much, for when a reporter asked her what effect the lawsuit would have on their relationship, she broke down. What a brave young woman, though. I never thought I'd live to see a white person sacrifice her own happiness for black people. She's a very special person."

She is indeed, Makhado thought.

SHAKA, the second askari, watched Liefling's press conference with great interest. Like Gideon, Shaka was a black man, about six feet two inches tall, powerfully built, and wore an expensive Italian-made suit and a pair of perfectly round designer glasses. The glasses gave him a scholarly air, even though he was one of the CCB's most ruthless assassins. He was sitting in the expensively furnished den of a huge brick house in Thohoyandou, the former capital of the defunct Venda homeland.

Shaka was completely baffled as to how Liefling had obtained such specific details about the Thathe Vondo death squad. Such information could only have come from someone on the inside. Who? At first Shaka was inclined to believe that the information had indeed been provided by the Afrikaner members of the Thathe Vondo death squad who were about to squeal. But he had later dismissed the idea when he recalled how racist the Afrikaners members of the Thathe Vondo death squad were. They were unlikely to betray Kruger, the man who'd done them many favors after apartheid ended. And, most important, they still believed in *Baaskap*.

Shaka actually smiled when he finally guessed who could have provided Liefling with the information. He marveled at Gideon's courage. But he also knew that by breaking the code of silence to expose the Thathe Vondo death squad, Gideon had signed his death warrant, and that he, Shaka, would be ordered to kill him, just as he'd been ordered to kill all the other askaris who'd squealed.

As Shaka watched Liefling's press conference, he waited for the call from his control. He wondered if the orders would be that he only kill Gideon, or if Liefling, David and Thando would have to be killed too, for knowing too much.

LIEFLING and Thando entered the small office adjacent to the conference room.

"Sorry I became emotional," Liefling said.

"You wouldn't be human if you hadn't," Thando said comfortingly. "I know how close you are to your mom."

Doris, a large black woman with two missing front teeth sat behind a scratched and cluttered desk. Doris was busy answering the phone, which had been ringing off the hook since the press conference began.

From her cheery disposition, one could hardly tell that Doris was a survivor of spousal abuse. Only her missing teeth attested to the fact that her unemployed and alcoholic husband had used her as a punching bag. Thando had intervened and he was now in jail.

Doris looked up when Liefling and Thando entered.

"Hold on, Mrs. Kruger," Doris said cheerily into the phone. "She just walked in." Turning to Liefling she said, "Your mom's on line one."

Liefling dreaded taking the call. "She's calling about the lawsuit," she murmured to Thando. "She's probably furious."

"Didn't you tell her about it yesterday?" Thando asked.

"I meant to," Liefling said, heading for the phone on a small side table near the faded sofa by the open window. "But when I called her I couldn't bring myself to mention the lawsuit."

"Why not?"

"She would have begged me not to file it. And I wouldn't have had the strength to say no."

"Now what are you going to do?"

"Talk to her I guess."

Liefling took a deep breath, picked up the phone and in as calm as a voice as she could muster under the circumstances, she said, "Hi, Mom."

FREDA, barely able to contain her anger, demanded fiercely, "Why did you do it?"

Her breath came in spurts as, cordless phone in hand, she paced up and down the eclectically furnished living room with its Italian leather sofas, oriental statues, thick Persian rugs and contemporary paintings. The TV was on but the sound was muted.

"I had to, Mom," Liefling said softly, after a brief pause.

"Had to? And you didn't even have the decency to tell me yesterday when you called?"

"I'd planned to. I'm sorry."

"Sorry!" Freda exploded. "Fine thing to say you're sorry after telling the whole goddamn world that my husband is a torturer and a murderer! Is this how you repay me for all I've done for you?"

"He left me no choice."

"No choice! What choice did you bloody want? Did you even think of what this would do to my marriage? Don't you care about my happiness?"

"Of course I do."

"You sure have a strange way of expressing it."

"Magnus can stop the lawsuit from going to trial, you know."

"How?"

"By testifying before the TRC."

"Why should he?" Freda said, her voice rising, almost shrill. "Didn't he tell you he did nothing wrong?"

There was a long and awkward pause. Freda continued pacing. She came to an abrupt stop in front of the large bay window overlooking a spectacularly landscaped garden overshadowed by majestic blue-gray Mountains.

"Did David put you up to this?" Freda demanded.

"David didn't put me up to anything," Liefling said defensively. "I filed the lawsuit based on the facts."

"What facts? I know Magnus, Liefling. He may have been part of the CCB, but he'd never authorize the torture and murder of innocent human beings. If he'd done that, do you think I'd have married him? What do you take me for?"

"But, Mom, when you married him you knew nothing about his years in the CCB," Liefling countered. "The CCB was a secretive organization. It sponsored death squads that tortured and killed scores of innocent men and women. How could Magnus have been highly placed in the organization and not have known about its activities?"

Freda, tears in her eyes, was too angry and confused to reply. Under normal circumstances she would have followed her daughter's reasoning. She would have understood that there was more to apartheid and those who'd served it than met the eye. She would have remembered her own persecution by nameless and faceless instruments of its terror within BOSS, who'd poisoned her pets, tapped her phones, called her in the middle of the night to harass her psychologically in an attempt to force her to divorce Christiaan or commit suicide.

She would have remembered the harrowing testimony that had emerged from countless TRC hearings, testimony that had revealed that people like her husband, who on the surface seemed normal and personable and even charming, had, in secret and when vested with unrestrained powers, committed abominable crimes that had led most of the world to declare apartheid a crime against humanity and to liken its enforcers to Nazis.

But Freda recalled none of this. All she was thinking about was the effect of her daughter's lawsuit on her marriage to a man she absolutely adored, a man who had smoothed the way toward her once more becoming a respectable member of the tightly-knit Afrikaner community.

If the lawsuit wrecked her marriage she was certain she couldn't endure the disgrace and the ostracism from the Afrikaner community that was sure to follow. Not after what she went through following Christiaan's rejection of apartheid.

And now, more than ever, she needed to belong to that community. It provided her with an anchor. She needed the Afrikaner culture and traditions she'd grown up with to reassure her that all was well amid the bewildering changes taking place in the new South Africa. Particularly at a time when she was disillusioned by what had followed the destruction of apartheid. She'd hoped that in the new South Africa racism and violence would be a thing of the past, that a black government would ameliorate the condition of the impoverished masses and bring about racial healing and reconciliation –

ideals for which her first husband had sacrificed his life.

How wrong she had been! Violence and crime was endemic. Racism of a different kind had reared its ugly head. Whites were now discriminated against in jobs and in schools. Even liberals like herself found themselves suspect and called racist by black militants. And instead of improving, the lot of poor blacks had worsened in many cases, as corruption and nepotism siphoned public resources that should have been earmarked for their desperate needs.

In such a maelstrom, Kruger stood like a rock: confident, steadfast, strong, wealthy and, above all, a proud Afrikaner. She wasn't about to let anyone destroy her marriage to such a man.

As if reading her mother's mind, Liefling said, "I know what you went through, Mom. And I know what Kruger has done for you. He's made your life comfortable and has given you respectability. I know you're worried about your marriage. But think of what Dad sacrificed his life for."

"Don't tell me about your father," Freda snapped. "Not after the hell I endured following what he did."

"Then think of the victims of apartheid. Think of the families who lost loved ones to death squads. Think of the hundreds of children who've been orphaned. You yourself once worked with those children in Alexandra. You know of their heavy loss. You felt their pain. You worked long and hard to help them rebuild their shattered Ubuntu. And they responded because you showed them you cared. Is it too much to ask Magnus to shed some light on what happened to their fathers and mothers?"

It took Freda a while to respond. She *was* thinking of those orphaned children with their wide smiles and bright eyes, with such a love for life, despite having witnessed horrors that would have harrowed adult souls.

In a voice wrung by anguish, Freda said, "But where's the proof that Magnus knows about death squads, Liefling? All you said at the press conference was that several policemen are planning to come forward and implicate him. Why did you refuse to give their names?"

Liefling found it difficult to lie to her mother. She wondered if she should confess the truth about having made up the story about there being policemen who planned to implicate Kruger in secret testimony.

If I tell her the truth, Liefling thought, *Kruger will certainly end up knowing about it.*

Suddenly an idea occurred to Liefling. If she told Freda the truth, and Freda told Kruger, then it might make him complacent. He might stop searching for informers within the Thathe Vondo death squad, a search that, she was certain, would expose their mystery witness. She didn't know if the idea would work. Accustomed to taking chances, she was willing to give it a try.

"Mom, can you keep a secret?"

"What secret?"

"I have no witnesses against Magnus."

"What!"

"I made up the story about several members of the Thathe Vondo death squad having approached me offering to testify against Magnus. I said it because I want to pressure him to testify. For your sake, I don't want to drag him to court."

The truth had exactly the opposite effect on Freda.

"How dare you file a frivolous lawsuit against my husband!" she screamed.

"It's not frivolous."

"It is! Didn't you just admit that you lied about having witnesses?"

"But that doesn't change the fact that Magnus knows about death squads."

"Listen to me, Liefling," Freda said in a voice laced with bitterness and desperation. "I'm not going to let you ruin my husband and destroy my marriage with a pack of lies."

"I'm not lying, Mom. Please believe me."

Freda ignored the plea. She was no longer thinking. She was now speaking purely out of anger. "Magnus will never yield to such blackmail. He'll fight you in court. And when he does, I'll fight on his side."

"I'm sorry you feel that way," Liefling said, her voice breaking. "Believe me, I didn't do this to hurt you in any way."

"Sure you didn't," Freda said, then slammed down the phone.

She took a deep breath, collected herself, then went over to the wet bar and poured herself a stiff drink. She normally didn't drink in the afternoon but she felt she needed one. She swallowed it in one gulp.

How dare she file a frivolous lawsuit, Freda thought, pouring herself a second drink. *I'd better tell Magnus.*

Freda drained her second drink, picked up the phone and dialed Kruger's number in Johannesburg.

26 GIDEON, the phone still in his hand, debated whether to make the fateful call. *What if I confide in Shaka and he turns around and betrays me?* He thought.

Gideon remembered how ruthlessly effective an askari Shaka had been. The art of double-crossing had been central to the dirty work he'd done for Kruger. As a turned senior MK officer, he'd passed on to Kruger highly damaging information regarding ANC cells in the townships; he'd given booby-trapped grenades to militant youths clamoring for weapons to fight against apartheid; he'd carried out the assassinations of anti-apartheid activists; and he'd lured dozens of unsuspecting MK guerillas into deadly traps set by the Thathe Vondo death squad.

Gideon thought of another reason not to trust Shaka. Unlike Gideon, Shaka's dirty work for Kruger hadn't ended in 1993 when the Thathe Vondo death squad had disbanded. On the contrary. Under the ANC government, Shaka had been rewarded for his "heroic service" on behalf of the liberation struggle with a cushy job within the reconstituted South African National Police Force. He'd used that position for the benefit of Kruger's security firm by providing it with sensitive intelligence to run its nationwide operations, for which he was paid handsomely.

Gideon pondered this for several moments. He stared at Shaka's number in his open address book. He was convinced there were definite risks in confiding in someone as ruthless and treacherous as Shaka, whose services were for sale to the highest bidder.

Yet somehow he felt that, in this particular matter, Shaka could be trusted. Gideon felt that Shaka had compelling personal reasons to want to see Kruger and his death squad brought to justice. Besides those personal reasons, Gideon felt that Shaka could be trusted because both of them had grown up together. Gideon had moved in with Shaka's family in Alexandra in order to finish high school after his own family was endorsed back to Venda in 1979. They'd been bosom buddies at mountain school and later roommates at the Turfloop, the tribal university apartheid had set up for blacks from the North.

Their bond had been further strengthened after both were detained and tortured by the Venda security forces following the Soweto Uprising for organizing demonstrations calling for the abolition of segregated education and the homeland system.

But would friendship and shared suffering prevail in a situation of such high stakes, where the wrong move meant death? Gideon didn't know the answer. But he was willing to take a chance with Shaka. He prayed that he was right in thinking that his friend was as eager as he was to see Kruger brought to justice.

Gideon slowly dialed Shaka's number.

KRUGER stood by the window. Viljoen and Barnard fidgeted in their seats around the conference table. To ease their nervousness, they poured themselves glasses of whiskey. There was no doubt in their minds that a successful lawsuit would bankrupt the firm and send them all to Pretoria Central prison for the rest of their lives.

Only Botha managed to remain calm. He had faith in Kruger's abilities, particularly when his back was against the wall. Botha had seen those abilities amply demonstrated during their years together at John Vorster Square, and later on in the way Kruger had single-handedly waged a ruthless ten-year war against MK and its key cell in Alexandra.

For largely personal reasons, Viljoen didn't share Botha's confidence in Kruger. Petrified of prison and of being rendered penniless by the lawsuit, he had his own idea about what they should do to save their skins before it was too late. Since Kruger's arrival from Sun City, Viljoen had been meaning to broach the idea but had lacked the courage. The more whiskey he drank, the more courage he felt.

Sufficiently drunk, he puffed on a cigar. After blowing a thin trail of smoke toward the fretted ceiling, he said, "General, don't you think the best way to take care of Liefling's lawsuit is for all of us to apply for amnesty? We still have time, you know. And the government would pay all our legal costs."

Kruger did not reply. His eyes remained fixed on John Vorster Square. Viljoen elaborated on why he thought applying for amnesty was their best option. "The National Reconciliation and Promotion of Unity Act clearly states that anyone who applies for amnesty can never be charged with any crime by the State or sued for human rights abuses by victims or their families. And Liefling has said she'd drop the lawsuit if you agree to testify. What do we have to lose?"

Kruger's chest heaved and his broad shoulders straightened but still he said nothing. He continued staring out the window at John Vorster Square.

This time it was Botha who spoke. His voice dripped with scorn. "I can't bloody fucking believe you said that, Piet," he said indignantly. "Do you mean to tell me we should confess that we firebombed houses, and that we tortured and killed God knows how many kaffir communists and terrorists? You want us to admit that we secretly buried dozens of bodies in mass graves all over the fucking bushveld camp? Is that what you're saying?"

Testily, Viljoen said, "Of course not."

"Then what exactly are you saying?"

"We'd offer sanitized versions of what our unit did. Just like other CCB units have been doing."

"What makes you think the bloody TRC will grant us amnesty if we lie?" retorted Botha, a dismissive sneer on his thin lips. "Don't you know that one of the conditions for amnesty is confessing everything?"

"Who would contradict our sanitized testimony?" Viljoen shot back, glaring at Botha. "There were no witnesses. And every member of the Thathe Vondo death squad will be glad to sign onto a common version of what happened."

"I agree with Viljoen," said Barnard. "Applying for amnesty is our best option."

Kruger had heard enough. Slowly he turned away from the window and faced the three men. A transformation had come over him. His eyes blazed and his nostrils flared. The muscles of his thick neck were corded like ropes. He resembled an enraged bull ready to charge. His expression instantly sent a chill through them.

With deliberate, unhurried steps Kruger walked toward a large oil painting at the far end of the room. Gilt-framed and covering most of the wall, it depicted the treacherous murder of Voortrekker leader Piet Retief by Dingaan, King of the Zulus, on February 8, 1838.

Dingaan, who ten years earlier had treacherously murdered his half brother Shaka, had invited the unsuspecting Retief and his men to his kraal, *Mngugundlovu,* Place of the Great Elephant. The Boers naively believed that Dingaan would finally give them vast tracts of Zulu territory in exchange for a mere 63 cattle and 11 rifles. Apparently not trusting

Dingaan, or thinking him a fool, the Boers brought only the cattle – but not the guns. When they arrived at Mgungundlovu, the cunning Dingaan had requested that the armed Boers leave their guns outside the kraal as a mark of good intentions and join him in toasting their new friendship.

The Boers had fallen for the trap. While his armed warriors were dancing in front of their drunken and carousing guests, Dingaan shouted, *"Bulala Abathakathi!"* (Kill the Wizards!)

Retief and his men were instantly grabbed, tied and dragged up a nearby hill, where their bodies were stoned and mutilated. Shortly thereafter two unsuspecting laagers were attacked by Zulu impis at dawn at a place Afrikaners later called "Weenen" (Weeping). Approximately 500 people, mainly servants, were killed and the Zulu impis seized 25,000 head of cattle and thousands of sheep and horses.

"This," Kruger bellowed, thrusting a finger at the painting, "is why I'll never bow down before kaffirs and ask for forgiveness for what we did."

"But asking for forgiveness isn't a requirement for amnesty, General," Viljoen said, surprising even himself by the quickness of his reply, which was prompted in part by a deep-seated fear of prison, especially after hearing rumors that black prisoners were sodomizing white prisoners as payback for apartheid.

"I don't bloody care," Kruger snapped. He strode back to the table. "If we testify before the bloody TRC we'll be desecrating the memory of our Voortrekker forefathers. We'd be saying that the sacred blood they shed in carving a Vaderland for us out of the Dark Continent was in vain. And never – I repeat, never – will I do that."

He slammed his fist on the table for emphasis, making the drinks and bottles of Scotch wobble.

"Twenty-eight thousand Afrikaner women and children died in British concentration camps when our people fought for their homeland," Kruger continued, breathing heavily. "They included my grandmother and three great aunts. They didn't die in order for us to prostrate ourselves before bloody kaffirs."

He paused and gazed across the room at the credenza behind his massive oak desk. On it were photos of his mother, a British concentration camp survivor, and his two younger sisters.

"Don't any of you ever forget that ours was a righteous struggle," Kruger said sternly, in the tone of a dominee chastising wayward members of the Dutch Reformed Church. "We were fighting for the survival and purity of the Afrikaner race. We were defending the Afrikaner way of life, language, identity and culture. And when we resume the struggle to reclaim our birthright – as soon we shall – the only leaders of the Fourth Boer Revolution will be men who didn't grovel before kaffirs. The choice is yours. Do you want history to number you with the traitors and cowards who sold out the *Volk*, or do you want to be known as Afrikaner patriots who, from the ashes of apartheid, created a new Vaderland?"

There was total silence. Eyes lowered, Viljoen and Barnard puffed furiously on their cigars. The room reeked of acrid tobacco and cigar smoke, overpowering the sweet fragrance from a bouquet of fresh roses, orchids and irises in a blue vase in the middle of the table.

It was Viljoen who broke the silence. "So how do you propose we handle your stepdaughter's lawsuit? If she wins, she'll bankrupt the firm. And without money there won't be any Fourth Boer Revolution. Instead we'll all be rotting in Pretoria Central Prison. And considering what the Thathe Vondo death squad did, I wouldn't be surprised if the ANC brings back the death penalty just for our benefit."

Kruger glared at Viljoen.

"How can she win?" he demanded fiercely.

"You heard what your stepdaughter said about having witnesses," Viljoen said.

"What witnesses?" Kruger shot back. "Didn't I make damn sure that no one we interrogated ever lived to tell about it?"

"I'm not talking about those kinds of witnesses," Viljoen retorted. "I'm talking about members of the Thathe Vondo death squad who are so desperate they've approached your daughter and asked her to help them apply for amnesty before the May 10th deadline. And I don't blame them. Who would pass up such an unbelievable TRC deal? It grants you immunity from any lawsuit forever in return for merely testifying? I'd accept their deal and testify if worse comes to worse."

Viljoen stopped abruptly. He couldn't believe he'd uttered the last statement. Feeling suddenly hot for betraying his latent fear and wish, he hurriedly poured himself a tot of whiskey.

"I see," Kruger said. "So you, too, plan to turn traitor, is that it?"

Viljoen said nothing.

Kruger turned to Barnard. "Are you too planning to turn traitor?"

"Of course not," Barnard said. "And I don't think Viljoen plans to do that either. He's just worried about the lawsuit, that's all. I am too."

"Don't you idiots see she's bluffing?" Kruger said.

"But how can we be sure she is, General?" asked Barnard. "After all, during the press conference she provided specific information that could only have come from an insider. And Viljoen and I talked to several members of the Thathe Vondo death squad when we were in Venda a couple of weeks ago. They are desperate, General. And I can understand why. Unlike us, they have families to consider."

Kruger abruptly returned to his chair at the head of the table. "I never thought I'd recruited a bunch of cowards to fight for the Vaderland," he sneered. "Can't anyone see that the kaffir-lover is bluffing? Of course she has no witnesses. She's simply playing a psychological game with me. She's using the same tactic used by TRC investigators in exposing the policemen who killed Steve Biko."

"Why would she be bluffing, General?" asked Barnard, twirling his cigar between nicotine-stained fingers.

Kruger abruptly looked up. "To make fools like you panic."

"But what if she does have access to evidence against us?" Viljoen ventured to ask. "I sure as hell don't want to spend the rest of my life in prison running from kaffir rapists. I say we apply for amnesty as a preemptive measure. We have everything to gain and nothing to lose."

"I'm very surprised by what a coward you've become, Piet," Kruger said. "Very surprised. You of all people. What happened to your guts, huh? Has liquor and women made you soft? You used to execute dozens of ANC communists and terrorists without so much as blinking an eye. I'm beginning to have serious doubts about putting you in charge of organizing the Boer Army."

"I'm not a coward, General. I just want to make sure nothing derails the Fourth Boer Revolution."

"Nothing will."

"General," said Botha, who'd been silently weighing everything that was being said. "I have a suggestion."

Kruger looked at his right-hand man.

Botha took a sip of his brandy before speaking. "I think you should call a meeting and explain to the men why they're better off not applying for amnesty. It's not logical to expect them to run the risk of being sued and possibly sent to jail when they could apply for amnesty and be immune from prosecution. You need to tell them about the Fourth Boer Revolution. Unless they know and are reassured, they'll think it's every man for himself."

Viljoen and Barnard nodded. Kruger pondered this for a while. "Okay, arrange a meeting with the men as soon as possible."

"For where?"

"The Thathe Vondo private game reserve."

"I can arrange one for this coming Monday," said Viljoen.

Suddenly the telephone rang.

Kruger picked it up and said rather brusquely, "I thought I told you I didn't want to be disturbed, Helena. Who is it?"

"It's a reporter from *The Star*. He wants your reaction to the lawsuit."

"Tell him to contact my lawyer."

Kruger had barely replaced the receiver when it rang again. Frowning, he expected it to be some obnoxious reporter.

"Mrs. Kruger is on the line," Helena said. "I told her you were in an important meeting. She says it's urgent."

27

GIDEON, heart pounding, said to his fellow askari, "Hullo, is that Ndwakhulu?"

"Ja," responded a suspicious voice. "Who's speaking?"

"This is Thanyani. How are you?" Because Gideon and Ndwakhulu had attended the same mountain school, they were required by tradition to address each other by the names they'd been given after being circumcised. Ndwakhulu meant "Big Wars," and Thanyani meant "The Wise One."

"Hi, my friend," Ndwakhulu cried exuberantly. "Howzit? I can't believe you called. I've just been thinking about you."

"Really?"

"Ja. I just finished watching a very interesting press conference. Is that what you're calling about?"

"As a matter of fact, yes."

"I must commend you, Thanyani."

"What for?"

"For exposing Kruger and his death squad."

"I don't know what you're talking about."

"Come on. Who else could have provided Liefling with such specific and damning information about the Thathe Vondo death squad."

"Any of the fifty Afrikaner members."

Ndwakhulu laughed. "No, my friend. I know those fucking Boers. They wouldn't turn on Kruger, even if they are scared shitless. They worship the bastard like a god. Only one of two persons could have provided that information. You or me. And I didn't. But don't worry, I'm with you. You haven't forgotten how much I hate Kruger, have you?"

Gideon's antennas immediately went up. He wondered if he was talking to Ndwakhulu his friend or Shaka the treacherous askari.

"If you hate them why are you still working for them?" Gideon asked.

"I'm working for the bastards so I can find ways to destroy them," Ndwakhulu said. "I'm waiting for the perfect moment. Because of Kruger I'm living in hell, despite the money he's paying me. It can't restore my soul."

How right, Gideon thought, recalling his own inability to find peace because of what he'd done.

"I could have refused to become an askari," Ndwakhulu went on. "Instead I let the bastard turn me into a killing machine against my own people. You can understand, can't you, why I'd want to see him brought to justice?"

The explanation sounded plausible but Gideon didn't know whether or not to believe it. Ndwakhulu was, after all, a cunning askari, superbly skilled in the art of double-talk. That's one reason he'd been so effective as an double agent and had avoided exposure.

"And Liefling's lawsuit is a brilliant way to do that, my friend," Ndwakhulu said. "First we bankrupt the pigs, and then we send them all to jail. I love it."

"Are you really with me?" asked Gideon.

"Of course. Fill me in on what you've done so far."

Again Gideon became suspicious. Why was Ndwakhulu so eager to join forces with him? He had more to lose – a job that paid him six figures, a fine house, a fleet of imported cars and plenty of money in the bank. Should he risk telling Ndwakhulu the rest? Operating purely on instinct, Gideon decided to play it safe.

"What do you want to know?" he asked.

"A couple things. Did you give Liefling your real name?"

"No, and I also spoke in Afrikaans."

"Brilliant stroke," Ndwakhulu said. "That way if the bastards were listening, they'll think you're one of the Boers."

"Do you think they were eavesdropping?"

"You never know. But I'd be very careful if I were about what you say over the phone."

"I was careful."

"Did you give David any concrete evidence?" Ndwakhulu asked.

Gideon thought of the diaries and the items he'd retrieved from the bodies of victims and hidden in a cave. He'd collected the items – ID cards, glasses, shoes, and pieces of clothing – after the executions, when he'd been ordered to clean up the bloody mess. He was about to mention the diaries and the items, but then changed his mind. Something told him to withhold such vital information until he had further proof of Ndwakhulu's trustworthiness.

"No. I told him only what Liefling mentioned at the press conference."

"Good. You never want to reveal your entire hand, my friend, even to allies. Does your wife know that you plan to testify against Kruger?"

"No."

"Very good. You don't want to unnecessarily endanger her life. Well, it seems you've made all the right moves so far. So when can we get together and plan the next move?"

"What about this Sunday?" Gideon said. "I'll be in Venda visiting my folks. I can stop by and see you. Will you be in town?"

"Certainly, my friend. I'll be here waiting for you. In the meantime I'll be gathering my own evidence to help Liefling nail the psychotic bastard."

KRUGER switched on the speakerphone. Botha, Viljoen and Barnard eagerly leaned forward to listen.

"Oh, Magnus," Freda was heard over the speakerphone, sniffling.

"What's wrong, my dear?" Kruger asked in the honeyed voice of his other personality.

"I'm so sorry."

"About what, honey?"

"About the lawsuit."

"Don't worry, dear. Prinsloo will take care it."

"He should have no problem doing that."

"What do you mean?"

"The lawsuit is bogus."

There was a pause. Articulating each word slowly, Kruger said, "Did you say bogus?"

"Ja. I just spoke to Liefling. She confessed to making up that story about policemen who plan to testify that you know about death squads."

It would be an understatement to say that Kruger and his henchmen were stunned by this revelation. They stared at each other and smiled with undisguised relief. Viljoen and Barnard, their faces showing signs of contrition, looked at Kruger with renewed awe. How could he possibly have known that Liefling was bluffing?

"Did you say you spoke to her just now, my dear?" Kruger asked with a self-satisfied smile.

"Ja. I called her in Alexandra."

"And she told you she made up the story about having witnesses?"

"Ja."

"Did she say why?"

"She thinks she can pressure you into testifying."

"I see."

"I don't know what's gotten into Liefling, honey. I thought you two had hit it off so well at the wedding. She danced and joked with you, and after the reception she told me I couldn't have married a better man."

As always, Kruger's Machiavellian mind, sharpened by constantly ruminating over the tactics and stratagems in Sun Tzu's *The Art of War*, was already thinking ahead. It suddenly dawned on him that his wife would make the perfect alibi in a scheme he'd been hatching on how to eliminate Liefling without implicating himself.

"I think I know what made her change her mind about me, my dear," he said smoothly.

"You do?"

"Certainly. Remember what I told you about David?"

"Ja."

"I'm sure he's the one who got Liefling to file the lawsuit. After all, she did so after talking to him. And remember what I told you about his having a vendetta against me?"

"Ja."

"This lawsuit is clearly his way of settling scores. And he's using Liefling to do it because she's gullible."

"I think so too. But I told her in no uncertain terms that if the lawsuit ever goes to trial, I'll be on your side."

"Thank you, my dear. But I doubt very much that it will. Not after what you just told me about Liefling making up witnesses. I wouldn't be surprised if during the preparatory examination (preliminary hearing) the judge dismisses the lawsuit. So don't worry, okay?"

"Okay."

There was a pause.

"Magnus?" Freda said.

"Yes dear?"

"I love you very much. I won't let anything come between us."

"I love you too, Freda. See you tonight."

Kruger switched off the speakerphone. Smiling broadly, he faced Viljoen, Botha and Barnard. "Didn't I tell you the kaffir-lover was bluffing?" Kruger poured himself a drink, downed it in one swig and beamed in apparent satisfaction.

"You were right," Viljoen said apologetically. "I'm sorry I doubted you."

"Me, too," Barnard said.

"I'm not so sure she's bluffing," Botha said, a pensive look on his chiseled face.

Kruger looked up at him. "Explain yourself," he demanded brusquely.

"If Liefling has no witnesses, why would she admit it to your wife, of all people? She certainly knows that Freda is madly in love with you and would tell you in a minute."

Kruger frowned. He hadn't thought of that.

"My feeling is that she told your wife for a reason," Botha said.

"What reason?"

"To throw you off the trail, for one. The kaffir-lover knows that once you believe she doesn't have any witnesses, you'll become complacent."

"Ludwig has a good point, General," Viljoen said, his fear of prison returning. "She must have something up her sleeve."

Kruger was silent for a long while. Finally, he said, looking at Botha, "So what do you propose we do?"

"I suggest we wire Liefling's flat and car, along with David's and Thando's," Botha said. " That way we'll be able to monitor their discussions about the lawsuit. And if there are really any witnesses, we'll be sure to pick that up too and go after them."

"Brilliant," Kruger said. "Get Swanepoel to do the wiring immediately."

Kruger glanced at his gold Rolex. It was almost five. He'd meant to leave at four-thirty. He grabbed his attaché and rose from the table. "I'd better be off. I must be in Stellenbosch by seven. I'm already running late and Freda is expecting me for dinner. See you Monday night at the game reserve."

"Jesus fucking Christ," Botha cried as Barnard and Viljoen followed Kruger in getting up from the table. "What fools we are!"

Everyone turned and stared at Botha.

"Of course," Botha went on, clapping his hands. "Why didn't I think of it before?"

"Think of what?" Kruger demanded. He was impatient to get to the Lear for the hour and half flight to Cape Town.

"Gideon," Botha said.

"What about him?"

"He's the one who plans to squeal, not our fellow Afrikaners."

"Gideon?" Kruger said, almost laughing. "What gave you that crazy idea?"

"Why wouldn't he? After all, he knows everything about the Thathe Vondo death squad. And he turned down the job you offered him, remember?"

"It's because he loves teaching," Kruger said, resuming his seat. "He's not a fool, Ludwig. I've done him a lot of favors. I built a school and installed a water tap for his father's village. And after the unit disbanded, I gave him a bonus of R450,000. On top of that, I got Viljoen to hire his old man, Makhado, as foreman at the game reserve."

"Barnard and I stopped by the old kaffir's kraal several weeks ago," Viljoen said. "There was no indication he knows anything about his son planning to testify."

"And Gideon wouldn't take such a big step without first consulting his father," said Barnard, the self-proclaimed expert on black culture. "Venda tradition requires him to. His father has to make sacrifices to the spirits of *Midzimu*. Otherwise they will be angry and stop protecting Gideon on any dangerous mission."

"And I know the old kaffir," Viljoen said. "He won't let Gideon testify. If he did, he knows I'll fire him and the ten women on the spot. And they need the money."

Botha was unconvinced. "There's a lot more money in the lawsuit than the pittance you're paying them. And as far as *Midzimu* are concerned, westernized kaffirs like Gideon don't believe in them."

"You forget, Ludwig," Kruger said, "that Gideon has a wife he cares deeply about. And also he cares about his reputation as a teacher. There's talk that he might be offered a top education post in the next ANC government. Surely he wouldn't risk all that by revealing that he's a former askari."

"But if he exposes the most ruthless CCB death squad and stops the Fourth Boer Revolution he'd be a big hero to kaffirs," Botha countered. "They'll forgive him his treachery. And the TRC will be more than glad to grant him amnesty."

Apparently Kruger hadn't thought of that either. He looked troubled for a moment, then said confidently, "I understand what you're saying, Ludwig. But, I repeat, Gideon is not a fool. He knows what I did to those ten askaris who wanted to be big heroes by breaking the code of silence."

"Kaffirs are notoriously cunning and treacherous, General," Botha said. "Even the most loyal ones. Don't forget my father was betrayed by a kaffir he'd done a lot of favors for. Someone he treated like a son."

"Should we eliminate Gideon?" Kruger asked.

"No, not yet. Let's watch him carefully between now and the deadline for applying for amnesty."

"How?" Viljoen asked.

"I'll ask Swanepoel to wire his house and car. If it turns out that Gideon is innocent, we'll leave him alone. We might even give him a little bonus to keeping his mouth shut. But if he's in cahoots with your stepdaughter, then I have the perfect person to quickly eliminate him."

"Who?" Kruger asked.

"Shaka."

"Why won't Shaka, too, turn against us?" Kruger asked.

"Because he's one of us. He's got blood on his hands. I trained him myself to be a ruthless assassin, remember. Gideon merely spied for us; Shaka killed for us. And don't forget, Shaka used to be a senior officer with MK, for which the ANC rewarded him with a cushy job in the South African National Police. He won't squeal. Especially when we're still paying him R20,000 a month."

Barnard and Viljoen nodded in agreement. They were familiar with Shaka's formidable reputation as a CCB killer.

"If we need him to, Shaka can also eliminate Liefling, David and Thando."

"Brilliant, Ludwig," Kruger said with evident satisfaction. "Absolutely brilliant."

Kruger felt immense pride in his right-hand man. He trusted Botha's instincts because Botha harbored such an intense hatred of blacks that he was suspicious of even those who'd served apartheid well. Of the ten askaris Kruger had ordered executed over the years, it had been Botha's cunning that had exposed their treachery before they had had time to squeal.

"Okay, gentlemen," Kruger said, getting up. "We have plenty of work to do. All the rats and traitors must be dead by the time we meet Monday night at the game reserve. The lawsuit must never get to trial."

28 TINA's white Volvo pulled into the circular driveway of Kruger's large estate shortly before five. She parked it next to the spouting fountain. Emma, whose cherubic face looked quite worried, met her at the top of the stone stairs.

"Madam is upstairs changing," Emma said softly in Afrikaans. "She asked me to tell you to wait for her in the living room."

"Thank you, Emma," Tina said as Emma led her across the marbled foyer to the huge living room.

Tina was busy admiring some of the rare paintings adorning the off-white living room walls when Freda walked in. She was wearing brown slacks and a pink hand-woven sweater. Her normally radiant face looked drawn and tired.

"I hope you haven't been waiting long," she said quietly.

"Not at all. I just arrived."

Freda turned to the maid, who'd been standing at a discreet distance by the door, in case she was needed. "Emma," she said softly.

"Ja, Madam?"

"Can you please make us some tea?"

"Certainly, Madam."

Emma left for the kitchen. Freda and Tina sat down on the tan Italian leather sofa in front of a blazing fire in the marble fireplace.

Freda sighed. "So, what do you think of Liefling humiliating me in front of the whole world?"

"I don't know what to say without knowing all the facts," Tina said cautiously. "What exactly led her to file the lawsuit?"

"Well, she's trying to help about two hundred families of victims of death squads in Alexandra. I have no problem with that. I know she's obsessed with finishing the work her father was doing when he was murdered. But a week ago she went completely off base."

"What did she do?"

"Two days after Magnus and I returned from our honeymoon, I invited her over to spend the night. I wanted to tell her all about the honeymoon. I could sense something was wrong as soon as she arrived. She wasn't listening to me. She seemed quite absent-minded. At breakfast the next morning, out of the blue, she accused Magnus of knowing about CCB death squads. As you can imagine, I was completely shocked. So was Magnus."

"But he *did* belong to the CCB."

"He doesn't deny that. But he was a mere advisor. He insists he knew absolutely nothing about death squads. But Liefling doesn't believe him. She filed the lawsuit in order to force him to testify before the TRC."

"If he used to belong to the CCB why won't he testify?"

"Why should he? He's done nothing wrong."

"So you believe him?"

"Of course."

"Listen, Freda," Tina said, leaning forward. "I know how much you love Magnus, and how much he's done for you. But that shouldn't blind you to whatever mistakes he may have made in the past. I know Liefling. She's a very careful lawyer. She wouldn't have filed the lawsuit without evidence."

Freda became defensive. "What evidence? She has none."

"But during the press conference she said – "

"She lied," Freda interjected. I called her after the press conference and she admitted that she fabricated the story about having witnesses."

Tina raised her eyebrows. "She lied about that?"

"Ja," Freda said emphatically.

Emma brought tea with shortbread biscuits then left.

"I wonder why she'd lie," Tina said, pouring a little honey into her tea.

"She's desperate, that's why."

Tina stirred her tea. "I find it hard to believe that a high-ranking member of the CCB couldn't have known about death squads. I've been closely following the TRC hearings. I'm convinced that many of the generals are lying when they deny any knowledge of what their minions were doing."

Freda poured cream into her tea. "So what can I do?" Her voice was full of confusion and despair. "I'm caught in the middle. If the lawsuit goes to trial, whose side should I take?"

"If I were you, I'd remain neutral until all the facts come out."

Freda carefully sipped her hot tea. "But I told Magnus I was going to take his side."

"You did?"

"I was speaking out of anger at Liefling. But I did tell him that."

"Liefling is your daughter, Freda, no matter how much you may disapprove of what she's done."

"So what do you suggest I do?"

"Wait a few days for everything to settle down. If Liefling's lawsuit is without foundation, it will soon become apparent."

"Magnus thinks it will be thrown out during the preparatory examination."

"All the more reason to wait," Tina said. "And if I know Liefling, she'll be the first one to apologize to Magnus for having falsely accused him."

"Thanks for the advice," Freda said. "I feel much better about this now."

"I guess this is the best time to tell you something that's been bothering me," Tina said.

"What is it?" Freda said, setting down her cup.

Tina cleared her throat. "I'm very uncomfortable around Magnus's friends."

"Why?"

"They're so *verkrampte*. At the wedding several of them were downright insulting."

"How so?"

"They gave Paul a hard time over the fact that he's *verligte*. One of them was particularly obnoxious. His name, I believe, is Piet."

"You mean Piet Viljoen?"

"Ja, that's his name."

"He's one of my husband's business partners. What did he say to Paul?"

"He called Paul a kaffir-lover."

"What!"

"Apparently he and Paul were arguing about the idea of an Afrikaner-only homeland. Paul called it racist. That's when Piet called him a kaffir-lover."

Visibly upset, Freda said, "Why didn't you tell me this before?"

"I didn't want to spoil your wedding."

"You should have told me. Piet Viljoen has absolutely no right to insult Paul like that."

"Also, I was very offended by how many of Kruger's friends were constantly accusing blacks of ruining the country. That's hypocritical. Afrikaners ruined the bloody country." Tina was becoming more passionate now. The old activist in her was coming alive. "We are to blame for the crime and violence."

Freda looked shocked. "What on earth do you mean? We aren't criminals and robbers and carjackers."

"Who *are* the criminals? Most of them are uneducated and unskilled black youths. And why are they uneducated and unskilled? Because apartheid, a system that we Afrikaners created, defended and benefited from, rammed an inferior education system down their throats. When they rebelled, we teargassed them, beat them and shot and killed hundreds of them. We closed down their schools and threw them in jail where we brutally tortured them. The violence of apartheid taught them to be violent and to hold life cheap. Now the chickens are coming home to roost."

"I'm surprised to hear you say that," Freda said.

"Why?"

"Those carjackers who murdered your husband and almost killed you didn't care that both of you were *verligte*. They didn't care that you'd never wronged them. They didn't care that you'd been persecuted for fighting for their rights. They could at least differentiate between good and bad white people."

"Why should they, when apartheid didn't differentiate between the innocent and the guilty?" Tina said.

"What do you mean?"

"Most blacks are law-abiding and hard-working," Tina said. "But under apartheid we treated them like criminals. No, worse than animals. We took away their ancestral lands. We uprooted their communities to make way for whites. We confined them to miserable ghettos like Alexandra. We relegated them to menial jobs. We made it a crime for migrant workers to live with their families in so-called white South Africa. We arrested them for not having pass books and for having the wrong signatures in them. We made it a crime for them to walk on whites-only beaches, to enter through whites-only doors, and to ride whites-only buses."

"You keep on saying 'We,'" Freda said. "I never did any of those things."

"Didn't you vote for the National Party in election after election, like most white people?"

Freda said nothing. She sipped her tea.

"You can't claim you didn't know," Tina said. "We *are* to blame for what's happening in South Africa now. The seeds of all these pathologies were planted during apartheid. And it'll take generations to undo the damage."

"You were always a bleeding-heart *verligte*," Freda said. "But I agree with you on the issue of Magnus' friends. I don't particularly like a lot of them either. But they're his friends, not mine. As long as he doesn't interfere with my friends, I don't interfere with his."

"To tell you the truth, Freda, I still can't believe you married him."

"You forget, Tina, that Magnus and I were once engaged."

"But that was more than 35 years ago. You've changed a lot since then. You're no longer that *verkrampte* young girl who won the Miss Voortrekker contest three years in a row."

The contest, which Freda won for her leadership qualities, beauty and nationalistic fervor, had been held at the Voortrekker Easter Competition Camp near the Voortrekker monument on a hill outside Pretoria. Run by members of the Broederbond, it had included competition in shooting, tracking, sentry duty, assault courses, knowledge of Afrikaner history and a heavy dose of political indoctrination. Prior to winning the competition, Freda had successively gone through the three levels of the Voortrekker movement, the *Penkoppie* (cub), *Verkenners* (scout) and the *Staatmakers* (stalwarts).

"I haven't changed as much as you think," Freda said.

"If you're still that *verkrampte*, why didn't you divorce Christiaan after he started speaking out against apartheid?"

"I almost did, but Liefling begged me not to. She said Christiaan needed me. But he had no right to put us through the hell we went through. No right at all."

"But Freda, Christiaan was just obeying his conscience. What did you expect him to do?"

"Keep his mouth shut."

"And condone the murder of innocent school children whose only crime was to refuse to be taught in Afrikaans, the language of their oppressors?"

"He wasn't a politician," Freda said without much conviction. "He was a dominee."

"That's rubbish and you know it," Tina said firmly. "Our dominees were as political as any politician. They're the ones who blinded us to the evils of apartheid. They're the ones who made us its willing accomplices. Why do you think apartheid lasted as long as it did? It's because every Sunday morning, when we flocked to church, we were reassured by our dominees that the Afrikaner people were God's chosen race, that apartheid was God-ordained, and that black people were the inferior descendants of the cursed Ham. That's why we never questioned what the government did to blacks in order to give us one of the highest standards of living in the world."

Tina paused. Freda suddenly rose from the sofa and walked to the window. She repeatedly twirled the blinds open and closed with nervous fingers. She was clearly disturbed by what her friend was saying. She knew that she was speaking the truth, that her love for Magnus blinded her to the truth about apartheid and the Afrikaners' role in propping up the evil system. For some time she said nothing. She simply stared outside at and the fading late afternoon sun. Then she turned to Tina and said, "Your first husband was a *verkrampte*."

"I was young when I married Joubert," Tina said. "I didn't know any better. And besides, like you I was obeying my parent's wishes. But then I went to England and America to play on the tennis circuit, and everything changed. I saw films and read books that were banned in South Africa, including *Cry the Beloved Country*. I befriended black tennis players who were among the best in the world. I ate and socialized with them. I gave tennis lessons to black children and was amazed at how quickly they mastered the game. I couldn't help remembering that in South Africa black children were denied the opportunity to become an Arthur Ashe or Althea Gibson, not because they didn't have the talent, but because of apartheid. It was then that I realized how wrong and evil the system was. And why we white South Africans were hated around the world. When I came back, I knew I had to take a stand. I could no longer pretend I didn't know. And when I found out that Joubert had joined the AWB, I divorced him."

"Magnus isn't a member of the AWB."

Tina emitted a short laugh. "Don't fool yourself, Freda. There isn't that much difference between racists who wear business suits and those who parade around in brown-shirts carrying swastikas flags and mouthing racist and anti-Semitic slogans. The AWB is simply more crude that's all. If Magnus isn't of the same ilk, why does he insist on Afrikaners having their own homeland?"

"What's wrong with us having our own homeland? The Constitution grants us that right if we want to preserve our culture, language and heritage."

"That's a racist cop-out."

Freda turned and looked at Tina, who was pouring herself a second cup of tea. "Racist?"

"Ja," Tina said. "We are running away from problems we helped create. The irony is that we can't run away at all. Our fate is inextricably tied to that of blacks. No Afrikaner homeland can survive if the rest of South Africa goes up in flames. We have to keep South Africa unified and make democracy work."

"How can we make democracy work when we have no real power?" Freda countered. "Whites are now a marginalized minority. Blacks have all the power."

"Then let's join forces with open-minded and progressive blacks. Most blacks are reasonable, Freda, once you prove to them that you are sincere about no longer believing in *Baaskap*."

Freda walked back to the sofa and sat down. "Magnus isn't a racist, Tina. He really cares about blacks. During the apartheid era he built them wells, clinics and schools. And his firm employs hundreds of them as security guards. Do you think he'd have done all that if he were an AWB neo-Nazi? And do you think I'd have married him? What do you take me for? I'm not that stupid."

"I know you aren't," Tina said.

"You just need to get to know Magnus a little better," Freda said. "You and Paul should come to the braai on Sunday so you can talk some more with him about his views."

"What is braai about?"

"Magnus is launching a foundation in honor of his mother. It will be devoted to preserving the Afrikaner culture and identity."

"No, thank you. Paul and I are leaving tomorrow morning for Pretoria to visit his sick mother." Tina glanced at the clock. "As a matter of fact I'd better be leaving. I need to start packing."

The two friends rose and walked together to the front door. Tina paused in the marble foyer.

"As for Liefling, remember that she's your daughter. Your only child. I know you love her very much."

"I do."

"And she loves you too. She used to tell me during tennis lessons that she had the greatest mother in the world. You've been through a lot together. And I'd hate to see you sever all ties with her without giving her a chance."

"I won't. In fact now that I've talked to you I'll call her and try and clear the air. I don't want her thinking I've abandoned her."

"Please call her," Tina said. "And in case you need to reach me while I'm in Pretoria, here's the number where Paul and I will be."

She wrote it on the back of her business card and gave it to Freda.

As the two friends embraced in the doorway, Freda said, "Thanks for your advice, as always."

29 **KRUGER**, his face pensive, closed the well-thumbed copy of Sun Tzu's *The Art of War* and stared out the small window of the Learjet. He recalled how Hunter had given him the book as a birthday present over thirty-five years ago, when the two white supremacists began corresponding after meeting at the University of Alabama in Tuscaloosa, where Kruger had been an exchange student.

Sun Tzu has never failed me, he thought as he stashed the little manual inside his briefcase and shoved the briefcase under his plush leather seat. Since leaving Johannesburg International airport an hour earlier, Kruger had been engrossed in reading several of the manual's thirteen chapters, searching desperately for clues on the best strategy for eliminating Liefling.

A day never passed without his perusing the practical guide to strategy written over 2,500 years ago by a Chinese philosopher-general. Its advice had served him well as a military man, businessman and lover. *The Art of War* had led Kruger to believe that the world in which people work and live is a network of actual and potential combat zones, that struggle is the primary mode of being, that individual lives are expendable, that no one is to be completely trusted, that survival depends upon unconditional victory, and that those who seek such a victory must be willing to risk everything.

Kruger was prepared to risk everything to ensure the survival of the Afrikaner *Volk*. And if it meant killing his stepdaughter and destroying his marriage, so be it. But he was confident that he could eliminate Liefling and save his marriage, thanks to the plan he'd hatched while speaking to Botha.

Kruger checked his watch. It was almost seven. In less than half an hour he'd be landing in Cape Town. He couldn't wait to talk to Freda, who was central to the success of his plan.

The private phone rang. He picked it up, thinking it was Freda. He was surprised, almost shocked, to hear a familiar voice say, "Hullo, *bloedbroer*."

He tensed. His throat felt dry. For a few seconds he could not speak. When he finally did, his voice had a fake cheerfulness, "Hullo Reggie. What a surprise. Where are you calling from?"

"North Carolina," Hunter said tersely. "I just got off the phone with the Cali Cartel. They're threatening to scrap the deal. What happened?"

Kruger sat up straight. His heart was racing. He reached for his drink and took a sip before explaining the day's extraordinary events, from his meeting with the South American in Sun City to his discussion with Botha, Viljoen and Barnard after Liefling's stunning press conference. He ended by mentioning the possibility that Gideon, whom Hunter had met at the bushveld camp in 1986, might be planning to expose him and the Thathe Vondo death squad.

Hunter said, "I warned you not to use askaris. You can't trust niggers."

"They were an invaluable counterinsurgency resource," Kruger said. "Without them I wouldn't have been able to penetrate and neutralize the ANC's MK cell in Alexandra."

"Then you should have eliminated Gideon as soon as he'd served his purpose."

"On hindsight, I should have. But back then I had a policy of not killing valuable askaris, Reggie. They were hard to find and train."

"Look at the mess you're in because of a nigger. I've never trusted niggers and never will. What do you plan to do now? If Gideon rats the Fourth Boer Revolution is dead."

"He won't. We'll eliminated him."

"How?"

"Remember Shaka?"

"You mean that nigger Botha trained to be an assassin?"

"Ja. I plan to use him to eliminate Gideon. But first I have to find out how much the kaffir bastard has told Liefling."

"What if he's told her everything?"

"Then Shaka will eliminate her too."

"Now you're talking like the old Magnus I know. The Magnus whose bible is *The Art of War*."

"But I need a little help from you in the meantime."

"What kind of help?"

"Can you get the Cali cartel to give me about a week before calling off the deal? I'll need that much time to get rid of the lawsuit."

"Okay. That shouldn't be a problem. The Cali cartel owes Von Schleicher and me a big favor. If you take care of the lawsuit, they'll keep their end of the bargain. I'll see to that."

"Thanks, *bloedbroer*."

"But take care of Gideon quickly, okay," Hunter said. "He's the only witness against you. If he's still alive by next Friday, the deal is dead."

"Don't worry, I'll take care of him."

GIDEON, Nomhle and their two children were sitting around the kitchen table eating spaghetti when the phone rang. Gideon got up and answered it.

He listened to the caller for a minute or so. "Thanks for calling," he said. I'd forgotten about it. I'll see you soon."

"Who was that?" Nomhle asked.

Gideon said, "It was the mayor. I'd forgotten about an important meeting he'd invited me to tonight."

Gideon put on his black leather coat and hurried out the door. He got into his Ford Explorer and drove several blocks. But he didn't go to Bovet. Instead he drove about a mile to a pay phone, and dialed the number the caller had given him.

"What's going on?" he said.

"I couldn't talk to you on your phone," Ndwakhulu said.

"Why not?"

"I'm afraid Kruger and his men may have tapped it."

"Tapped it? Oh, hell. Do they know?"

"I'm not sure. But I don't want to take any chances. Be careful from now on about what you say over the phone. Are you still coming to Venda Sunday?"

"Ja."

"Is your family coming with you?"

"No. Nomhle and the kids are going to Soweto to attend her sister's wedding."

"I can't wait to see you, my friend. And I can't wait for us to nail Kruger."

SHAKA, after talking to Gideon, dialed his controller's number in Johannesburg.

"I just spoke to Gideon. He'll be in Venda on Sunday visiting his parents, and his wife will be in Soweto attending a wedding. So there won't be anyone in the house. Swanepoel should have plenty of time to wire it."

"Are you sure?" Botha asked. "Could he have lied to you?"

"I'm positive. He trusts me completely."

GIDEON and Nomhle were in their master bathroom getting ready for bed.

"I won't be able to attend your sister's wedding on Sunday," Gideon said, brushing his teeth with Colgate mint toothpaste.

Nomhle stared at him. "Why not?"

"I'm going to Venda. My father is conducting the annual ceremony to honor our ancestors."

"Why didn't you tell me before?"

"I forgot." Noticing the disappointment on Nomhle's face, Gideon added, "I wish I could be at the wedding, honey, but I can't let my father down. As his only surviving son it's important that I be present."

"When will you be back?" Nomhle asked.

"Late Sunday night. I'm teaching morning class on Monday."

KRUGER called Botha at the firm as the plane approached the Cape Town International airport.

"I just spoke to Hunter," he said. "He's assured me that the Cali Cartel will give us a week to take care of Gideon. Have you given Shaka his instructions?"

"Ja. He's ready to move whenever you give the word."

"Good."

"And Swanepoel's people plan to wire Gideon's Explorer sometime tonight. The Cape Town crew is busy wiring Liefling's flat and car."

"Isn't the kaffir-lover home?"

"No. She's still in Jo'burg. They're also working on David's and Thando's. The two of them are with Liefling at the Market Place as we speak."

LIEFLING, Thando and David had Tandourri dinner together at an Indian restaurant at the Market Place in downtown Johannesburg. After dinner they went to Kippies Bar for drinks and the best of South African live jazz.

"So when are you flying back home?" David asked Liefling.

"Tomorrow morning," she said. "I have to prepare for Sunday's fund-raising party."

"Who's coming?" Thando asked.

"A lot of activists from the Cape area, along with my friends from UCT."

"I wish I could be there," Thando said. "But Sidney will be in town and plans to stop by."

"Are you two back together again?" Liefling asked.

"No. But our daughter wants us to be."

"Why don't you get back together?" David asked. "He's such a nice guy. I was very impressed by the testimony he gave on your behalf during your amnesty hearing."

"Despite the testimony, I don't think he's forgiven me for what happened to his brother."

Liefling's cell phone rang.

"Excuse me," she said, getting up. She stepped outside the noisy bar. Minutes later, she came back.

"Was that Sipho?" Thando asked.

"No. It was my mom."

"Your mom?"

"Ja. She wants me to come to her place on Monday. She wants us to talk."

"About the lawsuit?" Thando asked.

"She didn't say. But I guess it's about the lawsuit."

"Interesting," David said, sipping his beer. "Will Kruger be there."

"No."

"Will you go?" Thando asked.

"Ja. She told me she spoke to her friend Tina after we had that disastrous exchange on the phone. Tina apparently suggested that we talk."

"Who's Tina?" David asked.

Liefling drained her glass of red wine. "She's a remarkable Afrikaner woman. A former tennis pro. My mother met her at the multiracial school I attended in Sandton. Tina taught tennis there. What's so amazing is that she was married for three years to a professor at the University of Pretoria, who was a member of the AWB."

"Really?" David exclaimed.

"Ja. He was so *verkrampte* and controlling he forbade her to even read English newspapers. Tina divorced him after she returned from a year of playing tennis in America, where she became radicalized after learning the truth about apartheid. And you know what she did after divorcing him?"

"What did she do?" asked Thando, intensely curious. She pushed aside her empty wineglass and leaned forward on the small table with the flickering candle to listen more attentively.

"She joined the Black Sash," Liefling said. "Shortly afterwards she married James, an English-speaking journalist for *The Rand Daily Mail*. They met when he interviewed her for a story about Afrikaner members of the Black Sash."

"Joining the Black Sash and then marrying an Englishman," David said, "Wow, that's quite radical."

"She paid the price," Liefling said. "The marriage so infuriated her parents so much they disowned her. And BOSS persecuted her for belonging to the Black Sash. They tapped her phones, opened her mail, and constantly played vicious hoaxes on her, calling her in the middle of the night to tell her that her husband had been killed in a car accident, or had been caught with a black prostitute. But to her credit, Tina never backed down. She continued fighting against apartheid. Even the murder of her husband two years ago during an attempted carjacking didn't make her abandon her belief in black majority rule."

"Quite a remarkable woman," Thando said. "I'd like to meet her someday."

"I'll be glad to introduce you."

Liefling glanced at his watch. "Wow, can you believe it? It's almost eleven."

"It's still very early," David said.

"For you, night-owl. I have a six-thirty flight to catch. I need some sleep."

The three paid for their drinks and left Kippies Bar. It had rained and the streets were wet. Because it was dangerous to drive at night in Johannesburg, David and Thando had left their cars at home. David took a taxi for the thirty-minute ride to his house in Diepkloof, a section of Soweto, and Liefling and Thando took a taxi to Thando's flat in Alexandra, where Liefling was spending the night.

FREDA lay awake in the darkness. The only light came from a sliver of moonlight streaming in between the drawn drapes. She was lying next to Kruger on their king-size waterbed with its lace canopy. It was around eleven-thirty.

"Magnus?" she said.

"Yes darling?" Kruger said.

There was a pause as Freda pondered if she should go ahead and say what she'd resolved to tell her husband after her talk with Tina earlier that afternoon.

"You know I don't approve of what Liefling has done," Freda said, her voice trembling slightly. "But at the same time, she's my daughter. My only child. I don't want to see her hurt."

"What do you mean, dear?" Kruger turned on the light and sat up against the headboard. He looked at Freda.

"Well, I won't rush to judgment and condemn her without knowing all the facts."

"What facts, my dear? You yourself said the lawsuit is bogus."

"If it is, then the court will throw it out."

Kruger didn't answer. He wanted to explode in anger but he restrained himself. He knew the importance of maintaining his calm in order to retain Freda as an alibi in his plan to kill Liefling. He was silent for a long while, wondering what had caused Freda's sudden change in attitude.

"Did you talk to anyone after we spoke this afternoon?" he asked.

Freda realized she couldn't lie. Kruger would find out from either the maids, butler or gardeners, if he hadn't done so already, that Tina had been there.

"Ja. I spoke to Tina."

Kruger jaw muscles tightened and his pale blue eyes flickered in anger.

"But she didn't influence my decision," Freda said quickly, sensing her husband's displeasure. "I'm responding as a loving mother and wife. I'd like to see this matter settled out of court. That's why I called Liefling shortly before you arrived. I invited her to come here on Monday."

"You what?"

"I know you said she should never set foot on your property again. But I want to talk to her about dropping the lawsuit."

"I see. And did she agree to come?"

"Ja."

Kruger pondered this for a moment. His anger seemed to melt, softening his expression. He leaned over and kissed Freda. "You did the right thing in inviting her to come here, my dear. Hopefully you can reason with her. I'd like to see this matter settled out of court as much as you do."

Freda smiled at him, pleased that he was no longer angry.

"My main concern is David," Kruger said. "As long as Liefling is under his influence, I doubt she'll drop the lawsuit. There's no doubt David is out to get me. And he's getting desperate because he has no evidence. And desperate men can do desperate things."

Freda gave Kruger a worried look. "What do you mean?"

"David once murdered an innocent woman in order to silence her. If I were Liefling I'd be very careful around such a man. You don't know what he might do when his back is against the wall."

Freda was alarmed. "Do you think he might harm her?"

"As I said, my dear, desperate men do desperate things.

30 GIDEON, dressed in a tweed suit and a black fedora hat, entered through the wooden gate of Makhado's kraal. He struggled to balance a fat briefcase and several brimming grocery bags from Checkers Supermarket. Two barefoot little boys with nappy black hair spotted him.

"Uncle Gideon is here! Uncle Gideon is here!" they shouted at the top of their lungs. At the cry about a dozen youngsters, between eight and fourteen years old, abruptly stopped playing soccer and jump rope in the dusty courtyard and raced each other to the gate in an attempt to reach Gideon first.

"Where are Pinkie and Joshua?" one of the girls asked excitedly.

"They didn't come along this time," Gideon said to his nieces and nephews as they crowded eagerly about him. He handed them the packages. "Is your Grandpa home?" he said.

"Uh-uh," said a boy with a runny nose. "He's in the big hut."

"And your Grandma?"

"She's not home," said a little girl with big brown eyes and a wide disarming smile. "She went to visit great-grandma at the hospital."

Gideon heaved a sigh of relief. He didn't think he had the courage to confess the truth before his mother, for fear of breaking her heart. He handed the bag containing packets of candy, biscuits and fish and chips to a girl with braided hair. She was thirteen but a meager diet of cornmeal, greens and chicken intestines made her look no older than ten.

"Mpho," Gideon said, "give these out. No fighting, now. There's plenty to go around."

"We won't fight, uncle," Mpho said, bubbling with excitement.

Gideon, briefcase in hand, proceeded to a large rondavel hut with circular mud walls. A pointed metal spike protruded from the top of its thatched roof. The spike was meant to ward off evil spirits that, according to the Vendas, one of South Africa's most superstitious tribes, often rode bolts of lightning and slithered in through unprotected roofs during severe thunderstorms to harm those within.

The hut was surrounded by four others, slightly smaller in size, in which slept the wives and children of Gideon's two older brothers and sister, all of whom were now dead. Both brothers were killed in 1987 when the elevator in which he was riding snapped a cable and plunged 200 meters down a mining shaft, killing all ten miners packed inside. His sister died in 1991 from AIDS. The deaths of his three siblings devastated Gideon and made him feel an enormous responsibility to provide for their children.

As Gideon approached the main hut, Makhado emerged through its low door. He was wearing a pair of faded bib overalls and held a hammer in his left hand.

"*Ndaa*, Baba," Gideon greeted him in Venda.

"*Ndaa*, my son," Makhado said. "Nice to see you again. Can I get you something to drink? You must be thirsty after the long drive."

"Yes, Baba."

Makhado summoned a wiry dark-skinned boy wearing khaki shorts choked around the waist with a piece of string made from the fibers of a Baobab tree.

"Vutshilo, run to the kitchen and ask Luambo to bring your uncle something to drink."

"Yes, Grandpa," Vutshilo said and off he went.

"Please have a seat," Makhado said, pointing toward a wooden bench under the shade of a Marula tree. Next to the bench was a woodworking table Gideon had bought him three years earlier. On the table were a crosscut saw, a chisel, a carpenter's gauge, a set of screwdrivers, a sander and several boxes of nails.

"Still working on the kitchen table?" Gideon asked.

"No. That's long done. I'm now working on a couple of benches for the village school."

Gideon leaned his leather briefcase against the table, took off his jacket and sat down. Makhado sat down beside him, chest erect.

"So how's Nomhle and the children?" Makhado asked.

"Fine. They went to a wedding in Soweto."

"Whose?"

"Nomhle's sister's."

Gideon saw movement out of the corner of his eye and turned to see a sweet-faced young woman, about eighteen, who was dressed in a colorful *mucheka* and carried a tray with two tall tumblers filled with orange Kool-Aid and floating ice-cubes. She crossed the courtyard and came to where Gideon and Makhado were sitting. She kneeled before Makhado, a sign of respect, her legs bent sideways, as she handed him the tray.

"Thank you, dear granddaughter," Makhado said.

"You're welcome, grandpa," Luambo said demurely.

"*Ndaa,* uncle," she said to Gideon.

"*Ndaa,* Luambo," Gideon said. "How's school?"

"Fine," Luambo said with a shy smile.

"Have you decided which university you want to attend after Matric?" Gideon asked.

"I'd like to go to Venda University," Luambo said.

"Provided we can get the money to send her there," Makhado said.

"I'll pay for her," Gideon said without hesitation.

Luambo looked up at Gideon with surprise. "You will?"

"I promise."

"Oh, thank you, uncle," she cried as tears of gratitude filled her eyes. "Thank you. You don't know how much this means to me. God bless you, uncle."

"And may He bless you too, Luambo."

She got up and hurried excitedly to one of the huts, to share the good news with members of her extended family.

"You've made her very happy, my son," Makhado said proudly.

"I can afford it now that I've finished paying the mortgage for the house."

"She wants to be a doctor."

"She'll make a good one. She has the brains. I'm very impressed that she always comes out number one in her classes."

Gideon sipped his drink. It was hot and humid, and the air shimmered with heat waves along the dusty ground.

"Baba," he said, suddenly avoiding eye contact with Makhado, "I came here to confess terrible things I've done."

"What terrible things have you done, my son?"

Gideon swallowed. His throat suddenly felt dry.

"For ten years I was an askari," he said, his words barely audible.

"An askari?" Makhado cried, stunned.

"Ja. I spied for General Magnus Kruger and his death squad."

KRUGER felt a surge of pride as he entered the huge white tent erected on the manicured lawn of his estate. Inside, a hundred well-heeled guests, spiffed up in tuxedos and evening gowns, chatted in small knots, sipped wine and nibbled delectable hors d'ouvres. Kruger was pleased to notice that among the guests were the elite of Afrikanerdom – politicians, businessmen, educators, lawyers, journalists, judges and ministers. On a flower-decked stage ringed with bunting and fluttering flags of the former Boer Republic, a professional brass quartet played music by Wagner, along with patriotic Afrikaner songs.

The weather was glorious. The evening sky was a mellow magenta. A cool gentle breeze fanned the leaves of the stately oak trees and wafted the fragrance from the nearby gardens bursting with a variety of flowers. To Kruger's guests this was what their ancestors had sacrificed their blood, sweat and tears to achieve for their posterity. This was what successive generations of Afrikaner nationalists, schooled in the mythology of Baaskap, had sworn a sacred covenant with the Almighty to preserve at whatever cost.

It was an understatement to say that Kruger's guests loathed those Afrikaner politicians who'd negotiated the surrender of white power and privileges to blacks. In the final days of apartheid many of Kruger's guests had openly supported various right-wing and neo-Nazi groups that had demanded the creation of an all-Afrikaner homeland. When an all-Afrikaner homeland failed to materialize, they'd secretly applauded efforts by CCB death squads to derail negotiations between the government and the ANC.

Since the TRC – which they regarded as nothing but a Star Chamber and the Nuremberg Tribunal combined – began its inquisition, they'd rallied behind men like Kruger for refusing to appear before it. And the braai to celebrate the launching of The Henrietta Foundation, which was dedicated to the preservation of the language, culture and heritage they deeply cherished, was yet another example of the need to support men like Kruger, *regte* Afrikaners.

Kruger smiled as he spotted Freda. She was wearing a turquoise evening gown that beautifully accentuated her eyes. The diamond and ruby necklace glittering about her neck was a recent gift from Kruger. Freda was moving effortlessly from group to group, trying to be the perfect hostess, but thought of Liefling kept intruding.

As she tried to make small talk with Kruger's guests, she silently wondered how in the world they'd acquired such rabidly racist and anti-Semitic views. She was used to hearing Afrikaners bemoan their loss of power and privileges, but this was too much. As she moved along, she caught snippets of conversations.

"The bloody kaffirs are ruining South Africa. My Mercedes has been stolen three times. I can't get insurance on my new one."

"We used to have law and order under apartheid. Now it's total chaos. And the bloody ANC refuses to bring back the death penalty."

"The maids and garden boys have become so cheeky. They want pay raises."

"It's because they now have unions. They had none under apartheid."

"We are seriously thinking of leaving South Africa."

"Where will you go?"

"America."

"But aren't there kaffirs there too?"

"There are. But at least they aren't running things."

"But the Jews are."

Freda noticed that her guests abruptly switched topics whenever she joined them. She wasn't surprised. Most of her guests knew her from her days as an outcast. To them she was the Afrikaner who'd dared belong to the ANC, an organization they regarded as nothing but a den of communists, terrorists and race mixers. On top of that she had been the wife of Christian Malan – a Benedict Arnold who'd undermined apartheid by questioning its moral legitimacy.

Freda knew that to be accepted back into the laager, she would have to give up all her *verligte* ideas, something she wasn't prepared to do.

Freda was startled by a voice behind her. "How are you, my dear?" She turned and was surprised to see Wilhemina, dominee Muller's wife.

"I'm fine, thank you."

"I'm *so* sorry to hear about what Liefling did."

"You mean the lawsuit?"

"Ja. How could she do such a thing to her own stepfather?"

"I'm as mystified as you are."

"I don't want to speak ill of the dead," Wilhemina said, her heavily made-up green eyes darting about furtively, her voice lowered, as if she half-expected Christiaan's ghost to appear and upbraid her. "God says we should forgive all sinners. But to tell you the truth Christiaan was mad to repudiate the church's teachings against race mixing. Look at what his liberalism has done to the poor child. It's absolutely heart-breaking. How devastated you must feel."

Wilhemina reached out and tenderly touched Freda's hand. Despite being infuriated by Wilhemina's condescending attitude, Freda felt obligated to put up appearances.

"I warned Christiaan about the consequences of repudiating apartheid," Freda said safely.

"I'm sure you did, my dear. What loving, God-fearing Afrikaner woman wouldn't? What in heaven's name did Christiaan hope to gain by rejecting his own people for natives? After all, they are a different specie than whites."

Freda didn't know what to say.

Wilhemina fingered her pearl necklace, looking into the distance thoughtfully. "Did you know that before he became a dominee, my husband Koos was a top government scientist during the 1950s?"

"I didn't know that."

"Not many people do. His work was top secret."

"What did he do?"

"He used to conduct IQ experiments on pickaninnies."

"Really?"

"Ja. Prime Minister Verwoerd himself commissioned the experiments as a way of proving the necessity of natives having their own education system."

"You mean Bantu Education?"

"Ja. Koos found that natives actually have smaller brains than whites, and that from childhood they have an aptitude for just two things."

"What two things?"

"Immorality and criminality."

Freda stared at Wilhemina, realizing for the fist time how thoroughly apartheid had conditioned whites to believe in their supposedly innate, God-given superiority over blacks. Wilhemina's attitude sickened her. Freda suddenly felt alone amid the crowd. These racists and anti-Semites were not her people. She wanted nothing to do with them. If it meant she would have to spend her life socializing with the like of Wilhemina, she didn't want to be admitted back into the laager.

"The blacks I know are neither immoral or criminals," Freda said, surprising herself by her boldness. "On the contrary, they are full of Ubuntu, something many whites lack."

"If they're so full of humanity why did they necklace your first husband, my dear? And why are townships dens of all kinds of iniquities?"

"Have you ever been to one?" Freda asked, sipping her wine and eyeing Wilhemina.

Wilhemina stared at Freda as if she were out of her mind. "Never."

"I have," Freda said. "I used to work with orphaned children in Alexandra. And I'll never forget the love and kindness we received from blacks after Christiaan rejected apartheid. It was more than we'd ever received from whites. And after Christiaan died, nearly half a million blacks turned out for his burial at the Alexandra cemetery."

Wilhemina turned pale. "Don't tell me he's buried in a kaffir cemetery."

"He sure is. His God-fearing relatives refused to have him buried next to his mother, as she'd requested before she died."

"Oh, my God!" Wilhemina said, visibly shaking. "If anyone ever buries me in a kaffir cemetery, I'll haunt them."

I bet you would, Freda thought.

Freda was about to say something when she noticed Kruger leave a group of about six former SADF generals and majors who'd refused to testify before the TRC and bound up the stage. She grabbed the opportunity to escape from Wilhemina's clutches by moving closer to the stage to better see and hear her husband as he prepared to speak.

31

LIEFLING looked thinner than usual as she sat on the wrought-iron balcony of her flat talking to detective Malusi. A bottle of red wine and a tray of raw vegetables with a tangy dip sat on the wicker table between them. Inside the flat a roaring party was in progress.

"I'm so glad you could make it," Liefling said. "How did the hearing on muti-killings go?"

"Very well. The government pledged to provide us with all the help we need to tackle the problem nationwide."

"I'm glad. I can't believe that in this day and age women are still being burned as witches."

"Ignorance is largely to blame. That's why the task force plans to hold town meetings all over the country to educate people on the issue."

"There's no doubt education is key. It's the key to so many of our problems, including AIDS and crime. The worst crime apartheid committed was to deprive black people of a decent education."

"I agree."

Suddenly the balcony's French doors opened and Sipho stepped out. Looking exhausted, he was dressed in a pair of khaki Docker pants, black turtleneck and a green cotton sweater. Liefling's eyes lit up when she saw him.

"I'm glad you could make it, honey." She kissed him as they briefly hugged.

"I'd have been here earlier," Sipho said, "but we were inundated with trauma victims." He placed the Adidas duffel bag he was carrying on an empty chair. "The violence in the townships is really getting out of hand."

"Blame it on drugs and gangs," Malusi said.

Sipho was about to say something when a large, light-skinned Xhosa woman named Sibongile appeared at the French doors. A sociologist and classmate of Liefling's at UCT, she'd helped Liefling organize the party.

"Hi Sipho," she said.

"Hi Sibongile. Nice to see you."

"Nice to see you too." Sibongile turned to Liefling. "We're out of drinks."

"All the wine and beer is gone?"

"Ja. Don't forget there are more than fifty people inside. And they all guzzle."

"Shit, and the bottle stores are closed now," Liefling muttered.

"I know where to get some drinks, honey," Sipho said.

"Where?" Liefling asked. "It's Sunday evening."

"The shebeens. They never close. I'll be back in fifteen minutes."

"Are you sure it's safe?"

"I know where to go. Don't worry."

"I'll come with you," Malusi said.

"No, stay and talk to Liefling."

After Sipho left and Sibongile returned inside, Malusi said, "Sipho tells me that Bishop Tutu has agreed to intervene in the lawsuit."

"Ja," Liefling said, picking up her wineglass. "I asked him to. I don't want the lawsuit to go to trial if I can help it."

"Do you think he can convince Kruger to change his mind and testify?"

"I hope so."

"What if he doesn't?"

"Then I'm afraid the case goes forward. The preparatory examination is set for Wednesday."

"How strong is your case?"

"Frankly, it's quite weak without witnesses. That's why the testimony of our mystery witness is so crucial."

"Who is he?"

"He won't give his name. He claims to have been an askari for a CCB death squad operated by my stepfather. But what's frustrating is that so far he's declined to come forward or be interviewed. And time is running out. His evidence is crucial for an effective presentation of the case at Wednesday's preparatory examination. Otherwise I'm afraid the judge will dismiss the lawsuit as frivolous."

"If I can be of any help please let me know. I know a lot of former askaris from my former days with the security branch."

"Thanks."

Sibongile reappeared. "Come on, Liefling, people are asking where you are."

"I'm coming," Liefling said, rising. She and Malusi rejoined the crowd inside the flat. The make-up of the group reflected Liefling's liberal politics. She had friends from every racial and tribal group in what Nelson Mandela called "a rainbow nation" of 43 million people. There were Zulus, Xhosas, Afrikaners, Pedis, Tswanas, Coloreds, Sothos, Ndebeles, Indians, Jews, Shangaans, Muslims and Vendas. The throbbing beat of Johnny Clegg's music vibrated from the stereo speakers, enlivening the festive atmosphere.

"Here comes our Joan of Arc," Sibongile said, leading Liefling by the hand through the crowd. "Comrades, let's give our sister Liefling a big African send-off. We want to make sure she can bring Kruger to justice, no matter how many high-powered lawyers he has."

"That's right," some one said.

"You nail him, Liefling," said another.

"We know you can do it," said a third.

Smiling, Liefling stood in front of the group, next to the cold fireplace. The din gradually subsided. Someone turned down the loud music.

"I'm glad to see all of you here," Liefling said. "Without your support, I couldn't have made it this far."

An appreciative murmur ran through the crowd. "Hear! Hear!" a lone voice said drunkenly.

"Many of you know how hard this lawsuit has been on me," Liefling continued. "I'm estranged from my mother, a person very dear to me. And I've received dozens of obscene phone calls and death threats."

Liefling paused for several moments as she felt the full weight of all she'd been through. "But you, my friends," she continued in a quavering voice, "have urged me not to give up. You've reminded me of the victims of apartheid, and of the importance of fighting for what is right. I invited you here tonight to let you know that whatever the outcome of Wednesday's preparatory examination, there's nothing for me to be ashamed of. Yes, I've been called all sorts of names, and it hurts." Liefling started to choke up. "But you, my friends, know who I am. And, most important, I know who I am."

Sibongile wrapped her arm comfortingly around Liefling.

"Thank you for all your support and friendship," Liefling said.

Sibongile spontaneously broke out singing *Nkosi Sikelel' Afrika*, the national anthem. Instantly everyone joined in the singing. People clenched their right fists and thrust them into the air as they'd done so many times as activists during the struggle against apartheid. As Liefling sang, the song's haunting lyrics reminded her of her father, who'd sacrificed his life for the cause of racial equality and social justice. Tears came to her eyes as she thought of the miracle of a multiracial democracy having been born without recourse to a bloody revolution because of the transcendent moral leadership of Nelson Mandela.

To her and to those packed inside the flat, *Nkosi Sikelel' Afrika*, composed by a Xhosa teacher named Enoch Sontonga in 1897, evoked South Africa's great potential for progress and prosperity, provided reconciliation and forgiveness go hand in hand with truth and justice.

Few eyes were dry as the group sang the first part of the anthem in Zulu, as was customary, and the second part in Sesotho.

Zulu

Nkosi Sikelel' i Afrika	Lord, bless Afrika
Maluphakamis' uphondo lwayo	Let her horn be raised
Yizwa imithandazo yethu	Listen to our prayers
Nkosi, sikelela--	Lord bless,
Thina luswapho lwayo	We her offspring
Woza Moya	Come Spirit
Woza Moya Oyingcwele	Come Holy Spirit
Nkosi sikelela	Lord Bless,
Thina lusapho lwayo	We her children

Sesotho

Morena boloka	God Bless
Sechaba sa heso	Our Nation
O fedise dintwa le matswenyeho	Do away with wars and troubles
O se boloke, o se boloke	Bless it, bless it,
O se boloke morena	Bless it, Lord
Sechaba sa heso	Our Nation
Sechaba sa heso	Our Nation

KRUGER leaned into the mike and said in a hearty and booming voice, "Fellow Afrikaners, this is a great day for our people. The Henrietta Foundation will do for the Afrikaner people what the National Party and all the other so-called Afrikaner parties have failed to do. It will fight for their rights and protect their vital interests."

Kruger, skilled in art of using gestures for emphasis and to manipulate emotions – like his idol, Adolf Hitler – swung his hands about like an orchestra conductor with each sentence.

"Our people continue to be victims of crime, violence and affirmative action. Our language, culture and heritage continue to be trampled upon. And patriotic members of the security forces, *your* very sons, who did their utmost to defend *your* way of life, continue to be humiliated and persecuted by the TRC. That must and will stop."

Kruger paused. The crowd went wild. People clapped and whistled vociferously.

"I pledge to you today that the Afrikaner nation will rise again, in pride and in strength," Kruger went on. "I'll fight to the bitter end to ensure its survival. No one will stop me. Not even my stepdaughter's frivolous lawsuit."

The audience booed at Kruger's allusion to Liefling, who'd been the main topic of conversation throughout the afternoon.

"I've assembled the best legal team in the country," Kruger said, "led by the incomparable Prinsloo."

There was loud clapping as Kruger pointed at the silver-haired Prinsloo, standing with his plump wife to the left of the stage. Next to Mevrou Prinsloo stood her son Derek, who was lovingly holding the hand of his fiancée, the blonde-haired daughter of a wealthy Afrikaner investment banker.

"And Prinsloo tell me that Liefling doesn't have a case. Not even a circumstantial one. I've even heard rumors that she's thinking of dropping the lawsuit."

"If she does, counter-sue her for defamation of character!" Dominee Muller shouted. He was standing just below the stage. Mrs. Muller, who was standing next to her husband, smiled proudly.

"I've thought of that," Kruger said with a smile. "But out of deference to my dear wife" -- he cast a look in Freda's direction -- "I'll resist the temptation. I'm not, after all, a vindictive man. I know a wayward and misled child when I see one. There's little doubt in my mind as to who's really behind the lawsuit, which, clearly, is intended to prevent me from rebuilding the Afrikaner nation."

"The ANC!" the audience shouted.

Kruger squared his shoulders and grabbed the mike tighter, readying himself for his peroration. "But the enemies of the Afrikaner people won't succeed in their blackmail, my friends. I'll never volunteer to humiliate myself by appearing before the TRC when I've committed no crime. And I'll never ever betray the brave and patriotic members of the security forces who prevented South Africa from falling into Marxist-Leninist hands."

His eyes swept the audience, a group whose support he knew he would need when the time came to launch the Fourth Boer Revolution. Everyone was silent and attentive as during a sermon.

"There's a lot of revisionism going on about what actually happened under apartheid," Kruger said. "People conveniently forget that we were facing a total communist onslaught. On direct orders from Moscow, Peking and Cuba, the ANC gave orders to its supporters in the townships to destroy all semblance of law and order so as to prepare the ground for a People's Revolution. Do you remember when ANC terrorists exploded bombs in crowded shopping centers, churches, bus-stops and restaurants, killing innocent people?"

"We remember!" the captive audience shouted.

"South Africa was on the verge of anarchy, ladies and gentlemen," Kruger continued. "And to prevent the total disintegration of our society, the SADF had no recourse but to use covert operations by CCB Special Forces. The men who carried out their duties in this context are bonafide heroes. They deserve medals, not humiliation. Without them there would have been no peaceful transition. Mandela would have inherited a wasteland."

Even before Kruger completed his harangue, the audience clapped thunderously. Kruger, smiling broadly, wiped his brow, which was beaded with sweat. Someone handed him a drink.

"By the way," he continued as he sipped, his voice now soft and soothing, and less strident, "I received a call from Bishop Tutu this morning. Apparently my stepdaughter spoke to him. In the interest of reconciliation, he says, he wants to talk to me about preventing the lawsuit from going to trial. Isn't that nice of the Bishop?"

"What about Mandela?" Dominee Muller said. "Has he called too?"

"I haven't heard from him yet," Kruger said with an ironic smile. "But I wouldn't be surprised if he offers to personally escort me into the Star Chamber."

The crowd laughed.

Kruger turned and signaled to the orchestra to strike up *Die Stem Van*

Suid Afrika, which, along with *Nkosi Sikelel' Afrika,* was now part of the dual national anthem. The decision to have a dual national anthem had been reached in the spirit of Ubuntu. Its aim was to heal the nation by forging a common heritage out of what was dear to Afrikaners and to blacks, erstwhile enemies.

Yet Kruger's neo-Nazi regarded *Die Stem* as their exclusive national anthem. To them it was a rallying cry for the faithful to keep the faith, and to support to the bitter end uncompromising Afrikaner patriots like Kruger. Therefore it was with uncommon fervor, as they saluted the huge Vierkleur flag draped across the stage, that Kruger and his merry band of fascists sang:

> Uit die blou van onse hemel, uit die diepte van ons see,
> Oor ons ewige gebergtes waar die kraanse antwoord gee.
> Deur ons ver-verlate vlaktes met die kreun van ossewa -
> Ruis die stem van ons geliefde, van ons land Suid-Afrika.

> Ons sal antwoord op jou roepstem, ons sal offer wat jy vra:
> Ons sal lewe, ons sal sterwe -- ons vir jou, Suid-Afrika.

> In die merge van ons gebeente, in ons hart en siel en gees
> In ons roem op ons verlede, in ons hoop of wat sal wees,
> In ons wil en werk en wandel, van ons wieg tot aan ons graf -
> Deel geen ander land ons liefde, trek geen ander trou ons af.

> Vaderland! ons sal die adel van jou naam met ere dra:
> Waar en trou as Afrikaners - kinders van Suid-Afrika.
> In die songloed van ons somer, in ons winternag se kou,
> In die lente van ons liefde, in die lanfer van ons rou,
> By die klink van huweliksklokkies, by die kluitklap op die kis -
> Streel jou stem ons nooit verniet nie, weet jy waar jou kinders is.

> Op jou roep sê ons nooit nee nie, sê ons altyd, altyd ja:
> Om te lewe, om te sterwe - ja, ons kom Suid-Afrika.

> Op U Almag vas vertrouend het ons vadere gebou:
> Skenk ook ons die krag, o Here! om te handhaaf en te hou -

Dat die erwe van ons vad're vir ons kinders erwe bly:
Knegte van die Allerhoogste, teen die hele wêreld vry.

Soos ons vadere vertrou het, leer ook ons vertrou, o Heer -
Met ons land en met ons nasie sal dit wel wees, God regeer.

(Ringing out from our blue heavens, from our deep seas breaking round;
Over everlasting mountains where the echoing crags resound;
From our plains where creaking wagons cut their trails into the earth -
Calls the spirit of our Country, of the land that gave us birth.

At thy call we shall not falter, firm and steadfast we shall stand,
At thy will to live or perish, O South Africa, dear land.

In our body and our spirit, in our inmost heart held fast;
In the promise of our future and the glory of our past;
In our will, our work, our striving, from the cradle to the grave -
There's no land that shares our loving, and no bond that can enslave.

Thou hast borne us and we know thee. May our deeds to all proclaim
Our enduring love and service to thy honor and thy name.

In the golden warmth of summer, in the chill of winter's air,
In the surging life of springtime, in the autumn of despair;
When the wedding bells are chiming or when those we love do depart;
Thou dost know us for thy children and dost take us to thy heart.

Loudly peals the answering chorus; We are thine, and we shall stand,
Be it life or death, to answer to thy call, beloved land.
In thy power, Almighty, trusting, did our fathers build of old;
Strengthen then, O Lord, their children to defend, to love, to hold --
That the heritage they gave us for our children yet may be;
Bondsmen only of the highest and before the whole world free.
As our fathers trusted humbly, teach us, Lord, to trust Thee still;
Guard our land and guide our people in Thy way to do Thy will).

Following the singing of *Die Stem,* various speakers, led by Dominee

Muller, climbed onto the stage and delivered tirades against liberals, Jews, Communists and the TRC, while pledging to never to forsake *Bittereinders* like Kruger to its mercy. Afterward the speeches, everyone retreated to the tent for a sumptuous dinner.

The whole proceeding left Freda with little doubt that she didn't belong among such people.

Tina was right, she thought. *These people, despite their normal appearance, are nothing but a bunch of neo-Nazis.*

32 MAKHADO had never cried as an adult. His father and the mountain school had taught him that it was unmanly to cry, no matter the extent of the personal tragedy suffered. Even when malaria killed his mother, brother and two sisters, he never shed a tear though his heart was breaking. But Makhado came very close to weeping as he sat listening for several hours – with a mixture of horror, astonishment and rage – to Gideon's incredible confession of his double life as an askari for General Kruger's death squad.

"Please say it's not true, my son," Makhado pleaded. Tears pricked the corners of his eyes.

Gideon lowered his head and said in a contrite voice, "It's true, Baba. And it's all in those diaries." He languidly pointed to the two thick notebooks with sturdy black vinyl covers he'd just removed from his briefcase. They were sitting on Makhado's lap, cradled between his work-gnarled hands.

"Every atrocity the Thathe Vondo death squad committed while I was an askari is in there," Gideon said. "How many houses we firebombed. How many anti-apartheid activists and MK guerrillas we killed. When they were killed. How they were killed. And what was done with their corpses."

Makhado's chapped lips trembled. He tried to speak but no words came out. He gazed with pained eyes at his thirty-seven-year old son, now a total stranger to him. It was almost seven o'clock, and Gideon had been pouring his heart out for more than two hours.

"Why did you do it, my son?" Makhado demanded.

Gideon didn't know what to say.

"How could you have betrayed your own people?"

Sensing his father's fury, Gideon thought it best to say nothing. He simply reached down, picked up a whittled stick and began drawing figures in the red dirt. His brain feverishly searched for an answer that would explain, if a satisfactory explanation were possible, how he could have been one of Alexandra's most beloved teachers and respected activists and an askari at the same time.

"Did you ever think of the families of the men and women you betrayed?" Makhado demanded hotly.

Gideon gave no reply. His face wore a mask of indescribable guilt as he continued prodding the red dirt.

"Answer me. Did you?"

"I tried not to," Gideon murmured softly.

"I can see why. How could you live with yourself knowing that you spied for ruthless killers who – "

Makhado choked on the rest of the sentence. He clenched his fists. He turned and glared fiercely at Gideon, eyes awash with contempt.

"You even stood by and watched as they were being tortured and murdered," he said bitterly. "You heard their screams of pain, their pleas for help. And yet you did nothing."

"I'm not proud of what I did, Baba," Gideon said in an anguished voice. He broke the stick in two and then, confounded that it was broken, flung the pieces away. "I never wanted to become an askari."

"Then why did you become one?"

"I had no choice."

"No choice!" Makhado exploded. He gripped Gideon by the shoulders with both hands and shook him violently. "What choice did you want? Aren't you the son of Venda warriors?"

"I am," Gideon mumbled.

"Didn't your great-grandfather slay a dozen Boers at the Battle of Hangklip, armed only with his spear and shield?"

"He did."

"And when they captured and tortured him, didn't he choose death rather than betray his fellow warriors?"

"He did."

"Then why did you dishonor his memory?"

"I wasn't myself, Baba," Gideon said, swallowing hard.

Makhado let go of his shoulders and said scornfully. "What a lame excuse. Only cowards make such excuses. Not men who've been to the mountain school."

"I was a broken man, Baba," Gideon said.

Makhado stared at his son, uncomprehending.

"Torture broke me," Gideon went on. "I was arrested during the second state of emergency for giving a speech at a mass funeral. An askari who'd infiltrated the MK cell in Alexandra fingered me as a member. General Kruger immediately brought me to the interrogation center in Venda."

"Here in Venda?"

"Ja. As a matter of fact, the interrogation center is at the very private game reserve where you now work. It's about five miles from the main lodge, near the Crocodile Lake."

The revelation jolted Makhado. He'd seen the place. It consisted of four small thatched-roof huts surrounding one large one. But he'd taken it for a remote bushveld camp.

"Shortly after I was brought to the interrogation center, I was taken to one of the huts and chained to a wall. There were about a dozen MK guerrillas in the hut, men and women. Most of them had been caught trying to infiltrate back into the country through Zimbabwe. The hut was dark and reeked of feces and urine. The walls of the hut were thin, and throughout the night we could hear bloodcurdling screams and cries as our comrades were being tortured and murdered in the *waarheid kamer* – the truth hut."

"What is the truth hut?" Makhado asked.

"It's the large hut. That's where prisoners were brought for interrogation. They were tortured until they confessed. Afterwards they were executed."

"Executed?"

"Ja. No one brought to the interrogation center ever left it alive."

"So what happened after you were brought to the interrogation center?"

"For six days straight I was repeatedly punched and kicked, given little food, and forced to sleep while standing under a harsh bright light with my hands and feet chained." Gideon shuddered at the memory. "They attached electrical wires to my testicles and shocked me repeatedly. But I refused to betray my comrades. On the seventh day, when I thought I was losing my mind, Viljoen and Barnard came for me. They again dragged me to the truth hut. It was pitch dark. It must have been well past midnight. Inside the hut I found Viljoen interrogating three MK cadres by the glow of a paraffin lamp. General Kruger was sitting at a nearby wooden table, supervising the interrogation and taking notes. The shackled hands and feet of the cadres were hooked to a power generator, the kind used to pump water for animals. I recognized them. They were former students I'd helped flee the country back in 1985. I was supposed to rendezvous with them in a few days and lead them to an MK hideout at the Alexandra graveyard, from where they could carry out their mission of making the ghetto ungovernable."

Gideon paused, still horrified by the memory of what he'd witnessed that awful night.

"Their faces were swollen and bloodied," he continued, his voice cracking. "One of them had a busted eardrum. Another's nose was ripped open. Viljoen had shoved a knife into it. Blood was all over the place. It looked like the three cadres had been tortured for several days. But they wouldn't talk. I saw General Kruger give Viljoen a nod. With a maniacal grin on his fat face, Viljoen calmly flicked on the generator switch. Electricity instantly surged through the body of the first cadre. His name was Thabiso. He writhed and screamed. Blood foamed out of his ears and mouth as electricity fried every part of his body."

Gideon paused. He was now shaking. Beads of sweat glistened on his hot brow. Somehow he managed to continue. "Then something amazing happened. The two remaining cadres suddenly stood up and thrust their shackled fists high into the air. They saluted their dead comrade in the name of the struggle. Then they began singing *Nkosi Sikelel' i Afrika*. Then Mzamani, the group's leader, turned to Kruger and said defiantly, 'You can kill us, but we'll never betray the struggle. And someday the ANC shall rule South Africa."

"General Kruger laughed. 'Not if I have anything do with it, kaffir,' he said scornfully. 'This is a white man's country. And it shall remain that way.' He then turned to Viljoen and nodded. The next cadre to be electrocuted was Dladla. At seventeen he was the youngest. Yet he too met his fate like a true African warrior. Then it was Mzamani's turn. Before he died, he said something that has haunted me ever since."

RIAAN SWANEPOEL sat inside a 4,000 square foot bunker with soundproof walls in the basement of the headquarters of Arm, Protect & Secure Inc. in downtown Johannesburg. This was the firm's surveillance center. It consisted of five large rooms equipped with secure phones, faxes, printers, computers, and giant television monitors that were used to project tracking maps, photo images from satellites, maps of premises and details about any neighborhood, city or town in South Africa. There were four workstations in each room, manned by highly trained technicians, all of them white, Afrikaner and former policemen and security officers.

The first room was used for monitoring residential burglar alarm systems; the second for monitoring alarm systems on business premises; the third for communicating with the firm's thousand security guards deployed around the country; the fourth for communicating with the firm's specially equipped vans and sedans that patrolled neighborhoods and business areas protected by the firm.

The fifth room was accessible only through a thick steel door that opened only after someone had peered into a high-definition eye-scanner mounted on the right side of the door. The scanner automatically matched the striation and vessel patterns of the retina with on-file retinal patterns stored inside a supercomputer named *Voortrekker*.

As director of the surveillance center, Swanepoel reported directly to Botha. Since getting instructions to keep tabs on Liefling, Thando, David and Gideon, Swanepoel had been working overtime. The beefy fifty-one-year old ex-bouncer at a Pretoria nightclub didn't mind that. He was obsessed with surveillance, to the point where he had no private life whatsoever, which is why Botha had put him in charge of surveillance. The move allowed Botha the playboy time to indulge himself without fear of missing out on critical information.

Swanepoel was perfect for surveillance work. During the '70s he had headed a secret department within the South African Bureau of Racial Affairs, charged with investigating violations of the Immorality Act.

Swanepoel had been famous within the department for his sting operations. He'd hide in closets, plant hidden cameras and microphones in bedrooms and peep through keyholes, all in an effort to catch lovers of different races in the act. Sometimes he'd take the lovers by surprise, gleefully blinding them with the flash of his Olympus camera as it snapped away. As the terrified couple, naked and clinging to one another, looked on, his goons would seize sheets, panties, briefs and other incriminating evidence.

Everything would be hauled off to special labs for analysis to determine if any coitus had taken place. And Swanepoel loved conducting the definitive test of whether the Immorality had indeed been broken: probing the woman's vagina for the presence of contraband semen. It was Swanepoel who had arrested David and Dikeledi on charges of breaking the Immorality Act back in 1979.

Swanepoel was busy monitoring the bugs in Liefling's flat, Thando's office and David's Soweto house when the phone rang. It was Botha checking in.

"Are you coming to work tonight?" Swanepoel asked.

"No," Botha said. "I'm going out on a date. Has anything important happened since we talked this afternoon? I want to update the General before I go out."

"No. Liefling's race mixing orgy is still going on. And Thando is at the office working late. As for Jew-boy, his girlfriend just arrived and will be spending the night."

"What about the mystery witness?"

"He hasn't called Jew-boy in two days."

"Has *Voortrekker* confirmed if he's really Gideon?"

"He's still working on his profile. I'll go and check to see if he's done."

Swanepoel rose from the compact swivel chair in front of the console and walked toward the humming supercomputer squatting in the middle of the room. In it were stored the names, addresses and profiles of hundreds of thousands of individuals, including policemen, politicians, employees of the firm and its clients. Arm, Protect & Secure Inc. routinely used much of this information in conducting its legitimate business of providing protection for its clientele.

But the computer contained other information from hundreds of top-secret files which had mysteriously disappeared from John Vorster Square and other police stations across the country shortly before Nelson Mandela became president. These files contained the names of impimpis, askaris, collaborators and other agents of CCB death squads.

Swanepoel pressed a couple buttons on the specialized keyboard and watched the flickering monitor for a couple seconds. He frowned. He got back on the phone.

"Nope," he said to Botha. "No confirmation yet. But I'm certain its Gideon."

"Where's the bastard now?"

"In Venda visiting his father. I had my men attach a powerful transponder to the rear bumper of his Explorer. It sends microwave signals every ten seconds, which are triangulated by our surveillance-satellite uplink to pinpoint the Explorer's exact location around the clock."

"And has Shaka checked in yet?"

"He's on his way. And I have everything ready for him."

"Good. I'll check back with you in about two hours or so. Should you need to reach me in case of any emergency, dial my cell number."

"Okay."

KRUGER, Freda, the Mullers and the Prinsloos were enjoying a sumptuous candlelight eight-course dinner inside the tent when Emma came and summoned Kruger to the phone. The call was urgent. Kruger excused himself, rose from the table and hurried to his study on the second floor.

"Sorry to disturb you, General," Botha said. "But I wanted to give you an update."

"Go ahead," Kruger said impatiently. "I'm in the middle of dinner."

"I spoke to Swanepoel about ten minutes ago," Botha said. "He spent all day at the monitoring station."

"Anything unusual?"

"No. Jew-boy is at home with his girlfriend. Thando is at the center working late. Shaka is already in Jo'burg. And your stepdaughter is having one of her rainbow orgies."

Kruger muttered a curse. There was nothing he hated more about Liefling than her multiracial parties.

"Has *Voortrekker* confirmed if Gideon is Shaka?"

"Not yet. Swanepoel says he needs one more voice stress analyzer result to make a definitive identification."

Kruger frowned.

"Give me a ring as soon as that happens," he said. "If Gideon is indeed the kaffir-lover's mystery witness, he must be captured immediately and taken to the interrogation center. We must find out who else knows."

"I'll let you know, General."

"And is everything set for tomorrow's meeting?"

"Ja. I spoke to Viljoen and Barnard earlier in the day. They told me that every member of the Thathe Vondo death squad will be present."

"Excellent. Talk to you later."

33

GIDEON couldn't continue. He broke down into piteous sobs. Makhado held his hand tightly. "It's okay, my son. It's okay."

"Before he was electrocuted," Gideon went on with great effort, "Mzamani said, 'Professor – my students called me Professor because I always carried books with me – you were my favorite teacher because you were tough. You were tough because you wanted us to be strong men and women so that someday we'd smash apartheid. Please, Professor, don't disappoint me. Let me die knowing that you'll never break, that you'll never betray the struggle.'"

Gideon paused. His throat felt dry. He swallowed. He then continued. "Mzamani then thrust a clenched right fist into the air and shouted, 'Amandla!' while staring straight into my face. He expected me to respond, 'Awethu!' But for some reason I couldn't. It was as if fear had made the 'Awethu' stick in my throat. It was as if I knew I'd break."

Gideon wrung his hands, as if the act might wash away the blood of the comrades he'd betrayed. "When I didn't respond with 'Awethu,' General Kruger smiled. He signaled to Viljoen to zap Mzamani. I shook with horror as I stared at the three crumpled and lifeless bodies of my comrades.

"General Kruger then turned to me. 'Gideon,' he said, speaking almost like a father to me. 'I know you care very much about your wife and two children. I also know that your father, who was hard hit by the recent drought, relies on you to help him take care of the families of your sister and two brothers who are dead. A lot of people would suffer if you died.'

Having said that, General Kruger made me an offer he knew I couldn't refuse, especially given my state of mind. He had a way of knowing when someone had reached the breaking point. I'd reached that point.

"'Turn askari for us,' he said, 'and your life will be spared. And I'll find ways to help your father take care of your extended family. I'll also build a well, a clinic and a school for your village. But if you refuse, you'll die like the three terrorist dogs you see crumpled in front of you. Not only that, but afterwards I'll send vigilantes to kill your wife and two children. You don't want their pretty faces hacked to bloody pulps with machetes, do you?'"

Gideon could barely speak now, but he forced himself to go on. "You know how much my family means to me, Baba. I couldn't bear the thought of their being hacked to death. So I told General Kruger that I'd cooperate. What else could I do?"

Gideon noticed that tears were now flowing freely down his father's hollow cheeks. He was very surprised. He'd never seen his father cry before. Makhado made no effort to wipe away the salty tears. For several long moments he stared in silence at the pitiless evening sky. The sun had now almost completely vanished behind the mountains. Dusk was furtively creeping in. Lights came on in several of the huts, and the hot and humid air reverberated with the din of insects.

"I forgive you, my son," Makhado said with a heavy sigh. "Now I understand. You were faced with an impossible choice."

He wrapped his arm comfortingly around Gideon's hunched shoulders. "Warrior that I am, I don't know what I'd have done if I'd been in your shoes. But you must reclaim your lost honor, my son."

"I know, Baba," Gideon said, looking up at Makhado. "That's why I came to talk to you. I want your advice."

"About what?"

"I'm thinking of testifying at General Kruger's trial. As a matter of fact, I've already contacted David Schneider, one of Liefling's partners."

"Have you told him what you just told me?"

"No. I wanted to talk to you first. There are risks involved."

"What risks?"

"I might be killed."

Makhado was silent for several minutes before he said, "You should testify, my son. Despite the risks."

"I have one more thing to confess, Baba," Gideon said, avoiding eye contact with Makhado. "And please don't be angry with me. I'm not a warrior like you. I'm afraid to die. If General Kruger finds out that I'm planning to testify against him, he won't hesitate to do to me what he did to the other askaris he wanted silenced."

"What did he do to them?"

"He cut out their tongues and fed their bodies to the crocodiles at the lake near the truth hut."

Makhado shuddered. "Holy *Midzimu*. What had they done?"

"One of them – his name was Moses – was planning to testify at an inquest into the death of a student activist named Dikeledi. She was murdered while in detention at John Vorster Square. The bogus police report said she'd died from an epileptic seizure. But Moses was present when Kruger and Botha interrogated Dikeledi. He saw Botha inject her with a drug he said was insulin that Dikeledi was refusing to take despite being a diabetic. Moses told the two other askaris that he was going to reveal the truth because he wanted to stop being an askari. His wife and four children had left him because being an askari had made him violent and abusive. The two askaris, apparently thinking they'd be rewarded for turning Moses in, told Botha, who was their controller. He told Kruger, and Kruger had all three of them killed."

"Despite the fact that two of them were innocent?"

"Kruger didn't want to take any chances. He's that ruthless. If you ask me, I think he's mad."

"I understand your fear, son," Makhado said. "But testifying is the right thing to do. Your eyewitness testimony can convict this madman. And his conviction might give a measure of justice to the grieving mothers and fathers of all the people he's killed. Most important, they'll find out where their loved ones' bodies were buried after they were murdered. They'll be able to exhume the bodies for proper burial, and perform the rites of purification so their wandering souls can be welcomed into the realm of their ancestors."

"I know, Baba. That's one reason why I want to testify."

"And as for you, my son," Makhado said, squeezing his hand. "Testifying will restore your Ubuntu. You'll be able to look yourself in the mirror. And I'll be very proud of you."

"I wish for nothing more than to have my Ubuntu restored, Baba," Gideon said.

"The truth *will* restore your Ubuntu, my son. I'm convinced of that. Only the truth can make the Midzimu forgive you for what you've done." Makhado reached into the pocket of his overalls and brought out a round tin of snuff. He opened it, inhaled a pinch and then sneezed violently, a propitious sign.

"Bless you," Gideon said.

"Thank you," Makhado said. He put the tin of snuff back into his pocket. He blew his nose hard into a brown handkerchief, then said, "Tell me one thing, son. Why did General Kruger target Alexandra?"

"The ghetto was a powerful symbol of black resistance to apartheid,"

Gideon said. "The ANC was very active in Alexandra in the 1980s. And after I joined, my task was to help arrange safe passage out of the country for dozens of students who daily fought running battles with the police and troops."

Gideon paused. His mind's eye was suddenly flooded with memories of the brave boys and girls, some as young as ten, who took on the most powerful army on the African continent, armed only with rocks, slingshots, petrol bombs, the dented lids of trash cans as shields and an unconquerable spirit.

"General Kruger's mission was to crush the growing rebellion in Alexandra," Gideon continued, his voice growing more impassioned. "There was fear that it might spark a people's revolution, and that blacks might start attacking whites in the nearby suburbs."

"Why did General Kruger use the bushveld camp as an interrogation center? It's six hours from Alexandra. Weren't there other places nearby? John Vorster Square, for instance?"

"He wanted a place as far away from the township as possible. Also, a lot of MK guerrillas who ended up in Alexandra infiltrated back into South Africa from Zimbabwe and Mozambique through Venda. And a remote bushveld camp covering thousands of acres of thick forest was an ideal site for mass murder."

Makhado shook his head in bewilderment. "Why did General Kruger build the village a school and dig us a well if he's such an evil man?"

"It was part of his strategy to pacify the village so it wouldn't harbor ANC and PAC guerillas. Also, he did it to ensure my loyalty. General Kruger was like a father to his askaris, as long as we were loyal to him. Over the years he used a CCB slush fund to help us whenever we or our relatives needed help with housing or work permits. And when he disbanded the death squad in 1993, he gave me a bonus of R450, 000. I used the money to build the new house, buy the Explorer and help you and mama through hard times."

"Are you the only askari left?"

Gideon hesitated. He didn't know if he should tell his father about Ndwakhulu. But then he remembered that he'd already confided in Ndwakhulu about his plans.

"No," he said, "I'm one of two left."

"Who's the other one?"

"Ndwakhulu."

Makhado was stunned. "Ndwakhulu Mavhungu!" he cried. "The one you went to mountain school with?"

Gideon nodded.

Makhado shook his head. "I don't understand."

"Kruger recruited us about the same time. He trained me as a spy and Botha trained Ndwakhulu as an assassin. He killed a lot of people. And when the death squad was disbanded, he continued working for Kruger."

"Did you tell him about your plans to testify?"

"I did."

Makhado stared at Gideon in disbelief. "Why in the world did you do a foolish thing like that?"

"I trust him."

"Trust him?"

"Ja."

"What makes you so sure he won't betray you if he's still working for Kruger?"

"He told me that he's been thinking of exposing the Thathe Vondo death squad too."

"He may have been lying in order to trap you."

"Maybe. But it's a gamble I'm willing to take. Besides, I have reasons for believing he won't betray me."

"What reasons?"

Gideon glanced at his watch. "They're too complicated for me to explain. I have to be going. I promised Ndwakhulu that I'd stop by his house so we can go over the evidence we have against Kruger and his death squad before we give it to the human rights lawyers. Trust me, Baba, Ndwakhulu won't betray me."

"I hope you're right, my son."

Gideon grabbed his briefcase and stood up. Makhado also got up and they walked across the courtyard toward the gate.

"Son, tomorrow I intend to tell Viljoen that I'm quitting."

"Why?"

"I don't need blood money."

Gideon grabbed his father's arm.

"Don't quit, Baba," he begged. "At least not now."

"Why not?"

"It'll make them suspicious. Ndwakhulu said that they might be watching me. I don't want them to start watching you too. It might be dangerous."

Makhado thought for a while. "Okay, I'll think about it."

Makhado and Gideon reached the Explorer, which had a tan leather interior, a CD player and a radar detector. Gideon opened the passenger door and was about to climb in when a thought arrested him. He turned and faced Makhado.

"Baba," he said.

"Yes, my son?"

"If anything should happen to me and Ndwakhulu before we testify, please make sure those diaries get to Liefling and David."

"I will. Is this the only copy?"

"No. The other one is in the car. I plan to stop in Soweto and give it to David after I talk to Ndwakhulu."

"Be very careful, my son."

"I will, Baba."

Makhado, who seldom openly expressed affection, gave Gideon a big hug. They hugged for a very long time. Finally Gideon climbed into the Explorer, started the engine, made a sharp U-turn and drove off.

Midzimu, please protect my son as he does his duty, Makhado murmured as he watched the Explorer bump its way down the winding, rutted rural road.

He hurried back to the main hut. He was halfway there when a thought stopped him. He wondered if he'd ever see his son alive again. He turned and looked down the road. The Explorer had disappeared.

GIDEON'S Explorer pulled up the cobbled driveway of Ndwakhulu's 5,000 square-foot bricked mansion, which he shared with his mother. The mansion was in an exclusive section of Thohoyandou, a neighborhood that was home to lawyers, business leaders, doctors and various other professionals, many of whom had prospered during the homeland's short-lived independence and were now employed by the ANC-led government. He bounded up the steps to the huge front door, above which was mounted a close-circuit security camera.

He rang the bell. No one answered. He rang it again. Still no answer. He looked about, puzzled. He was about to turn and leave when the door creaked open and he saw Ndwakhulu's mother – a wizened old woman wrapped in a colorful blanket and leaning on a carved walking stick.

"Hullo, Mrs. Mavhungu," Gideon said loudly, aware that Mrs. Mavhungu was hard of hearing. "Remember me? I'm Thanyani."

"Yes. I've been waiting for you. Ndwakhulu is not home."

"Not home?"

"Ja. He left last night for Johannesburg."

Gideon was stunned. "For Johannesburg?"

"Ja."

"Did he leave any messages?"

Mrs. Mavhungu slowly lifted her gnarled hand toward Gideon. "He gave me this letter to give to you."

Gideon took the letter. "Thank you," he said.

"Won't you come in?"

"No, thanks," Gideon said, a bit flustered by the sudden turn of events. "I'm in a bit of a hurry."

Once inside the Explorer he ripped open the letter and turned on the reading lamp. On a single sheet of notebook paper was written the following cryptic message in Ndwakhulu's sloping cursive:

Dear Thanyani:

My plans have changed. I had to leave immediately for Jo'burg. I will be staying at the Sandton City Hotel. Room 1130. Meet me there as soon as you get to Jo'burg. Do not under any circumstances use the phone to call me. Come in person. It's a matter of life or death.

Your Comrade,

Ndwakhulu

34

THANDO was in her office at the Phutadichaba Community Center busy reviewing several affidavits she'd gathered that afternoon when she heard a faint knock on the door.

"Come in," she said, raising her eyes toward the door expecting to see another shaken woman seeking refuge from an abusive boyfriend or husband.

The door slowly opened. A tall, broad-shouldered man in a charcoal gray double-breasted suit, brown Stetson hat and snakeskin boots walked in. Thando's heart skipped a beat at the sight of the visitor, who was carrying a slim, expensive-looking leather briefcase.

"Sidney!" she cried.

"Hi, Thando," the man said, flashing a smile which dimpled his left cheek.

"Please come in," Thando said, getting up from behind the cluttered desk. She eagerly shook Sidney's hand. She wanted to give her former husband a hug but felt it would give her feelings away. They were divorced, after all, and divorced couples had to keep enough emotional distance to avoid complications.

"How was your drive?"

"Not bad," Sidney said. "I made excellent time." Sidney glanced at Thando's cluttered desk. "I hope I'm not disturbing you."

"No, not at all," Thando said, resuming her seat behind the desk piled with affidavits and TRC transcripts. "I'm getting ready for Wednesday's preparatory examination. Please sit down."

Sidney grabbed the stack of newspapers and books on a chair and placed them on the nearby sofa.

"Sorry the place is a mess," Thando said.

"You should see my office," Sidney said, sitting down.

"Did you stop by the flat?" Thando asked.

"Ja. I found Mkondeleli and a friend studying for exams. Our daughter has grown a lot since she last visited me."

"She sure has. When people see us together they think we're sisters." Sidney laughed.

"Can I get you something to drink?" Thando asked.

"A Coke will do," Sidney said.

Thando took two chilled Cokes out of the small refrigerator in the center's kitchenette. She handed one to Sidney.

"Mkondeleli told me she's doing very well in school," he said, opening the can with a loud fizz.

"She thinks she'll come out number one again," Thando said, opening hers. "I told her not to be overconfident."

"She will. She's very smart. After all, she inherited her mother's brains."

Thando smiled shyly. "By the way," she said, "thanks a lot for all the help with the school fees, books and uniform for this term. I hate to impose like that on you."

"You aren't imposing," Sidney said. He sipped his Coke. "It's my responsibility as her father."

Thando was pleased that he felt that way.

"She told me that after exams their class is going on a trip to Cape Town to visit Robben Island and the Parliament buildings," Sidney said.

"In two weeks. But I might not be able to afford money for the train and hotel. I just paid taxes and bought new furniture for the flat. And I'm not earning much."

Without hesitation, Sidney whipped out a checkbook from his doeskin wallet and wrote a check for R2000. He handed it to Thando. "I didn't want to give it to her. I want her to think it's coming from you."

Thando hesitated before accepting the check. "Why?"

"Well, I don't want her thinking that her mother isn't a good mother because she can't afford to provide for her needs. You're a very good mother. You're giving so much of your time to very worthy causes that don't pay you much. I'm making a lot more money than I need."

Tears came to Thando's eyes. It was just like Sidney. Always generous, always understanding. For a brief moment she thought of old times. It had been nearly three years since their amicable divorce. The judge had initially ruled that Sidney should have primary custody of Mkondeleli, since he had a stable job and could provide for her, but Sidney had declined. He'd insisted that Thando have primary custody, adding that she'd be the better parent of a young girl, who needed a female role model. Not only that, but with his six-figure salary, he'd offered to pay generous child support and when Thando was still unemployed, he'd loaned her money and paid the deposit and first month's rent for her apartment.

It was clear to Thando, as she sat across from Sidney and once more felt that lump in her throat she'd felt when they'd first met, that she was still very much in love with him. She'd dated other men since the divorce, but she knew that none could ever replace the father of her only child, the man who'd been by her side during the struggle against apartheid. She was convinced she'd remarry Sidney in a minute if it weren't for the heavy guilt she still felt.

That guilt had to do with the death of his younger brother, Nelson, who'd been a member of her underground MK cell in Alexandra. Thando blamed herself for Nelson's death. As cell leader, she'd ordered him executed after he'd been exposed as a spy for the security forces. The decision had been the most agonizing of her life.

Sidney had been deeply pained by his brother's death, but he'd told Thando that he didn't blame her for it. He'd said that Nelson would have betrayed more of their cadres and compromised their mission if she hadn't acted. Sidney had even testified in her behalf during her amnesty application before the TRC for Nelson's death.

But there was no amnesty for guilt. Unable to bear the thought of staying married to a man whose brother she'd ordered killed, Thando had felt compelled to end their ten-year-old marriage.

But each time she saw Sidney, she wondered if she'd done the right thing in asking for a divorce. Especially considering the fact that she still loved him dearly, and that their daughter yearned for them to get back together. Yet Thando knew that the only way they could ever get back together was if she could overcome her feelings of guilt. And the only way she could do that was to find out who'd turned Nelson into an askari.

"So how's life been treating you lately?" Sidney asked.

"Okay. Busier that ever," Thando said, nervously tapping the edge of the desk with a red ballpoint pen.

"Still fighting an uphill battle to protect women's rights, I see," Sidney said, glancing at the feminist posters plastering the whitewashed walls.

"No other battle is more important," Thando said. "Did you know that a thousand rapes are committed in South Africa each day? Over 60 percent of husbands routinely beat their wives. And every six days in Gauteng alone a woman is killed by her male partner."

"It's tragic," Sidney said. "I'm afraid it will take a lot of time to change the culture of violence among men. Patriarchy and apartheid have seriously damaged them. Remember the debates we used to have over this issue with our comrades at the graveyard hideout?"

"I sure do," Thando said, smiling.

"Do you still go there?"

"From time to time. For old time's sake."

Thando recollected the dangerous and exhilarating times she and Sidney had spent as part of the MK cell. Whenever cell members were not out on bombing and assassination missions, or planning strategies on how to make Alexandra ungovernable, Sidney would preside over what they called "Freedom University," during which they heatedly debated issues of freedom, justice, and equality.

The pain of remembrance made Thando abruptly change the subject. "So, what did you want to see me about?"

"I came to warn you, Thando."

Surprised, Thando straightened. "What about?"

"Stay out of the lawsuit against Kruger."

"Why?"

"It's too dangerous. You could get killed."

Thando rolled her eyes. "You should know me better than that. Have I ever been afraid of dying?"

"Thando, think of our daughter. She needs you. These neo-Nazis are ruthless. They won't hesitate to kill you if they feel threatened. Have you forgotten how many of our comrades were brutally murdered by CCB death squads? I don't want anything to happen to you."

"Thanks. But I can take care of myself," Thando said with determination.

"So many of these CCB bastards have gotten away with murder," Sidney said. "Kruger isn't the first one."

"But he's a big fish," Thando said. "And I have personal reasons for wanting to see him prosecuted if he refuses to testify."

"What reasons?"

"I believe his death squad killed many of our cadres."

"Do you have proof?"

"Ja. We have a secret witness who's confirmed that Kruger's death squad killed Mzamani, Dladla and Thabiso. I also have reason to believe that Nelson was the person who betrayed them, and that he was working for Kruger."

Sidney raised his eyebrows. " And on what grounds do you believe that?"

"Our witness says that Kruger's death squad operated from Venda. And as you know, I used to send Nelson and Gideon to Venda a lot to arrange safe passage for our cadres who were infiltrating back into the country from Zimbabwe. Most of them never made it because their escort, your brother, was an askari. It was only after Gideon came forward with evidence proving that Nelson was indeed the reason why so many of our cadres were disappearing that I felt compelled to act. Even after that, I still had doubts about his guilt. Now this witness will hopefully put an end to all the doubts. And when he does, maybe I'll stop feeling so guilty. "

"Has this mystery witness come forward?"

"No."

"How can you trust him if he hasn't come forward?"

"He'll come forward."

"What if he doesn't?"

"Then we've got no case against Kruger. And we'll look foolish at Wednesday's preparatory examination."

Sidney shook his head. "I don't understand why you'd risk your life to prosecute such a dubious case."

"You should be the last person to ask me that question," Thando said looking into her former husband's face. "You know what the CCB did to men like your brother. And you know that if I hadn't ordered him executed I wouldn't have asked for – " Thando couldn't bring herself to utter the word "divorce."

Sidney was silent for a long while. "Please be careful," he said finally.

"I'll be careful."

"If you need any help while you're working on the case, let me know. The holidays are coming up. I can arrange for Mkondeleli to come and stay with me and her grandma."

"Thanks. I'd appreciate that. Especially because if the lawsuit goes to trial, it's likely to be a long one."

"I guess I'll be on my way then," Sidney said, rising.

"How long are you in Jo'burg for?"

"About a week. If you don't mind, I'd like to take Mkondeleli shopping one afternoon next week. Her 14th birthday is coming up soon."

"That will be nice."

Thando accompanied Sidney to the door..

Sidney looked into her eyes. "Take care of yourself, Thando."

"I will."

He smiled shyly then said, "Would you mind if I kissed you goodbye?"

"Not at all."

When their lips met, Thando felt a surge of warmth and longing she'd never felt in a long time. She stood in the doorway and watched as Sidney descended the stairs, got into his new black Mercedes and drove away.

Still pondering his warning, she was halfway to her desk when the phone rang.

"Thando speaking."

"Hi, Thando. This is David."

Thando's face brightened. "Hi."

"Our mystery witness just called again."

"He did? Great. Is he finally willing to come forward?"

"More than that. He has the evidence we need to nail Kruger."

Thando's heart started pounding. "What kind of evidence?"

"Diaries. Apparently he recorded every atrocity committed by Kruger's death squad. He's bringing them over."

"When?"

"Tomorrow morning at ten."

"I'll be at your place. Have you called Liefling?"

"I'm about to. And don't forget to pick up the affidavit from Vusi's mother. Our mystery witness says he knows who murdered him. He also says he knows who set up your brother-in-law, Nelson."

35 LIEFLING and Sipho snuggled together on the living room couch, exhausted. But neither felt sleepy yet. It was about 11.30 a.m. The last of the guests had departed. The lights were off; an aromatic candle burned in a crystal dish on the coffee table, next to two wineglasses. A light breeze from the nearby Atlantic Ocean fluttered the lace curtains of the open window. In the distance the imposing facade of Table Mountain shimmered a hazy gold under powerful spotlights.

Sipho gently caressed Liefling's flushed cheek, smoothing away a loose strand of silky hair from her eyes. She closed them, enjoying the tender touch of his fingertips.

"That was some party," Sipho said. "I enjoyed meeting your friends."

"They told me they really enjoyed meeting you too."

"You know, we've been together almost three months," Sipho said, drawing intricate lines and circles on Liefling's smooth well-tanned arms. "You've met my brother, but I've yet to meet a single one of your relatives."

"Well, my mom was planning to take us out to lunch, but then the lawsuit messed things up."

"What about your other relatives? You told me you had aunts and uncles around the Western Cape."

"It's unlikely they'll agree to meet you," Liefling said, her eyes fluttering open. "They're opposed to any kind of interracial relationship. Black-white. Colored - white, Indian -white. It doesn't matter. They don't even approve of English-Afrikaner marriages. They're *verkrampte* members of the Dutch Reformed Church who still believe in all that Tower of Babel nonsense. After my father repudiated apartheid, they wanted nothing to do with him or his family."

"What exactly made him turn his back on apartheid?"

"I did."

Sipho looked puzzled. "You did?"

"Ja," Liefling said, sliding her hand slowly across Sipho's muscular chest. "On June 17, 1976, I turned him from Saul to Paul."

"How?"

"It's a long story."

"I'm eager to hear it."

"I was seven at the time," Liefling began. "School was out for the summer holidays and I was with my parents in Holland, where my father was attending the World Council of Churches conference. My father and I were alone in the hotel watching Wimbledon on TV. My mom was out shopping. Suddenly a news bulletin interrupted the matches. It showed pictures of South African riot police opening fire on unarmed schoolchildren in Soweto. Horrified, I cried, '*Kyk, hulle skiet skoolkinders! Hoe kom, Papa?*' " (*Look, they're shooting schoolchildren! Why, papa?*)

Liefling paused.

Sipho felt her tremble slightly. He hugged her closer.

"My father had no answer to my question," she went on. "He was just as horror-struck as I was. He suddenly fell to his knees and began praying. I was bewildered. I could tell my father was in torment. His eyes were shut and his face was contorted with anguish. He kept on praying. Finally, after the massacre was over and bodies lay strewn all over the dusty street, he opened his eyes. They were wet with tears. He hugged me tight. Tighter than he'd ever hugged me. He said, in a trembling voice, 'Our lives will never be the same, my Liefling.'"

"Amazing," Sipho said.

"The next day we flew back to South Africa. It was a Friday. That Sunday we went to church. I remember it was packed. People had been shaken up by the escalating violence in the townships. They wanted to be reassured that all was well. Their stricken consciences wanted soothing. And in the past, my father had done a great job of justifying any draconian measures taken by the government to maintain law and order. Among the congregation were members of the Broederbond, including several cabinet ministers."

Liefling paused. The flame of the candle dipped and bobbed in a sudden breeze flowing in through the open French doors.

"But this time my father was in no mood to let them off the hook. I remember his strong voice filling the room when he began denouncing apartheid. He called it a sin, a crime against humanity. He urged his fellow Afrikaners to abandon the suicidal policy before it was too late. 'I cannot in good conscience,' he said, 'support policies which result in the cold-blooded murder of innocent schoolchildren whose only crime is to want a decent education.' At the end of the sermon there was stunned silence. No one moved. All eyes followed my father as he slowly made his way down the aisle toward the door. I clung to my mother, who was seated in the front pew. I noticed she was ashen-faced and weeping. My father stood next to the door, ready to greet parishioners as they went out, as he'd done so many times in the past. No one shook his hand."

"What?"

"Not a single person shook his hand. One man even spat in his face. My father later told me that the man was a senior member of the Broederbond."

"The bastards."

"That night my father was visited by a delegation of dour-looking church elders. He was asked to recant his heresy or face the consequences. He refused. He was instantly fired as dominee of the *Moederkerk* and we were ostracized."

"It must have been hard on your family," Sipho said compassionately, curling a strand of Liefling's hair around his pinkie.

"It was hell," Liefling said softly. "I wasn't prepared for it. Nobody was. Not even my father. I lost all my friends. So did my mother. Even relatives shunned us." Liefling's voice grew bitter as she spoke. "Soon after my father was fired, we left Stellenbosch and moved to Jo'burg. But things didn't get any better. The Broederbond wanted to make an example of my father. It unleashed BOSS on us. The bastards tapped our phone, poisoned our pets and got pro-government papers to print malicious editorials about my father. BOSS even went so far as to regularly phone my mother – who was very depressed at the time – and tell her that the reason my father had repudiated apartheid and taken the job in Alexandra was because he had black lovers."

"You're kidding?"

"I'm serious. It was a common tactic. One time the caller even suggested that my mother would be better off killing herself and me to spare us the shame of what my father had done."

Her throat dry, Liefling paused and swallowed. Sipho noticed that her eyes were moist with tears. He gently kissed her forehead. It felt a bit warm.

"And then came the series of banning orders," Liefling continued. "My father was prohibited from meeting with more than one person at a time. He even needed permission to talk to his wife in public and to attend my birthday party. He couldn't publish anything. He couldn't be quoted. He couldn't even leave our block to go anywhere. He was even forbidden to preach."

A loud car raced past the window. After its noise had died down, Liefling continued. "But my father refused to be silenced. He'd send me to represent him at political meetings in the townships. That's how I came to know Alexandra so well."

"How did he earn a living if he couldn't preach?"

"Charity. Every weekend my father's congregation in Alexandra would take out a collection for our family. And strangers would bring us food. And these were people who had very little."

"They must have really admired your father."

"They did. He was the only white person who could enter Alexandra in the middle of a riot. I remember one time *Comrades* who'd just necklaced an *impimpi* hoisted my father on their shoulders and paid him homage as they danced around the charred corpse. Of course my father was weeping."

"Why?"

"A police patrol had prevented him from entering the ghetto in time to save the *impimpi*."

"Incredible. How did your mother take all this?"

"Not too well, I'm afraid," Liefling sighed. Shivering a bit, she pulled up the cotton quilt draping the sofa and covered her bare shoulders. "She was really bitter. She blamed my father for ruining our lives. They fought a lot. Many times she threatened to divorce him."

"That must have been a rough time for you?"

"It was. But to my mother's credit, she never left my father. She slowly got over her bitterness. It was the mid-1980s and more and more Afrikaners were beginning to openly question apartheid. Especially after President Botha publicly admitted that Verwoerd's idea of creating independent homelands was impractical, given the fact that most of the homelands were not economically viable."

"I remember the furor Botha's statement caused among *verkramptes*," Sipho said.

"But the genie was out of the bottle," Liefling said. "In universities and churches, people, especially the young, were asking questions previously considered taboo. They no longer believed the Big Lie. My mother even joined a group of Afrikaner women in Jo'burg who were spending two evenings a week teaching black domestic servants how to read and sew. Shortly after that, she began going to Alexandra itself and working with orphaned children. As for my father, he slowly regained a measure of respect among progressive Afrikaners. But right-wingers hated him. Particularly when he called for an end to segregated education."

"I guess right-wingers thought that mixed schools would lead to interracial dating and marriages," Sipho said.

"But my father stuck to his guns," Liefling said. "As a result, he made a lot of enemies. Especially within the security forces, which was full of *verkramptes.* Particularly when he started accusing the SADF of sponsoring death squads. He received a lot of death threats."

"He was a brave and remarkable man," Sipho said. "No wonder Bishop Tutu eulogized him as *Ighame lama Qhame*, the hero of heroes."

"You know what his favorite word was?"

"No."

"Ubuntu," Liefling said. "He said it was the most meaningful and spiritual word he'd ever heard. He used to pepper his sermons and speeches with it. He'd tell his black congregation that Afrikaners lacked Ubuntu, that's why they'd embraced apartheid as a way of ensuring their survival. If they'd had Ubuntu, he said, they would have recognized that the only way to ensure their survival was to acknowledge and affirm the humanity of others."

"That's so true," Sipho said.

"My father was fond of saying that the reason Afrikaners don't believe in Ubuntu is because they are basically an insecure people. They have this nagging feeling that no one loves them, that they are alone on a hostile continent. But my feeling is that if they truly embrace the spirit of Ubuntu, they'll find out they're accepted and loved. I'm convinced that blacks would welcome them with open arms as fellow human beings."

"You're right," Sipho said. "Blacks are very forgiving. Sometimes too forgiving."

Liefling turned and glanced at the clock above the fireplace. It was ten minutes past midnight.

"I'm ready to go to sleep," she said, yawning.

"Me too. But first I'd like a little rooibos. Care for some?"

"Sure."

Sipho and Liefling got up and went to the kitchen. They were seated at the table sipping their mugs of steaming rooibos tea when suddenly the phone rang.

"Aren't you going to answer it? Sipho asked. "It might be important."

Liefling shook her head. "Let the answering machine pick it up. It's probably an obscene call or death threat. I've been getting a lot of those lately in the middle of the night."

On the seventh ring, the answering machine on the kitchen counter started recording a message. Liefling lunged for the phone when she heard

David's excited voice.

BOTHA sang along to the screamed lyrics of a white supremacist rock band blasting from the CD player. He was in a particularly good mood. He'd just dropped off his date – a large-breasted, platinum blonde who'd been a runner-up in the segregated Miss South Africa beauty contest during the apartheid era – at her condo in the suburb of Rivonia. They'd had dinner at his favorite restaurant, did some sweaty bump and grind at a disco in Sandton City, and then had wild sex at her condo after watching an X-rated video.

His craving for pleasure now sated, his thoughts turned to Swanepoel. He wondered if his right-hand man had already confirmed the mystery witness's identity. If it was indeed Gideon, he couldn't wait to tell Kruger about the brilliant scheme he'd come up with for eliminating Gideon, Liefling, David and Thando, and then using drugs to cover up their deaths, just as he'd done in the old days.

Botha's car phone rang. He turned down the music and flipped open the phone.

"Ludwig speaking."

"Ludwig, this is Riaan."

"What is it?"

"Jew boy just received another call from the mystery witness."

"Who is he?"

"It's Gideon all right."

"Are you sure?"

"Without a doubt. The voices match, despite the fact that the kaffir again spoke in Afrikaans."

"What did he tell Jew boy this time?"

"Plenty. Not only does he intend to testify against the general and expose our unit, but he has the evidence to back up his story."

"What evidence?"

"A set of diaries in which he recorded everything the Thathe Vondo death squad did during his years as an askari."

"Jesus fucking Christ!" Botha slammed on the brakes. With tires screeching, he swerved sharply to the right into a deserted OK Supermarket parking lot.

"Did you say diaries?" he demanded, his heart beating fast.

"Ja. He also has pieces of clothing, ID cards, shoes, glasses and various other items he collected from the corpses of the communists and terrorists we executed."

"Oh, hell. Are you sure?"

"I heard him loud and clear. I planted only the most sophisticated bugs in the Jew-boy's shack. They give us a front row seat. Jew-boy even has his girlfriend over tonight. They were busy fucking the brains out of each other when Gideon's call interrupted them."

"Shit. Where's the kaffir bastard now?"

Swanepoel glanced at the TV monitor.

"According to the tracking system, he's in Venda."

"What's he doing there?"

"Visiting his parents."

"I'd better come over and call the General immediately."

With that Botha snapped the phone shut, started the engine and roared off toward the surveillance center in downtown Jo'burg.

36

BOTHA stormed into the surveillance center, flustered and breathless.

"Quick, I need a secure line!" he said.

Swanepoel swung his swivel chair around. "Room 3."

Botha was on his way to Room 3 when he remembered Kruger's instructions to apprehend Gideon before he left Venda. Botha turned to Swanepoel and asked, "Is Viljoen at the game reserve?"

"I'll check." Swanepoel picked up a yellow phone and made an encrypted call. He talked rapidly in Afrikaans. As he listened to the response he flashed a wide grin, revealing uneven, smoke-stained teeth. He covered the mouthpiece and turned to Botha. "He's there. Along with Barnard and five other members of the unit. They're having a party at the lodge with a couple of broads."

"Hand me the phone," Botha said. Swanepoel complied.

Botha spoke animatedly into it for several minutes, gave it back to Swanepoel, and then, grinning, entered Room 3 to make the call to Kruger.

KRUGER sat a desk in his dimly-lit study, crying. The study's door was locked to prevent Freda from coming in and finding him in such distress. The cause of his tears was an old letter nestled between the dog-eared pages of the Afrikaans Bible in front of him. The letter was from his mother. She'd written it before committing suicide one wintry day in 1961, shortly after Kruger joined the army following his return from America, where he'd been an exchange student at the University of Alabama in Tuscaloosa, studying agriculture.

He'd read the letter several times, along with verses from the Bible, since cloistering himself in the study an hour earlier. He'd told Freda, whom he'd left sleeping in the bedroom down the hall, that he needed to prepare himself for the morning meeting with a delegation from the TRC, led by its chairman, Bishop Desmond Tutu.

Kruger dried his eyes with the back of his hand and read the letter one more time.

My dearest Magnus,

The time has come for me to kill myself. And please, don't blame yourself for my death, my son. After what you told me about your father, I've concluded there's nothing left for me to live for. What he's done can never be undone, nor can its shame be overcome. He's committed an abomination, a sin that the Bible says is contrary to the laws of God, and for which there can be no pardon.

As the daughter of a dominee, I was raised to believe in the Bible. It is God's infallible word. It is the rock on which the Afrikaner people have leaned throughout their history on the Dark Continent. And as a dutiful and loving wife and mother, I believed that our family had a special duty to be exemplary by obeying God's will in everything we did, especially when it came to our behavior.

Many of our Afrikaner brethren, before apartheid was established, had lived in moral turpitude. I remember accompanying my father during the Great Depression on visits to minister to fellow Afrikaners who were so poor many of them were living in sin with Coloreds and kaffirs. I remember how this caused my father great pain. He vowed to devote the rest of his life to shaping a new morality for the Afrikaner people, so as to ensure the purity of the Volk, on which its survival hinged.

I married your father and didn't become a missionary as I'd planned because he told my father that he too believed in the importance of shaping this new morality that would purify the Volk. When, through hard work and devotion to apartheid, he was chosen dominee of the *Groetekerk*, I rejoiced. I knew that he was now in a powerful position to shape this new morality because he had the ear of the Prime Minister himself, who was a regular member of the church.

I remember how hard your father labored, along with other dominees from across the country, to urge swift passage of the Immorality Act and the Prohibition of Mixed Marriages Acts. I even sat up late at night stuffing envelopes containing a pastoral letter he was sending to poor Afrikaner families providing Biblical justification for the Immorality Act and the Prohibition of Mixed Marriages Act.

No one is perfect, my son. Only God is. But your father is nothing but a monster. May his damned soul rot a grain a day in hell! Your father lied to me about why we had to leave Cape Town so abruptly. He said that he'd been posted to Venda as a missionary. Now, thanks to you, I know the bitter truth. I know why the Broederbond made its decision in the utmost secrecy. I also know – and it breaks my heart to know this – why Freda's father forbade her from ever seeing you again when you two were so much in love and everyone expected you to get married.

I don't blame Freda's father. What father would permit his daughter to marry the offspring of such a devil as your father?

It was hard for me to decide to take Leta and Erika along with me, my son. But I'm convinced your sisters will be better off in Heaven. And given their purity and innocence, I'm sure that they'll be numbered among the angels. I couldn't bear the thought of leaving them behind after what your father had done. Can you imagine the shame, the scorn, the shunning, that would have attended them the rest of their lives with a father like that?

Again, my dearest Magnus, don't blame yourself in the least for our deaths. It's God's will. By telling me the truth, you did the right and honorable thing. I'll always remember your love for me. I wish you all the happiness that's possible in a world full of temptation and sin. Resist it with all your might, my son. Devote yourself to the Afrikaner people. Safeguard their purity so as to ensure their survival. And I pray that when it comes time for you to marry, you may find someone like Freda.

Goodbye, my beloved son.

Your loving mother,
Henrietta

P.S. I've left you the Bible my father gave me before he passed on to a better world, where your sisters and I shall soon join him. During my years at the Kroonstad concentration camp, its message kept me alive. It solaced my soul after I watched my mother and two little brothers die of typhoid. Read it diligently, my son, and let it be your absolute guide, especially in times of trouble and doubt and despair. Above all, let it be your guide in seeking ways to protect the interests of the Volk, God's chosen people.

After writing the letter while sitting on the sunny verandah of the family farm outside Louis Trichardt, Henrietta had bundled her twelve-year-old twin daughters into the family's stationwagon and driven it off the top of a cliff about six miles away, killing herself and her children.

Kruger again glanced at the letter.

I should never have told you about him, Mom, he thought, struggling to prevent tears from flowing. *I should have quietly taken care of the bastard. If I had, you, Leta and Erika would still be alive. And you would have been proud to see me finally bring Freda home as my wife. But I promise you, Mom, I'll never forsake the Afrikaner people.*

Kruger was still transfixed by his mother's letter when the phone on the antique desk rang. He quickly grabbed it.

"General, this is Ludwig. We've finally confirmed the mystery witness's identity."

Kruger sat up straight in his leather chair.

"Who is he?" he demanded.

"Gideon."

Kruger's face reddened. "That bloody double-crossing kaffir." He clenched his teeth. "After all I did for him."

"I know."

"How do you know he's the one?"

Botha told him about the intercepted phone calls and the results of the voice-stress analyzer. "And he has diaries and photos," he added.

Kruger's turned pale.

"Where is the kaffir bastard?" he demanded icily.

"He's still in Venda. I've ordered Viljoen and Barnard to go after him."

"Good. He must not get away."

DAVID said excitedly, "I hope you're sitting down."

Phone in hand, Liefling walked back to the table and sat down.

"I'm sitting down," she said.

"Our mystery witness is ready to spill his guts. Not only that, he has physical evidence proving everything he's told us so far about Kruger's death squad."

"What evidence?"

"Diaries in which he recorded every atrocity Kruger's death squad committed, and items he's retrieved from the bodies of its victims. And these items include pieces of clothing, shoes, ID cards, glasses."

"Unbelievable," Liefling said.

"And he's on his way to my place with the diaries."

"Right now?"

"Ja. He's driving from Venda right this minute."

Liefling turned to Sipho, who stood leaning against the tiled kitchen counter.

"Our mystery witness has diaries. And he's on his way to David's place."

"YES!" Sipho cried triumphantly, throwing back his head and clapping his hands together.

"Did our mystery witness say when he'd be there?"

"Around 10.00 a.m."

Liefling turned to Sipho. "What time is your flight to Jo'burg?"

"Eight-thirty."

"That's too late."

"There's an earlier flight at six. I've caught it several times."

"Great." Liefling returned to the phone. "There's a flight leaving at six. I can be there before our mystery witness arrives. If those diaries are legit, they must be kept in a bank vault."

"I agree."

"Have you told Thando?"

"Ja. She's coming around ten as well."

"Can you ask her to pick me up at Jan Smuts on her way to your place?"

"Sure."

"And David?"

"Ja?"

"Great instincts. I wouldn't have filed the lawsuit without any witnesses. Your conviction that our mystery witness was legit swayed me."

"It took courage on your part to trust me. And I appreciate that."

SWANEPOEL smiled as he removed the headphones from his large ears. He'd just finished listening to the conversation between Liefling and David. He quickly rose, went to Room 3 and peered through the glass window. He noticed that Botha had just finished talking to Kruger on the phone.

He entered. "You won't believe what I just overheard," he said to Botha, and then proceeded to relate the intercepted conversation between David and Liefling.

Botha smiled wolfishly.

"Wonderful job, Riaan," he said. "I'll call the General right away. This information fits perfectly with my plan to eliminate Liefling, David and Thando in one fell swoop."

	MAKHADO could not sleep. He lay staring into the inky
37	blackness. Mudjadji, his wife of forty-nine years, lay next
	to him, snoring rather loudly. The two were on a double
	bed elevated about two feet from the cowdung floor by
	cement blocks, a practice the Vendas believed prevented

the sleepers' souls from being whisked away in the middle of the night by
malevolent half-human, half-ape spirits called *Thikoloshes*. Makhado slowly
rolled over and gently prodded Mudjadji with his left elbow.

"Mother of Gideon," he whispered softly.

Mudjadji moaned sleepily. "What is it?"

"I have something important to tell you."

"Can't it wait until morning?"

"No. It can't."

Mudjadji rolled over and faced her husband.

"Gideon was here," Makhado said.

"The grandchildren told me," Mudjadji mumbled. She squinted in an
effort to adjust her eyes to the semi-blackness. "I wondered why you'd
withheld news of his visit. Is anything wrong?"

Makhado made no reply. Instead, he shifted uncomfortably under the
thin blanket. He stared out the small window at the full moon which,
throned in a cloudless starry sky, rained silver beams over the peaceful
courtyard.

He sighed heavily, then said, "I don't know how to say it."

"Say what, Father of Gideon?" Mudjadji asked. She fumbled for a box of
matches on the nightstand and lit a candle. Now fully awake, she searched
her husband's dark face in the flickering candlelight for clues as to what was
weighing heavy on his heart.

Again, Makhado sighed heavily. He knew that what he had to say would deeply hurt the woman he dearly loved. Mudjadji idolized their only surviving son. That's why it had taken him this long to bring up the matter of Gideon's visit.

"Remember back in 1986 when Gideon was detained without trial for three months by the security police?" Makhado said. Normally very direct, he felt he had to be roundabout.

"How can I forget that terrible time?" Mudjadji said. "It was during the second state of emergency. Across the country hundreds of people had been killed and tens of thousands more detained. We were burying people every week. And our support group marched to the police station in Louis Trichardt every day to demand the release of detainees."

"Well, our son was brought to a bushveld camp not too far from here to be interrogated by General Kruger."

"The same General Kruger who's being sued by his stepdaughter?"

"Yes."

"So our son plans to testify against him, is that it?" Like her husband, Mudjadji had been closely following the news about Kruger's upcoming trial, which had riveted all of South Africa.

"Yes."

"He should testify," Mudjadji said. "If General Kruger operated a death squad that tortured and murdered innocent people, the truth must be told. He must be brought to justice."

"It's not that simple."

"What do you mean?" Mudjadji asked.

Makhado started to say something and then abruptly stopped. He suddenly felt like an executioner, wielding an assegai and about to plunge it into the heart of the woman he loved. He knew that after hearing the truth about their son, Mudjadji would never be the same again.

"Our son was an askari for General Kruger," Makhado said.

Mudjadji emitted a tiny gasp. Her small frame shuddered.

Makhado proceeded to tell her everything. "He informed on the ANC. And the information he provided led to the abduction, torture and murder of many activists and MK guerrillas by General Kruger and his death squad."

Makhado felt Mudjadji's body suddenly become rigid. For a moment he thought she'd suffered a stroke or a heart attack. In the flickering yellow light of the candle, he saw Mudjadji clutching the silver cross dangling from her neck. She stared with unblinking eyes at a framed picture of a crucified black Christ hanging from the far wall. Gideon had bought her the picture to replace the picture of a white Christ the missionaries had given her when she was baptized. Her lips kept moving as in silent prayer. Tears formed in the corners of her brown eyes, then dripped onto the cross she was clutching.

Makhado clasped his wife's arm. It felt icy cold. "I knew this would come as a big shock to you, Mother of Gideon. That's why I was reluctant to tell you."

Several moments passed without a word from either Makhado or Mudjadji. Finally Mudjadji managed to stammer faintly, "Father of Gideon, tell me how our dear son could have betrayed his own people?"

Makhado's lips quivered. "Kruger threatened to kill him, Nomhle and the grandchildren if he didn't co-operate."

Again Mudjadji shuddered. Tears now flowed freely down her wrinkled cheeks. Makhado gently dried them with the palm of his hand.

Mudjadji said softly, "Has Gideon told Nomhle?"

"No. He plans to tell her when he gets back."

"You say our son is planning to testify against Kruger. Has he contacted any lawyer?"

"Yes. He's already contacted one of the lawyers involved in the case. As a matter of fact, he plans to stop by his house and give him a set of diaries he kept as an askari. The diaries contain everything: names, dates, the location of mass graves, how many people were fed to the crocodiles, how many were burned alive, how many were shot, how many were strangled to death, how many were electrocuted and how many had their bodies blown to smithereens by limpet mines."

"Oh, my God!"

"He also mentioned having stored other evidence in a cave near the place where the interrogations took place. He also has pictures."

"Pictures?"

"Yes. Of the huts where victims were tortured, and of some of the corpses before they were buried, burned, blown to bits or fed to the crocodiles."

"Where was Kruger and his men when our son took the pictures?"

"He says that Kruger always left by helicopter after the interrogations. He left the dirty work to his men. They in turn would order Gideon, who was the only one of the askaris who didn't drink, to clean up the mess, while they caroused in the main lodge. Gideon said the Boers always began the interrogations with a braai and then would gather for drinks after the killings or go out in search of prostitutes."

"Did our son take part in any of the torture and killings?"

"No. But other askaris did. He was mainly a spy."

Mudjadji sighed deeply. Clutching the cross tightly against her drooping breasts, she muttered, "Thank you, Jesus. Thank you Lord."

"I'm worried about our son testifying," Makhado said.

Mudjadji raised her eyes and looked anxiously into Makhado's.

"Kruger and his men are ruthless," Makhado said. "They've killed many of men and women in cold blood. If they found out that our son plans to testify, they'll kill him too."

Makhado felt his wife start to tremble again. He held her tighter.

"But I swear by my *Midzimu*," he vowed, "if they harm our son, I'll make them pay dearly."

"How, Father of Gideon?" Mudjadji asked.

"I'm not called Makhado for nothing." His dark eyes smoldered with a determination and anger Mudjadji had never seen before. "I'm a descendant of warriors. I survived malaria when everyone thought I'd die. And at the mountain school, when I became a man, I killed two lions, armed only with a spear."

"But you're no longer young, Father of Gideon," Mudjadji said with the utmost respect. "You're almost sixty-five. And the Boers have guns."

"I may no longer be young, Mother of Gideon. But my strength is not gone. Certainly not my intelligence. Around white people I pretend I'm weak and ignorant. I shuffle about like a servile fool and say 'yes, baas' because I don't want them to know the real Makhado. The Makhado who isn't afraid of any white man. Tomorrow I'm going to work, despite the fact that Viljoen is one of them. I'll be on my best behavior as a deferential kaffir. But I'll be watching."

GIDEON pulled his red Explorer into the deserted and dimly-lit parking lot of a rest area near the Thathe-Vondo Sacred Forest, the burial ground for Venda chiefs. The forest was about two miles from Lake Fundudzi, home of the python god, which holds a special place in the rites of the Venda matriarchal culture, and requires the permission of a nganga priestess to enter. According to Venda lore, the lake is supposed to be inhabited by the furtive Ditutwanes, half-human spirits with one eye, one leg and one arm. The forest is infested with snakes, including the deadly black mamba, and by baboons, which once warned Venda warriors of approaching enemies.

Gideon was reluctant to stop near such a place, but he had to relieve himself. It was almost midnight, half an hour after he'd left Ndwakhulu's mansion. He killed the engine, reached into the glove compartment and retrieved a long-stemmed flashlight. He got out and began walking briskly toward the lavatory in the rear of the hut. His footsteps echoed in the still night air. He shone the flashlight at the lavatory's door.

"Shit," he cried, noticing it was padlocked. A sign in the middle of the door read, "Sorry, Out of Service" in Venda, Afrikaans and English.

"Well," he muttered to himself, "I just have to be brave and go in the Thathe-Vondo forest."

Flashlight in hand, Gideon entered the dense foliage of the Sacred Forest. He was glad he'd taken precautions against malaria, ticks and mosquitoes, scourges throughout the swampy lowveld. He disappeared behind a clump of bushes. Untying his cowhide belt, he lowered his pants and cotton jockey trunks. He was about to squat on his haunches to relieve himself when suddenly he saw headlights in the distance. Two cars were approaching at high speed. The lead car – a bakkie splattered with red mud – abruptly stopped behind Gideon's Explorer.

Who could that be? Gideon thought as he hurriedly pulled up his pants. He wondered if he should reveal his presence. He decided to wait. He was glad he'd turned off the flashlight.

The second car – a minivan – pulled up behind the bakkie. About a dozen men carrying flashlights and assault rifles jumped out of the two vehicles.

Must be the police, he thought. He recalled reading about increased police patrols in rural areas due to a recent spate of killings of white farmers.

Three of the men walked over to Gideon's Explorer. They slowly circled it, searching its interior with the bright beam of the flashlight. One tried the driver's door. It was open. He peered inside; seconds later he emerged. Gideon's heart stopped beating when he noticed that the men were wearing combat fatigues and hooded black masks called *balaclavas*, garb similar to that worn by members of the Thathe Vondo death squad on missions.

"*Hy is nie hier nie,*" said man who'd just peered inside the Explorer. The voice jolted Gideon like an electric shock. It was Viljoen's.

"I thought I saw a light as we were approaching," a second man said, also in Afrikaans. It was Barnard. Gideon's heart pounded wildly.

"I did too," echoed Viljoen.

"It was over there," said a third man, pointing in the direction of the forest.

"Maybe he's taking a piss," Viljoen said.

"Should we wait or go after him?" Barnard inquired.

"Let's go after him," Viljoen said. "He's probably seen us by now. Put on your night-vision goggles."

Doors opened and slammed. Within minutes Viljoen and the men had donned their night-vision goggles, which registered thermal images in red and everything else in dark green. As Gideon, bathed in sweat and heart racing, crouched behind the bushes, he heard the clicking of R4 and R5 automatic assault rifles. He saw the men heading toward him.

BOTHA gave Swanepoel a thumbs-up when Kruger answered the phone.

"General," Botha said. "Riaan just intercepted an amazing bit of information. Your stepdaughter will be on the first flight out of Cape Town to Jo'burg."

"What for?"

"She wants to be there when Gideon delivers the diaries. Thando will be picking her up from the airport and taking her to David's place in Soweto. That means David, Liefling and Thando will be together in Soweto. So Shaka can easily eliminate the three of them and initiate a brilliant cover-up I've come up with."

"Explain it."

"Well, all I need is to have Viljoen ask one of the men to bring down Gideon's red Explorer to Jo'burg after he's captured. The trip should take about six hours. Shaka will drive the Explorer to David's house tomorrow morning pretending to be Gideon."

"Pretending to be Gideon?"

"Ja. David won't know the difference since Gideon hasn't yet revealed his identity."

"I see," Kruger said, chuckling.

"I'd suggest that Shaka eliminate David first, then Liefling and Thando after they arrive from the airport. As soon as the job is done, he'll leave behind a briefcase full of cocaine and crack with the three dead bodies. I'll then call our friends at the Jo'burg police department and tell them to go to a certain address in Soweto to investigate three drug-related executions. How does that scheme strike you?"

"Brilliant, Ludwig," Kruger said. "Absolutely brilliant. I heartily approve of it. And while all this is happening, I'll be a thousand miles away, meeting with Bishop Tutu. No one will connect me to the killings."

"That's the plan."

"I like it. Call me as soon as Shaka has completed the job."

"I will."

38   **GIDEON** ran blindly through the dark forest, frantically groping for a way out. He saw what seemed like a faint light beyond the thick trees. He dashed toward it. Stepping out into a clearing, he was immediately blinded by the glare from what seemed to be a thousand flashlights.

He blinked rapidly. When his eyes finally adjusted to the harsh bright light he found himself surrounded by members of the Thathe Vondo death squad. Viljoen, grasping a shotgun, hovered over Gideon, who fell to his knees and used his arms to shield his eyes from the harsh lights.

Viljoen pointed the shotgun at the forehead of the cowering Gideon and said slowly, in guttural Afrikaans, "You know the penalty for snitching, kaffir."

"NO! Please, don't kill me!" Gideon begged as he attempted to crawl away. Viljoen pulled the trigger. The shotgun went off with an ear-shattering noise, blowing Gideon's head off.

Makhado cried out. He sat bolt upright in bed, breathing hard. His body was drenched with sweat. His scream awoke Mudjadji.

"What's the matter, Father of Gideon?"

"I had a nightmare," Makhado said, shaking.

"What kind of nightmare?"

Makhado, after a long silence, answered, "I dreamed Gideon was dead."

KRUGER remained in his study for some time after speaking to Botha, mulling over a scheme for ensuring that he had in Freda a perfect alibi once Thando, Liefling and David had been killed. At ten minutes past midnight, he left for the bedroom. He was surprised to find Freda awake, having left her fast asleep. He wondered how long she'd been awake, and if she'd eavesdropped on his conversation with Botha.

"What's wrong, dear?" Kruger asked as he took off his robe and got into bed.

"There's something I've been meaning to talk to you about," Freda said, rolling to face him.

"What is it?" Kruger said. He tried to hide his nervousness by snuggling up against Freda.

"I felt extremely uncomfortable at the braai this afternoon," Freda said.

"Why?"

"A lot of the people who came are racist. They blame everything wrong in South Africa on blacks. That's not true. We Afrikaners are partly to blame."

She's been talking to that verligte traitor Tina again, Kruger thought angrily.

"But, my dear," he said smoothly, "blacks are now running the country. And look what a mess they've made of things. Compare that to the law and order we used to have when Afrikaners were in charge."

"Do you hate blacks, Magnus?" Freda said suddenly, looking her husband straight in the eye.

The question took Kruger aback. But skilled in hiding his true feelings whenever the occasion warranted, he said, "Of course not, my dear. Why do you say that?"

"It's just that the people you hang out with are so racist."

"I don't hate blacks, my dear. I have a lot of black friends. And I hang out with all sorts of people. Sure some of them are racist, but there are racists among blacks, too."

"I'm glad you don't hate blacks," Freda said, "because Liefling is in love with a black."

Kruger abruptly withdrew his hand from Freda's. "Dating a black?" He'd wanted to use the word 'kaffir' but refrained, aware of Freda's sensibilities.

"Ja. His name is Sipho Radebe. He's a surgeon. One of the best in South Africa."

"Do you approve?"

"Liefling is a grown woman, Magnus."

"You didn't answer my question," Kruger said tersely.

Freda let out a troubled sigh. "It's not a matter of approving, Magnus. I have no business passing judgment on my daughter's love life. After all, she's responsible for her own happiness."

Ever quick to seize an opening, Kruger said, in a voice that was calm, despite the deep rage he felt. "You're right, my dear. Liefling is a grown woman. And she's responsible for her own happiness. She can date whomever she wants. The reason I asked if you approved his dating a black man is because I care very much about her happiness. After all, she's the only child of a woman I deeply love. That's why I'm worried about her continued association with David. I don't want anything to happen to her."

"What do you mean?" Freda asked anxiously.

"For the past week I've had private investigators dig further into David's background. The report they brought back is shocking. I was just going over it in the study."

"What did they find out?"

"Remember what I told you about his involvement with drugs?"

Freda nodded.

"I thought it was on a small scale. But I was wrong. He's very heavily involved. My private investigators found out that he's a major distributor of cocaine, heroin, Madras (Quaaludes), dagga and Ecstasy. You name the drug, he sells it."

Freda was aghast. She stared at Kruger.

Kruger caressed Freda's arm and said, "In fact, while I was in the study, I got a call from one of the investigators. Tomorrow morning David is meeting with another major drug dealer from Alexandra, who happens to be a schoolteacher."

"A schoolteacher?"

"Ja. And do you know why they're meeting?"

"Why?"

"David is apparently deeply in debt. He owes about one million rands to Colombian drug lords. And they're after him."

"After him? You mean they intend to kill him?"

"I'm afraid so, my dear. Unless, of course, he comes up with the money. My private investigators believe that David intends to ask the other drug dealer for a loan of about one million rands. And you know how he plans to pay it back?"

"How?"

"By blackmailing me."

"Blackmail you?"

"Ja. Liefling's lawsuit is nothing but an attempt by David to blackmail me. He knows that a group of South American investors are interested in purchasing the firm. I believe Liefling told him after she heard about it at the breakfast table, remember?"

"I remember."

"So David thinks that I'll rush to settle the lawsuit in order to avoid an embarrassing court battle that might torpedo the deal. Then from the settlement fee, he'd easily be able to pay off the drug lords."

"It all makes sense," Freda said. "I wonder why Liefling is so gullible."

"She's naïve and idealistic, my dear," Kruger said. "She doesn't suspect anyone she believes to be a friend could be capable of hurting her. And my private investigators tell me that David is a desperate man. And, like I said before, desperate men do desperate things."

"I must warn Liefling. I'll tell her tomorrow when I meet her for lunch."

" In the meantime, I'll be meeting with Bishop Tutu. Hopefully between the two of us we can put an end to the lawsuit. I want nothing more than to reconcile with Liefling. And as for Sipho, I look forward to meeting him. I may be *verkrampte*, my dear, but I'm not a racist. If Liefling is in love with a black man, that's her business. As long as he treats her with respect."

"I knew you weren't a racist, darling."

"And I love you more than anything in the world," Kruger said, reaching over and kissing Freda. "I won't let anything come between us."

Strangely, Kruger was speaking the truth. In his own twisted way, he indeed did love Freda more than anything in the world. That's why he felt absolutely no compunction lying to her in order to keep her love. Lies had been his way of gaining and keeping the most precious things he'd sought throughout his life.

But the lies will soon end, one way or the other, Kruger thought as he began fondling Freda's breasts. Like Macbeth, Kruger knew that he'd "supped full of horrors." He'd reached a crucial turning point in his quest to achieve his life's ambition: gaining the woman his mother had worshipped and ensuring the survival of the Volk. He knew that Botha's plan for eliminating Liefling, Thando and David would either be his salvation or sound his death knell. And having long sold his soul to the devil of apartheid, and being unwilling to reclaim even a piece of it back by confessing his abominable crimes before the TRC, he put little value on life – unless that life was spent with his beloved Freda, in an Afrikaner-only Vaderland.

39 GIDEON scrambled down the slippery trail. He paused behind a thick-trunked tree, breathless

Where do I run? Gideon wondered. He'd been running for more than ten minutes. Despite a full moon, it was dark in the forest because of the towering, big-leafed trees and thick underbrush. The rush of water told him that a river was probably nearby. He realized he was near the Thathe Vondo private game reserve.

He listened for sounds of Viljoen and his posse. Nothing. Suddenly baboons nearby began to howl. Abruptly, they stopped. He listened carefully. To his left, he heard the snapping of twigs and the crunching of leaves.

He froze. He fought hard to suppress a sneeze. Suddenly a shot rang out. The bullet ricocheted off the trunk of a bluegum tree about a foot away. Beams of yellow light flashed between the dense foliage of the trees in his direction.

"Daar is hy!" he heard Viljoen yell.

Startled by the close proximity of the men, Gideon turned and plunged deeper into the woods. The posse followed. He waded across a small stream. He scrambled up the bank and ran blindly through the forest. Baboons howled all around him. Thorns and sharp branches tore at his disheveled tweed suit and scratched his perspiring face. The water inside his shoes squished as he ran. His breath came in spurts.

"Gideon!" he heard Viljoen shout. He sounded very near. "There's no use running away! We can see you even in the dark."

Another bullet whizzed past his head. It bounced off a boulder to his left, inches from his head.

"If you don't give yourself up immediately," Viljoen bellowed, "the next bullet will be through your thick skull!"

Gideon ignored the call to surrender. He knew full well the fate that awaited him if he did. He wondered how they'd found out he was in Venda and that he'd be driving along that road. He was certain Ndwakhulu had betrayed him. He zigzagged between trees to avoid presenting an easy thermal image for the night-vision goggles. He felt like a hunted animal. His mouth was dry and his tongue and throat felt coarse, as if he'd swallowed sand. His brow dripped with sweat. His lungs felt like bursting. His desperate flight reminded him of how the MK guerillas he'd betrayed must have felt when members of Kruger's death squad were hunting them down through the very same forest.

Gideon had been running for what seemed like forever when he saw dim lights ahead. It was the rest area hut. He'd run full circle and was back at the parking lot. He could see his Explorer. If only he could reach it. He felt in his coat pocket and realized he still had the keys. He was about to dash in the direction of the parking lot when he saw a hooded figure in the front seat of his Explorer. He instantly changed direction and tore down the road.

"Daar is hy!" he heard Viljoen shout as he and the posse emerged from the woods and spilled onto the road.

Gideon knew he was faster than his pursuers, most of whom had beer-bellies. He'd been a track star at both high school and university, specializing in long distances. Panting hard, arms flailing and his jacket billowing, he raced down the steep and winding road, praying that a car might drive by and come to his aid. He heard the sharp rev of an engine and the squeal of burning tires. He glanced over his shoulders. Several men were running down the road after him, while others were scrambling into the back of Viljoen's bakkie.

He gritted his teeth and lengthened his stride. He saw the lights of an approaching vehicle in the distance. His hope swelled. Suddenly shots rang out. Gideon screamed in pain. He staggered several feet and then collapsed, clutching the back of his right leg. Blood oozed just above the calf muscle, where a bullet had penetrated. He attempted to crawl into a nearby gully called a *donga,* but Viljoen was already upon him, breathing hard.

"You fucking kaffir bastard," he screamed as he repeatedly kicked Gideon in the face and stomach with hard-toed boots.

The bakkie arrived and several hooded men leaped out. Barnard pulled Viljoen away from Gideon, who had curled into a ball to protect himself from the blows.

"Take it easy, Piet," he said. "Ludwig said the General wants him alive. We need to find out who else knows about the diaries."

"We're taking you to the truth hut, you bloody kaffir rat," Viljoen shouted as the neo-Nazis bundled Gideon into the back of the bakkie. "And you'll tell us everything. I'm going to interrogate you, and you know my methods."

LIEFLING hardly slept. By five she was already up and packed. Sipho was still asleep. He moaned sleepily when she lightly kissed his cheek. She left him a brief note on the kitchen table, then quietly slipped out of the flat. Within an hour she was at Cape Town International Airport. Before boarding South African Airways Flight 215 bound for Johannesburg, she called Thando and gave her the flight information and arrival time. She couldn't wait to get her hands on the diaries detailing the activities of Kruger's death squad.

SIPHO woke up around seven-thirty. Realizing that he had less than an hour to get to the airport for his flight to Johannesburg, he jumped into the shower. He read Liefling's note while sitting at the kitchen table having a quick breakfast of cereal with fruit and apple juice.

> *Hi honey,*
>
> *Wish we had the same flight. See you in Jo'burg.*
>
> *I love you,*
> *Liefling*
>
> *P.S. In case you need to reach me, David's number is 759 – 4869.*

Just as Sipho was getting ready to leave the flat for the airport, the phone rang. He answered it on the second ring, thinking it was Liefling. It was Freda.

"How are you Mrs. Kruger?" Sipho said cheerily.

"I'm fine, thank you. Can I please talk to Liefling?"

"I'm afraid she's already left."

"Left? For where?"

"For Jo'burg."

"Jo'burg? But we're supposed to be having lunch together."

"It was a last-minute decision. She has an important meeting with David at ten."

Sipho heard Freda gasp.

"Is anything wrong?"

"No," she said hastily. "Do you have David's number?"

"Ja." Sipho gave it to her.

NOMHLE, whose Zulu name meant "Beautiful," sat at the oak kitchen table and poured skim milk into her coffee. The worried look on her face didn't escape her two children, Pinkie and Joshua, who were sitting across from her eating a hearty breakfast of whole-wheat pancakes, scrambled eggs and orange juice.

She sighed. "I wonder where your father is."

"Don't worry Mama, he'll come," said twelve-year-old Pinkie, who had her mother's smooth, oval face and large, clear, black eyes. She was wearing Bovet's school uniform, which consisted of a pleated black gym dress, white shirt, wool sweater and shiny black shoes.

"Why hasn't he called?" Nomhle asked, absentmindedly sipping her tea.

"Maybe his car got stuck or something," said fourteen-year-old Joshua, draining his orange juice. "It's been giving him problems lately."

Joshua had his father's prominent brow and expressive brown eyes. He was also neatly dressed in his school uniform, which consisted of long gray pants, a white shirt, a blazer with a school badge, and shiny black shoes.

"I have a feeling something's wrong," Nomhle said.

"You always have a feeling something's wrong, Mama," Joshua said. "Our teacher calls that being superstitious."

"There you go using big words again," Pinkie said.

"It's because I want to be a teacher, just like Papa."

"Papa doesn't use big words when he talks."

"He does when he talks to me."

Pinkie made a face at Joshua, who threatened to hit her with a spoon.

"Stop it you two," Nomhle said impatiently, rising from the table.

"You haven't touched your breakfast, Mama," Pinkie observed.

"I'm not hungry. Please hurry and clean up or you'll be late for school."

"Yes, Mama," Pinkie and Joshua said simultaneously.

Nomhle headed down the hallway to the bedroom, one of three in a seven-room house in Eastbank, where many of Alexandra's professional class lived. Gideon had bought the house with the bonus he'd received from Kruger. Pinkie cleared the table and Joshua completed his math homework.

"Why do you always do your homework in the morning?" Pinkie asked as she washed the breakfast dishes under warm soapy water. "You should do it in the afternoon like me instead of running around chasing girls."

"I do it in the morning so I can avoid doing dishes, you fool," Joshua said with a puckish grin.

"I heard that," Nomhle said from the bedroom. "From now on, Joshua does the dishes."

"I was only joking, Mama," Joshua said.

"That wasn't a joke," Pinkie said, drying the dishes with a *fie-doek* cloth before stacking them on the dish-rack. "He always avoids doing dishes."

"I chop wood and make the fire. Dishes and cleaning are for girls."

"Who told you that?" Nomhle said, checking her white nursing uniform for wrinkles in the carved hallway mirror.

"My friends don't wash dishes," Joshua said.

"You live in this house, not at your friends'," Nomhle said. "And in this house you do dishes, just like Pinkie."

At precisely seven-thirty, Nomhle and her two children were strapped into seatbelts inside the family's black 1997 Ford Taurus with leather seats. Gideon had bought her the car for her thirty-sixth birthday. She backed out of the two-car garage, electronically shut the iron gate, turned right, and drove about three hundred yards before turning left and crossing the concrete bridge spanning the Jukskei River. The short drive to the bridge put her in another world. Gone were the nice brick houses with their manicured lawns, garages, paved streets, running water, electricity and sewers. Now she was in an area teeming with *mkhukhus* – shacks made from corrugated tin, sheets of plastics and cardboard.

The jungle of shacks stretched as far as the eye could see along the banks of the swollen and fetid river. The shacks were home to tens of thousands of blacks, mostly Mozambican refugees who, incredibly, considered places like Alexandra paradise compared to their impoverished and war-ravaged country.

To avoid dwelling on the widespread misery, which never failed to depress her spirits, Nomhle always listened to tapes when driving through this part of Alexandra. This morning she inserted an English vocabulary-building tape for her children. Whenever they complained about not having enough Nintendo games, about too much homework, and about why they had to study hard instead of watching their favorite American-made TV shows, Nomhle always reminded them that education was the key to a future in the new South Africa.

"Without it," she'd say, "you'll end up living in shacks like these."

The Taurus made its way through the labyrinth of rutted streets interlacing the jungle of shacks, headed for Bovet, her children's school.

The streets were already clogged with their usual morning traffic. Uniformed students, faces glistening with Vaseline to ward off the morning chill, trotted to overcrowded schools rimmed with barbed-wire fences. Stern-faced workers, many carrying *scufftins* (food for work) in plastic containers, hurried to jobs in the suburbs and firms around Alexandra. And hordes of unemployed men, mostly teenagers, huddled in clusters around fires of burning tires and trash, trying to keep warm. Many of them had cell phones – a status symbol which was also used in drug dealing – stashed deep inside the pockets of their baggy pants.

Nomhle dropped Pinkie and Joshua outside the school gate then proceeded to her widowed mother's home. On the way she called Makhado on her cell phone.

<table>
<tr><td>

40

</td><td>

MAKHADO and the group of ten Venda women arrived at the Thathe Vondo private game reserve at about eight. The group had left their village, which was twenty miles away, just before sunrise and trudged on foot through the dark forest and over steep mountains on foot.

</td></tr>
</table>

Throughout the journey to the game reserve, Makhado was deeply troubled. He took dreams very seriously. He regarded them as omens through which one's *Midzimu* communicate things to come.

Makhado was also troubled by another problem. He didn't know how he was going to act in front of Viljoen, now that he knew him to be torturer and a killer.

I'll avoid him as much as possible, Makhado thought as he and the women reached the entrance to the game reserve. To his horror, Makhado found Viljoen waiting for them on the verandah of his office.

"Makhado," he said tersely, "I'd like to see you in the office."

"Yes, baas," Makhado said with lowered eyes and dutifully followed Viljoen into the office. The women, casting them troubled looks, headed for the kitchen.

I wonder what could be wrong, Makhado thought. *He usually sleeps in on Mondays.*

"How are you this morning?" Viljoen said cheerily, speaking in Fanagalo.

The greeting took Makhado by surprise. Viljoen seldom condescended to talk familiarly with his servants. He preferred barking orders at them as a way of reminding them who was in charge.

"Fine, baas," Makhado said hesitantly.

"Good," Viljoen said. "And your family?"

"They're doing fine, baas."

"I'm glad to hear that."

To what do I owe this sudden friendliness? Makhado wondered suspiciously.

Makhado's survival instinct told him to search for hidden clues that might reveal Viljoen's true motive for being so friendly.

"I'll be gone most of the day," Viljoen said.

Head deferentially cast down, Makhado furtively scrutinized Viljoen's face through the corners of his eyes. He noticed huge bags under Viljoen's bloodshot eyes, suggesting that he'd hardly slept.

Sleep-deprived white people are notorious for their tempers, Makhado thought. *Where's Viljoen's?*

"While I'm gone, I want the braai pit prepared," Viljoen said.

"Yes, baas." Makhado decided to say as little as possible.

"That's all," Viljoen said.

Relieved, Makhado turned to leave. He was already out the door when the phone rang.

"Viljoen speaking."

He turned and called out to Makhado. "It's for you."

Bewildered, Makhado shuffled back into the office. Viljoen handed him the phone. "It's your daughter-in-law."

"Thank you, baas," Makhado said in his most servile tone. He had several of these, geared toward Viljoen's various moods.

Viljoen watched Makhado attentively.

Makhado's face clouded as he listened. "But he did leave early yesterday evening," he said into the phone. "He should have arrived by now."

Makhado listened some more, then said, "Yes. Please call me as soon as he gets there....I'll be leaving around four..."

A troubled look on his face, Makhado handed the phone back to Viljoen.

"What's wrong?" Viljoen asked.

"It's Gideon, baas."

"What happened?" Viljoen said, feigning surprise and great concern.

"He came to visit me yesterday. He left around sunset to return home. He still hasn't arrived."

"Why didn't he stay overnight? It's dangerous driving at night. What with carjackings, robberies and muti-killings. Anything could have happened to him."

Makhado said nothing.

Viljoen shrugged. "Well, I hope he's all right."

"I hope so too, baas." Makhado turned to leave.

"Oh, I almost forgot," Viljoen said. "I want the special lodge next to the

Baobab tree opened and thoroughly cleaned."

"The one used by baas Kruger when he's here?"

"Ja. He's coming for an important meeting tonight."

"I'll make sure it's spic and span, baas."

"Thanks. You can go now. And I hope Gideon's all right."

I bet you do, you bloody neo-Nazi bastard, Makhado thought.

"Thank you, baas," Makhado said, bowing.

Why is Kruger coming here tonight? Makhado thought as he went out the door. *He hasn't been to the game reserve in ages. Could his visit be connected with the disappearance of my son?*

Makhado had barely gone halfway down the wooden steps leading from the verandah to the courtyard when the office phone rang a second time. He was headed back to the door, thinking it was Nomhle calling to say Gideon had arrived, when through the half-open window he heard Viljoen say, "Hi General. I'm fine, thank you."

Makhado stealthily crept closer to the window and crouched below it.

"We've got him, General," Viljoen said. "We caught him near the Thathe Vondo forest. No, we haven't interrogated him yet. He's in the truth hut."

Makhado heard the words as if in a dream. Pain stabbed the pit of his stomach. But anger and hatred checked it.

"I'll make him talk all right," Viljoen said. "I just spoke to his old man.... Ja, Gideon stopped by to see him yesterday.... No, I don't think he knows about the diaries...I can tell when a kaffir's lying, General...He's a harmless old kaffir....Sure, I'll make Gideon reveal who else knows about the diaries....Good luck with your meeting with Tutu....See you tonight."

That was all Makhado needed to hear. He hurriedly crept down the steps. As he trudged back to the kitchen, tears streamed freely down his cheeks.

They're going to kill my son, he kept muttering.

Overwhelmed with grief, and no longer in view from the office, he staggered toward a towering Mopane tree. Suddenly feeling hot and faint, he leaned heavily against the tree's rough trunk. He slowly dried the tears in his eyes with the back of his hand. But his weakness was fleeting. As he thought about the fate that awaited his son in the truth hut, the son he loved the more for his courage in risking his life by agreeing to testify, he knew he had to act.

I have to come up with a plan to rescue my son—if he's still alive, Makhado thought as he hurried to the kitchen. *Or die trying.*

NOMHLE said, "I'm worried about Gideon, Mama."

She was speaking to her 56-year-old overweight and diabetic mother. The two were sitting at a small kitchen table covered with a plastic tablecloth. "He hasn't returned from Venda."

"Didn't he call?" her mother asked in Zulu.

"He called late last night saying he was on his way."

"Have you tried calling his father?" said her mother as she stirred Nutrasweet into her black coffee, which she was having with pieces of fruit.

"Ja. On the way here I called him at the game reserve. He said that Gideon left last night."

They heard a car pull up outside and a moment later there was a knock on the front door.

"Maybe it's Gideon," Nomhle's mother said hopefully, struggling to get up.

"I'll get it," Nomhle said. She rose and went to the door. She opened it a crack, and then said with a smile, "Hi, Thando."

"Hi Nomhle," Thando said.

"Is your mom in?"

"Ja. She's in the kitchen. Please come in."

"I'd love too," Thando said. "But I'm in a bit of a rush. I have to pick up Liefling from the airport."

"Who's that?" Nomhle's mother asked from the kitchen.

"It's Thando."

"Oh," Nomhle's mother said, rising. "I almost forgot. Tell her I'll get the package."

She went into her small but neat bedroom. Tears came to her eyes as she opened a small cupboard below a framed picture of Christ on the cross. From inside, she removed a thick package wrapped in brown paper, which was next to the jar containing the pickled right hand of Vusi, her only son. For years she'd been searching for the truth about what had happened to the rest of his body. She didn't know that Vusi had been part of MK or that Thando had given him the responsibility of arming the township's self-defense units during battles with the police and soldiers.

But she vividly remembered the terror she'd felt when about a dozen men wearing balaclavas and combat fatigues had barged into her house one night back in 1989. They had grabbed Vusi, who normally was in hiding but on that night had stopped by to make sure his mother was all right. Despite her screams, protests and pleas, they had whisked him away in an unmarked car. A few days later, she'd received his severed right hand in a jar. She'd kept the hand in the hope of someday burying it with the rest of his body.

She'd prayed everyday that the TRC would finally expose his murderers.

She didn't hate them. She cherished her Ubuntu too much to contaminate it with hatred. She didn't even want them prosecuted. Her faith in Christ had led her to forgive even her enemies and to hope for justice in the hereafter. She simply wanted her son's remains.

She dried her tears, and, package in hand, returned to the kitchen.

"Please take care of these photos and letters," she said, handing Thando the package.

"Thank you," Thando said. "Don't worry, Mrs. Mavundla, we'll take good care of them."

Thando was about to head back to her Toyota when Nomhle said, "Gideon didn't come home last night."

"Where did he go?"

"To Venda to visit his father. He was supposed to be back early this morning."

"Don't worry," Thando said, "he'll show up."

Nomhle felt somewhat reassured.

41 **THANDO** rolled down the windows of the Toyota as she and Liefling left the bustling Johannesburg International Airport and entered Elecktron Highway, headed for downtown Johannesburg. The usually polluted air smelled fresh and crisp following cleansing overnight thunderstorms.

"I finally got all the affidavits," Thando said.

"Great. Including the one on Vusi?"

"Ja. I picked it up this morning."

"I'm worried," Liefling said, fishing in her handbag for her cell phone.

"About what?"

"Our mystery witness. He sounds too good to be real. I hope he shows up with the diaries."

"He will."

Liefling dialed David's number. The phone rang six times, then an answering machine picked up. She left David a message informing him that they were on their way.

"I wonder where he is," Liefling said.

"Hannah spent the night over there, so he probably drove her to work."

"I like Hannah," Liefling said, reclining her seat to a more comfortable position. "David seems very much in love with her."

"I really respect David for sticking with her through her drug problem," Thando said. "Most men would have left."

"He's very caring."

"What about you and Sipho?" Thando asked, switching lanes on the four-lane highway.

"He spent last night at my place."

"I bet you had a nice time."

Liefling smiled, then laughed when she saw Thando gazing at her expectantly. "Well," Thando said.

"Well what? Yes, we had a nice time. End of story."

"No juicy details?"

"I'd have more to tell if Sipho and I had more time together. But he's been working seven days, commuting between Bara and the clinic in Guguletu. In fact. he's on his way to Bara as we speak. We'd have been on the same plane but he couldn't change his ticket without a penalty."

The Toyota drove past Bruma Lake. Joggers plodded along leafy paths in the dazzling morning sun.

"What about you and Sidney?" Liefling asked. "Do you think you'll ever get back together again?"

"I hope so. I still love him a lot. "

"How did you two meet anyway?"

"During military training in the Soviet Union."

"You were in the Soviet Union?"

Thando nodded.

"What part?"

"Odessa in the Ukraine. MK sent me there for training in urban guerilla warfare. For six months I was the only black among members of other liberation movements – including members of the PLO and the Red Brigade. When Sidney came for advance training in intelligence, we started hanging out together."

"How did Sidney end up with MK?"

"Same way I did," Thando said, switching lanes. "The injustices of Bantu Education turned us into revolutionaries."

"How?"

"In high school Sidney excelled in math and science and wanted to study electrical engineering. The job at the time was reserved only for whites, so none of the tribal colleges offered courses in engineering. And under the Extension of University Education Act, he couldn't apply to any of the white universities. So he applied to study abroad. He received several scholarship offers from American universities. He chose MIT. In 1975 he applied for a passport. The government refused to grant him one. He was told he could only apply for an exit permit, which meant he would automatically lose his South African citizenship and become an exile."

Thando paused as the Toyota slowed due to thickening traffic.

"What did he do?" Liefling asked.

"He didn't apply. He was afraid he'd never see his family again. So he enrolled at Turfloop University, planning to become a science teacher. The

Soweto Uprising radicalized him, as it did many of our generation. He organized student boycotts and protests. When the security forces came after him, he fled the country and joined MK."

Liefling shook her head. "So someone who wanted to become and engineer ended up waging war," she observed.

Thando nodded. "After eight months in the Soviet Union we returned to Africa very much in love. Sidney popped the question and I accepted. MK posted us together to Harare. We had a traditional wedding at his grandparents' village near Victoria Falls. It was so romantic."

"I can imagine," Liefling said. "I once flew a helicopter over the falls. They were awesome. There was this huge rainbow across."

"You can fly helicopters?"

"Ja. My former boyfriend taught me how."

"Sidney too can fly," Thando said. "He even trained members of the Zimbabwean airforce on how to fly Soviet Migs. But in Harare his work was intelligence-gathering. I worked mainly with MK cadres who were about to infiltrate back into South Africa. In 1985, two years after Mkondeleli was born, the ANC intensified the armed struggle. Sidney and I were sent to Alexandra, with instruction to establish a key MK cell, from which to make the township ungovernable. I left Mkondeleli with her grandparents. A year after we established the cell the Nelson tragedy happened."

"How did Sidney's brother become part of your cell?"

"He ran a trucking service between Venda and Alexandra. And Sidney used him to transport MK cadres from Zimbabwe to Alexandra. What we didn't know was that Nelson was already a spy for the security forces."

"How did you find out?"

"Gideon exposed him."

"Gideon?"

"Ja. But not before Nelson had betrayed dozens of MK cadres. That's why I had no alternative but to have him executed."

"You did your duty as a commander."

Liefling noticed there were tears in Thando's eyes. She reached over and held her hand. The Toyota had slowed due to bumper-to-bumper traffic on the approach to downtown Jo'burg.

"I'm sorry for bringing up the issue," Liefling said. She could tell Thando was still suffering, still grieving.

"It's okay," Thando said as the Toyota reached Hillbrow.

*****

SWANEPOEL switched off the eavesdropping machine tuned to an Infiniti bug planted under the dashboard of Thando's Toyota. Smiling, he strode toward Room 3, where Botha was sitting across the table from Shaka, who was wearing Gideon's clothes: tweed suit, white shirt, red tie and black shoes.

"They've left the airport," Swanepoel said to Botha. "They're on their way to David's house."

"Excellent," Botha said. He turned and faced Shaka. "You know your orders, right?"

"Sure," Shaka said impassively.

"I don't want any foul-ups."

"Have I ever failed to execute?"

"No. But this is different. The timing has to be perfect."

"It will be perfect. All I need to know is when Liefling and Thando are likely to get to David's house."

Botha glanced at his watch. It was ten to nine. He turned to Swanepoel and said, "When do you think they'll get there, considering traffic?"

"Let me find out," Swanepoel walked over to the computer. He pressed a couple of keys and a tracking map appeared on the monitor showing traffic patterns along Johannesburg's main arteries.

"They're in Hillbrow and traffic is quite congested," Swanepoel said. "I'd say about thirty-five minutes."

"That should give you plenty of time," Botha said to Shaka. He reached down at his feet and picked up a large, heavy-looking brown suitcase.

"This is Gideon's," Botha said.

"What's in it?" Shaka asked.

Botha grinned. "Cocaine and crack. Leave the suitcase on the table after the job is done."

Shaka grabbed the suitcase.

"Gideon's Explorer is in the underground garage," Botha said. "One of the boys drove it down from Venda. Remember, after you do the job, drive away leisurely. There should be plenty of witnesses to notice Gideon's Explorer leaving David's house so they can describe it to the police later."

"What about the money?" Shaka asked.

"Five million rands will be wired to the account number you gave me as soon as I inform the General that David, Liefling and Thando are dead."

42

BOTHA contacted Kruger as soon as Shaka left on his mission.

"He's on his way, General."

"Good. Call me when the mission is complete. I'll be at my office meeting with Tutu."

Kruger replaced the receiver, rose from behind his desk, walked out of his study and descended the spiral staircase to join Freda for breakfast in the morning room. As he approached the door he heard Freda dialing the phone. Curious, he stopped and listened.

"David, this is Freda, Liefling's mother," she said sternly. "I know that my daughter is coming over to see you. And I know the truth about your using my daughter to extort money from my husband in order to pay drug dealers. If anything happens to Liefling, I'll make you pay dearly."

Freda slammed down the phone.

Kruger smiled. *Perfect alibi,* he thought. He paused a bit before entering the morning room so Freda would not realize he had overheard.

"Good morning, my dear,' he said suavely.

"Hullo, honey," Freda said, looking up. "I guess I won't be having lunch with Liefling after all."

"What happened?"

"I called her flat a little while ago. Sipho answered and said Liefling is on her way to Jo'burg."

"Really?"

"Ja."

Kruger sat down. "I wonder why she didn't call to let you know about her sudden change of plans."

"I know why. It's because she's meeting with David."

"With David? When?"

"At ten."

"Where?"

"In Soweto, of all places."

"Hmm." Kruger pursed his lips.

"I'm terribly worried about her going to Soweto after what you told me about David. So I called his place."

"What did you say to him?"

"He wasn't in. I left a message. I told him I knew about his plan to extort money from you to pay off drug debts. Oh, Magnus," she said, glancing at him worriedly, "what if the drug lords come and find my poor Liefling there?"

"Relax, dear," he said, squeezing her hand. "I'll make a few call to some of my friends in the police force in Jo'burg. They'll make sure she's safe."

"Oh, thank you, darling."

Emma brought a silver tray with two plates of spinach omelets and piping hot scones. She set the plates before them, poured their tea and returned to the kitchen. They started eating.

"When are you leaving for Jo'burg?" Freda asked.

"After my meeting with Tutu," Kruger said. He swallowed a mouthful of his omelet. "Why?"

"Do you mind if I came along?" Freda said, ignoring her food. She had little appetite. "I want a face-to-face talk with Liefling about David. Once she knows the truth about his involvement with drug dealers, I'm convinced she'll abandon the lawsuit."

"Okay." Kruger looked at his watch. "In that case you'd better get ready. We'll leave immediately after my meeting with Bishop Tutu."

DAVID heard the phone's shrill ring just as he walked in through the front door. He raced to the kitchen, almost stumbling over a thick law journal on the floor. He ransacked the clutter on the kitchen table for the cordless phone. He found it buried under a pile of books on the intricacies of South Africa's mixture of Roman Dutch and Common law.

"Hullo, David speaking," he said eagerly, thinking it was the mystery witness calling for directions.

"Where have you been?" Liefling asked, relieved to hear his voice. "I've been calling your place since Thando and I left the airport."

"I just returned from dropping Hannah at the theater for a rehearsal. I got caught in traffic."

"Got my message?"

"No. I just walked in."

"Have you heard from the mystery witness?"

"Not yet." David glanced at his watch. "He should be on his way. He said he'd be here at ten. And it's nine-thirty. Where are you?"

"Caught in traffic. But we're already in Hillbrow."

"When do you think you'll get here?"

"In about half an hour or so."

BISHOP DESMOND TUTU got out a limo in front of the entrance to the Cape Town offices of Arm, Protect & Secure Inc. The diminutive chairman of the TRC was wearing his trademark purple robes, golden cross pendant and tinted shades. He was accompanied by two white men in suits, Dr. Alex Borraine, the TRC vice-chairman, and Chris De Jager, a former acting judge who was also a member of the TRC.

At the sight of the three men a pack of reporters surged forward and surrounded them, shouting questions, waving microphones, focusing cameras and jockeying for position.

"Bishop Tutu! Bishop Tutu!" they cried, trying to outshout each other.

"You guys should get a life," Bishop Tutu said with an impish grin as reporters thrust microphones and cameras into his face. "You mean to tell me you've got nothing better to do on a such a beautiful Monday morning than to scare three little guys like us."

Borraine and De Jager smiled.

"Bishop Tutu, do you think the meeting with General Kruger will avert a criminal trial?" shouted a reporter.

"We sure hope so."

"But General Kruger has repeatedly refused to appear before the TRC. He accuses the Commission of being a tool of the ANC."

This was a charge that infuriated Tutu. He stopped to answer it. His eyes, behind their tinted glasses, shone passionately. More mikes and cameras were thrust into his face. He swatted a couple of them away when they came close to knocking his glasses off.

"Nothing could be farthest from the truth," he said, slowly and deliberately. "The Commission is as fair as fair can be. We've listened to testimony from all sides. We are a Commission for all South Africans."

"What about the charge that the Commission is out to humiliate Afrikaners because they're responsible for apartheid?"

"Not true either," Tutu said. "We aren't out to humiliate anyone. We are interested in finding out the truth, pure and simple. That's why asking for forgiveness isn't an amnesty requirement. What the Commission wants is for all who appear before it to confess what they did fully and with candor."

"Do you think General Kruger is afraid he'll be found guilty if he appears before the TRC?"

"The Commission is not a court of law. Neither are we a Nuremberg Tribunal. The twenty Commissioners do not sit in judgment of anybody. We're only interested in the truth. If people confess the whole truth about the human rights abuses they committed during the apartheid era and can clearly show that the acts, no matter how heinous, occurred in pursuit of a political objective, the Commission is duty-bound to grant those people amnesty."

A reporter from *The Star* spoke up. "General Kruger has said that he stands a better chance defending himself in a court of law than before the TRC. He says that in a court-of-law, witnesses can be cross-examined, but not before the TRC."

"I'll let Dr. Borraine answer that," Tutu said, glancing at his colleague.

"That's absolutely false," Borraine said. "The Commission's proceedings aren't based on witnesses giving evidence against someone applying for amnesty. They are based on the applicant voluntarily – and I must emphasize, voluntarily – telling the Commission the truth about what he or she did."

"And no one has to apologize for apartheid," De Jager added. "The Commission has granted amnesty to people who were clearly unrepentant about what they did. Nevertheless, they did comply with the requirements for amnesty spelled out under The Promotion of Truth and Reconciliation Act."

"And I should add one very important reason why it's in General Kruger's best interest to grab this golden opportunity to appear before the TRC before the deadline expires, rather than defend himself in a court-of-law," Tutu said. "Amnesty expunges any criminal or civil liability a person is likely to have. If you confess the truth, you cannot – I repeat, you cannot – be sued by the State, or by anyone in a court of law. This is one of the toughest provisions to have been included. The TRC's critics regard the provision as a loophole that lets killers get away with murder. But the Government, though acutely aware of the enormous suffering of the victims of apartheid, felt that in order to be able to put the past behind us and to foster the healing of our beautiful nation, it should go the extra mile in the interests of reconciliation. Now if you'll excuse us, General Kruger is waiting for us. Please let us through."

More questions were shouted but Tutu, Borraine and De Jager ignored them as they made their way among cameras, mikes and bodies. Finally they reached the guarded gate leading to the Victorian mansion.

KRUGER stood by the window of his second floor office, his hands clasped behind his back. He smiled wryly as he watched the media spectacle outside the gate.

Tutu loves entertaining the media, he thought. *But he won't do so at my expense.*

Kruger returned to his desk. A minute or so later, his secretary knocked and entered.

"Bishop Tutu and the delegation are here."

"Show them in."

DAVID sat at the cluttered kitchen table, head in his hands, deeply troubled by the message Freda had left on his answering machine. He wondered why she persisted in believing that he was a drug dealer. He couldn't wait for Liefling to arrive so together they could call her mother and straighten things out.

David's eyes filled with tears as he gazed at the framed photo in front of him. It was of Dikeledi Motsei, a gorgeous pre-med student he'd dated while at Wits University. Tall, well-built and with smooth chocolate-brown skin, Dikeledi, as a student leader during the 1976 Soweto Uprising, had participated in the necklacing of a white police sergeant who'd headed Soweto's notorious security branch. It was the brilliant defense of David's father, a prominent lawyer and a secret member of the South African Communist Party, that had saved Dikeledi from the hangman's noose in a high-profile trial presided over by the then Judge Prinsloo.

David's eyes rested on a copy of the official report from the inquest that he and Dikeledi's family had demanded after her death in police detention. Judge Prinsloo had found the security branch at John Vorster Square not guilty on charges of manslaughter.

David looked at the black and white photo again. *I know the bastards killed you, Dikeledi. And I won't rest until they're brought to justice.*

The doorbell rang. David hurried to the door and opened it a crack, expecting to see Liefling and Thando. Instead his jaw dropped. In front of him was a tall black man wearing a tweed suit, a black fedora hat and dark shades. A trench coat muffled his face against the cold winter air. He was carrying a leather suitcase in his right hand. David looked beyond the man and saw a red Explorer parked in the driveway.

"You're here," David stammered in disbelief.

"Ja," Shaka said. "Sorry I'm a little late. May I come in?"

"Sure," David said with alacrity, opening the door wide and welcoming his assassin.

43 SHAKA hurriedly stepped into the room. His eyes darted about quickly to see if there was anyone else inside. Botha had assured him that David would be alone and that Swanepoel's eavesdropping had detected no other person. Always cautious, Shaka wanted to make sure.

"Do you mind locking the door?" he said.

"Not at all," David said, bolting it. "I can't believe this," he gushed as he pulled down the alabaster blinds. He flicked on the light switch. "I was beginning to doubt you were real."

"I'm real," Shaka said. "It took me longer to get here than I thought."

"Please sit down," David said, leading Shaka to the cluttered kitchen table. "May I get you anything to drink?"

"What do you have?"

"What would you like?" David said. He opened the refrigerator. "I have beer, wine, Fanta, Coke, Ginger beer, Perrier."

"Ginger beer, please," Shaka said. The kitchen was well lit, but he never took off his shades or hat.

"Are you expecting anyone?" Shaka asked, despite the fact that five minutes earlier he'd received a call from Botha that Liefling and Thando were about ten minutes away, and that he had to kill David quickly in order to have time to prepare an ambush for them.

David hesitated before answering. "Yes. I hope you won't mind. My colleagues, Liefling and Thando, are on their way here as we speak."

"I don't mind. May I use the bathroom?"

"Sure," David said, placing the Ginger beer and a clean glass in front of the person he thought was their mystery witness. "It's down the hallway to your left."

"Thanks," Shaka said. He rose, leaving his suitcase on the table.

David watched him enter the hallway bathroom. He noticed that his visitor still hadn't taken off his hat or dark shades.

Of course he's suspicious, David thought. *So would I if were carrying such explosive evidence.* David eyed the suitcase gleefully. He couldn't wait to see the sensational diaries. He heard the gurgling sound of a toilet flushing. At the same time he heard a car stop outside.

The bathroom door opened. Shaka reappeared. David stared, slack-jawed, in utter disbelief and horror at the person he'd thought was their mystery witness. Gone were the fedora and the dark glasses. In their place Shaka was wearing the dreaded balaclava hood worn by members of the Thathe Vondo death squad. His gloved right hand was holding a nine-millimeter pistol with a cylindrical silencer screwed to its snout.

KRUGER eyed Tutu, Borraine and De Jager critically. The men were seated around a deal table in a private study just off Kruger's office.

"So the TRC wants me to confess crimes I never committed, is that it?" Kruger asked with a touch of sarcasm.

"The TRC is not about crimes, General," Tutu said emphatically. "It's about the search for truth."

"You mean the ANC's version of the truth," Kruger said.

"You're mistaken, General?" Borraine said, trying hard to mask his irritation. "The uniqueness of the TRC is its independence. Though an ANC-dominated government formed us, we don't give any special treatment to ANC members. They're required to testify about human rights abuses they've committed – even though they committed them in the pursuit of a very just cause: the destruction of apartheid."

"Come on, Dr. Borraine," Kruger said with a small laugh. "Everyone knows what the TRC really is. It's nothing but the ANC's way of settling scores against us Afrikaners. They didn't defeat us on the battlefield. Now they want to humiliate us before the whole world under the guise of searching for truth."

To Kruger's surprise, it was De Jager who responded. "Permit me to contradict you, General Kruger. I'm an Afrikaner too. I wouldn't have agreed to serve on the TRC if I'd had the slightest indication that the Commission was not what it was intended to be: an independent and fair-minded body whose sole interest is in healing our country. Don't forget, General Kruger, that the National Party was a part of the Government of National Unity, and a signatory to the Constitution that established the TRC."

Kruger hated Afrikaners who sided with the enemy, but he did his best to mask his abhorrence of De Jager. Traitors like him were to be barred from the Vaderland.

"Didn't the National Party withdraw from the Government of National Unity in 1996 precisely because it perceived the TRC as biased, Judge Jager?" Kruger said in a tone of feigned reasonableness. "It's easy to pervert a good thing. What we Afrikaners agreed to was reconciliation, not witchhunts."

Tutu spoke. "With all due respect, General Kruger, you grossly misunderstand the law that established the TRC."

Anger flashed briefly in Kruger's pale-blue eyes. "Do I?" he said with barely disguised disdain.

"Yes," Tutu said firmly.

"Then please refresh my memory," Kruger said indulgently, leaning back in his chair and folding his arms across his chest.

"I'd be more than happy to."

Kruger smiled sardonically as he watched Bishop Tutu reach for his briefcase. He knew the law. He actually wanted to say, "There's no need to read me the law, Bishop. I've long made up my mind not to testify. Good day." But he had a reason for prolonging the charade. He knew that any minute now, he'd receive a call from Botha informing him that Shaka had accomplished his mission.

Once the damn lawsuit is history, Kruger thought as Tutu fumbled for the booklet titled <u>Justice in Transition</u>, *then the firm will be sold and I'll have the money to proceed with plans for the Fourth Boer Revolution.*

Kruger only half-listened as Tutu said, "As you know, General, the TRC is based on the final clause of the Interim Constitution, which was unanimously adopted in 1993. That clause states:

> *This Constitution provides a historic bridge between the past of a deeply divided society characterized by strife, conflict, untold suffering and injustice, and a future founded on the recognition of human rights, democracy and peaceful co-existence and development opportunities for all South Africans, irrespective of color, race, class, belief or sex.*
>
> *The pursuit of national unity, the well-being of all South African citizens and peace require reconciliation between the people of South Africa and the reconstruction of society.*
>
> *The adoption of this Constitution lays the secure foundation for the people of South Africa to transcend the divisions and*

*strife of the past, which generated gross violations of human
rights, the transgression of humanitarian principles in violent
conflicts and a legacy of hatred, fear, guilt and revenge.*
   *These can now be addressed on the basis that there is a need
for understanding but not for vengeance, a need for reparation but
not for retaliation, a need for Ubuntu but not for victimization.*

Bishop Tutu closed the booklet and gave Kruger a pleading look.

"We've come here in the spirit of Ubuntu, General Kruger," he said. "We know you have every right to defend yourself in court against your stepdaughter's lawsuit. But we hope that you also recognize a duty to the nation to help us find the truth about such matters as CCB death squads and the disappearance of anti-apartheid activists and MK guerillas."

"Are you suggesting that I had anything to do with death squads, Bishop Tutu?" Kruger said, looking quite appalled and indignant.

"No. I'm suggesting no such thing. But since you were a high-ranking member of the CCB, I thought you might be able to shed some light on the issue. Especially because so little is known about this clandestine group. Few of your colleagues have come forth and testified."

"Let me get it straight," Kruger said, rising. "You want me to betray the honorable men I served with by revealing the activities of the CCB."

"If such activities were illegal and constituted gross violations of human rights," Borraine said, "then yes, you're obligated to divulge them."

"And if I refuse?"

"Then your stepdaughter's lawsuit goes to trial," De Jager said. "And not only that, but the TRC may subpoena you to testify, if it considers it in the national interest."

"Now I see," Kruger said triumphantly. "You're here to blackmail me."

"Far from it," Tutu said. He chose his words deliberately and, as always, gave them a moral bent. "We are here to beg you to do the right thing. If you love your country, and I believe you do, General Kruger, then appear before the TRC. You'll be making an immense contribution toward its healing if you do. There's also an advantage for you, General Kruger, in case you've overlooked it."

"What is the advantage, I pray you?"

"In a court of law you may lose," Tutu said sternly. "But before the TRC, if you tell the truth, you're guaranteed to win. Not only that. No one – not the state Attorney General, not the victims or their families – can ever take you to court. Isn't that a good deal? If I were you, I'd grab it."

Suddenly the phone rang and Kruger answered it. He listened for several minutes, then said, "Are you sure?" and "I'm not surprised." Kruger slowly replaced the phone. A somber look on his face, he turned to Tutu, Borraine and De Jager and said, "That was my lawyer, gentlemen. He just informed me that he's planning to file a motion with the court to have the lawsuit against me dismissed on the grounds that it is part of a blackmailing scheme."

Tutu, Borraine and De Jager looked at each other, stunned.

Kruger said, "I'm not as surprised as you are, gentlemen. I know Liefling. She's a good girl. She was very happy that I married her mother. You should have seen us dance together at my wedding. She didn't strike me as someone who would file a lawsuit against me on her own volition. I even told her mother of my suspicions that someone must have put her up to it. Now my lawyer's investigators have confirmed that she was indeed blackmailed."

"Blackmailed!" Borraine asked, looking skeptical.

"Ja. By a drug dealer."

"A drug dealer?" Tutu said, looking puzzled.

"Yes, gentlemen, a drug dealer who'd hoped to extort money from me so he could pay off his huge drug-dealing debts. My lawyer told me that the evidence of this blackmailing scheme will be presented to the judge during the preparatory examination."

Tutu, Borraine and De Jager exchanged bewildered glances.

Kruger glanced at his watch. "I'm sorry to have to cut our meeting short, gentlemen. But I have a plane to catch. I have a meeting with my lawyer in Jo'burg to discuss this unexpected turn of events. Thank you for coming and have a good day." Kruger rose and cordially shook hands with Tutu, Borraine and De Jager, who still looked quite confused.

After they'd left, Kruger strode to the window. Minutes later he saw Tutu, Borraine and De Jager get into their limo without stopping to talk to any reporters. All they said to the shouted questions was "No comment."

Kruger returned to his desk. He'd hardly sat down when the phone rang. Kruger grabbed it.

"Hullo, darling," Freda said. "Is the meeting over?"

"Ja."

"How did it go?"

"As well as can be hoped."

"Are you ready to come pick me up?" Freda had been shopping at the Waterfront.

"I was just about to leave," Kruger said. He hastily packed his briefcase and put on his coat. He decided to call Botha before leaving.

"Is the job done?" he demanded.

"I haven't heard from Shaka yet," Botha said.

"The meeting with Tutu just ended."

"How did it go?"

"I set up the drug angle perfectly. You should have seen the stunned looks on their faces. Once Shaka executes, everything should fall into place."

"He will."

LIEFLING rang David's bell a third time, growing impatient. "David, are you in there?" she shouted, rapping the door loudly with her knuckle.

Shaka jabbed the pistol into David's ribs, indicating he should answer in the affirmative. "Ja, I'm in here," David said, his knees shaking. "I was in the bathroom."

"Well, aren't you going to open the door?"

"Open the door," Shaka whispered.

"I'm coming," David said as he slowly walked to the door, Shaka behind him, the gun pointing right at David's heart. David unbolted the door, opened it a crack and peered at Liefling.

"My!" Liefling said at the sight of his pale face. "It's as if you've seen a ghost. What's wrong?"

"Oh, nothing. I'm just not feeling well."

"Are you alone?"

David hesitated, then feeling the pistol in his ribs, he said, "Ja, Ja, I'm alone. Who else would be here?"

Liefling immediately sensed something was wrong. She noticed the red Explorer in the driveway.

Obviously someone is in there with him, Liefling thought. *Then why is David denying it? And why is he so petrified?*

"May I come in?" Liefling asked.

David hesitated. Again feeling the jab of the cold pistol, he said, "Ja. Of course."

Something's definitely wrong, Liefling thought, as she hesitated. *David's acting out of character. Normally, he'd have flung open the door and given me a bear hug.*

"Oh, wait," Liefling said, "I almost forgot the affidavits. I'll get them from the car."

| 44 | **GIDEON** was slumped on a wooden chair in the middle of a large windowless room lit by a single bulb dangling from the cobwebbed rafters. His hands, swollen and bleeding at the wrists, were strapped behind his back. He'd been stripped naked. The wound in the back of his swollen leg |

was festering. Drenched in blood and sweat, he was running a fever.

Viljoen stood before him, grim-faced. He was wearing camouflage fatigues. Barnard, also in camouflage, stood beside a fish tank filled with rancid and bloody water. Both were seething with anger. For the past several hours they'd been torturing Gideon trying in vain to force him to talk. They'd smashed his face with brass knuckles. They'd repeatedly dunked his head in the tank and held it underwater until he felt his lungs bursting for air. They'd covered his head with a sack until he had nearly suffocated. They'd placed electrodes on his testicles and zapped them until he screamed in agony. Still, he'd refused to talk.

Now Viljoen prepared to use a method that had never failed to make his victims talk. He loaded one bullet into the revolver in his right hand.

"Are you going to talk or do you prefer to die, kaffir?" Viljoen snarled.

Gideon said nothing. He simply stared at Viljoen and Barnard with swollen but defiant eyes. He blinked away the blood trickling down his forehead.

Viljoen spun the chamber once and then pressed the cold muzzle of the pistol against Gideon's right temple. Now it was Russian Roulette time, Viljoen's favorite interrogation technique. Gideon shuddered. He remembered the many times he'd seen the brains of victims splattered all over the floor after they'd refused to talk, thinking Viljoen was bluffing.

"Even the most stubborn kaffir eventually talks inside the truth hut," Viljoen said. Without warning, he pulled the trigger. There was a loud click. Gideon's heart pounded wildly.

"You're one bloody lucky kaffir," Viljoen said, grinning. He spun the chamber a second time. Again he placed the pistol against Gideon's right temple. He was about to squeeze the trigger when Gideon mumbled, "What do you want to know?"

Grinning, Viljoen lowered the pistol. "That's better."

He pulled up a chair and sat down facing Gideon. He prepared to begin grilling him on who else knew about the diaries so they also could be eliminated.

THANDO was about to step out of the Toyota when Liefling gently nudged her back inside.

"There's something wrong with David," Liefling whispered, getting inside the Toyota and closing the door.

"What do you mean?"

"There's someone in there with him. But he denies it."

"Denies it?" Thando said, surprised. "Isn't Gideon in there with him?"

"Gideon?"

"Ja. Gideon Munyai, the schoolteacher. Makhado's son."

"Why do you think it's Gideon in there?"

"That's his Explorer in front of us," Thando said, pointing.

"That's his?"

"Ja."

"How can you tell?"

"I recognize the number plates. He let me use it one time to transport women to a march against rape in Pretoria."

"What's Gideon doing here?" Liefling said. "And why is David so scared?"

"There's only one way to find out," Thando said. "Let's go in."

"Do you think Gideon might be our mystery witness?"

Thando gave Liefling a stunned look.

"Gideon, an askari? No way. He was a trusted member of MK." She shook her head from side to side for emphasis, making her braids bob.

"Wait a minute," Thando cried. "I saw Nomhle this morning. She said Gideon had gone to Venda but hadn't returned. And David said the mystery witness was coming from Venda, didn't he?"

"Ja."

"Then maybe Gideon gave him a ride."

"That's possible. But it doesn't explain why David looked terrified," Liefling said, biting her lower lip. "After all, he knows Gideon."

Liefling looked at the door, which was now closed. "I'm going in," she said, reaching into her purse for her loaded Beretta – the gun she had bought for self-protection at her mother's insistence.

"Wait a minute," Thando said, grabbing Liefling's arm. "You can't just walk to the door holding that gun in the open, like you were John Wayne."

"Why not?"

Thando smiled. "Don't forget I used to command guerrilla fighters. I know a lot more about ambushes than you do. Hide the gun under this stack of affidavits." She handed them to Liefling. "Walk normally to the door. Pretend nothing's wrong. Be on the alert for any sign of movement. I'll keep an eye on the door and window."

"Thanks."

"One more thing. When you get to the door, kick it wide open in case there's someone hiding behind it. I'll keep you covered." Thando removed her Magnum from the glove compartment.

Liefling hid the Beretta beneath the affidavits and got out.

"Good luck," Thando said.

"I'll need it."

Liefling walked as normally as she could toward the door, which seemed miles away. Her heart pounded.

"Keep calm, keep calm," she kept muttering to herself. Suddenly, halfway to the door, an idea occurred to her. She pretended to struggle with the heavy load of affidavits.

"David!" she yelled, "I need some help."

For about a minute nothing happened. Suddenly David screamed, as if in deep pain. Liefling dropped the stack of affidavits, threw herself to the ground and rolled under a nearby shrub. Thando flung open the car door and, head bent low, zigzagged toward Liefling.

"Are you okay?" she asked.

"Jesus Christ!" Liefling cried. "What was that?"

"Sounds like David's hurt."

"I'm going in," Liefling said. "Keep me covered." Bent low, she started inching toward the door, using the shrubs as cover. Thando kept the Magnum aimed at the closed door, reading to fire.

VILJOEN said, "We want you to answer just one simple question. Did you tell anyone else besides David about the diaries?"

"No," Gideon said through bleeding and swollen lips.

"Do you really expect us to believe that?" Without warning, Viljoen smashed the pistol into Gideon's face. Gideon's face burned with pain, but he didn't cry out. Knowing he was going to be killed anyway, he was determined to die like a true African warrior.

"Why would I tell anyone else?" he mumbled.

"You're lying, kaffir," Viljoen hissed. He placed the cold muzzle of the pistol underneath Gideon's chin and jerked his bloodied face upward. "You did tell your wife. You once told me she's your best friend. Why wouldn't you tell her?"

"You know why," Gideon mumbled. "I betrayed her brother Vusi."

Viljoen and Barnard looked at each other in mutual remembrance of how Gideon had betrayed Vusi. They recalled how Gideon had told them when Vusi would be visiting his mother, how they'd ambushed him, and how Botha had chopped off Vusi's right hand and then executed him after he'd refused to reveal where he'd hidden the cache of AK-47s that were destined for Alexandra's self defense units.

"What about the old kaffir?" Viljoen asked.

Gideon's heart skipped a beat. He remembered the diaries he'd given his father. He decided to feign ignorance. "What old kaffir are you talking about?"

"You know who I'm talking about," Viljoen said. "Your fucking old man."

"What about him?"

"Did you tell him?"

"No."

"Don't lie, kaffir," Viljoen snapped. "Shaka told us everything. He told us that you visited your old man before you came to him and tried to persuade him to testify with you."

Viljoen smiled as he noticed the look of shock on Gideon's face.

"Shaka is a good kaffir," he said. "Unlike you. Now I'll ask you a second time: Did you tell your old man about the diaries?"

"If I'd told him, do you think he would have come to work today?"

Gideon knew he was taking a gamble. Perhaps his father had changed his mind and quit his job, as he'd threatened to do. Gideon's swollen eyes strained to make out Viljoen's reaction. For a long time Viljoen said nothing. He simply stared at Gideon. He could tell Gideon was no longer afraid to die. He was a different man from the one they'd turned into an askari. That fact made Viljoen very angry.

"If you told him, kaffir," Viljoen hissed, "we'll find out. And when we do, we'll wipe out your entire fucking family."

FREDA and Kruger sat side by side in the back of a limo, headed for Cape Town International airport where his Learjet was parked.

"I called David's house several times while I was at the Waterfront," Freda said. "There's no answer."

"I hope Liefling's okay," Kruger said, thinking how perfectly his plan was unfolding. Freda would be the perfect alibi. He couldn't wait for the call from Botha informing him that Shaka had accomplished his mission, that Liefling, Thando and David were dead, and that the police had concluded that drug lords had killed them. He imagined breaking the news to Freda in a voice full of sorrow but still firm, calming her hysteria, commiserating with her on the loss of a special daughter, and reassuring her that he would take care of her.

LIEFLING kicked open the front door and rushed in, Beretta raised, ready to fire. Her eyes darted about the room. She saw no one. Then her eyes fell to the floor.

"Oh, my God!" she cried in horror.

David was lying face down in a pool of blood on the beige carpet. She rushed toward him and turned him over. She flinched at the sight of the gaping gunshot wound in his belly. Nausea rippled up from her stomach. She lifted his limp right wrist and searched for a pulse. There was none.

Thando stormed through the door and saw Liefling leaning over David. "Oh, no," she stammered. "Please, God, no. Is he dead?"

"I can't find any pulse. Call an ambulance – quick! I'll check the rest of the house."

Thando grabbed the phone on the kitchen table and called for an ambulance. Liefling, gun drawn, cautiously went from room to room. She searched all five rooms, including the closets but found no sign of anyone. Then she realized why. The kitchen's rear door was ajar. She rushed into the backyard but saw no one. There was no way to tell in which direction the gunman had fled given the intricate alleys interconnecting Soweto's tiny matchbox houses and shacks.

"Damn." Frustrated, she went back inside and began searching for clues as to who the gunman might have been. The suitcase on the kitchen table caught her attention. She opened it. Her eyes widened as she stared in disbelief at the contents – several cellophane bags and plastic vials of white powder.

"I don't believe it," she murmured, picking up one of the packets of cocaine.

Suddenly she heard Thando scream. She raced back to the front door and found Thando kneeling beside David, cradling his languid head in her hands.

"He's alive, Liefling!" Thando cried. "He's alive!" Tears of joy streamed down her cheeks. "I did CPR. I was able to get a faint pulse. Feel."

Liefling squeezed her thumb against the radial artery in David's wrist. Yes, there the was a faint pulse.

"Thank God!" Liefling cried.

Sirens screamed outside. Thinking it might be the police, Liefling grabbed Thando's Magnum and her Beretta. She rushed back to the suitcase, tossed the guns inside, closed the suitcase and hid it in a nearby closet, just as two black paramedics came rushing through the door carrying emergency kits and gear.

"I managed to revive him," Thando said as the paramedics attended to David. "I did CPR."

One of them looked up at Thando. "You just saved this man's life."

"Who shot him?" asked the other.

"We don't know," Liefling said. "Whoever it was fled through the back door."

Within minutes the paramedics had stabilized David, placed him gently on a stretcher and wheeled him out to the ambulance.

"Which hospital are you taking him to?" Liefling asked.

"Bara."

"We'll follow in our car."

The ambulance roared away, siren screaming.

"Where are the police?" Liefling asked.

"Don't bother," Thando said. "There's so much violence and crime in Jo'burg that it takes them hours to respond to a call for help, if they ever do."

"That's a relief."

Thando gave Liefling a puzzled look. "It is?"

"Follow me. I'll explain."

Liefling retrieved the mysterious suitcase from the closet, placed it on the kitchen table and snapped it open. Thando's large brown eyes grew even larger at the sight of the cocaine and crack. "Holy ancestors! Where did you find it?"

"On the kitchen table."

"Do you think David is involved in --"

"I don't know," Liefling said. "There's a lot I don't understand. Gideon's role in all this for instance. But there's no time to argue. Let's get the hell out of here before the police come."

Liefling grabbed the suitcase and she and Thando left for Bara.

45

BOTHA paced nervously inside Room 3. From time to time he stopped and starred at the phone. Suddenly it rang. He snatched it up on the first ring. "Yes?"

"This is Shaka."

"Where the hell have you been?" Botha demanded. "I've been waiting for a call from you for the last half hour. The General just called. He's on his way to Jo'burg and wants to know how the mission went."

"There were problems."

"You fucking stupid kaffir bastard!" Botha screamed. He almost slammed his fist on the table but restrained himself. "I told you no foul-ups! What happened?"

Botha suddenly felt hot. He loosened his tie and lit a Lucky Strike.

"Everything was going well until David tried wrestling the gun out of my hand when I wasn't looking."

"Where were your big eyes looking, kaffir?"

"I was watching Liefling as she came to the door. Instead of entering, she went back to the car. She seemed to suspect something. She talked to Thando for a little while and then came back. Halfway to the door she called out to David for help. That's when David tried to snatch the gun. I shot him in the stomach."

"Is he dead?"

"I don't know. He's in surgery at Bara. As a matter of fact, I'm calling from a phone booth across the street from the hospital."

"Are you fucking crazy? What if someone recognizes you?"

"No one saw me. I was wearing a balaclava."

There was a pause.

"What happened to the briefcase?"

"I saw Liefling carrying it into the hospital."

"Dammit!" Botha resumed pacing. He puffed furiously.

"Stay there. I'll give you a call as soon as I've talked to the General."

Botha slammed the phone down. He wiped his sweaty brow with the back of his hand. He opened the door and called out to Swanepoel, who'd just gotten off the phone with Viljoen and Barnard.

"The bloody kaffir bungled the mission," Botha said.

"Oh, shit!" said Swanepoel.

"Has Gideon talked?"

"No," Swanepoel said. "Piet and Jan just finished working on him in the truth hut. They tried everything - electric shock, the wet bag, brass knuckles – nothing worked. They think only the General can make him talk. They want to know what time he's arriving tonight."

"He just left Cape Town and is on his way here. I have to think of some way to fix Shaka's fucking mess before he arrives."

Botha took another long drag on his cigarette, then exhaled slowly, staring at the swirling smoke. His eyes shifted back to Swanepoel.

"Thando's Toyota is bugged, isn't it?" he asked.

"Ja."

"Good. Is one of the firm's special vans available?"

The firm owned a fleet of more than one thousand vehicles nationwide, used in the normal course of providing private security for clients. The majority of these vehicles – mostly vans and sedans – bore the company logo. But there were about two hundred specially equipped vehicles that had been designed to appear identical to the sedans and vans used by the police and members of the security forces in their battle against endemic crime and robberies. These were equipped with police sirens, radar detectors, laptop computers and other equipment used in secure communications.

Of course it was illegal for the firm to impersonate the police. But such impersonation was indispensable to the firm's success. Given the fact that it often took forever for the real police to respond to emergency calls, it was extremely comforting for the firm's clients – and discomforting for would-be robbers and carjackers – to see the "Police" show up at the scene minutes after being summoned. As a result, none of the firm's hundreds of clients were killed during robberies or had their businesses burglarized or their expensive cars hijacked.

The firm's tactics had never been exposed because Kruger had friends in high places. A timely and discreet bribe was enough to keep things quiet in a police department in which one in four policemen were corrupt.

It was one of these special "Police" vans that Botha was inquiring about.

"Let me check," Swanepoel said. He punched a couple of keys and an inventory list appeared on the computer monitor.

After scanning it, he frowned. "There's been an unusually high number of attempted burglaries, heists and carjackings. Most of the special vans are being used. I don't see anything available in the Jo'burg area at the moment."

"Then look outside Jo'burg. If you can't find one, tell one of the men to get his bloody van back to headquarters immediately."

Swanepoel said. He hit a few buttons on the keyboard and another longer list scrolled down the computer screen.

He scanned the master list. "Aha!" he cried. "I think I've found one."

"Great. What type?"

"It's a van similar to those used by the anti-hijacking squad."

"Excellent. Where is it?"

"It's on its way from Pretoria. And it's fully loaded. It even has the latest tracking system."

"When can I have it ready?"

"In about an hour."

"Good. Put a dozen AK-47s in it. You know, the ones from the stockpile we seized from the MK cell in Alexandra during the apartheid era. I'm driving to Bara to pick up Shaka. He and I will trail Liefling and Thando. I have a brilliant plan on how to clean up this mess before the General arrives."

THANDO lay on a stretcher in a sterile operation room. A needle stuck into her right arm drew blood from her vein and pumped it directly into David, who was lying on the operating table, amid a tangle of EKG and IV wires.

"Please, God, save him," she mumbled as a surgeon, his assistant and two nurses operated on David. The atmosphere was tense. David's abdomen gaped open as the surgeon tried desperately to repair massive internal damage done by the bullet that, after entering through the navel, had ripped parts of his stomach and the right lung before exiting just below his rib. Miraculously, in its diagonal trajectory, the bullet had missed the superior mesenteric artery, the Hepatic artery and the lower Aorta. And that's what had saved David from instant death.

But there was no doubt his wounds were life-threatening. His system had suffered severe shock and he'd bled profusely. Thando had volunteered to donate the blood he needed to survive. She was glad her blood type was O-negative, making her a universal donor.

The delicate operation was entering its fourth hour but the surgeon's hands remained steady, his eyes focused despite the harsh operating lights turned on above the table. Every skill he'd ever learned as a surgeon was in use. He knew that a lot was riding on his ability to save David. He was not just another victim of a gunshot wound. He was the friend and co-worker of Liefling, the woman he dearly loved.

"Suction please," Sipho said to the nurse in a calm voice.

With the suction machine hissing noisily, the nurse proceeded to suction the blood that had pooled in David's abdomen. Some of the blood had dribbled to the floor and the towels at Sipho's feet were saturated. Yet he kept working. Another nurse wiped the sweat off his brow.

Don't die on me, David, Sipho thought as he continued repairing David's damaged internal organs.

MAKHADO waited until nightfall before stealing his way to the small thatch-roofed hut at the back of his kraal. No one but his wife saw him leave. Inside the hut he lit a candle and proceeded to put on his warrior garb. He hadn't worn the gear since his youth. His grandfather, who'd served under the Great Makhado, the legendary Venda warrior after whom he'd been named, had worn the same gear.

First he placed an impressive conical helmet on his head. It was set on a toque made of animal skin and held in place by a chinstrap. Ostrich feathers trimmed the helmet. Three long and slender feathers, taken from the *sakabonyi*, or the widow bird, plumed the sides and front of the helmet, making it appear twice its natural size. Porcupine quills protruded from its sides, enhancing its ferocious appearance.

Next, Makhado tied around his neck a necklace made from the teeth of a wild boar and plaited thongs from the tawny skin of the lion he'd killed when he was sixteen, shortly after he was circumcised. Then he ornamented his bulging biceps and powerful legs with braided bands of long white hairs that had been carefully plucked from the tail of an ox in the prime of its virility.

He girded his loins with a richly decorated belt. Its front was made from strips of leopard skin and hung down to the middle of his strong thighs. Its back was made of small antelope skin. Makhado then covered his calves and ankles with bracelets made of black seeds as large as cherries. The bracelets enhanced the width of his legs so that when he stamped his bare feet on the ground, the rattling of the black seeds mimicked the thunder of charging elephants.

His warrior attire now complete, he walked to the corner of the hut and stooped to pick up his shield, battle-axe and spear. The shield was similar to those made famous by the Zulus in their memorable battles during the *Mfecane*, (the Crushing), when Shaka, Africa's Genghis Khan and Napoleon combined, had forged the mighty Zulu nation.

The massive shield was oval in shape and made of ox-hide. On either side of its central line, from top to bottom, ran two parallel rows of square incisions through which were woven strips of different colors. The axe was made of a narrow and elongated blade attached to a wooden handle. The formidable spear, his main weapon in hand-to-hand combat, was made from a razor-sharp, double-edged steel blade about fourteen inches long that had been bound with an iron wire onto a wooden handle about four feet long.

After inspecting his weapons, Makhado placed them on the cool cowdung floor. He picked up a weathered canvas satchel and looked inside. It contained a pair of second-hand binoculars Gideon had bought him several years earlier after learning of his bird-watching hobby. He slung the satchel over his shoulder and picked up a calabash containing the war-medicine he'd brewed shortly after returning from work. He took several swigs. He opened his snuffbox and took a pinch. Kneeling down before several totems, sprinkled snuff over the totems and poured a libation into a small bowl in front of them. He muttered incantations to his ancestral spirits.

"*Midzimu*, please be by my side as I battle the white man," he said solemnly, his eyes fixed on the totems. "I promise never to disgrace your hallowed names."

Suddenly he heard a faint cough outside the door of the hut.

Without turning, he said, "Come in, Mother of Gideon." Makhado uttered the words in a low voice, signifying the solemnity of the occasion.

Mudjadji lifted the flap covering the doorway. Slowly, she stepped into the hut, dimly lit by the flame of the flickering candle. She silently stood by the door, holding something in her small callused hands.

"What is it, Mother of Gideon?" Makhado said.

"I know you must go back to the Thathe Vondo game reserve tonight, Father of Gideon," she said softly. "But my heart wishes you wouldn't go. It is trembling with fear at what awaits you there."

Makhado made no reply. His face stoic, he gazed at the totems arranged in the order of their prominence on the reed mat in front of him.

"The white men are too many," Mudjadji said. "And they have guns."

"I know all that, Mother of Gideon," Makhado said. "But I must find out what they did to our son."

He paused.

"If they killed him, it is my duty to avenge his death."

Makhado's tone left no doubt about his resolve.

"What if you're killed, Father of Gideon?"

"It is a great honor to die in battle, Mother of Gideon. My grandfather died in battle. So did his father before him."

Mudjadji lowered her head.

"How will I cope without you, Father of Gideon?" she said softly.

For a long while Makhado made no reply. Finally he rose and faced his wife.

"You'll cope just fine, Mother of Gideon," he said. "You have the strength of five women. That's why I never took more wives, even when my relatives urged me to."

Makhado walked over to Mudjadji and took her in his arms.

"If I'm killed tonight, Mother of Gideon, my spirit will always be with you. You're my better half. A part of my soul. I remember the day I first met you by the purling stream. You were as beautiful as the rising dawn. You became my bride, the woman of my dreams. Over the years you've brought great joy to my home. You've borne me many children and worked very hard. And you've always given me good counsel."

Mudjadji's lips trembled with emotion. Her eyes shone with tears and the memories of many years. She managed a weak smile.

"You too are my better half, Makhado," she said. "You're the only man I've ever known. When I first laid my eyes on you, I knew why they'd named you after the Great Makhado, Lion of the North. You are strength, courage, pride and defiance personified. It seems only yesterday that your aunts and uncles came to my father's kraal and paid fifty fat cattle as *lobola* for me. It was the highest dowry ever paid for any girl in my village. You made me very proud."

Makhado kissed Mudjadji. She clung to him.

"But I'm so afraid, Father of Gideon," Mudjadji whispered in his ear. "You're no longer as strong as you were in the old days when you slew lions and rescued fellow miners buried under rockslides. Why don't you go to the police instead and let them handle the matter?"

"I do not trust the police, Mother of Gideon," Makhado said. "Don't forget that most of the men who tortured and killed our people were policemen. Besides, the white men are gathering at the camp tonight. Viljoen said Kruger will be there. He's the evil one I'm after."

"I understand, Father of Gideon," Mudjadji said, sighing with resignation.

Makhado felt his heart break at the thought that he might never see his beloved Mudjadji again. A part of him wanted to weep, but now he was a different man. He was Makhado, an African warrior. And on the eve of battle, African warriors never expressed any emotion except dauntless courage and strength.

"I must go now," Makhado said. "It's grown dark enough. If I do not come back alive, know that the *Midzimu* have willed it so."

"As always, Father of Gideon," Mudjadji said in a voice filled with pride, "they hold our lives in their hands."

Makhado again kissed his wife. Then he gathered his shield, battle-axe and spear.

"Father of Gideon," Mudjadji said respectfully. "I know that those weapons are formidable, but at a time like this, it won't hurt to bring more weapons along."

"What weapons?"

Mudjadji removed the cross from her neck and handed it to Makhado along with a copy of the Shangaan Bible she'd brought.

"You know I don't believe in the white man's God," Makhado said.

"I know. But He's a God of Justice," Mudjadji said. "Don't forget that my father was also a formidable Shangaan warrior, but he never went into battle without this Bible, which he gave to me before he died."

Makhado took the cross and the Bible. He put the Bible in the satchel and let his wife tie the cross around his neck.

"I'm doing this only because I love you, Mudjadji."

"I know."

Makhado walked outside. The night was soft and warm. Bright stars bejeweled the sky. A waxing moon rested lazily on the brow of a distant hill.

Makhado turned and looked at Mudjadji one last time, silhouetted against the door of the hut. A gentle breeze rustled the branches of the tall trees rimming the kraal. Without uttering another word, he firmly grasped his shield and spear, then turned and jogged at a steady pace into the night, headed for the Thathe Vondo private game reserve, in search of his beloved son.

46

LIEFLING was oblivious to the high-stakes drama taking place inside the OR as Sipho fought to save David's life. She was busy trying to comfort Hannah, who sat hunched forward on a faded brown sofa in the corner of the waiting room, crying inconsolably.

"Don't worry," Liefling said, hugging her tight. "He'll pull through."

"How could anyone want to kill David?" Hannah sobbed, covering her face with her pale delicate hands. "He never harmed anyone. He was always helping people." She looked at Liefling with tear-filled brown eyes. "Practically everyone in Soweto knew him."

"I know," Liefling said, then thought of the drugs.

"Hannah, I know this is an unfair question to ask you at this time," she said. "But it's important. Was David involved in drugs?"

A wounded expression clouded Hannah's elfin face. "And I've been clean ever since I met David."

Liefling's cell phone rang.

"Excuse me," she said, grabbing her purse on the sofa. She retrieved her cell phone and flipped it open.

"Liefling?" a familiar voice said.

"Mom," Liefling cried in surprise. "How are you?"

"I'm fine. Listen, I must talk to you. It's urgent. Are you alone?"

"Just a minute. " Liefling stepped into the corridor and spoke to her mother for several minutes. When she returned to the waiting room, her face was ashen. She put the cell phone back in her purse and sat down next to Hannah.

"Is anything wrong?" Hannah asked.

Liefling was about to say something when the waiting room door clicked open and Thando entered, looking weary.

"Is he --?" Hannah said.

"He'll make it," Thando said with a deep sigh.

"Thank God!" Liefling cried. She flung her arms around Thando. Hannah hugged her as well.

"For a long time it was touch and go," Thando said. "I'm exhausted from the blood transfusion."

Sipho appeared at the door, still wearing his pale green scrub suit. He smiled as he watched the three women embrace.

Liefling was the first to see him. Tears in her eyes, she ran toward him and kissed him. "Thank you, honey."

"David's very lucky," Sipho said. "The bullet passed within half a centimeter of his aorta. It's a blessing that Thando was around to give a transfusion. We're very low on O-negative because of all the violence in the townships."

"It's the least I could do," Thando said weakly.

"Can I see him, Doctor?" Hannah asked anxiously.

"Certainly," Sipho said. "The anesthesia should wear off soon."

Liefling was about to say something to Sipho when they heard an announcement over the intercom, "Dr. Radebe, Code blue in the ICU. Dr. Radebe, Code Blue in the ICU."

"I'm afraid I have to leave you, honey," Sipho said to Liefling. "How can I reach you?"

"I'll leave my cell phone on. Thando and I are going to Alex. We need to find Gideon."

"Good luck. And please be careful."

He kissed Liefling, hugged Thando and Hannah and then hurried down the hallway to the ICU.

"Hannah," Liefling said. "Thando and I plan to run to Alex to talk to someone who might be able to explain who could have shot David. In case of an emergency, here's my cell phone number."

"Okay," Hannah said, taking Liefling's business card.

After accompanying Hannah to the Recovery Room where she took a seat beside David, who was heavily sedated, Liefling and Thando headed for the elevator.

"My mom called while you were in the operating room," Liefling said.

"What about?"

"She knows about the suitcase full of drugs."

"She does?"

"Ja. And she said my life is in danger if I keep it."

"In danger from whom?"

"Colombian drug lords. She thinks they are the one's who tried to kill David."

"My God. How does she know?"

"She wouldn't say. All she said was that she wants to talk to me tonight. If I don't show up, she's threatened to tell the police about David and the drugs."

"Damn," Thando muttered.

They reached the elevator and stepped in with a crowd of people. No longer free to converse, they merely exchanging worried glances. A minute later the elevator reached the ground floor.

"Where's your mother?" Thando asked as they hurried down the hall, headed toward the parking lot.

"In Sandton."

"Is Kruger with her?"

"No. He's away at a business meeting."

"Will you go?"

"I have no choice," Liefling said. "Otherwise she'll carry out her threat and tell the police."

SHAKA focused a pair of high-powered night binoculars on Liefling and Thando as they hurried across the crowded parking lot to where Thando's Toyota stood on the far side, near an overflowing and stinking Dumpster.

"Here they come," he said to Botha, who was sitting in the middle of the retrofitted van, huddled in front of a console complete with sophisticated electronic equipment used in surveillance. The back of the van was a holding cell, sectioned off by a three inches thick one-way mirror.

"Anyone with them?" Botha asked without looking up from the eavesdropping machine.

"No."

"Excellent."

"They're getting into the Toyota now," Shaka said.

Botha grabbed a pair of headphones and slapped them on. His right hand turned on the digital tuner, activating the infinity bug under the driver's seat of Thando's Toyota. "Let's go," he said.

Shaka started the van marked "Police," then pulled away from the curb of the deserted, dimly lit side street about a block from the hospital. Its huge antenna swaying in the wind and its siren off, the minivan followed the Toyota at a discreet distance as it headed toward Alexandra.

*****

LIEFLING noticed that Thando kept glancing at the side-view mirror. The Toyota was cruising along Louis Botha Avenue.

"What's wrong?" Liefling asked.

"I think we're being followed."

The Toyota came to a stop at the corner of Louis Botha and 9th Avenue, about half a mile from Alexandra.

Liefling raised her eyebrows. "Followed? By whom?"

"A police car."

"Oh, my God!"

"Don't panic."

"Don't panic?" Liefling glanced at the suitcase next to her. "Don't panic with drugs in the car! If they stop us we're done for."

"Just do as I say, okay?" Thando said calmly.

"Okay, okay." Liefling's heart started racing. She tried in vain to calm herself.

Thando threw a quick glance into the side-view mirror. "As soon as the traffic light changes to green, take off at top speed."

"Flee from the police! Are you crazy?"

"We must get to the hideout. It's our only chance."

KRUGER, dressed in a light-brown safari suit, embraced Freda by the door to their lavish townhouse in the exclusive suburb of Sandhurst, about two blocks from Sandton City.

"Have a good trip," Freda said. "I hope you clinch the deal with the South American investors."

"I'm sure I will," Kruger said. "And I hope you have a productive meeting with Liefling. When did she say she was coming over?"

Freda, dressed in a white Adidas warm-up, glanced at her wristwatch. "She said she'd be here in about forty-five minutes."

"Are you sure she'll come?"

"I told her that if she doesn't, I'll go straight to the police."

"I hope she comes. And don't forget to watch the news tonight. My sources at the station said there will be a story about David and his involvement with Colombian drug lords."

"I won't forget."

Kruger kissed Freda on the lips. "See you tomorrow evening when I get back. And please," he said, giving her a second kiss and smiling, "give me a call as soon as you've spoken to Liefling."

"I will."

Kruger picked up his leather attaché, descended the stone steps and got into his chauffeured limo that would take him to a private airstrip outside Jo'burg where his Learjet was parked. He couldn't wait to hear from Botha, and to leave for the Thathe Vondo death squad's meeting in Venda, which he hoped would turn into a glorious celebration of the vanquishing of his enemies.

THANDO yelled, "Faster!"

"I have the gas pedal all the way to the floor!" Liefling yelled back.

The Toyota swerved right onto 9th Road. The "Police" van was in hot pursuit, siren screaming. About a quarter of a mile away was the teeming one-square-mile ghetto of Alexandra, which had a population of more than 600,000. A blanket of smog from braziers, coal stoves and trash fires, shrouded the ghetto, as usual.

"Take a left!" Thando yelled.

Liefling turned sharply onto 2nd Avenue, crossed the Wynberg London Road, and was in an area packed with shacks made of corrugated tin, sheets of plastics and pieces of cardboard.

"Take that street over there!" Thando yelled as she glanced back. The "Police" van was hot on their heels.

"What street?"

The shacks were so tightly packed it was hard to spot any street.

"On your left!"

"But it's too narrow!"

"Take it!"

Liefling swerved sharply to the left. The Toyota's tires screeched. It teetered on two wheels around the curve but didn't topple. Cars and taxis slammed on brakes and honked. The gap between the Toyota and the "Police" van widened a bit.

"Go down that street!" Thando yelled.

"What street?" cried Liefling. She saw no street -- only row upon row of tightly packed shacks.

"There, between those two shacks leaning against each other!"

Thando pointed to a tiny crack between two structures made of pieces of corrugated tin.

"But it's not wide enough!"

"It'll widen when you get to it!"

Liefling couldn't believe she could squeeze the whole Toyota through so narrow a crack without smashing into the shacks on either side. The shacks, due to overcrowding, had been built on parts of the street, choking it like rank weeds.

"Oh, my God!" Liefling screamed as the Toyota whipped so close to the shacks it ripped off their flimsy roofs. Chickens, goats, pigs, sheep and cows scuttled out of the way, as did barefoot children who'd been playing soccer and hopscotch.

An elderly man in a broad-brimmed straw hat festooned with stickers sat on an empty crate peacefully strumming tunes on a Jew's harp as he hawked one of the ghettos delicacies – *walkways* (chicken feet) and *spaghetti* (chicken intestines) – at a makeshift store called a *spazza*, which he had built in front of his shack. He gaped and the Jew's harp fell out of his toothless mouth as the Toyota came flying straight at him. He dove into the shack. He was just in time. The Toyota smashed his *spazza* into a pile of splintered wood and tangles of corrugated tin. The windshield of the Toyota was splattered with *spaghetti*.

Liefling was struck blind by the pink oozing goo.

She turned on the windshield wipers.

They didn't work.

"Sorry," Thando said, throwing open the palms of her hands. She shrugged and grinned. "I swear I meant to fix those."

They looked at each other and burst out laughing.

"Watch out!" Thando cried.

Liefling swerved just in time to miss an astonished cow.

She glanced in the rear-view mirror and was surprised to see the "Police" van make the same turn and race down the same narrow alley, knocking down even more shacks and food stands. But she was relieved to see that the gap between the Toyota and the "Police" van was widening.

Thando felt sure they'd soon be able to disappear in the Alexandra labyrinth. "Take a sharp right!" she cried.

"But there's a river -!"

"Take it!"

Liefling swung the wheel to the right with all her might.

The tires skidded, squealed and burned against the pavement. The Toyota almost plunged over the steep embankment into the reeking murky waters of the Jukskei river filled with floating garbage and sewage. Its tires spun in the mud as it slid closer to the river's edge.

"Throw the wheel to the left or you'll miss the bridge!"

Too late. Liefling screamed. She had completely lost control of the Toyota. Thando instantly reached over, grabbed the wheel and swung it hard to the left. The Toyota's tires caught the edge of the rickety bridge, but its momentum catapulted it over the bridge. Miraculously it missed the murky water and landed on dry land on the other side.

Thando glanced back. The "Police" van was still in hot pursuit.

The Toyota rattled its way up a dirt road full of potholes, headed toward what appeared a vast graveyard. Shacks lined both sides of the narrow road, which seemed to grow narrower and narrower.

Liefling gasped in horror.

Ahead the street dead-ended against a high barbed wire fence enclosing the graveyard. And the "Police" van was right behind them, about three hundred yards away.

47   **MAKHADO** finally reached the little knoll he'd selected as his watchpost, two hours after leaving his kraal. The knoll was about 500 yards from the entrance to the Thathe Vondo private game reserve. He rested his shield and assegai against the gnarled trunk of the towering Mopane tree, whose butterfly-shaped leaves smell of turpentine when crushed.

He climbed up the tree. He was quite agile for his age. Within seconds he'd reached one of the middle branches where he planned to wait in quiet watchfulness until the guests arrived. He unzipped his satchel, pulled out the pair of binoculars, pressed them to his eyes and studied the camp in the spectral moonlight, searching for any sign of Viljoen or Barnard. All seemed quiet. The main lodge and its surrounding huts and chalets were dark. In the middle of the courtyard, a fire burned in the grill he'd prepared for the braai. There were no lights in Viljoen's office and his bakkie was not in the parking lot.

He and Barnard must be at the truth hut, Makhado thought.

He was about to climb down and head there when he heard a rustling noise in a bush below. A male lion appeared. Makhado could tell by the way the lion hunched his shoulders that he was hungry and on the prowl for live flesh. His black nostrils flared, apparently catching the scent of a human. He sniffed Makhado's shield and assegai. His gleaming golden eyes, which can see perfectly in the dark, stared longingly up the Mopane tree.

The lion lay down under the tree, apparently prepared to camp out for as long as it would take for Makhado to come down.

How will I get down? Makhado wondered anxiously.

He recalled that a family of six, part of the waves of Mozambican refugees who daily fled starvation and desperation in the land-mine ravaged Mozambican countryside, had been eaten by lions a week ago, when they'd tried crossing illegally into South Africa through Kruger National Park. All that was left of the family, which included two small children, were a heap of gnawed, blanched bones.

Makhado remained motionless, praying the lion would leave. It was not that he was afraid of the lion – armed with his battle-axe he could take it on. He just didn't want to expend any energy in battling a wild animal when a still more formidable foe – white men with guns – awaited him.

I have no choice but to fight him, Makhado thought.

LIEFLING slammed on the brakes about a hundred feet from the barbed wire fence surrounding the graveyard. She and Thando scrambled out of the Toyota.

"Follow me!" Thando yelled as she headed for the fence.

Suddenly bullets whizzed over their heads and ricocheted off the grave stones beyond the fence.

"Where are we going?" Liefling asked as she stumbled after Thando, head bent low.

"You ask too many damn questions – even for a lawyer," Thando said, crouching before the fence. "Now shut up and follow me or we'll soon be dead."

She grabbed the bottom of the fence and lifted it with ease. Apparently the fence had been cut to create a hole large enough for an adult to wriggle through. Liefling went through first, followed by Thando.

"Stop! Police!" Botha screamed through a loudspeaker mounted on top of the van as it screeched to a halt behind the Toyota.

"Ignore him!" Thando said. "This way!"

"It's so dark," Liefling said. "I can't see where the hell I'm going."

"Grab my hand."

Thando led Liefling down a narrow, gravel path winding through the graveyard.

MAKHADO was devising strategy to fight the lion when he heard the muffled, distant sounds of oncoming vehicles. He quickly grabbed his binoculars and trained them in an easterly direction. A huge cloud of dust sparkled in the moonlight from the winding dirt road leading to the entrance of the Thathe Vondo private game reserve. His heart started racing. The neo-Nazis were arriving.

A bakkie roared out of the bush about fifty yards from Makhado's stakeout tree. Startled, he quickly trained his binoculars in the direction of the bakkie. It was Viljoen and Barnard. They'd been to the truth hut. He wondered if they'd gone there to kill Gideon. He chastised himself for not having gone there first.

The lion, apparently startled by the sudden noise, rose and disappeared into the bush. Makhado wondered if the lion had indeed gone away or was simply lurking behind some bush, waiting for him to climb down. He knew that hungry lions had all the patience in the world.

But he had to climb down. His hour of reckoning had arrived.

THANDO fell to her knees when she reached a rectangular tombstone in the middle of the graveyard. She shoved it aside, revealing a gaping hole where there should have been a grave.

"Get in," she whispered to Liefling.

Liefling hesitated. She was about to protest when Thando said, "At the bottom of the steps, take a right. Walk about two feet then reach down on the left. You'll find a lantern."

Liefling shuddered. "Where are we going, to some ghost party?"

"Yeah, it's Casper's birthday. Now go on! They're coming!"

Briefcase in hand, Liefling clambered down the steps.

Thando got in and heaved the tombstone back into place, burying them alive.

MAKHADO watched as the stream of minivans and bakkies drove through the iron gate into the private game reserve. Their lights dimmed, they resembled a procession of witches arriving for some infernal midnight rendezvous.

Makhado counted them. One, two, three...There were ten in all. Floodlights suddenly illumined the dark night. He could see the courtyard clearly now through his binoculars. The vehicles parked in a row next to the main lodge, about a hundred yards from the helipad.

Car doors opened and slammed as the men got out. Makhado saw Viljoen and Barnard jump out of their bakkie and greet the men with hearty handshakes. He noticed that the men wore combat fatigues and were heavily armed with rifles, shotguns and pistols. Heart pounding, Makhado slowly panned the group with his binoculars. There was no sign of Kruger.

Where is he? Makhado wondered, disappointed.

He panned the group again, then dejectedly lowered his binoculars. The evil man he was after wasn't there. Then he recalled Gideon telling him that Kruger always arrived last and by helicopter. The neo-Nazis streamed into a large, square thatched-roofed lodge known as *Voortrekker Laager*. They left their guns and rifles outside the door, in obedience of one of Kruger's rules not to hallow a place he'd named to commemorate the scene of the treacherous massacre of Piet Retief and his Voortrekker followers by Dingaan's Zulu impis.

Minutes later, Makhado heard boisterous noise coming from the lodge. The men sang patriotic Afrikaner songs, as if celebrating some great victory. He knew Afrikaans, and some of the songs were familiar to him. They were about the white man's sacred mission in Africa, his Covenant with God, his role as protector of Western Civilization, and the imperative need to preserve Baaskap.

He heard another song. It was about how, in the early hours of dawn on December 16th, 1838, their 468 of their Voortrekker ancestors had used 57 wagons to form a laager on the banks of the Ncome River to defend their women, children, servants and livestock against an inundation of 10,000 Zulu warriors. The Voortrekkers, under the leadership of Andries Pretorius, after whom Pretoria was named, and with the advantage of muskets, cannon fire and 120 black scouts (a fact not mentioned in Afrikaner legend), had mowed down 3,000 Zulus. The carnage was so great that the Ncome River ran red with Zulu blood. Only three trekkers were wounded, none fatally. The triumphant Boers had renamed the river Blood River. December 16th was celebrated as a great national holiday until the democratic elections of 1994 ushered in a black government that honored the slain Zulus.

While the men sang about the need to recapture the spirit of Blood River, Makhado climbed down. His eyes carefully scouted the thick woods. There was no sign of the lion. He stretched to relieve the numbness in his right leg, then grabbed his shield and began jogging at a steady pace toward the truth hut, about four miles away, where he hoped to find his son.

Midzimu, Makhado prayed, *let him still be alive.*

48 THANDO showed Liefling around the underground bunker.

"This used to be MK's main cell in Alexandra from 1986 through 1993," she said, holding up the lantern. "I lived here for most of that time."

Noticing the cleanliness of the Spartan-looking place, Liefling said, "It's so well-kept."

"I still come here from time to time, so I've had to keep it clean." Thando said. Her voice crackled with emotion. "There are many memories buried here. A lot of cadres who lost their lives in the struggle stayed here at one time or another. I guess preserving this place is my way of preserving their memory. With everything these days a priority – health care, education, housing, crime and so forth – very little is being done to remember all the fearless warriors who lost their lives so we could be free. Someday I hope we can honor them with a decent memorial."

Liefling wrapped her arm around her friend. "I agree," she said.

Thando resumed walking about the bunker. "This is where we kept our weapons, " she said, pointing to a small room to her left, which was now empty. "Mostly AK-47s and limpet mines."

"Where did you get them?"

"We smuggled them into the country via Zimbabwe, Mozambique and Swaziland. It was an extremely dangerous. The regime had askaris and impimpis everywhere. As a result many MK cadres transporting weapons were captured by the security force, killed and buried in unmarked graves."

"How large is this place?"

"About two thousand square feet."

"All beneath the graveyard?" Liefling asked, incredulous.

"Not really. Only the entrance and the tunnel we just came through are under the graveyard. To avoid desecrating the graves, we dug the tunnel parallel to the main road. This bunker is actually underneath the veld east of the graveyard, near the river. This is the kitchen," she said as they entered a small square room with a gas stove, a crude sink, a pine cabinet and not much else. "We seldom had to cook, though. We found plenty of food in the township whenever we went out at night."

A worried look on her face, Liefling said, "Are you sure we're safe down here?"

"Yeah. No one knows about the bunker."

"Who came up with the idea to create a hideout so close to the graveyard?"

"Sidney," Thando said as they rounded a corner. "It was a desperation move on our part. All of our cells in the township had been penetrated. So when Sidney and I were sent back in 1985 by MK to coordinate plans to render the ghetto ungovernable, we talked about the best place for a hideout. He's a big fan of Dickens. And as you know, Dickens loved graveyards. Sidney happened to be reading *Great Expectations* at the time, and he was quite taken by the opening scene where Pip encounters the escaped convict living in a graveyard."

"And I suppose it's the last place the security forces would look."

"Exactly. And we could easily communicate with our contacts in the townships during funerals. During the 1980s and early 1990s, there were mass funerals practically every week for those people shot by the police or massacred by death squads."

"Yes, I know," Liefling said. "I attended several of them with my father. During one the police actually fired teargas at us. It stung like hell. Men, women and children were coughing and vomiting as they ran in all directions. Some actually fell into open graves."

"I spoke during one of those teargassed funerals," Thando said.

"You did?"

"Ja. From time to time one of our cadres, wearing a disguise, would address the mourners," Thando said, smiling at their bold ingenuity. "We would relay messages from the ANC high command in exile. At times we would pass out pamphlets listing the times and short-wave frequencies of *Radio Freedom*. At other times we would appeal to black policemen to refuse to serve. The soldiers would fire tear gas into the crowd in an attempt to nab one of us. But they never did."

"Quite courageous."

"You had to have courage in the movement," Thando said as they entered a third room. It was large and contained a dozen cots with bedding.

"This is where we slept," Thando said. "We couldn't have house more than twelve cadres at a time. The men slept on that side of the room and the women slept on this side. We developed a great sense of camaraderie – like a family of brothers and sisters. Above all, we were all disciplined soldiers."

They entered the fourth room, which contained a long wooden table, twelve wooden chairs and two bookshelves.

"This is where we held our strategy meetings on how to make the ghetto ungovernable. This also served as our *Freedom University*. Most of us were students when we went underground, and we took our studies seriously."

"I can see," Liefling said, perusing the titles of the volumes still on the bookshelves. In the bright light of the lantern she saw a complete set of The Encyclopedia Britannica, the entire works of Dickens, the complete works of Shakespeare, a few volumes of poetry, several copies of Fanon's *The Wretched of The Earth*, a volume of Mandela's speeches and Steve Biko's writings, a copy of Karl Marx's *Communist Manifesto*, and a copy of *The United States Constitution* and *The Declaration of Independence*.

"Quite an eclectic collection," Liefling said, impressed.

"Gideon is the one who got us the books," Thando said. "Many of them were banned at the time, so they had to be smuggled into the country."

"What was Gideon's actual role in MK?" Liefling asked.

"He was mainly our contact with student leaders and activists who organized marches, protests and fought against the police and soldiers. And later on, after we'd succeeded in smashing the regime's local governing structures and forcing black policemen to resign en masse, he helped the community set up street committees, People's Courts and self-defense units. He also helped Comrades who were on the run flee the country."

"Quite a lot of responsibility."

"He was our mainstay. That's why I said he couldn't have been an askari. If he were, this hideout, for instance, would have been discovered by security force members long ago."

"I still don't understand how his Explorer ended up at David's place."

"I'm baffled too. I'd better sit down." Thando pressed her hand against the wall for support. "I'm feeling a bit woozy. I guess I'm still not fully recovered from all that blood I gave David."

Liefling pulled a chair for her and helped her sit down, then hung the lantern from a hook on the beamed ceiling that hardly had any cobwebs. She took a seat next to Thando.

"Care for something to drink?" Thando asked. "Last week when I was here I brought a couple bottles of juice. They are in the cooler next to the kitchen cabinet."

"Sure."

Liefling got up and went into the kitchen. Seconds later she came back with two bottles of nectarine juice. She gave one to Thando.

"Thanks."

Liefling sat down and opened the briefcase.

"Guess how much the drugs are worth," Thando said.

"I don't know how to estimate their value," Liefling said. "I'd say about R200,000."

"Not even close. I'd say at least two million."

"Two million?"

"Ja."

"That's a lot of money."

Thando sipped her juice and said, "That's enough for someone to impersonate the police."

"Impersonate the police?"

"Exactly."

"But we were being chased by a real police car. It had sirens and everything."

Thando laughed. "Just because it screams like a police car doesn't make it one, Liefling." She sipped her juice. "I've spent a lot of time fleeing from the police, so I know how they behave during a chase."

"The people chasing us – how did they behave differently from the actual police?"

"One thing real police officers certainly don't do – at least in South Africa – unless they're stupid, is to chase dangerous suspects without calling for reinforcements. Alexandra is the most dangerous ghetto in Jo'burg. I purposely provoked that chase because I wanted to see if other police officers would get involved."

Liefling knitted her brow. "Why would that have made any difference?"

"Malusi, your boyfriend's brother, is high up in the police department. We could have explained to him about the drugs and he'd have believed us. But our pursuers apparently didn't want other police units getting involved. That's why I came all the way here."

"So who was driving the phony police car?"

"Probably some professional thugs hired by one of the drug cartels."

"What are you talking about?"

Thando smiled. "International drug cartels are very sophisticated operations," she said. "Big money is involved. And big money calls for powerful connections, particularly within law enforcement. Some of the people who are supposed to investigate crime are actually involved in committing it. Particularly former apartheid security force members. Didn't you read the recent report by the World Economic Forum that stated that South Africa's level of organized crime is second only to Colombia's?"

"I heard it discussed on the radio. But I thought the report exaggerates the problem a little bit."

"It may, but police corruption *is* widespread. One in four officers in the greater Johannesburg area is under criminal investigation, and there are more than 190 crime syndicates – "

Thando stopped speaking and froze.

"What is it?" Liefling asked.

"Shhh! I think there's someone above."

Liefling listened intently. The sound of muffled footsteps was unmistakable. "Do you think the bogus policemen are still around?"

"I thought we'd lost them for sure."

"Could they know about this place?"

"Highly unlikely," Thando said, rising and retrieving the lantern. "But I don't want to take any chances. This way," she said, heading for the bookcase. "Help me move this. There's a secret passage behind it."

Liefling and Thando heaved the bookcase to one side, exposing a piece of wood paneling about three square feet wide. Thando removed the paneling, exposing a hole wide enough for an adult to crawl through on all fours.

"This is an escape route we created just in case the hideout was ever discovered," Thando said, crawling in.

"Where does it lead?"

"To the bank of the Jukskei River, about thirty-five yards from here."

Liefling crawled into the dark tunnel after Thando, who was holding the lantern.

"Good thing I'm not claustrophobic," Liefling said.

They were halfway through the tunnel when the sudden glare of a powerful flashlight blinded Thando.

"I wouldn't come this way if I were you," Botha said, pointing a nine-millimeter pistol straight at Thando's face. "Now crawl backwards – slowly. My partner behind you is also armed, so don't do anything stupid or he'll blow your fucking heads off."

Liefling and Thando began crawling backwards. The heavy smell of damp earth filled Liefling's nostrils. Her knees and the palms of her hands ached from pressing down on rocks embedded in the soil. Her heart was pounding hard from sheer terror at the thought that they had been caught, trapped, like hunted animals.

They emerged from the tunnel backwards and straightened, coughing and brushing the dirt from their bruised knees and palms. They looked up to see a tall figure wearing the blue police uniform of the South African police and a black balaclava. Pointing an AK-47 at them, he gruffly ordered them to raise their hands above their heads and stand with their faces to the wall. The tall figure spoke in a voice that made Thando's heart almost stop beating. Her eyes grew wide with horror and surprise. She wanted to say something but words failed her.

Botha emerged from the tunnel. He brushed dirt from his blue police uniform, pulled off the balaclava covering his head, smiled and said, "You must be wondering how we found you."

Thando was still looking at Botha's tall companion. She slowly shook her head from side to side in shock and disbelief.

"No, it can't be," she muttered. "No, it can't be."

Liefling stared at her, confused.

"You can take off the balaclava, Shaka," Botha said with a grin. "I'm sure Thando is eager to see you again."

49 KRUGER entered the fifth room of the surveillance center and found Swanepoel sitting in front of a computer monitor, complacently smoking a cigar. He seemed quite pleased. He stood up and saluted when Kruger entered.

"Dispense with the formalities," Kruger said tersely. "Have you heard from Ludwig?"

"Yes, General," Swanepoel said, sitting down. "I spoke to him a while ago. He and Shaka were about to enter the MK hideout where Liefling and Thando are hiding. And they have the drugs with them."

"Wonderful," Kruger said, pouring himself a drink. He sat down on a swivel chair. He gulped down his drink. "And you relayed to Ludwig the instructions I gave you?"

"To the letter." Swanepoel looked at the clock on the wall. "As a matter of fact, he should be calling any minute now. He assured me that this time nothing would go wrong."

"I hope he's right," Kruger said, lighting a cigar. "A lot is riding on tonight."

"And our friends in the police force are ready to move as soon as you give the word," Swanepoel said.

"I will as soon as Ludwig calls," Kruger said. "Get me my wife on the secure phone line in Room 3."

"Yes, General."

FREDA was preparing to take a bubble bath. She'd just finished walking four miles on a treadmill and doing some light weights in the townhouse's private gym. As the Italian marble tub with gold fixtures was filling with scented warm water, she turned on the TV to watch the eight o'clock evening news on SABC. The lead story sent shivers down her spine.

"Earlier today we reported that human rights lawyer David Schneider was shot and critically wounded in his Soweto home. In a bizarre twist, the assailant has turned out to be Gideon Munyai, a friend of Schneider's and a well-respected Alexandra schoolteacher and community activist. The police found his red Explorer parked outside the victim's home in Diepkloof.

"At first the police suspected that Schneider had been a victim of an attempted robbery. But following an anonymous tip, police searched Schneider's house. They found cellophane bags of cocaine and crack stashed under the mattress. His girlfriend, a recovering drug addict, has been taken into custody. Police are keeping Schneider under heavy guard at Bara until he's recovered enough to be questioned.

"In another startling development concerning this strange case, Detective Malusi Radebe of the murder and robbery unit of the Johannesburg police said have mounted a nationwide search for Liefling Malan, the human rights activist who recently filed a three-billion-rand lawsuit against her stepfather, General Magnus Kruger.

– "Oh my God!" Freda cried, stunned. She clapped a hand over her small mouth in horror, trembling all over –

Miss Malan and her colleague, former MK commander Thando Khosa, are wanted for questioning in the David Schneider shooting. According to witnesses, the two were last seen fleeing in a white Toyota Hilux with Johannesburg registration plates. The police have reason to believe that the two have in their possession a briefcase containing drugs estimated to be worth two million rands which Munyai was apparently delivering to Schneider. Anyone with information about the whereabouts of the white Toyota Hilux should immediately contact the Johannesburg police. Both suspects are said to be heavily armed."

Feeling faint, Freda rose and staggered toward the wet bar, anxious for a stiff drink. She was halfway there when the red phone on the glass side table rang. She stared at it, afraid to pick it up, wondering if the police were calling to tell her that Liefling had been found dead. The phone rang four times before she picked it up with a trembling hand.

"Who is this?" she stammered softly.

"What's the matter, darling?" Kruger said.

"Oh, Magnus!" she cried, letting out a deep sigh of relief. "Thank God it's you."

"Who did you think it was?"

"The police."

"The police?"

"Yes. It's happened. Just as you said it would."

"What's happened?"

"I need a drink first. I'm afraid I'll go into shock. It's so dreadful."

"It's okay, honey. Take your time. Everything will be all right."

"David's been shot," Freda said.

She heard Kruger gasp. "Good God! When?"

"This morning. In his house."

"Is he dead?"

"No. He's still alive but badly wounded. He's at Bara."

"Was Liefling with him when he was shot?"

"Apparently."

"Is she okay?"

"I don't know. She's disappeared. The police are looking for her."

"Looking for her?"

"Ja. Apparently drugs were involved in the shooting, Magnus. Just as you predicted. And you won't believe what else. A schoolteacher from Alexandra is said to have shot David. A schoolteacher, for goodness sake. What's this world coming to?"

Freda poured herself another drink. "I don't know what to do, Magnus. I'm scared. For all I know my daughter might be dead."

"Calm down, honey," Kruger said, sensing that Freda was becoming hysterical. "Let me make a few calls to see if I can't locate her. I'll call you back as soon as possible."

SWANEPOEL gently knocked on the door to Room 3 when he saw that Kruger was off the phone.

"Come in."

Swanepoel opened the door. "Ludwig is on line 4, General. He and Shaka have Liefling and Thando cornered at the MK hideout in Alexandra. He wants to know what to do with them."

Kruger grabbed the phone and punched line 4.

"Excellent job, Ludwig. Kill the kaffir bitch and bring the kaffir-lover to the airport. I'll be waiting there."

*****

FREDA had barely finished talking to Kruger when the phone rang.

"Hullo?" she said in an anxious voice.

"Freda?"

"Tina!" Freda cried.

"Paul and I were just watching the news. We saw that awful story about David Schneider and Liefling. I just finished calling Stellenbosch. Emma told me you were in Jo'burg. What the hell is going on?"

"I have no clue. All I know is that David is mixed up with Colombian drug dealers."

"Have you heard from Liefling?"

"No."

"Are you okay?"

"I'm very scared, Tina." Her voice was cracking. "I don't want anything to happen to my poor Liefling."

"Is Kruger with you?"

"No. He's in Venda. I'm all alone. And I'm scared, Tina."

"Listen, Paul and I are about half an hour away. We'll come over, okay?"

"Thanks."

50

THANDO stared in horror as she stood face to face with her former husband.

"Sidney! So it was you who betrayed our comrades!' Her eyes were ablaze with hatred and contempt.

Botha grinned. "That's right. All along your beloved husband was our askari. Not his brother Nelson. He was as innocent as he claimed to be when you ordered him executed. General Kruger had him framed when it seemed that your husband's cover might be blown. Your husband was too valuable an asset for us to lose, Thando. As a senior MK officer, he kept us informed about the terrorist group's every move, and helped us pick and choose which terrorists to ambush and where."

Botha swept the bunker with his gun. "And we've long known about this terrorist nest," he said with satisfaction. "At one point we discussed torching it. But General Kruger decided it would be more useful left alone. Especially since Gideon was spying for us also."

Liefling was stunned. "So Gideon was an askari too?"

Botha looked at Liefling. "Ja, kaffir-lover. One of our best. He and Thando's husband helped us eliminate more communists and terrorists and learn more about MK's operations in the Jo'burg area and in Venda than any other askaris in the entire CCB."

The revelation struck Thando like a sledgehammer. It knocked all resistance out of her. She continued staring at her former husband. She felt such hatred for him that all she could say was, "Why, Sidney, why?"

"Because you were unfaithful to me," Sidney said without emotion. "You slept with Nelson when I loved you more than any other woman in the world. I endured torture rather than betray you. But when I found out that you were cheating on me with my own brother, I swore revenge."

"Cheating on you?" Thando cried in amazement. "With Nelson? Who told you such nonsense?"

Sidney looked at Botha, who quickly said, "Of course she'll lie to save her neck. You saw the evidence with your own eyes, didn't you?"

"I did," Sidney said.

"What evidence?" Thando said.

"Enough talking," Botha snapped. "The General is waiting for us at the airstrip. Let's get it over with and go. Don't forget the five million rands that's waiting for you."

"So that's it, you bastard," Thando cried. "You did it for money. I should have known."

Thando lunged at Sidney. But he was too quick for her. He stepped aside and at the same time swung the butt of the AK-47 into Thando's solar plexus. She yelled in pain and doubled over. A blow to the back of the head sent her crumpling to the floor like a sack of mealies.

"You bloody bastard!" Liefling screamed, lunging at Sidney. "You killed her!" Sidney was about to swing the AK-47 at Liefling when Botha grabbed Liefling and pulled her away. "I wouldn't if I were you. Sidney can hurt you real bad. I should know. I trained him. You don't want him to mess up that pretty face of yours, do you?"

Liefling stared at Thando's motionless body.

"No, she's not dead," Botha said. "But she'll soon be."
Liefling stared at Botha, then at Shaka.

Botha grinned. "I see you're amazed. I'm not surprised. You didn't know what you were getting into when you took on your stepfather, did you? He's a different man than you, your mother or the world knows. He's ruthless when it comes to protecting the interests of the Afrikaner people. He'll let nothing stand in the way of what he considers his mission in life: to protect the interests of Afrikaners. He's prepared to destroy anything that stands in the way."

Liefling shook her head in disbelief.

"You better believe it. I've known your stepfather for over twenty years. I served under him at John Vorster Square. He's the Afrikaner equivalent of Shaka Zulu. He has no conscience. No Ubuntu as you moralists like to say. Apartheid needed men like him to enforce its brutal laws. When you filed that lawsuit, you effectively signed the death warrants of everyone involved in it. Thando will be the first one executed. And Sidney has requested the privilege of being her executioner."

Groaning, Thando opened her eyes and blinked, then rolled onto her side and tried to get up, despite the hot pain in her stomach. Botha shot Shaka a stern look. "Finish her off."

Shaka moved toward Thando.

"And David will be next," Botha said to Liefling. "And your stepfather has agreed that I should be his executioner, since I have a personal score to settle with the Jew bastard. For your information, he'll die in his hospital bed at precisely midnight."

Liefling was aghast. She felt numb. Her head swam in a fog of disbelief.

"Nothing is beyond your stepfather," Botha said. "He considers himself a God, just like Shaka did. Apartheid gave him the power to decide who should live and who should die. And since you're going to die, I'll tell you a little secret. General Kruger also executed your father."

The revelation staggered Liefling. Dizzy with shock, she collapsed on one knee.

"No, no!" she whimpered, looking up at Botha with tears welling in her eyes. "He didn't kill my father! That's not true! How could he have killed my father and then turned around and married my mother?"

Botha grinned. "For someone who majored in literature I'm amazed by your ignorance of the classics. Didn't Hamlet's uncle kill his own brother in order to marry his wife? And didn't Oedipus kill his father and marry his mother? Why do you find it hard to believe that a man who was treated badly by your father's family would kill your father and marry the woman he adores?"

Liefling had no answer. She slowly struggled to her feet. Her legs felt like lead and she was trembling.

"He's eager to tell you the whole story during the plane ride to the Thathe Vondo private game reserve, your place of execution," Botha said. Then turning to Thando, he said, "But your place of execution, adulteress, is here. Are you ready, Shaka?"

"Wait for me outside," Shaka said grimly. "I want teach the fucking whore a lesson first."

"Of course," Botha grinned. "But don't take too long. The General is waiting for us." He turned to Liefling and said, " Let's go." Liefling hesitated. Botha placed the muzzle of the gun to her temple. "I said MOVE!"

Liefling remained defiant.

"Go, Liefling," Thando pleaded with her.

Liefling clenched her right fist, thrust it into the air and shouted, "Amandla!" Tears streamed down her cheeks.

"Ngawethu!" Thando shouted back with a clenched right fist raised high.

"Enough of this tribal shit," Botha said, slapping a pair of handcuffs on Liefling. He prodded her with the nine millimeter. Reluctantly, her eyes still on her doomed comrade, she staggering toward the dimly-lit hallway.

The last she saw of Thando was her shrinking away to a corner as Sidney raised the AK 47 and shouted, "This is for making a fool of me, you fucking whore!"

Liefling staggered up the steep steps into the chilly night. The graveyard was filled with old tombstones and crosses, many of them of fallen heroes and heroines of the liberation struggle, including Liefling's father, whose simple grave was under the shade of a Jacaranda tree. The vast graveyard was now bathed in the eerie light of a full moon. In the distance, intermittent screams, gunfire and police sirens punctuated the noise of township revelry.

"We'll wait here," Botha said, holding Liefling's arm tightly. The chill wind whipped against her face. Eddies of dust stung her eyes and made her eyes water. She sneezed.

After waiting for several minutes, Botha impatiently glanced at his watch and then peered into the bunker. "Hurry up, Shaka!" he shouted.

Suddenly Thando screamed "No, please, no!" Several shots rang out in quick succession, shattering her scream.

Liefling screamed in horror and collapsed to the ground, hyperventilating. Botha jerked her back onto her feet. "That should teach you not to become too friendly with communist kaffir bitches."

A minute or so later Shaka emerged up the steps. His face was impassive.

"Good job," Botha said, hovering at the mouth of the bunker. He grinned. There was a glint of treacherous cunning in his eyes. "Here's your reward, kaffir," he said, raising the nine millimeter. He fired twice. Sidney didn't have time to react. The bullets smashed into his chest and flung him back into the bunker.

"You bastard! You murderer!" Liefling screamed hysterically.

"Don't curse me," Botha said, closing the trap-door and replacing the gravestone. "Curse your stepfather. He's the one who said no witnesses. Besides, isn't it appropriate for them to be together in death? Like Romeo and Juliet. When our friends in the police force find them with the briefcase, they'll file a nice report about a pair of drug-dealing lovers who were killed in their hideout by a Colombian hit squad."

"Where are you taking me?" Liefling asked as Botha marched her toward the "Police" van.

"Like I said, your stepfather is very anxious to talk to you."

"About what?" Liefling demanded brusquely.

"About your perversion, kaffir-lover. Afterwards, he plans to feed you to his favorite and perpetually hungry pets: his pack of Nile crocodiles."

Liefling shuddered.

Botha grinned. "I wish I could be there to see them devour your soft kaffir-loving flesh, but I have your friend David to take care of."

51

LIEFLING sat on a swivel armchair in front of a square folding teak table. The handcuffs chafed her wrists as she twisted her hands about, trying to make them less painful. Kruger, the man she hated at that moment more than anyone in the world, sat across from her, wearing military fatigues with a triple-7 swastika armband. The two were aboard Kruger's Learjet, which was flying over the sedate mining and agricultural town of Pietersburg, the capital of the Northern province, headed for the tiny airport at Thohoyandou.

"How could my mother have married a fiend like you?" Liefling said, shaking her head in disbelief.

Kruger grinned. "Considering that you'll soon be dead, I'll share a few secrets with you about myself. But first – "
Kruger rose and went to the liquor cabinet. "What would you like drink? A martini? I love martinis and so does your mother."

"Nothing," Liefling said tersely. Her throat was dry but she didn't trust Kruger. She knew poisoning was a common method of murder.

"I'd untie you," Kruger said as he mixed himself a martini. "But I don't know what tricks someone as desperate as you are might try. I was on a military plane once with an ANC activist. She was a middle-aged woman. I was taking her to the bushveld camp to be interrogated. She looked quite harmless, you know, slightly fat and near-sighted. Out of courtesy I'd left her hands untied. You know what she did? While I was scribbling notes about something important she'd revealed about the ANC, she lunged for my throat. I was amazed by what powerful hands she had. She'd have choked me to death if Ludwig hadn't knocked her out cold with a pistol. Since then I've made it a rule to keep all prisoners handcuffed."

"I wish she'd strangled you," Liefling said.

Kruger laughed. "Destiny hadn't willed it, my dear. I'm a man of destiny."

Liefling stared at Kruger. He was a far cry from the kind and charming man her mother had raved about before marrying. She now saw a racist fanatic, a madman, a psychopath. Despite feeling repulsed by him, she willed herself to speak in a normal tone of voice so she could get answers to the many questions racing through her mind.

"Why did you kill my father?" she asked with muted anger.

Kruger leaned back in his swivel chair and sipped his drink. "Why did I kill your father?" he said slowly, as if speaking to himself. "The answer is rather complex, my dear. You see, he was morally perverted. And I detest moral perverts." He put particular emphasis on the word "detest."

"It's you who's morally perverted," Liefling shot back. "Not my father."

Kruger chuckled. "You're entitled to your opinion. But mine is backed by solid facts. And as a lawyer, you should know the importance of facts. It's a fact that on June 20, 1976 – the Sunday after communists incited students to riot in Soweto – your father preached a blasphemous sermon titled 'Obedience to God.'"

"I heard that sermon, Magnus," Liefling said fiercely, glaring at him. "I was sitting in the front pew. My father was obeying God when he called for the abolition of apartheid. The moral perverts were people like you – people who defended apartheid."

Kruger swiveled his chair. "No, Liefling, you don't know what apartheid meant to Afrikaners. It had nothing to do with discriminating against blacks. Apartheid was our only way of insuring our survival as a people by protecting ourselves against the ultimate genocide: miscegenation. If you mix black and white, what color do you get?"

"Human."

Kruger scoffed. "Don't be stupid. You get a mongrel. And mongrels are not white, no matter how white their skin color may be. Without apartheid, given the weakness of human nature, more Afrikaners would have been tempted to commit the same abominable sin that my own father committed."

Kruger paused. Liefling noticed for the first time that he was showing signs of strong emotion. A transformation was gradually coming over him. His nostrils flared, the veins in his neck bulged and his eyes blazed with maniacal fury.

"And what sin was that?" she asked.

"Fucking kaffir women," Kruger said viciously.

Liefling gaped.

"And I caught him in the bloody act," Kruger said, gnashing his teeth.

"Not once, mind you. I could understand if he'd made a mistake one time. But four times. Four times. In the very same bed he shared with my mother. I was such a dutiful son that when he asked me to lie to protect his marriage and reputation, I did. After all, he was my father and dominee of the most powerful church in the country. He served as a spiritual leader to prime ministers and members of the cabinet. He was regarded as a staunch guardian of apartheid. He'd been the strongest champion of the Immorality Act. Yet he, of all people, turned out to be a moral pervert."

Overwhelmed with emotion, Kruger abruptly rose. He paced up and down the carpeted aisle, clasping and unclasping his hands. Liefling's eyes followed him.

He's a sick, tormented old man, Liefling thought.

"So that's why your family left Cape Town so suddenly," she said.

"The Broederbond forced us to leave," Kruger said, pouring himself another drink. "They knew the damage that would be done to the Immorality Act if one of its chief proponents, a dominee at that, were charged with violating it."

Kruger paused. He sipped his drink.

"And do you know who cast the deciding vote to oust my father?" he asked, sitting down.

Liefling said nothing.

"Your grandfather, Francois Diderick Malan," Kruger said.

"My grandfather?"

"Ja. He told the Broederbond Executive Council that the Immorality Act was key to preserving the purity of the Afrikaner people, and that anyone who violated the law should be punished, no matter how important. I agreed with him. That's why when my father persisted in violating the Immorality Act, I had no choice but to kill him."

"You killed your own father?"

"He deserved to die."

"Why?"

"Because his moral perversion caused the deaths of three people I loved the most in this world – my mother and two sisters."

Kruger paused, overcome with emotion. Liefling noticed that his eyes had the pathetic look of a wounded doe.

"How did they die?" she asked with pity.

"They committed suicide," Kruger said. "We were living in Venda at the time. I thought my father had given up his repulsive perversion of fucking kaffir women. But then I found out that he was still doing it. And the fact that Venda maidens went about bare-breasted during their lascivious *Domba* initiation dance drove him nuts. He'd sneak into their huts deep in the woods on the pretext of bringing them the gospel. Yeah, that was some gospel he gave them – right between the legs."

Kruger paused, looking sickened at the mere thought of a white man with a black woman. Liefling wondered what he thought of her and Sipho.

"One day, while my mother was away visiting relatives in Cape Town," Kruger said, "I caught him in the act again. I threatened to tell my mother when she came back. 'You don't want your mother to kill herself, do you?' he said, again trying to blackmail me into keeping quiet. He knew I loved my mother and wouldn't do anything to hurt her."

Kruger paused. He bit his lip. Tears came to Liefling's eyes. Now she understood how the Immorality Act could have been one of the most immoral pieces of legislation ever enacted anywhere. Even Afrikaners were its victims. She remembered the furor caused by a study conducted by a reputable Afrikaner professor that found out that many Afrikaners had black ancestors, and that they'd gone to great lengths to deny and hide the fact, suffering untold psychological damage as a result. She somehow sensed that Kruger's psychosis had its origin in such denial and repression.

"My mother came back," Kruger continued. "She looked quite exhausted. I knew she was suffering. She was only forty-six but looked eighty. One evening, while my father was away doing 'missionary' work, I told her. She simply let out a deep sigh. She didn't cry or tear at her hair. She simply said, 'I knew it would happen.' When I asked her how she knew, her reply was cryptic. 'There's something about your father that makes him lust after kaffir women. I thought his sickness would be cured if I married him.' Puzzled, I asked, 'What is it that makes him lust after kaffir women?' my mother replied that it was better I didn't know. 'Why don't you leave him?' I asked. She replied that my father had threatened to reveal the secret if she left him. 'The scandal that would follow would ruin your sisters' chances of getting Afrikaner husbands. And they would end up marrying kaffirs. And I can't let that happen.' That's when I realized what I had to do."

Kruger looked out the window of the Learjet. "We'll soon be landing in Thohoyandou, my dear."

Liefling had been hanging on his every word, and wanted him to continue. "Okay, now I understand why you felt you had to kill your father. But how did you do it?"

"It was very easy, actually," Kruger said. "There's a small lake near the game reserve where we're going. My father often rode his horse past it on his way home from his so-called missionary work. It's full of Nile crocodiles. A week after my mother drove her car over the cliff, killing herself and my two sisters, I ambushed him near the lake. I struck him on the head with the butt of a rifle. He passed out. I bound his hands and feet. When he woke up, I interrogated him. I wanted to know the secret my mother had alluded to before she committed suicide.

"'If I told you,' he said, 'would you kill me or would you spare my life?'

"'It depends,' I said.

"He told me. The truth was so shocking I had no choice but to kill him in order to bury the past. He actually had a smile on his face as I clubbed him to death. Afterwards I tossed his body to the crocodiles."

"What was the shocking secret?" Liefling couldn't help asking.

Kruger didn't immediately reply. He looked at Liefling for a long time, unsure whether to reveal a secret no one else knew. Knowing that the secret would die with her, he decided to tell her.

52

MAKHADO shook Gideon, whose bloody head was slumped over his naked chest. "Can you hear me, my son?"

"I didn't break, Baba," Gideon mumbled deliriously through torn and swollen lips. "They tortured me, but I didn't break."

"I know, my son," Makhado said, his jaws tense with anger, tears in his eyes. "You've regained your honor, my son. You're a true African warrior."

He tenderly daubed the blood from Gideon's lips with a wet rag.

"Viljoen and Barnard came again, Baba," Gideon said between sips of water from the bottle Makhado was holding to his mouth. "They battered my face with brass knuckles. They covered my head in a wet plastic bag until my lungs nearly burst. They dunked my head in water. They shocked my testicles. But I didn't break, Baba. I didn't tell them I'd given you the diaries."

"You were very brave, my son," Makhado said with deep emotion. He quickly sliced the thick ropes around Gideon's swollen wrists with the sharp blade of his assegai.

"They threatened to feed me to the crocodiles," Gideon mumbled. "But then Viljoen's cell phone rang and he and Barnard rushed out."

"They are back at the main lodge, my son," Makhado said. "Their fellow neo-Nazis have arrived. But I have a feeling they'll be back. That's why we must hurry. Can you walk?"

Gideon tried standing but his leg gave way beneath him and he collapsed. Makhado helped him up. Despite his battered and swollen face, his swollen wrists and right leg, the high fever that made him lapse in and out of delirium, the presence of his father somehow renewed Gideon's strength. Leaning against Makhado's broad shoulders, he was able to hobble a few steps at a time.

"My neighbor Nzhelele runs a mountain school near here," Makhado said as he half-dragged, half-carried the wounded Gideon out of the truth hut. "Once we get there we'll find help."

The air was oppressively humid. The full moon made it seem daylight, but beyond the clearing the forest loomed dark and menacing, and reverberated with the din of insects, the cries of hyenas and the howls of baboons. Makhado, with his arm firmly wrapped around his wounded son's waist, struck out for the dark forest, searching for the trail that would lead him across the river to the mountain school about eight miles away.

53

KRUGER gazed steadily into Liefling's eyes as he made his grand confession. "My father was half-kaffir," he blurted out.

Liefling was stunned. For several minutes she stared at Kruger from across the folding table. The plane was now thirty miles from the Thohoyandou airport. The sky outside was cloudless and filled with bright stars. Below the plane was nothing but thick jungle.

"That's shocking, isn't it?" Kruger said with a self-deprecating smile. "You can imagine my own shock."

"But you look so Afrikaner."

"Lots of Afrikaners have kaffir blood in them. But the Broederbond kept the information suppressed, afraid of what it might do to apartheid."

How true, Liefling thought.

Kruger sipped his martini. "The kaffir blood entered the family because my grandfather was a *bywoner*. You know what that means?"

"Yes," Liefling said. "In primary school we were taught that most Afrikaners were forced off their land by industrialization and the commercialization of farming in the 1890s and became squatters."

"Not all of them could eke out a living as *bywoners*," Kruger said. "What the Broederbond's National Christian schools didn't reveal, of course, was that a lot of poor Afrikaners ended up living in slums with kaffirs and Coloreds. After his farm went under, my grandfather left his starving parents and two siblings in Craddock to look for work in Durban. He spent several years working as a porter, a stevedore and a post-cart driver. At one time even as a pimp to a stable of Kaffir and Colored prostitutes. But he soon grew sick and tired of city life and when he returned to Craddock he found that father and two siblings had died in a fire. His mother, who barely escaped alive, had moved to Grahamstown, and was now a maid in the home of a wealthy Cape Malay Colored who had a beautiful but dark-skinned daughter."

Kruger shifted in his seat and fidgeted with his empty glass, appearing reluctant to reveal more. But after a pause, he glanced at Liefling and went on.

"My father saw great opportunity in this arrangement. He proposed to the daughter. The Colored landowner agreed to the marriage with alacrity. My grandfather was handsome, well read and well traveled, despite his apparent poverty, so the landowner knew he'd bring enormous respectability to his daughter. Shortly after my father was born, the landowner, his wife and daughter were drowned during a boating accident. But there's reason to suspect foul play."

"You mean your grandfather killed his own wife?" Liefling said.

"No one really knows. But why should it matter? The only thing that matters is that my grandfather inherited the Colored man's vast wealth. He promptly sold the farm and moved with my father to Stellenbosch, where no one knew them. And no one suspected that my father was half-kaffir because he had curly, sandy blonde hair and blue eyes. My grandfather quickly remarried. This time his wife was the purebred daughter of a wine-growing Huguenot family. He sent my father to elite Afrikaner private schools and to the University of Stellenbosch, where he studied theology. That's where my father met my mother. She was the daughter of a professor of theology who was also an influential member of the Broederbond."

Kruger stopped talking. Liefling watched him sip his drink, riveted to his story.

"Then came the Great Depression and my grandfather lost everything," Kruger said. "But by then my father was well-established and influential within the Afrikaner community. Shortly after the National Party came to power in 1948, he became dominee of the Grootekerk in Cape Town. Life was great. My mother had borne him three children. All of them blonde and blue-eyed. He was a member of the Broederbond and advisor to prime ministers. Then the family curse caught up with him. I was in my second year at Stellenbosch University and dating your mother. In fact, we were planning to get married after I graduated. I found my father in bed with our Colored maid. I was so shocked I threatened to expose him."

"Why didn't you?"

"He blackmailed me into keeping silent. He warned about the consequences. And I had my own reasons for wanting to avoid a scandal. I didn't want to hurt my mother, and I didn't want to lose Freda."

Again Kruger paused. The confession was draining him emotionally. He took a deep breath, sipped his drink and then continued. "I kept his perversion a secret for over a year. But then your grandfather Francois found out."

"My grandfather?"

"Ja. He was a close friend of my father's. Both were inducted into the Broederbond the same year – 1925. Both married women who'd been interned in British concentration camps. Most important, both believed in racial purity and had been vociferous champions of the Immorality Act. One afternoon your grandfather stopped by unannounced to see my father. My mother and sisters were away visiting relatives and I was at the University of Alabama in America. Your grandfather found my father naked in bed with a Colored prostitute. He was so enraged that he forbade your mother to marry me. He also cast the deciding vote in the Broederbond's secret trial that stripped my father of his leadership position. I hurried back home from America only to find that my family had left the Cape and moved to Venda, and that your mother was forbidden to see me. We weren't even allowed to speak to each other on the phone. I was so hurt by our break-up that I abandoned plans to become a winegrower and went into the army. Two years after I did, I killed my father."

"Did anyone ever find out?" Liefling asked.

"No. His disappearance was blamed on muti-killers. His body was never found. Just as no one will find your body."

Liefling shuddered. She could tell from the look in Kruger's eyes that he meant to kill her.

"But before I kill you, my dear," Kruger said, as the Lear began its initial descent into the Thohoyandou airport, "I'll tell you how I killed your father."

54

THANDO awoke with a pounding headache. She stared confusedly about the bunker. All she saw was the flickering lantern on the table. She touched her left side. Her ribs throbbed dully. Her hair was matted with dried blood on the side where Sidney had struck her with the butt of the AK-47. She leaned against the table and hoisted herself up.

"Liefling!" she called out as she staggered from room to room. She was no one. She staggered toward the steps leading outside, then stumbled over something. She looked down and saw Sidney's corpse, his police uniform soaked in blood.

Then she realized what had happened.

"Oh, God," she moaned as she kneeled down and felt in vain for a pulse. There was none. She cradled Sidney's head gently in her hands and repeatedly kissed his serene face. Tears streamed down her cheeks. Over and over again she muttered in Zulu, "*Ngi ya gu thanda,* Sidney. I love you, Sidney."

Gradually she recalled the improbable sequence of events that had led her former husband to save her life by sacrificing his......

SIDNEY pressed his forefinger to his lips, signaling to Thando to be quiet. Liefling and Botha had just disappeared around the corner, headed for the steps. He came over to where she stood against the wall and whispered, "I'm sorry I had to do that to you, honey. But I had to make it look real or else the bastard would have executed you himself."

"What's happening?" Thando asked, bewildered.

"There's no time to explain," Sidney said. "I've explained as much as I can in this letter." He quickly removed a sealed white envelope from the left pocket of his police trousers and handed it to her.

She took it hesitantly.

"Hide it." She stashed it inside her bra.

Sidney glanced nervously down the long and narrow corridor. He heard Liefling and Botha going up the steps.

"Okay, now listen very carefully," he said. "I'm going to hit you on the side of the head to draw some blood. The blow will be hard enough to make you pass out. Just in case the bastard should decide to come down to sees for himself if you're dead. I doubt he will since he's in quite a hurry. I'll fire several bullets into the wall to make it sound like I've shot you. Plead for mercy before I do. You got that?"

Suddenly the truth dawned on Thando. "What about you, Sidney?"

"I can take care of myself," he said quickly. "Please take care of our little girl. If anything happens to me, tell Mkondeleli that even though her father was an askari and did many bad things, in the end he did the right thing by saving her mother's life." Sidney looked directly into Thando's tear-filled eyes. "As for you, my darling, I know you didn't cheat on me. I love you, I always have, and I always will."

Sidney gave Thando a quick kiss and then a hug. She clung to him.

"Hurry up, Sidney!" they heard Botha yell from the top of the steps.

"Goodbye, my love," Sidney said, wrenching himself loose. "Now plead for mercy and scream the loudest you've ever screamed."

Thando did so.

"I'm sorry, darling," Sidney said. He raised the AK-47 and struck her on the side of the head. Thando instantly passed out and slumped to the floor. Blood oozed from the side of her head.

Sidney hurried toward the steps and met his fate.

55

THANDO removed Sidney's letter from her bra. She tore open the envelope and read the letter with tear-filled eyes in the flickering lantern.

My dearest Thando,

I know they're going to kill me. They always kill their askaris, just as I believe they've killed Gideon. Before I die, I want you to understand why I did what I did. First, I became an askari because I loved you very much. I was turned on June 16, 1987, after being captured while leading a group of comrades across the border with Zimbabwe to a safehouse in Venda. Apparently one of the comrades was already an askari.

After I refused to talk following a brutal interrogation by Kruger at a bushveld camp in the Northern Transvaal, he said something that led me to break. He said that if I refused to become an askari, he would kill me and then spread rumors that you, my beloved Thando, were an askari too.

Knowing how readily our comrades believed such rumors, because MK was infested with askaris, I knew what would happen to you. You could have been executed. I couldn't bear the thought. So I agreed to turn askari. I didn't do it for the money. You know I'd never stoop that low. I did it out of love.

During my years as an askari, I was used mainly to lure unsuspecting MK cadres into traps set by Kruger and members of the Thathe Vondo death squad. I was also used as an assassin against prominent anti-apartheid activists. At other times I was given booby-trapped grenades to distribute to Comrades, that later exploded and either maimed or killed them. All this caused me deep pain and profound guilt.

But what caused me the deepest pain and the profoundest guilt was what they did to my brother Nelson. I wasn't involved in planting the evidence against him. I believe Botha did that. He only told me my cover was on the verge of being blown and that Nelson had to be sacrificed.

I do not in any way blame you for ordering my brother's execution. His blood is on my hands. It wrung my heart to see you suffer all those years from the guilt of having done what you had to do as commander of our cell. I would have done the same thing if I had been in your shoes, not knowing the truth. We were all victims, my beloved Thando. The apartheid regime knew how to divide us in order to conquer us.

You may ask why I didn't I leave. Well, I've asked myself the same question many times. One reason is that Kruger always held over me the threat of harming you and Mkondeleli. He used a similar threat with Gideon. Also, I remained an askari because I wanted revenge. I wanted to time it just right so I could destroy Kruger and his men. They must have sensed this, for after the death squad disbanded, they deliberately kept me in the dark about their plans, even after they hired me as a highly paid consultant to their security firm.

That's why I had to pretend I was still one of them, still an obedient askari, still a ruthless assassin. When Liefling filed the lawsuit, I knew the time had finally come for me to act. At first I'd planned to offer to testify, but then Gideon beat me to it. From then on things moved rather quickly. He and I were planning to testify together when Botha informed me that Kruger wanted me to kill Gideon, Liefling, David and you for five million rands. That's when I knew I had to come up with an alternative plan. One thing I knew from bitter experience was that Kruger seldom left any witnesses and that I'd be killed after I'd done their dirty work.

When I went over to David's place in Soweto, I'd planned to tell you the truth. I'd worked it out this way. As soon as you and Liefling came in, I was going to take off my balaclava and confess the truth. Then we'd all figure out a way to stay alive. But David surprised me by trying to wrestle the gun out of my hand. It went off accidentally and I fled. You know the rest.

I still love you very much despite what has happened between us . You continue to feel, to care, to love and to sacrifice for the greater good. Many former freedom fighters, on the other hand, are looking out for number one. They've sold the revolution for pieces of silver. They've forgotten the suffering and sacrifices of the masses and the true meaning of the impassioned cry, "Amandla! Ngawethu!"

But you haven't forgotten, my darling. You remain true to the cause. I can't tell you how proud I am of what you're doing to protect children, for whose future we first took up arms against apartheid, and to fight for the rights of women, whose contributions and sacrifices made the difference in the liberation struggle.

I feel very blessed to have known you, my beloved Thando. You are a true mother of Africa. Please pray for my soul. And please take care of my ailing mother and our beloved Mkondeleli. The struggle continues.

Your beloved,
Sidney
Amandla!

Thando had held back her tears while struggling to read the letter to the end. Now they came in a flood. She wept for what seemed an eternity. At last she rose and gently dragged Sidney's corpse back into the room. She covered him with the blanket from her bed – the one in which they'd snuggled together in the busy many years ago, reading Shakespeare under the moonlight.

Her face stern despite flowing tears, she saluted her dead husband in the name of the struggle. She clenched her right fist, raised it high into the air, and shouted, "Amandla!"

There was no "Ngawethu!" shouted back in response. But she thought she heard it being faintly whispered back by Sidney's spirit as it journeyed to the realm of his ancestors. She began singing 'Nkosi Sikelel' Afrika,' in a soft voice full of sorrow.

She sang the anthem three times, slowly, gazing down at her lifeless husband, recalling memories of their time together. Then she walked over to the chest at the foot of the cot where she had often slept. She opened it, removed her brown, neatly pressed MK uniform, complete with combat boots and black beret. She then retrieved the Magnum from the briefcase. She changed clothes, screwed the silencer onto the Magnum and loaded it with bullets.

She pulled up a chair and sat down. She checked her watch. It was 10:05 p.m. She still had time. She grabbed her cell phone and dialed the number of the person whose help she needed if her bold plan for revenge was to work.

56   **MUDJADJI** stopped and leaned against the trunk of the Marula tree. She had been trudging through the dark forest for over an hour, accompanied by her grandson Vutshilo, who was armed with a *knob-kierrie* club.

"I'm exhausted, my grandson," she said. "Let's rest a while."

"Okay grandma," Vutshilo said. "How far is the place?"

"Not much further. About two miles."

"Do you think we'll get help there for grandpa?"

"Plenty of it, my grandson. I only hope that your grandpa is still alive."

The thought of her husband induced Mudjadji, despite her aching legs, to resume walking. About half an hour later she and Richard finally reached the entrance leading to the mountain school.

"Wait here, child," Mudjadji said. "It's taboo for you to go any further because you haven't yet been circumcised. I'm permitted to enter only because I'm the wife of your grandpa, who used to be a great teacher at the school."

Mudjadji covered her gray head with her blanket to show respect. Following custom, she walked around the poles in order to reach the visitor's gate. Mudjadji had almost reached the gate when five young men suddenly leaped out of the darkness and surrounded her, their assegais pointed at her chest.

"STOP!" one of the young men bellowed.

Mudjadji froze. One of the young men yanked the blanket from her head. "It's a woman!" he shouted incredulously.

A group of twenty powerfully built *Shepherds* appeared from nowhere. Nzhelele was among them. He studied Mudjadji's face in the light of the flaming torch he held above his head. Startled, he said with the utmost respect, "This is Makhado's wife. What's the matter, Mother of Gideon?"

"It's my husband," Mudjadji said in a trembling voice. "His life is in danger. He needs help."

"What's wrong? Where is he?"

Mudjadji told Nzhelele about Makhado's nocturnal trip back to the Thathe Vondo private game reserve, and the reason for his trip.

Nzhelele turned to one of his fellow *Shepherds* and said, "Get the young warriors ready for battle. Makhado needs our help in fighting against the Boers and neo-Nazis."

57 VILJOEN stood before the barbecue pit, whose lurid flames licked the humid air. Around the pit the neo-Nazis sat on lounge chairs enjoying a sizzling braai of game Viljoen and Barnard had shot earlier in the day. They also guzzled plenty of Laager beer. It was just like old times, when they'd held a braai before torturing and executing the enemies of Baaskap. As the men were drinking, eating and cracking bawdy jokes, Viljoen made a suggestion.

"*Bloedbroers*," he said, a can of Laager beer in his hand. He spoke in an overly loud voice, as he often did when drinking heavily. "Do you remember our answer to necklacing?"

"You mean the barbecue?" someone asked.

"Ja. Is anyone in the mood to roast a pig tonight?"

"Sure," several of the neo-Nazis responded.

"But where's the pig?" someone asked.

"We have a fat one in the *waarheid kamer*," Viljoen said.

"Fetch it!"

Viljoen drained his Laager beer and then said, "Okay. Barnard and I will go fetch the pig. You guys stoke the fire."

57 MAKHADO made yet another stop so Gideon could rest. He gingerly placed him down on the ground, careful not to cause him any more pain in his wounded leg. Gideon's high fever was now under control, thanks to the fact that Makhado had found some leaves along the way that contained a chemical similar to aspirin, which he'd given Gideon to chew. Makhado also had made a thick paste from the medicinal leaves of another tree and used it to cover Gideon's serious leg wound to prevent gangrene. All this had slowed them down considerably. They had barely traveled more than a mile from the truth hut.

"Father, I'm slowing you down," Gideon said. "Leave me and save yourself."

"I'll never abandon you, my son," Makhado said.

58

KRUGER smiled as the Learjet touched down at the tiny Thohoyandou airport.

He and Liefling immediately transferred to a waiting helicopter for the remainder of their journey to the Thathe Vondo private game reserve eighty miles away. The helicopter seated four passengers and had a single engine. Liefling, still in handcuffs, was hustled into the backseat next to Kruger.

The pilot was the bearded and sallow faced Wolgang Erasmus, Kruger's regular helicopter pilot.

As the rotor blades spun at maximum speed and the helicopter lifted into the humid night air, Kruger turned to Liefling and said, "In exactly twenty minutes, my dear, your troubles will be over. Tomorrow the media will report the most sensational story in the history of South Africa. A conspiracy by two human rights lawyers involved in drug-trafficking to extort money from me. The media will report that David got you to file a bogus lawsuit against me in order to pay off his Colombian drug suppliers, and that Thando, Gideon and Shaka were working for him."

The helicopter banked to the right, then leveled as it began following the course of the mighty river on the last miles of its journey.

"No one will believe your story," Liefling said in desperation as the helicopter began its descent to the remote private game reserve, about fifteen miles away.

"It's a pity you won't be here to eat your words," Kruger said. He reached over the front seat and tapped the pilot on the shoulder.

"Erasmus!" he shouted, "Contact Viljoen and tell him I'm on my way."

"Ja, General," Erasmus said. He put on the headphones and adjusted the frequency.

Turning to Liefling, Kruger said, "It was really quite easy to kill your father. All I had to do was to get Gideon, whom your father trusted, to lure him into a trap. Gideon invited him to meet with one of my former askaris, telling your father that the man had evidence about death squads. When your father got to the house on Tenth Avenue in Alexandra, Ludwig and I were there waiting for him. I made him an offer I thought he'd never refuse. I told him it was possible for him to be forgiven for turning his back on the Volk by denouncing apartheid. I told him he could be welcomed back into the laager and given an even more prominent and lucrative position within the Dutch Reformed Church. I told him all he had to do was to repudiate the ANC as a communist front. You know what he said?"

"Go to hell," Liefling said.

"That's right. He said he'd die before he ever betrayed his brothers and sisters. So I proved him prophetic. I slit his throat. Ludwig and I dumped his body into the back of a sanitized van, drove to a veld on the outskirts of Alexandra, where we doused his corpse with petrol and set it on fire. Then I tortured two young black thugs who'd been arrested for killing a black policeman until they 'confessed' that they were ANC Comrades and had killed your father in obedience to the slogan 'One Settler, One Bullet.' And as you know, Judge Prinsloo, a dear friend and my personal lawyer, sentenced them to death. They were hung at Pretoria Central Prison, a verdict that won me your mother's undying gratitude and affection. And how do you like this for a denouement? It's your mother who's going to be my perfect alibi in your disappearance and death."

Liefling was about say something when Erasmus said in an agitated voice, "Viljoen's on the line, General."

Kruger slipped into the front seat and put on a pair of headphones.

"Viljoen, this is General Kruger. What's going on?"

"Gideon has escaped."

"Escaped? How?"

"Apparently his father helped him escape.'

"Makhado?"

"Ja. The kaffir left a satchel inside the truth hut. But they couldn't be far. Gideon is wounded. In fact, Barnard and I have picked up their trail."

"Good. Where are you?"

"We're about a mile from the truth hut. The men are back at the lodge having a braai. The trail is still fresh, so we should nab the kaffirs in no time."

"Bring them back alive, you hear?" Kruger bellowed.

"Don't worry, General. We'll bring them in alive. The men are eager to have a barbecue."

59

MAKHADO lay flat on the ground and pressed his right ear to the moist earth, listening intently.

A minute later he sprang to his feet. "Two men are coming this way," he said, rubbing the dirt from his hands.

"I bet it's Viljoen and Barnard," Gideon said.

Makhado leaned on his assegai and thought. "Son, there's no way we can outrun them. We must stand and fight."

"But there are two of them, Baba. They have guns and I'm wounded."

"That's true. But they don't know the forest as well as I do. I'll use that to my advantage."

"How?"

"You'll see."

Makhado again went down on his washboard stomach and pressed his right ear to the ground. He listened for almost a minute, then sprang to his feet and said, "I think it'll work. They've just split up. One of them has gone to the right, probably to cut off our access to the bridge. The other is still following behind us."

"Then we're trapped."

"No, my son." Makhado tapped his forehead with his long thin forefinger. "You must think like a warrior." He grabbed his assegai and gave the battle-axe to Gideon. "Take this. I'll hide you in that thicket over there while I backtrack and take care of the one who's following us. If the other one finds you, hurl the axe straight at his chest. Can you do it?"

"Yes, Baba," Gideon said, accepting the battle-axe, though he doubted he'd have the strength to throw it.

Makhado, assegai and shield in hand, retraced his steps so noiselessly that even Gideon wasn't aware he'd gone.

60

BOTHA peered out the window of the "police" van as it came to a stop under a clump of trees along a deserted side street behind Chris Hani Barangwanath hospital. It was a quarter to twelve. Swanepoel was driving.

"It should take me less than fifteen minutes to do the job," Botha said confidently.

"Do you want me to wait here?"

"Ja."

Botha, dressed in a light black tracksuit, thin black leather gloves and a black balaclava, grabbed his bulging backpack, silently opened the side door and slid out.

He looked about, saw no one, then darted toward the barbed wire fence rimming the sprawling hospital. Hidden by large leafy trees, he opened the backpack and removed a pair of wire cutters. Working quickly, he cut out a two-foot portion of the fence, wriggled through the jagged hole, and within minutes was on his way toward his target, whose room was at the back of the building.

61

KRUGER smiled at Liefling as the helicopter descended out of the black sky and landed on a helipad in the middle of the Thathe Vondo private game reserve's main courtyard. The powerful glare of spotlights illumined the courtyard. The spinning rotor blades raised a huge cloud of dust and swayed the branches of nearby trees.

"This is the end of your journey, my dear," Kruger said.

Having been informed by Viljoen that Kruger was on his way, the fifty neo-Nazis had made preparations to welcome their revered leader. They now stood in two parallel lines outside the entrance to *Voortrekker Laager*. Some of the men held aloft flaring torches as in one of their parades; others waved red flags with the AWB's triple-7 insignia.

"Who are they?" Liefling asked.

"My warriors," Kruger said proudly.

The helicopter landed. Kruger climbed out, dragging Liefling behind him by her handcuffed wrists.

At the sight of the man they idolized like a god, the man who'd stood by them through thick and thin, the man who'd vowed to bring back Baaskap, the neo-Nazis, as if following the cue of an invisible conductor, broke out into a triumphant chanting of *Die Stem Van Suid Afrika*.

Bewildered, Liefling thought herself in other world. It was as if apartheid had never died. She knew about AWB neo-Nazis and their fight for a white homeland. She knew about their contemptuous dismissal of parliamentary democracy as a "British-Jewish invention designed to weaken Afrikanerdom." She knew that the AWB, at the height of its power and appeal during the late 1980s, had boasted of a membership of more than 100,000, drawn mostly from blue collar white workers, the bureaucracy, farmers and members of the security forces – all of whom had felt that their birthright of one of the highest standards of living in the world was being sold to black terrorists and communists.

Like most South Africans, Liefling had initially dismissed the AWB as a group of racist buffoons. She'd started taking them seriously when a member of their *Wit Wolwe* (White Wolves) brigade went on a fifteen-minute shooting rampage in the center of Pretoria, killing seven blacks and injuring sixteen. Now she saw up close how dangerous and fanatical they were.

There was no doubt in her mind now that her lawsuit against her stepfather was legitimate. These men and their deeds had to be exposed. Those who were guilty had to be punished to the fullest extent of the law. She knew that some former AWB members had abjured their violent and racist past and applied for amnesty. But the men before her were clearly unrepentant. They'd never accepted and would never accept black majority rule, at least not while under the control of men like her stepfather.

They had to be stopped. But how? She shuddered and her heart pounded as her eyes saw the expressions of pure hatred on the faces of the neo-Nazis as they watched her being dragged by Kruger toward *Voortrekker Laager*. She wondered frantically how long she had to live.

62

NZHELELE led the fleet-footed *impi* regiment of about one hundred young men and their *Shepherds* through the forest, headed for the Thathe Vondo private game reserve, about eight miles away. Wearing the same warrior garb as Makhado, they chanted war songs as they jogged in single file. Their strong arms firmly gripped assegais, shields, knob-kierries and battle-axes. They were clearly thirsty for battle, eager to prove their manhood. Even though they'd been told that the neo-Nazis were heavily armed, they knew that at night, in the forest, they had the advantage.

The forest was their backyard. They knew it like the back of their hands. It was where they'd learned to hunt, to survive for days without food or drink, to know every tree and every blade of grass, every smell and every sound, to wade across swamps, to swim across rivers infested with hippos and crocodiles, to find their way by the stars, to identify medicinal plants and to disappear without a trace when necessary.

After jogging for nearly an hour, they reached the small bridge spanning the turbulent river.

"We should split here," Nzhelele said. "Makhado's wife said Makhado is likely to be at one of two places: the main compound or the truth hut. I'll take a group to the main compound. Limela will take another group to the truth hut. Remember now, young warriors, this is the real thing. Everything you've learned about warfare is going to be put to the test. Don't do anything rash. And don't forget that it's a great honor to die in battle."

With that, the impi split into two roughly even groups. One group jogged along the edge of the river, headed for the truth hut. The other, led by Nzhelele, continued through the forest, headed for the main compound. Both places were equidistant, about four miles apart.

As they neared the enemy, the impis stopped chanting war songs and moved with the silence of ghosts through the dark forest.

63

BOTHA finally reached the back of Chris Hani Baragwanath Hospital, using shrubs, parked cars, dumpsters and darkness as cover. He was salivating to kill David. It would be such sweet revenge for the death of his father. He recalled how ignominiously his father had died.

On the morning of June 16, 1976, after the police had opened fire on unarmed students demonstrating against being taught in Afrikaans, an angry mob of students from another school, led by Dikeledi Motsei, had boldly marched toward a police station in the heart of Soweto, which was commanded by Botha's father. From here, he'd overseen the pacification of the ghetto through an elaborate network of impimpis and a brutal, mostly black, police force. When he heard that a mob of angry students was on its way, Botha's father had begged an impimpi he trusted to safely spirit him out of the ghetto.

While his brethren fled, the impimpi had stowed Botha's father in the trunk of an unmarked police car. Then it occurred to the impimpi that this was an excellent opportunity to atone for the years he'd reluctantly spied for the security branch. He'd driven straight toward the advancing mob. Reaching it, he got out, sought out Dikeledi, and said triumphantly, "A fat Boer pig is in the trunk." The chanting students had immediately dragged Botha's father screaming, struggling and kicking out of the trunk.

An intrepid BBC TV crew had filmed his macabre death. Botha, then on leave from his military duties on the border, had watched his father's murder on TV with burning hatred and rage. Chanting students had stripped Botha's father naked, and then thrown a gasoline-soaked tire over his neck. They had shoved it down to his arms to prevent him from wriggling free.

Then Dikeledi had ignited the tire with a match. Her face was impassive as she watched the human fireball of the man who had tortured and killed her brother writhe and scream. Then its distended belly had exploded. While a dozen students danced the *Toyi-Toyi* war dance, township residents, including women and children, had thrown rocks, and spat on the charred corpse of the most hated man in their community, who'd terrorized them for more than twenty years.

Botha had never forgotten Dikeledi's role in his father's murder. Nor the fact that it was David's father who had saved her from being hanged. Nor that David had dated her.

And he'd never forgiven. Even though he'd tortured Dikeledi and injected her with contaminated heroin during her detention at John Vorster Square, his revenge wasn't satiated. He still watched the videotape of his father's necklacing regularly. It fueled his hatred.

Botha, his back against the wall, sidled toward Room 345. He surveyed the height of the square brick building and smiled. As a member of *Koevoet*, he'd gone on dangerous missions in pursuit of "ANC terrorists" in Angola, Botswana, Lesotho, Mozambique and Zimbabwe. He'd scaled walls of taller and more impregnable buildings in order to reach and eliminate his target.

Scaling the walls of Bara to the third floor would be easy. Especially since there were only two guards in this wing of the sprawling complex. He'd seen one of them dozing off in the booth by the entrance. He was confident he could handle them both, if necessary.

Botha reached into his backpack, removed a pair of suction cups and a coiled climbing rope with a four-pronged anchor and went to work. He threw the anchor and coil of rope upward. The spikes of the anchor lodged themselves into the metal gutter around the hospital's roof. He tugged it several times. It was secure. He donned his special climbing shoes and his large hands gripped the special suction cups. He was about to begin his ascent when he felt the muzzle of a rifle on the small of his back and heard a stern voice say, "Freeze."

It was one of the security guards.

"Raise your hands!"

64

VILJOEN paused in the middle of the trail and sniffed the night air. He smelled sweat and blood. Then he heard a twig snap. Gleeful, he plunged into the brush, using his shotgun to bushwhack. Suddenly he saw the whites of Gideon's eyes. At the same instant, he saw something gleaming spinning through the air as the battle-axe headed for his chest. Viljoen instantly stepped aside and the axe nicked his left shoulder.

"You bloody kaffir bastard," he yelled, rushing at Gideon. He smashed his hard-toed boot into Gideon's ribs as he lay on the ground. Gideon grunted as hot pain seared through him. His leg wound throbbed as he struggled back to his feet. He hugged a tree to keep from collapsing.

"I'd kill you right here on the spot, you black bastard," Viljoen said, hovering over Gideon with the shotgun. "But the General wants to interrogate you, and the men want their barbecue."

Viljoen was about to reach for his walkie-talkie and call Barnard to come and help him carry Gideon when suddenly a sharp scream pierced the still night air. It was followed by the sound of stampeding elephants.

Startled, Viljoen said, "What's that?

Gideon smiled furtively.

Hands shaking, Viljoen fumbled to tune his walkie-talkie to Barnard's channel.

"Jan, can you hear me? Are you OK?"

No answer.

"Jan, are you there?"

"Help!" Barnard cried frantically.

"What happened?"

"I'm hanging upside down from a tree. And a herd of elephants is coming my way!"

Viljoen was bewildered. "How did you get upside down?"

"How do I bloody know! It seems like some kind of booby trap. I'm about four feet off the ground. A rope is tied around my feet. My bloody gun is on the ground and I can't reach it. Hurry or I'll be crushed to death by elephants!"

Gideon smiled again. He knew his father was still alive.

"I'll be there in a minute," Viljoen said.

He prodded Gideon with the shotgun.

"If you can't walk you'll have to crawl back, kaffir. Now let's go."

Gideon said nothing. He simply turned and began limping in the direction Viljoen was pointing with his shotgun. They'd hardly gone five paces when a blood-curdling scream rent the humid night air. Again, the scream was followed by the sound of stampeding elephants.

Viljoen shuddered. "Good God, what was that?"

Gideon smiled.

Viljoen fumbled for his walkie-talkie.

"Jan, are you OK?"

No reply.

"Jan, can you hear me?"

No reply.

Suddenly, an inhuman gurgling sound came through the walkie-talkie.

"Jan! What happened?"

"Jan is trying to tell you that he's about to die," Makhado said coldly. "But he's lost his voice because his throat has been slit."

Viljoen's knees turned to jelly. He looked about wildly. He accidentally dropped his walkie-talkie then had trouble finding it again. With shaking hands, he managed to tune into Kruger's frequency.

"General," he stammered. "This is Viljoen."

"Do you have them?" Kruger's voice came crackling through the walkie-talkie.

"No. Barnard's dead."

"Dead?"

"Ja. Makhado slit his throat."

"Jesus Christ. Where are you?"

"I'm about a quarter of a mile west of the truth hut."

"Can you get to the hut?" Kruger said. "I'll come and pick you up."

"Sure."

Suddenly the sound of stampeding elephants broke out again, this time from nearby.

"What was that?" Kruger asked.

"I don't know," Viljoen said in a tremulous voice. "It sounds like a herd of elephants or something. And they're coming this way."

"Get to the truth hut quickly," Kruger said. "I'm on my way."

While Viljoen was talking with Kruger, Gideon disappeared behind some bushes. But Viljoen was in no mood to hunt for him in a spooky jungle. He turned and ran like a rabbit toward the truth hut.

65

BOTHA obeyed the security guard. He was calm and collected as he slowly raised his hands. When they were even with his broad shoulders, with lightning speed he whipped out a bowie knife sheathed across his collarbone and took one swipe at the guard's throat. It instantly severed the jugular. Blood gushed. The guard dropped his rifle and clutched his gaping throat. Botha wasn't finished with him. With one sharp upward thrust he drove the ten-inch blade into the stunned and dying guard's heart. The blade entered just below the ribcage. Botha jerked it upward until the entire blade was swallowed up in flesh and blood and bone. He twisted it around several times for good measure.

The guard twitched, his sphincter relaxed and his body waste flowed out. He collapsed like a sack to the ground. Botha smiled. He kicked the corpse and then dragged it behind a nearby bush. Kruger had trained him well during boot camp at Voortrekkerhoogte in the art of killing without remorse.

Botha clipped the aluminum caribiner to his climbing harness and began his ascent. The only audible sounds were his measured breathing and the muffled sucking sound made by the suction cups each time he lifted one hand off the wall. He'd then slap it against the wall higher up and haul himself upwards. The ascent was child's play compared to climbing the steep and rugged peaks of the Drakensberg Mountains during Special Forces training.

It took him less than three minutes to reach the window to Room 345. He'd reconnoitered the hospital earlier and knew that windows at the underfunded hospital were generally left open at night to save on air-conditioning costs. The window to David's room was half-open. Botha peered inside.

There was David, tubes still attached to his nose and arms. As noiselessly as a snake, Botha slithered sideways through the open window into the darkened room. He heard soft, even breathing and smiled. He debated whether to smother David with a pillow, pump him full of bullets or hang him out the window. Hanging won. He was fascinated with the way the eyes of the victims he'd hung during his death squad days had bulged, their tongues had lolled sideways, and their legs had thrashed about in the air as if they were dancing one last *Toyi-Toyi.*

Botha made a large noose with the rope. He tied one end of the rope to the radiator beneath the window. His gloved hands reached for David's throat.

66

KRUGER lowered his walkie-talkie. His face was solemn. The AWB neo-Nazis looked at him expectantly.

"Gentlemen," he said slowly. "Barnard has been murdered."

The neo-Nazis gasped, cursed and shook their heads in utter disbelief.

"How did that happen?" someone asked.

"I'm not sure," Kruger said. For the first time there was a hint of fear in his voice. "Viljoen mentioned stampeding elephants. It sounds to me like Makhado may have accomplices."

"Accomplices!"

The men started talking to each other, speculating on who could be helping Makhado. Some said the ANC. Others pointed their fingers at the PAC.

"Don't worry," Kruger said above the din. The crowd quieted immediately. "As your leader, I plan to rescue Viljoen myself." Kruger turned to Liefling and said, "You, kaffir-lover, are coming with me."

Kruger yanked Liefling off the chair and ordered her to march toward the helicopter.

By the door, Kruger turned and said, "Remember now, stay here until I return. I'll have this matter under control in no time."

The men didn't answer. It was clear they were afraid. Minutes later, Kruger was inside the helicopter as it lifted off, headed for the truth hut. Liefling sat beside him, without handcuffs, but with Kruger's gun aimed at her temple.

67

BOTHA was just about to wrap the noose around the prone body's throat when a combat boot smashed into his crotch. He yelled in pain and clutched his burning testicles. He gasped for breath then gaped at the body on the bed. Like a mummy's, its hands reached for *his* throat.

Botha shrank back in horror. Suddenly he heard shouts and footsteps. The door burst open, lights flicked on, and Botha found himself staring into the muzzles of two semiautomatics pointed at his head by Detective Malusi Radebe and his brother Sipho.

"Freeze, you fucking asshole!" Sipho said.

"Keep your hands away from that knife," barked Malusi, who, as a former security branch member, was familiar with the knife-sheathed-near-the-collar- bone trick.

Squid-eyed and openmouthed, Botha stared in utter disbelief at the bed as the prostate figure he thought was David threw aside the tubes and white sheets and hopped down. Before him stood MK commander Thando.

"I don't like strange men touching me," she said.

"But --" Botha stammered.

"The man you wanted to kill isn't here, you neo-Nazi bastard," Malusi said, as he reached for his handcuff. "He's safe in the other room. Thando contacted me about your plans to come here at midnight. So we laid a nice trap for you."

"How did you --" Botha said, staring at Thando.

"You may have turned Sidney into an askari and an assassin," Thando said, "but you couldn't destroy his love for me. It will be my pleasure to see you hang."

Botha turned and sprang for the open window like a cat. Before anyone could stop him, he was out of sight. Seconds later there was a bloodcurdling scream. Thando, Sipho and Malusi rushed to the window and stared down.

There was Botha dangling in mid-air, tongue lolling and eyes bulging, as if he were dancing the *Toyi-Toyi*. The noose he'd prepared for David's neck was strung tightly around his.

Thando spat at him.

"Have your people arrested the driver?" Thando asked.

"Ja. They found him waiting on a side street," Malusi said. "He offered no resistance whatsoever."

"By the way, Thando," Sipho said. "I've been informed that Hannah has been released and is being driven over here."

"Thanks," Thando said. "Now we have to get to Kruger before it's too late."

"There's a military jet waiting to take us to the Thathe Vondo private game reserve," Malusi said. "And the commander of the military base in Venda has already dispatched a rescue squad."

"What are we waiting for?" Sipho said impatiently. "Let's go. Every minute is precious."

Thando glanced at her wristwatch. It was twelve-thirty. "There's someone we should bring along."

"Who? Sipho asked.

"Liefling's mother."

68

VILJOEN stumbled through the dark woods, headed for the truth hut. Though he was solidly built and weighed nearly two hundred pounds, he was terrified. *I must get to the truth hut,* he panted.

From time to time he stopped and swept the woods, eager to locate the source of the noises and shrieks and howls and stampeding. He saw nothing. He kept blasting away with his shotgun at anything that moved. As a result he ended up shooting at hyenas, jackals, baboons, owls, leopards and meerkats. His shotgun empty, he tossed it away.

Suddenly he saw the truth hut looming in the distance. Even though he wasn't a fast runner, he sprinted toward it. He arrived breathless. He staggered up the creaky steps. He flung open the door. He threw himself inside and barricaded himself with three latches and a deadbolt. He peered through the window. There was no sign of anyone pursuing him. He checked his shotgun and cursed when he discovered that he was out of ammunition. He'd left his packet of cartridges in the woods. But he was glad to be inside the truth hut. All he had to do was wait for Kruger to arrive by helicopter and rescue him.

The room was pitch dark. He fumbled in his pocket for his pack of Benson & Hedges. He struck a match. It lit but then fizzled before he could light the cigarette. Cursing, he struck another. It too fizzled.

"Let me help you, baas," a disembodied voice said from somewhere behind him in the dark room.

Viljoen jumped. "Who's that?" he demanded, fearing it might be the ghostly voice of someone he'd tortured and killed.

"It's me, baas," Makhado said in a humble voice.

Viljoen relaxed. He still thought of Makhado as his servant, his obedient and shuffling kaffir. Apparently he must have been delirious, for he actually said, "Thank God, my boy. Light the lantern, will you? It's on the table. It's bloody dark in here."

"Sure, baas," Makhado said, lighting the lantern.

Viljoen said, still looking out the window, "There's a herd of stampeding elephants out there, you know, boy?"

Makhado smiled. "You mean these elephants, baas?" Makhado said, stamping his feet on the floor.

Viljoen spun around and faced Makhado. For the first time he noticed his tribal warrior garb and assegai. "YOU!" he cried, realizing who he'd locked himself in the room with. He fumbled with the latch, desperate to open the door.

Makhado raised his assegai, ready to pin Viljoen against the door with it. "I wouldn't do that if I were you," he said in a tone that left no doubt that he meant it.

Viljoen shrank away from the door.

"Sit down on that chair, you neo-Nazi bastard," Makhado said, pointing to the interrogation chair in the middle of the room.

Viljoen crawled toward the chair. Makhado tied his hands behind the chair with a thick rope.

"Where's my son?"

Viljoen was tongue-tied.

"Speak before I slit your throat!" Makhado said fiercely, raising the assegai.

"I left him back in the woods," Viljoen stammered.

"Is he still alive?"

"Ja."

"Say 'Ja, baas.'"

"Ja, baas."

"He'd better be, you piece of shit," Makhado said. "If he's dead I'll skin you alive."

Makhado left to search for Gideon.

69 FREDA paced nervously up and down the sunken living room, still wearing her Adidas outfit. Her face was ashen.

"I don't believe it," she kept muttering.

Freda had just been listening to Malusi tell her that Kruger was responsible for the murder of her husband, and that he'd tried to kill Thando and David, and that he'd abducted Liefling and planned to kill her too.

"It's true, Mrs. Kruger," said Thando, who was sitting between Malusi and Sipho on the Italian leather sofa in the middle of the living room.

Standing by a large bay window, Freda shook her head. Hoping for some reassurance, she turned her eyes to Tina, her friend and confidante, who was sitting next to her husband, Paul on the other side of the L-shaped sofa.

"I believe it," Tina said. "I've long suspected something was very wrong with Kruger. And I tried to warn you."

Freda stared out at the chill night. But it could offer her no answer to the many questions swarming through her confused mind.

Freda turned and faced the room. "How could someone I loved so deeply, someone who has showered me with nothing but love and kindness, turn out to be the very devil himself? How could I have been so naïve, so wrong, so gullible?"

A pained expression on her face, Freda looked pleadingly at the somber faces in front of her, hoping that one of them would offer her some plausible explanation as to how she could have so misjudged Kruger's character.

"Love made you see only the good side of him, Mrs. Kruger," Thando said in a sympathetic voice.

"He was a Jekyll and Hyde, if you ask me," Tina said.

"A psychopath," Paul said.

"But he kept telling me that he loved me," Freda said.

"I'm sure he does," Tina said. "But like I said before, that shouldn't have blinded you to the fact that he's a dangerous neo-Nazi. He murdered his own father and your husband. He tortured and killed scores of people during the apartheid era. And he's prepared to kill again in order to achieve his goals. He's even prepared to kill Liefling – your own daughter – if necessary."

The mention of her daughter, her only child, awoke in Freda an undying maternal instinct.

"Not if I can help it," she said fiercely. "Let's go stop the neo-Nazi bastard."

70

MALUSI, Freda, Sipho, Thando, Tina, and Paul sat inside a military jet, headed for the Thathe Vondo private game reserve.

Malusi glanced at his wristwatch. "We'll shortly be landing in Thohoyandou," he said. "There's a military helicopter waiting for us there."

"How long will it take us to get to the bushveld camp?" Thando asked.

"Fifteen to twenty minutes."

"I hope my daughter is still alive," Freda said anxiously.

"If Kruger has harmed her," Sipho vowed, "I'll kill him with my bare hands."

Everyone looked at Sipho, surprised to hear a doctor who'd taken an oath to preserve life, talk about killing. But everyone understood how Sipho felt about the woman he loved.

He'll make a good son-in-law, Freda thought.

71

NZHELELE and the impi, as soon as they saw Kruger's helicopter land, abruptly changed course and headed toward it.

"It must not leave," Nzhelele said to the young warriors. The helicopter was about two miles away. The impi of young warriors, muscles straining, sprinted toward it. The impi was within 500 yards away when Nzhelele noticed Kruger scrambling into the helicopter.

"Don't let the bastard get away!" cried Nzhelele. In a sudden burst of speed, the young men dashed toward the helicopter but it was already airborne. They hurled their assegais ineffectually at the helicopter barely cleared the treetops as it banked left and flew away into the dark night.

72 | **BEZUIDENHOUT** and his fellow neo-Nazis cheered when they saw the two transport helicopters of the South African National Defense Force land in the courtyard and about a hundred armed troops stream out. The neo-Nazis hugged each other and actually shed tears at the thought that they were now headed to prison instead of being at the mercy of the bloodthirsty impi of Venda warriors.

73 **MALUSI** jumped off the military helicopter shortly after it landed in the main courtyard of the Thathe Vondo private game reserve. Thando, Sipho, Paul, Freda and Tina remained inside. Malusi hurried across the courtyard toward the two transport helicopters.

"Any word about Liefling?" Malusi asked the tall black officer in charge of the troops.

"No, sir. We learned from the neo-Nazis that Kruger took her in a helicopter."

"Where to?"

"To a place called the truth hut."

"Where is it?"

"About five miles from here, sir."

Without delay, Malusi scrambled back into the helicopter. It took off in a northwesterly direction, headed for the truth hut.

74 KRUGER laughed at the frustrated young warriors as the helicopter rose above them and roared away over the treetops.

"Stupid kaffirs," he said. "They're like their brethren at Blood River, who thought they could fight guns and cannons with spears."

Still chuckling, he peered out the window again. Suddenly he noticed that the helicopter was headed not toward the airport at Thohoyandou, but toward the Crocodile Lake.

He stopped laughing abruptly. "Hey! Where the hell are you going, Erasmus? I told you to take me to the Learjet. The airport is the other way."

"Why are you running away, baas?" said a very familiar voice close to Kruger. In his haste to get away, and because it was dark, Kruger hadn't noticed that the person sitting beside him wasn't Liefling.

He looked up and almost had a heart attack.

75

KRUGER stared in horror and disbelief at Makhado, who was pointing the sharp blade of his assegai at Kruger's heart.

Makhado snatched Kruger's gun, then turned to the pilot and said, "Are we almost there, Liefling?"

"In a minute," Liefling said. Gripping the steering wheel with her left hand and resting her right on the control shaft, she checked their altitude and speed, then took a quick look back at the stunned Kruger.

"Where the hell is Erasmus?"

"Dead," Makhado said. "I stabbed him with my assegai. I guess you know where we are going to drop you, you piece of shit. Open the door." He pointed the assegai at Kruger's throat. "I read in my son's diaries that you loved tossing innocent people out of helicopters during what your twisted mind called the 'Crocodile Ride.' Now is your turn to enjoy the thrill of being eaten alive by crocodiles."

Kruger stared wildly out the window. It was dark, but the full moon was bright enough to reveal the scaly backs of several crocodiles floating like logs on the silver surface of the lake.

Kruger reluctantly turned the handle of the helicopter door. Makhado kicked it open.

"Jump!" he said.

Kruger stared down at the scaly backs of the floating Nile crocodiles.

"I thought you were a brave man, General," Makhado said with a sneer. "I thought only brave men murder innocent men, women and children."

Kruger looked down. He hesitated.

"I guess he's eager to testify before the TRC," Liefling said to Makhado.

76

KRUGER yelled "Never! I'm a *Bittereinder!*"

With that he jumped.

"Let's hope his kind never haunts South Africa again," Liefling said as she swung the helicopter around and headed back toward the truth hut, where Sipho, Freda, Thando, Malusi, Tina and Paul were waiting, along with Nzhelele and his impi of young warriors.

"I'm afraid people like Kruger will always exist, Liefling," Makhado said. "The only deterrence against their evil is to never violate the laws of justice. Yes, we should forgive where forgiveness is deserved. But those who tortured and murdered in the name of apartheid and refused to confess their crimes must be punished. Otherwise how can we expect young black men like the ones who almost hijacked your car to respect the law when they see those who committed crimes against humanity getting away scot-free?"

"I agree," Liefling said. "That's why I'll spend the rest of my life, if need be, hunting them down and bringing them to justice."

"I know you will *Ngwenyama* (Lioness)," Makhado said with a warm smile as the helicopter began its descent into the clearing in front of the truth hut. "I know you will because, though you are an Afrikaner, you are a true daughter of Mother Africa. You feel her pain and suffering and believe in her immense possibilities for rebirth. And as we say in Venda when welcoming back a long-lost relative, *Ndi ngani nohuma mashaka o vha o xela kale.*"

Acknowledgements

I'd like to thank all those friends and acquaintances who took time from their busy lives to read and comment on the manuscript of **Ubuntu** during its many transmigrations. They include Dawn Ziegenbalg, Gay Marrs, Linah Mathabane, Shandana Durrani, Marilyn Harless, Paula Robinson, Lisa Elmore and my agent at Fifi Oscard Agency Inc., Kevin McShane.

To my brother George and sisters Florah, Miriam, Linah, Diana and Maria – thanks for so patiently answering my many questions over the years about events and experiences in your lives in Alexandra and Venda that were often too painful to describe. Thanks also for keeping me informed on the Truth and Reconciliation Commission's hearings on a regular basis. Your experiences, opinions, hopes, disappointments, anger and ideas helped lend authenticity to the tone and texture of this book.

I'd also like to thank my friends Linda Twala and Beyers Naude. Your courageous lives, your refusal to compromise your principles during the apartheid era and after, your steadfast faith and love, and your invaluable work on behalf of the Alexandra community, amply prove that the spirit of **Ubuntu** can co-exist with that of justice.

A special thanks to my beloved mother, Mudjadji, for the inspiration of your Ubuntu and for sharing with me stories about my father and the Venda and Shangaan cultures. They made the difference.

To my dearest wife, best friend and severest critic – Gail. Honey, there are no words to describe the value of your support, encouragement, understanding, edits and feedback. To my darling and infinitely patient children – Bianca Nathan and Stanley. Thanks for being such good sports and putting up with Daddy's endless hours at the computer.

Enjoyed reading Ubuntu?

Here are other books by Mark Mathabane

You can order them via his website at

www.Mathabane.Com

Kaffir Boy

The Classic story of growing up under Apartheid

Price: $13

Autographed by the author

#3 on the New York Times Bestsellers List

#1 on the Washington Post Bestsellers List

Winner of the Christopher Award

Kaffir Boy is the true story of how Mark Mathabane was weaned on devastating poverty and schooled in the cruel streets of South Africa's most desperate ghetto, where bloody gang wars and midnight police raids were his rites of passage. Like every other child born in the hopelessness of apartheid, he learned to measure his life in days, not years. Yet Mark Mathabane, armed only with the courage of his family and a hard-won education, raised himself up from the squalor and humiliation to win a scholarship to an American university.

This extraordinary memoir of life under apartheid is a triumph of the human spirit over hatred and unspeakable degradation. For Mark Mathabane did what no physically and psychologically battered "Kaffir" from the rat-

infested alleys of Alexandra was supposed to do — he escaped to tell about
it.

Praise for Kaffir Boy

"Like Claude Brown's **Manchild in the Promised Land** ... in every way as
important and exciting."
— **The Washington Post**

"This is a rare look inside the festering adobe shanties of Alexandra, one of
South Africa's notorious black townships. Rare because it comes ... from the
heart of a passionate young African who grew up there."
— **Chicago Tribune**

"Powerful, intense, inspiring."
— **Publishers Weekly**

"An eloquent cry from the land of silent people, where blacks are assigned
by whites to a permanent role of inferiority."
— **John Barkham Reviews**

"Compelling, chilling, authentic ... an emotionally charged explanation of
how it felt to grow up under South Africa's system of legalized racism
known as apartheid."
— **Milwaukee Sentinel**

"Despite the South African government's creation of a virtually impenetrable border between black and white lives, this searing autobiography breaches that boundary, drawing readers into the turmoil, terror, and sad stratagems for survival in a black township."
— **Foreign Affairs**

"Told with relentless honesty ... the reader is given a rare personal glimpse behind the televised protests and boycotts, of the daily fear and hunger which is devastating to both body and soul."
— **The Christian Science Monitor**

"A chilling, gruesome, brave memoir ... Mathabane provides a straightforward, harrowing account of apartheid as it is practiced."
— **Kirkus Reviews**

Kaffir Boy in America
By Mark Mathabane

Price: $14
Autographed by the author
Not available through bookstores
New York Times Bestseller

Kaffir Boy in America is the best-selling sequel to Mark Mathabane's extraordinary autobiography, **Kaffir Boy**. The story begins with Mathabane's escape from South Africa to the United States, and recounts his coming of age in a country overwhelming in its immensity, luxuriousness, poverty and despair. From his early college days when he first discovered the great black American writers, to his emergence as the voice of a new generation, from his reflections on America's racial and social injustice to his celebration of its basic freedoms, **Kaffir Boy in America** is a moving saga of hardship and determination, insight and inspiration, informed, above all, my Mark Mathabane's compassion for his fellow man.

Praise for Kaffir Boy in America

"Inspiring...provides a better understanding of South Africa, of America — and of being human."
— **The New York Times Book Review**

"A triumphant and inspirational book with profound insights about race relations, perseverance and the complexity of the 'American dream.'"
— **San Francisco Chronicle**

"An inspiring story...The glitz of America hasn't made Mark Mathabane forget that the struggle to free his homeland is still his struggle — and ours."
— **Chicago Sun-Times**

"Relentless, open-ended, cautionary and quietly splendid."
— **Cleveland Plain Dealer**

Love in Black and White
By Gail and Mark Mathabane

Price: $20
Autographed by the authors
Not available through bookstores
First-edition hardcover

Mark Mathabane, author of the bestsellers **Kaffir Boy** and **Kaffir Boy in America**, grew up fearing and hating whites in a South African ghetto. Gail spent the first ten years of her life in lily-white communities in Ohio, and feared the people her Texas girlfriends casually called "niggers."
The two never dreamed of marrying outside their races. As many Americans gave up on the racial ideal of an integrated society, and two segregated, opposed, and hostile camps emerged—one black, one white—Mark and Gail fell in love.

Love in Black and White is the dramatic, revealing and riveting story of how they overcame their own prejudices, society's disapproval, family opposition and personal self-doubts to be together. Woven into their intimate account of falling in love, getting married and raising children in the fishbowl of an interracial relationship are the beautiful, complex and heartrending stories of other interracial couples in America and South Africa.

<u>Praise for Love in Black and White</u>

"A personal and candid account of what it means to break an intransigent taboo—and a heartwarming affirmation of love and commitment."
— **Kirkus Reviews**

"A courageous, painfully honest, captivating love story."
— **Miami Herald**

"Remarkable...A thoughtful exploration of the complexities of interracial relationships and a great love story."
— **Lynn Neary, National Public Radio's "All Things Considered"**

"Intriguingly structured with alternate accounts by husband and wife, Love in Black and White is a hymn of praise to the power of love in the face of deeply felt societal prejudices...Highly recommended."
— **Library Journal**

"The Mathabanes write well of the sweet, nervous first days of their love, and they don't flinch from the bad stuff...As they show, all it takes is love, and defending yourself at nearly every turn."
— **front page, Washington Post Book World**

"The honesty that is deeply rooted in every paragraph makes this book a moving one."
— **Newsweek**

African Women: Three Generations

By Mark Mathabane

Price: $14

Autographed by the author

Not available through bookstores

In **African Women: Three Generations**, the author of the highly acclaimed and bestselling memoir **Kaffir Boy** presents the deeply moving, often shocking, but ultimately inspiring stories of his grandmother, mother and sister. Coping with abuse, gambling, drunkenness and infidelity from the men they love or have been forced to marry, all three women defy African tradition, and the poverty and violence of life in a modern urban society, to make fulfilling lives for themselves and those they love in the belly of the apartheid beast in South Africa.

Praise for African Women

"The South African, nonfiction version of Terry McMillan's **Waiting to Exhale**...These stories show us that women's spirits refuse to be imprisoned forever."

—The Boston Globe

"What courage it took for these three black South African women to tell their stories — and to live their lives! — and for Mark Mathabane to weave their individual stories into this book."
— Deborah Tannen, Georgetown University professor and author of You Just Don't Understand

"A powerful piece of work...It is a pleasure finally to have a book concerned with issues of dire importance to women written sensitively by a man."
— Washington Post Book World

"Mathabane shifts his attention from the evils of racism to what may be the still more insidious and intractable problems of sexism as he describes in spare, moving prose the lives of his sister, mother and grandmother."
— The Wall Street Journal

"A finely crafted book that makes it easier to understand how the vicious cycles of abuse and oppression of women snowballed under apartheid."
— Christian Science Monitor

"A deeply shocking tribute to the historical struggles, sufferings and above all, the courage of women."
— Quarterly Black Review of Books

"Memoirs that speak in harrowing detail of growing up female in South Africa...There's no sloganizing; rather, the political is made personal in scenes of daily confrontation between women and men, between black and white."
— **Booklist**

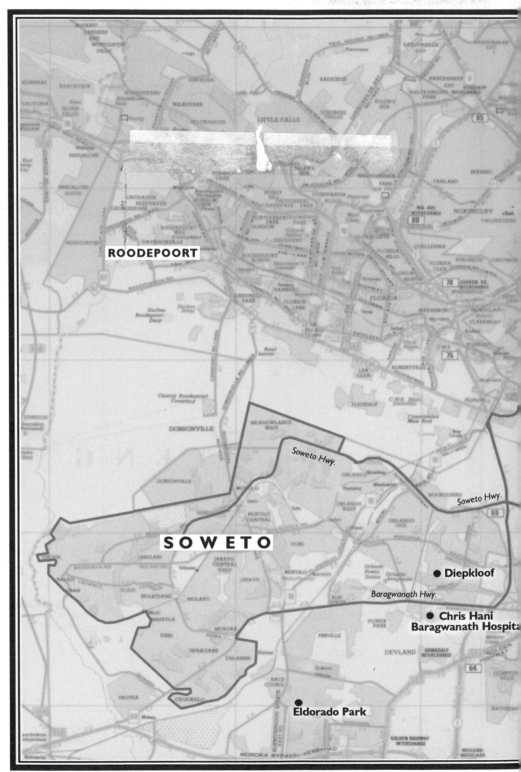

ROODEPOORT

S O W E T O

DOBSONVILLE

Soweto Hwy.

Soweto Hwy.

Baragwanath Hwy.

● **Diepkloof**

● **Chris Hani Baragwanath Hospital**

● **Eldorado Park**